"H

"One w your brothe for Lachlan."

"And ye kent his plan." Keenan's calm voice belied the tenseness she saw in his clenched jaw line. He wasn't as calm as he tried to present. Maybe she was learning how to decipher some emotions from his face, like normal people had to do. She studied him as he continued. "So ye sought the poisoned blades and used yerself as a shield."

"Not exactly." Serena held up her fingers and waved them. "I sought the blades, but only to pick them from his pocket."

"Ye were only able to pick one blade," he said. "Ye knew that ye couldn't grab them both." She watched his jaw line begin to tick. Amazing what one could discern from another without using magic. He was angry, perhaps furious inside.

"I had to do something," Serena said.

"I can protect my brother. I have since I could walk," Keenan replied flatly.

Serena looked up at him, her eyes narrowed. "I didn't grab the blade meant for Lachlan," she said and looked back at the cup in her hands. Her hands shook slightly as she held it to her parted lips and sipped the broth.

Serena nearly jumped when she felt his thumb touch her cheek. "Ye protected me." His words sounded calm, intrigued, so she looked back to him. But his eyes held fury, as if all of the emotion had drained from his words into them. "Doona do it again."

Praise for Heather McCollum

"*PROPHECY* is engaging and very well written. I totally enjoyed reading it."
~*Nancy Knight, co-owner, Belle Books*

"The title is good, the writing excellent, the story line works and you have a strong voice."
~*Rita Herron, author of the DEMONBORN series*

Love + adventure wrapped up in white magic! ♡

PROPHECY

Book One of
THE DRAGONFLY CHRONICLES

by

Heather McCollum

Heather McCollum

This is a work of fiction. Names, characters, places, and incidents either are the product of the author's imagination or are used fictitiously, and any resemblance to actual persons living or dead, business establishments, events, or locales, is entirely coincidental.

Prophecy: The Dragonfly Chronicles, Book One

COPYRIGHT © 2009 by Heather McCollum

All rights reserved. No part of this book may be used or reproduced in any manner whatsoever without written permission of the author or The Wild Rose Press except in the case of brief quotations embodied in critical articles or reviews.
Contact Information: info@thewildrosepress.com

Cover Art by *Tamra Westberry*

The Wild Rose Press
PO Box 708
Adams Basin, NY 14410-0706
Visit us at www.thewildrosepress.com

Publishing History
First Faery Rose Edition, 2010
Print ISBN 1-60154-723-4

Published in the United States of America

Dedication

This book is dedicated to my kids, who put up with
my constant "tap, tap, tap" at the computer.
And to Braden,
who has always been my real life hero.
I love you!

Prologue

On the Border of Alba and Strathclyde
On the Western Sea of Scotland
1005 A.D.

"My wards are weakening!" Serena's mother cried above the howling outside their small cottage. "I will hide ye, send ye away!" Her tone wavered against the noise like the lost voice of a person desperate to stay above the crash of waves. Serena had never heard her mother's voice so shaken, and it twisted in her little-girl stomach.

Serena's mother was Gilla, Great Wiccan Priestess of the Western Mountains, Keeper of the Earth Mother's magic. Her long braid swayed against her back like a pendulum as she paced across the gray floorboards to the barren hearth.

"How?" Serena asked. Her gaze darted to the rattling door. "With them out there. How?"

The demons flew along the perimeter just outside the standing stones that encircled the cottage, striking wildly at the protection wards her parents had erected with their combined magic. Serena was only nine years old but she knew that invasion meant death, probably the hideous death her father had endured. They'd found his broken body outside the stones, limp, swollen, bruised. Serena shivered and squeezed the hand of her younger sister.

"Please Earth Mother, my shields must last!" Gilla shouted at the ceiling. As if sneering against her prayer, something large dropped on the roof, and loose thatching floated down. Around the corners of the snug home, the wind laughed at their terror.

Gilla pulled a carved oak box from the mantel and turned toward Serena. "Starting with ye." Gilla's robes snapped around her as she whisked over to stand before the stone table in the center of the room. The legs of the center table anchored into the earth below the house, the floorboards cut and built around them.

"I'll send ye with my magic," Gilla continued, "all of ye," she said to her four daughters. "The demons stalk me now. They will steal the threads that hold our lives together in this realm," she said breathlessly. "The threads that I guard inside me."

Serena listened, rapt, ready to follow her mother's instructions. A tree beyond the window cracked against the eaves, and more thatching rained down upon them.

Her mother pulled something out of the box. "They've grown strong on your father's life force. But they need my magic strands."

With another series of thumps, small bits of dirt and straw sifted down upon the four girls. Serena covered her head and looked around the once tidy room.

Home. It had always felt warm, smelling of fresh baked bread. Now it was ice, a dusty prison of ice. Serena tried to swallow the dry grit she breathed into her mouth and coughed.

"I'll send one of my powers with each of ye. The magic the demons need to destroy our world will be far away, and all split up."

Nails scratching at the door mingled with the wild snapping of wolves. The girls screamed and grabbed onto one another.

"I need more time," her mother flicked her long fingernails toward the door. Yelps rent the air and coursed off into the shriek of the wind. "They send the beasts through my wards," she said, turning toward Serena. "They use Druce's magic against his own kin," her mother murmured. Wisps of her hair had come undone from her neat braid, sticking out haphazardly.

Gilla moved before Serena with unnatural speed, making her jump. "Ye must go now." Wild desperation warred with calm strength behind her mother's red-rimmed eyes. Bits of thatching spiked in her hair.

"Where, Mama?" Serena asked.

"To when," her mother countered and pulled Serena's hand into hers.

"When, then?" Serena whispered.

"Each of ye goes to a different place." Gilla paused, her eyes scanning her four daughters. "And a different time."

"How?" the second eldest, Merewin, asked.

"Drakkina, the Wiccan priestess and master, taught yer father and me how to uncoil our power threads and thread them through the planes of time." Her mother's words spilled over each other in haste. She took a deep breath and shook her head. "It's complicated."

"But," Serena started, "we willna be together. We'll be with strangers. Away from ye, away from our home."

"At first, but eventually ye will find home, find each other."

Large thumps pummeled the roof and then rolled down to the ground, squeaking and scurrying for shelter. "Rats." Gilla glanced at the walls as if testing their strength.

"But how will we know each other, how will we find each other?" Serena asked and pulled Merewin close against her with her free hand, not ready yet to let go of her family. "How will I find them if they're grown? They'll look different," she choked out.

Gilla placed a stone in Serena's palm. "Don't forget, ye all have my mark upon ye, the mark of the priestess, Drakkina." Gilla dropped Serena's hand and lifted the hem of her silver-green robe to show her leg where the brown pattern of a dragonfly lay against her pale skin. The dragonfly birthmark, they all had one somewhere.

"Serena," her mother said and took up the hand with the stone again. "Ye were born first and ye will leave first. I will thread ye into the future six hundred years. They won't find ye there." Gilla ran her finger along her daughter's firm lips and kissed her cheek.

Serena fell into her mother's arms and held tightly. She breathed in her mother's summery smell.

"I love ye, Mama," Serena avowed bravely and then stood back.

"Tha gaol agam ort, Serena." Gilla looked deeply into Serena's eyes. "Ye have your father's eyes, so bright, so unique." She breathed deeply. "I give ye my gift of sight, Child."

Serena looked down at the shiny red rock nestled into her palm. The rock contained coils of spun fibers wound tightly from the center to the very edges of the stone.

Her mother leaned over it, lips hovering just above its fiery surface. "I freely gift ye with my sight. On currents of my blood, on currents of my love, on currents of my fire power given by the Great Earth Mother, send her now within my thread of sight." She then opened her lips, took a deep breath, closed her eyes, and blew gently, so gently.

Serena watched the coils glow softly inside the orb. When her mother's breath ran out, she looked up at Serena.

"Deep sight is an immense power. Grow strong so ye do not lose yourself in it. Cherish it but be careful. Sight can be biased by yer perceptions." Her mother pulled a delicate blue feather from her pocket. She slipped it behind Serena's ear. She whispered, "Ye willna be alone, child."

Serena held the red rock carefully. It felt warm, almost hot, like the inside of what one's body must feel. "It feels...like I hold a part of ye, Mama."

"Ye do."

The room warped before Serena's eyes as her mother stepped back and her sisters grabbed hold for one last hug. Her mother produced another stone from a pocket and turned to Merewin, but the room wavered like the end of a dream, bending and fading.

The stone in her hand spread its heat up her arm and neck, up through the core of her skull and out along the skin of her face. Even her eyes felt hot. She blinked. Then the heat washed downwards through her stomach, sliding through thigh muscles, past knees to ankles and the very tips of her toes. Serena felt her body melt into liquid or light. Her weightless form watched the world quiver as through a pool of water.

Her body narrowed and lengthened and twisted into a single thread. She felt no pain, just different, fluid. Her altered self wasn't thick like a normal body, but thin and light. Serena stretched up through the roof of the house, up through a minute crack in the weakened thatch and out above the howling chaos.

Serena focused on the cottage at the center of the ten soaring stones, watching it shrink as she soared high above the home that had held the love of her family. She would have wept but didn't know if she had tears or even a face anymore.

She shot up through the clouds so that they lay roiling beneath her as the stars glittered above. She hovered there between heaven and hell.

Serena's thread twirled and twisted as sun and moon arched over, racing across the sky until they melded into one light, burning, flickering. Serena tried to turn from the sight but had no body to turn. When would it stop, the flashing, the twisting? How long had she been suspended? She would scream, go insane, die certainly if the flashing didn't end soon.

Heaviness grasped Serena's essence, pulling the red thread downward, back through a blue sky, back through the clouds. The earth flew to meet her as her body expanded and tingled, reforming in the air. The stone solidified in her hand.

A scream pushed up as she breathed in and exhaled once again. "Ahhh!"

Tree limbs brushed her robes that whipped around, slowing her plunge. Serena splashed through green pond scum. The cold water soaked through, and her toes sank into the bottom muck. She thrust upwards, sputtering and gasping. She flailed about for anything to help stay afloat and spat out the bitter water. Her long skirts, coupled with fatigue, trapped her movements. Serena's hands, one fisted around the stone, churned wildly at the musky water.

A boy's voice called out not far away. "She's an angel fallen from the sky," he said, in a strange language she somehow understood. "Grab hold," the boy said, and Serena's hand slapped against a rough branch. She grabbed it with her empty hand, and he dragged her toward the edge of the pond. Her feet squished into mud, finding rocks and sticks below the silt. She willed her legs to walk against the weight of exhaustion. Reaching the edge, her knees buckled, and she collapsed on the dirt. The boy turned her over.

"Help me," she whispered.

"I will help you," said the boy, and Serena's eyes focused on deep brown eyes that smiled down at her.

"You are an *àngelas*, an angel fallen from the sky." His lips formed words in another language, but she understood him. The rock warmed in her hand.

He had shiny dark hair, tanned skin, a firm smile and a kind heart. She had never seen him before. "Ye are William Faw," she said.

His brown eyes widened. He'd understood her. "You know me?" he asked.

Serena tried to focus again as a loud chirping sound hovered somewhere nearby. "Ye are to be my brother," she said, and then the pinpricks in her eyes turned everything black.

Chapter 1

Leeds, England - 13 Years Later
3 March 1746 A.D.

"You will dry to a ribbon of crust out here in the sun." Serena Faw, of the Faw Romany Tribe, flung her long hair back over her shoulder as she picked the wiggling pink earthworm off the sunny rock. "It's much cooler in my garden box." She nestled it amongst the tight confines of a miniature garden strapped to the back of her family's colorful gypsy wagon. "We don't stay long enough to grow gardens in the ground," she apologized to the burrowing worm.

Serena wiped her hands on a rag and glanced up at the rays of slanted sunlight filtering through the tall birch trees. "Now I'm talking to worms. Maybe I am going insane, like that old crone Petra told me about." Serena jogged to the front of the wagon. It was time to get ready for her performance at the faire. "I won't fit in any better if I'm caught talking to worms," she mumbled, and glanced around to make sure she was alone. She took the two large steps with gusto and squeezed into the tented wagon.

She plunged her hands down into the basin of cold creek water, then grabbed the scented bar of soap and scrubbed against the dirt. She'd lost track of time again while she'd tended the neat vegetable garden boxes. "Must try to act like a Faw," Serena mimicked her father's stern lecture voice. He was the king of their tribe and therefore needed his daughter, even one not of his blood, to act accordingly. She hadn't seen any of the tribe saving worms before.

Serena pulled her hands out of the water and dried them on her skirts. She leaned forward until her lips were level with a cold candle wick. She inhaled deeply and concentrated on slowing her rapid heartbeats. As she blew an invisible line of breath from her lips at the wick, she snaked out a thin tendril of power. The wick sparked to life.

She watched the flame flicker as it matured, a small pool of melted wax already growing at its slender base. She smelled the familiar incense and focused on the undulations of the rising and dipping flame. The noise of the gypsy faire continued to grow outside as darkness crept into camp. Serena pulled in another cleansing breath and watched the flame's little body dance. As she exhaled, the ribbon of fire bowed flat and straightened, then began to stir again.

Serena's gaze followed the flame until the noise of the people, the minds of the people, the emotions of the people nearby misted away. Control. Her clairvoyant sensitivity could crush her without it. Serena focused on the many hues of orange and yellow light sliding into one another. She must fortify herself before walking amongst so many people.

The bells at the wagon's door jangled. Serena funneled her senses in that direction, but did not shift her gaze.

"Yes, Shoshòy?" she asked softly, using her adopted brother's Rom name. His public name was William after his father. Romany sometimes had two names, one for private use and one used in public.

"King Will says you'll dance soon," he said, with his ever-present smile in his voice. "So stop staring at your candle and start getting dressed. I've seen many a foppish chub roaming about already. They drink more when you dance and then spend without care."

Serena blew at her candle, scattering the energy until it wafted up into a delicate swirl of smoke. She turned to William and smiled back. It was hard not to smile at her handsome brother.

"And chubs are easily parted with their moneys." She repeated William's favorite saying as she stepped behind a short screen to change into her dancing costume. She watched him over the top.

His exaggerated nod sent his chin-length, dark hair in disarray around his head. Serena knew that he must be older than her by several years, but he acted like he was a young boy. Which was probably why King Will hadn't matched him with any girl, yet. He still moved through the forest with bounding energy, like a rabbit, which had earned him his Rom name.

Serena pursed her lips and frowned. "No thievery, of course," she said.

He placed his hand against his chest in mock wounding, but then winked at her. "Of course not, King Will would have my hide. We just got here, and there's plenty of money to be made honestly."

Serena nodded and came out from the screen. "Tie these lacings," she said, and turned her back to him.

She heard him clear his throat as his cold fingers brushed against her bare back to tie the many laces of the purple and gold stays. "You know, Àngelas," he said, using her Romany name. "We are old enough now by far for someone else to be..." He hesitated and pulled hard on the stays. "...to be dressing you."

Darkness swirled around Serena's mind. His fingers against her skin washed cold dread down into her stomach as if someone were pouring a bucket of ice water down her throat. She shivered. William bled, a slick blackness oozed from his aura. She turned around and stared at him. "What?" she asked weakly.

"Duy should do it, or Petra. I'm a man. Have been for years."

Serena tried to follow his words. She shivered and attempted to redirect her feelings. "Of course, Shoshòy, I will talk to Petra. Let me see your hand."

William hesitated but then thrust out his hand. Serena didn't have to look at it. She only had to hold it. She clasped it in her naked palm. Serena tingled as the aura bled further into her. *Suspicion, despair, death.*

"Àngelas?"

Serena stared into William's eyes. "Stay away from the fools tonight. It doesn't feel right."

William stared hard at her, but then the playful twinkle flashed through his eyes again. He shrugged and pulled his hand from the cradle of her palm. "I'll help tend the fires." He smiled his charming smile and ducked to go out the door. "Hurry up, though, before King Will comes in here after you himself."

Serena tried to shake the itchy dread that spider-walked just under her skin. She finished fastening her scarves and bells, meant to catch the light of the fire, and hooked one last strand of painted jewels across her forehead. A sweet chirping melody from outside the wagon made her fingers flash as they looped and knotted. She stepped out into the night.

The melody called from a branch above her. She glanced around to make sure no one watched. "Chiriklò," she called, and the small sparrow landed on her hand. Serena stroked the smooth feathers of her pet. The bird crept closer to her and chirped loudly.

Serena laughed. "Yes, I have bread for you." She

pulled some bits from her pocket. The bird snapped one up and flew to a low branch nearby. "Aye, not at all like a Faw. Talking to worms and birds."

Even in the shadows, Serena could see the hint of blue in his perfect wings, the same unique blue of the feather her birth mother had gifted to her on that terrible night long ago. She had found the little bird, or rather it had found her, shortly after landing in the pond.

Coincidence? She didn't believe in coincidences.

Serena wasn't sure how long sparrows lived, but this one continued to thrive and follow her wherever she traveled. The bird's unusual color marked it unique and its ability to share information with her through its thoughts amazed her. Serena couldn't read the thoughts of animals. Sometimes she caught an image from one, but none could keep a conversation with her like the little blue sparrow.

After eating his bread, he twittered a short melody and let random thoughts of the day sift through his mind.

"Serena!" William called from near the fire.

"Sorry, Chiriklò, I am to dance tonight." The little bird flew higher up into the tree.

The scents, sounds, and thoughts from the faire pulsed against her like the wind before a storm, begging for her attention. But Serena easily thrust them from her, yanked on her soft leather gloves and wiggled her fingers down into each finger sleeve.

The first knowledge of her great sensitivity had crashed in on her upon awakening in the gypsy camp as Mari, her new mother, or duy, bathed her skin. She soon discovered that every inch of her skin could read the minds of those she touched. And many thoughts came to her without physical contact. Mari continued to help Serena master her power. Without control, Serena could lose herself to the onslaught around her.

She stepped between the wagons and smiled greetings to some of the Rom women nearby. They bustled around to set up their tin wares for sale. *Do not touch me. What new havoc will she bring? Shouldn't she be dancing? She scries the future more than is natural. Poor King Will.*

Their minds tumbled behind their polite smiles and nods. Serena shrugged inwardly and blocked their thoughts. Everyone thought she was strange, almost dangerous. Maybe it would be best if she lived alone. She clutched arms around herself and turned down another dark path toward the glow of the fire. She didn't belong with normal people.

Serena didn't even look Romany. They were dark of skin with beautiful shiny black hair. Her hair was red. Where their skin tanned under the sun, her paleness burned red. Even without her powers, she would always be an outsider. The stone from her mother had helped her understand their language at first. She had picked it up incredibly fast. Serena touched the red stone that hung on a cord around her neck. But her tribe still only saw her differences.

"Serena," she heard Mari call from near the fire, even though she called out Àngelas in her mind. William had given Serena her Romany name, Àngelas, when he saw her fall like an angel from the sky.

Her duy walked toward her through the shadows. Mari's concern penetrated Serena upon contact.

"I am fine," Serena said. "Just sad for a moment, is all."

Mari rubbed her back and sent soothing thoughts to her. *Àngelas, gift from God, with an amazing power to be cherished, not despised.*

"I know, Duy, I know. To be cherished, not despised." Serena looked at her mother who had still not uttered a word out loud. "But still, not normal."

Mari sighed. "You will find your path, Serena, and you will follow it to your happiness." Mari possessed a small measure of sight as well, but not near to Serena's ability.

Serena's eyes narrowed as she studied her duy. "You have seen this?"

Mari's chin bobbed just enough to be a nod. "It's in shadows, of course. There are happy paths and sorrowful paths," she warned.

"But there are happy paths?"

Mari laughed. "Of course, child."

From the distance, Mari and Serena heard a deep beat begin. Pipes, stringed fiddles, and the base harp joined in to roll together in a seductive melody. Serena dropped her outer shawl and handed it to Mari.

Mari frowned as she stared up at a little patch of stars shining down through the oaks. "The stars have worried me these last few nights. Be careful, Àngelas. Something dark comes."

Serena wanted to tell her about the taint on William's aura, but she had already missed the first cue. "Later, Duy, we'll talk of the stars." Serena broke away to run in her little leather slippers to the fire.

A crowd, mostly of men, gathered around the snapping bonfire that stretched up brightly in dancing shades of crimson light. Members of the tribe, including King Will, held the crowd back from the fire so that Serena could perform around its border. At the edge of the light Serena halted, closed her eyes, and filled her chest with warm air.

The fire crackled and huffed. Serena drew from the power within the flames. The noise of the people and the press of their thoughts dimmed as she funneled the magic of the fire through her body. She watched the flames flicker through her eyelids.

The thoughts of the crowd became a wall of noise that she held in its place away from her. She balanced it and diminished it until the noise was just part of the night wind blowing against her body.

The notes of the flute slowed, and Serena opened her eyes to stare at the flames. They pulsed with the night breeze, powerful and snapping. The flames beckoned her to dance with them. Serena's arms and torso moved in the same fashion. Her head rolled back along her shoulders, her arms extended, offering herself to the heat.

The heat, it was a familiar partner to her. She pulled from its energy the strength to force out the emotions of her audience. Fire magick infused her. Serena danced, shifting her body with the waves of heat, sometimes facing the blaze, sometimes facing the night chill where the people stood. She didn't see any of them, only the flame. It was her friend and partner. It accepted her, loved her.

Serena transitioned with the increasing tempo. Her body answered the music by mimicking its rhythm. Serena felt her hair wash around her shoulders as she turned, her arms languid and graceful. The core of her body warmed with fire and the thrill of the dance. She held a circle of silence around her as she moved. Here she could breathe, alone within the quiet, the peace.

****

"Bloody drunk fool." Keenan Maclean stood vigilant at the fringe of the crowd. His large frame usually relegated him to the back of an audience since at nearly six and a half feet, he could see above everyone. And tonight was no different. He watched his companion, soaked with royal whisky, ram and trip his way toward the front row, near the fire. As long as Keenan kept his eye on Gerard, he was technically guarding him. He certainly didn't appreciate any type of conversation with the man. If

Gerard wasn't so bloody crucial to the Jacobite cause, Keenan would have abandoned him to the gypsy faire much earlier. But Gerard Grant secretly supported Prince Charles Edward Stewart, Bonnie Prince Charlie, making him a surreptitious Jacobite. Plus, he nurtured a warm friendship with England's King George II. Gerard was worth his weight in whisky to the Jacobites.

Keenan, a loyal Scot down to the marrow of his bones, despised English rule as much as any other Scot. Having met the untried Prince Charles Stewart, Keenan couldn't support the radical Jacobite cause, either. His opinion didn't matter anyway since his laird supported the Prince.

Sworn to perform his duty to his family, Keenan needed to make certain Gerard made it home tonight and that the contents of his pocket remained intact. Keenan leaned against the trunk of a wide oak. One last onerous task to perform before heading back at dawn to his beloved Highlands. One more step closer to fulfilling his duty to the prophecy that ruled his existence.

The slow music increased in tempo before the hushed crowd.

A performance. Another drunk stumbled into him.

"Bloody hell," he cursed beneath his breath, his eyes searching the crowd near Gerard. He should carry the man out of here before their pockets were picked clean.

The audience remained motionless, entranced. Even bawdy Gerard studied the performer in stunned silence. Perhaps the dancer had talent. Keenan looked over a sea of heads towards the fire.

A woman danced from around the leaping flames. Her hair reflected the red of the fire with such intensity that it seemed to move as a twin flame. She wove her slender arms around her body;

white gloves were the only cloth to hide the perfect skin of her limbs. The loose folds of fabric swirled around her naked calves above delicate leather slippers. Silk swathed her middle, the fabric so thin and supple that it showed her softly rounded stomach as it moved like a wave under her flexible stays. The bells sitting low on her waist shook in time with the music as she snapped her hips. Her seductive, half-closed eyes scanned across the crowd but did not connect, as if she saw none of them. Her lips parted. As she whirled with the increased tempo around the fire, her full breasts rose and fell faster with her breath.

Keenan watched her sensual movements. His gaze ran the contours of her face. Her high cheekbones flushed, her translucent skin sparkled. *"Mo bhean,"* Keenan said in Gaelic. "My woman." The words filled his mind, thrumming through him with the sound of blood rushing in his ears. "Mine," he whispered roughly.

Keenan's thumb rubbed against his other fingers as if feeling her softness. Her skin would feel like the unblemished hide of a doe, tender, soft. "Mo bhean," he said again and took a step forward as if under a spell. Keenan's eyes followed the glimpses of her long bare calves, the taut muscles flashed by as she whipped the skirts back and forth. His hands fisted against his sides, and he shook his head, pushing out the ridiculous urge to hoist her up into his arms and carry her away. As if he was entitled to take her. As if she was his.

He could not turn away. Her arms held strength as she raised them up high. She was no young girl just blooming. She was a woman. Her body was shaped and rounded for the caress of a man. She rolled her head back, causing fire-colored hair to wash all the way down below her hips. It would run silky in his rough hands and smell of fresh night air and womanly warmth. Keenan felt a deep tightening in his loins. Bloody English trews gave no room to grow.

She danced toward the edge where Gerard stood. The bastard leered at the woman and licked his salivating lips.

"Move," Keenan demanded, his voice low and threatening as he elbowed through the dense cluster of people.

The dancer whirled away from Gerard's clenching fingers. But it was close, too close. Keenan wouldn't allow the bastard to touch her.

"Move aside," Keenan repeated.

Angry glares met his chest before climbing up to his fierce expression. The crowd parted. Keenan acknowledged none of them, but kept his attention on the dancer as he came alongside Gerard.

"Mmm, she's a luscious tart, she is," Gerard garbled and reached out once more.

It took all of Keenan's strength not to yank Gerard backwards. Instead, he stepped in front of him, blocking him with his body. "Get your arse out of my way, you bloody buffoon," Gerard called from behind him.

Keenan stood right along the perimeter as the dancer moved from side to side a few paces away on the other side of the bonfire. She swung her heavy tresses again, and Keenan could almost feel them. Like sun-warmed silk.

Keenan barely noticed Gerard's attempts to shove him aside. His entire conscious state focused entirely on the sensuous woman who pulsed like a flame, body bending as if an invisible lover swayed her. Keenan ran his hand roughly through his hair. "Insanity," he grumbled and closed his eyes for a long second. She was just a woman, a gypsy. He opened his eyes again. A gypsy woman who didn't look like any gypsy he'd ever seen before.

Prophecy

As long as the music played, Serena would continue to dance as the flame. She never tired as the serenity of the blazing ribbons of fire and the dance kept the voices, the unending thoughts of others, at bay. She heard them only as a whisper, saw them only as a blank wall surrounding her on the edge of light. Around and around she moved, watching with half seeing eyes the web of thoughts held out at the edge. She leaned against it evenly to keep the thoughts from seeping inward, into her circle.

As she rounded the fire once more, pushing against the wills of her audience, a hole in the wall appeared. Curiously she danced toward it. Reaching out with her mind, Serena leaned into the hole. Her mind fell through it, and her protective wall shattered. "No!" she whispered frantically.

Images bludgeoned her. Naked flesh, her naked flesh, pressed from behind, shoved into beds. Her mouth on the men, her lips skimming over sweaty skin.

"No," she gasped as if for air. Quickly she flung hard at the shards of carnal images. She took a wrong step, her body flailing. She felt it, or rather didn't feel it, the void. She fell against it, against him. She stared up at the dark, silent mountain holding her.

The man was a giant. He stood taller than any man she had known. His face glowed with the light of the fire, accenting a slash across his left cheek from his ear to his jaw. The scar accentuated the square set of his serious face. His eyes stared back into hers, they were light, but she couldn't tell the color. They narrowed as if trying to read her. Read her? Shocked, Serena realized that she could not read him. Not at all, as if he were a hole, silence in the noise of thoughts flowing around her.

His arms steadied her as he gazed into her eyes.

"Who are ye, lass?"

Serena was mesmerized. Never before had she met someone who was blank to her. Someone with whom she could not read their thoughts, their emotions.

"Lass, are ye hurt?" he asked, his sensual mouth forming the deeply accented words.

Serena glanced at his hands wrapped around her bare upper arms. Nothing, she read nothing from him. Serena snatched off her glove. His scar. Scars, chiseled into skin during battle, were extremely powerful. Even her defenses could not block the gruesome details.

Serena held her breath as she traced her finger down the length of the slightly puckered skin from his ear hidden in waves of dark hair to the rough squareness of his chin. The muscles in his jaw jumped at her touch. His lips opened on a ragged breath.

No jolt shot down through her arm and up behind her eyes. No visions of bloodstained iron, muddy grime and anguished cries of war victims. Just the void. He was the first person she had ever met whom she knew absolutely nothing about.

"What are you?" she whispered. "A demon?"

The man's face relaxed. "Some have called me worse."

Was he serious? She couldn't tell. Serena had never needed to learn the subtle ways a body tells when it speaks lies or jests. She had always been able to tell even before the lie was uttered. But now, now she was lost.

"What are ye called?" he asked, releasing her. The gently rolling brogue reminded her of the mountain people up north on the edge of the sea.

"Serena." She wondered what her name would sound like on his tongue.

"Move over, you oaf," said a man from behind

who nearly fell trying to push by the giant. "It is my turn to meet the lovely," he slurred and leered at Serena.

"Gerard, leave the lass alone. I ken it's time to take ye home, man," said the ruggedly sensuous giant. He smelled of open air, pine perhaps, leather, and warmth. It was strange to engage her other senses, but she tried. There wasn't enough time to fully study him, his smell, the deep roll of his voice, the feel of his muscles. Her other senses took much longer to fully see a person. She hadn't realized how easy it had been to sum up a person with her powers.

Serena's gaze moved over broad shoulders which pressed against the material of his shirt and then traveled down his chest to muscular thighs.

The one called Gerard grabbed Serena's bare hand and slid his clammy lips across her knuckles. His tongue snaked out and licked a trail of spittle across her hand.

She gasped. Waves of darkness rolled over her; lust, fear, pain, death. The ground wobbled as her vision blurred and she fell toward the void, somehow knowing, without knowing, that the void would catch her.

The giant caught her against him. "Bloody hell, Gerard, let her go," he said and clasped the man's arm.

"Listen, lovey, I have more money than this Scottish boor could even dream of having. And I know you Rom ladies like a little coin," he insinuated.

The giant finally pulled the lecherous hand from hers. Serena felt strangely numb, and pinpricks of light sparkled against the darkness. Just as her knees began to buckle, one strong arm went under them, and she was pulled up against a solid chest. Serena rested her cheek against the warmth and closed her eyes, relaxing in the strange silence that radiated from him. His warm, masculine smell enveloped her. Even without knowing him, Serena felt safe. Foolish, she thought, but kept her head against him and listened to the strong heart beat.

"Bloody damn Scot!" Gerard cursed after them as the mysterious man walked with her away from the fire toward the dark wagons.

"Put her down, now, English," Serena heard William say, and she lifted her head against the man's shoulder.

"I'm na English, lad." The arms holding her tensed.

"Whatever the hell you are, put my sister down," William demanded. Serena could feel the angry thoughts of her brother. As William brushed against her, she shivered. A slick inkiness surrounded him in her mind. Serena lifted her head and looked back at Gerard as he drank from a tankard. It had something to do with that man.

"William, this man helped me." She wiggled slightly to let him know that she wanted down, but he remained wrapped around her. She looked up into his face. His clear eyes studied her. "I'm fine now. Please let me down."

Slowly the giant let her slide down the length of his hard body. The friction against her torso and thighs let loose a slow flow of heat down into her stomach. She forgot to breathe as the tingle spread. "And what are you called?" she asked a bit breathlessly.

He stared a moment before speaking, as if weighing whether or not he should reveal his name.

"Keenan Maclean." Her stomach flipped. "Keenan Maclean," Serena repeated, slowly tasting it and trying to draw any information her senses could from his name. Pain in her chest, she must breathe. "Do you know my thoughts?" she asked softly. "What I'm thinking?"

His eyes narrowed slightly, his forehead furrowed. This was a look of confusion, wasn't it? He shook his head slightly. "Nay. Do ye ken my thoughts?" he asked and raised an eyebrow. Was that surprise? Maybe jesting?

"No," she said and frowned. Was he telling the truth?

"And this is troubling?" he asked. His hard eyes searched her face, but a faint grin played on his lips.

William stepped up beside her, his chest puffed outward. "Thank you, Maclean, for helping my sister. I will take care of her from here."

The Scot ran his eyes over William. "She is yer sister?" he asked and looked pointedly between their obvious physical differences.

"Not by blood." Serena felt the defensiveness in William. "But by every other way a man could be my brother."

Mari walked around the edge of the wagon. She stopped in front of the Scot and threaded her hand through the crook of her daughter's arm. To an onlooker it may have looked as if Serena held Mari up, but Serena felt the strength radiating alongside her, allowing her to lean gently into the warmth of her mother.

Mari scrutinized the man silhouetted by the campfire. She smiled pleasantly, but Serena felt her senses try to tune in to him.

The Maclean stood with his legs braced apart, his arms crossed. His eyes moved from Mari back to Serena, studying them. He wore English garb. An outer jacket of deep blue came down to his knees. His deeply muscled calves bulged sleekly in the fashionable court hose. The hilt of a short sword flashed inside his jacket against his ribs. He dressed the part of an English courtier, but his hair was his own, natural and dark, not powdered. Although handsome in the courtly attire, he looked too rugged for such finery. His physique and the scar marked him as a warrior.

"Thank you, for helping my daughter," Mari said and paused. "Sir?" She reached out to touch his arm, waiting for him to fill in his name.

"No 'sir,' just Keenan Maclean." The warrior tipped his head in response but did not smile. The firelight flickered shadows across his features. He looked fierce, dangerous, and incredibly powerful. Serena shivered.

Mari drew her hand back to her skirts. "You dress like the English, but you are not," she said in broken Gaelic.

"Aye."

He answered Mari, but his eyes remained on Serena. Had he lied before? Could he read her thoughts? By the Earth Mother, she hoped not. Serena rubbed her hands down her thighs through her skirts. Her skin still felt hot as if branded by his hard body during her slide to the ground.

"Perhaps from the mountains of the west," Mari said again in Gaelic.

"Woman, it is dangerous to speak the ancient tongue here," he said in English. "Ye best be careful."

Mari nodded and switched to English. "We traveled there several years ago, near the ocean."

"My home is Kylkern, near the sea," the man said.

Mari nodded. "Yes, yes, Kylkern Castle. I remember your laird well, the proud Angus Maclean. He was quite generous to us and allowed us to entertain. I would have you send him the kind wishes of King Will and the Faw tribe."

"He is dead," the man said swiftly, his eyes taking in all three of them.

"I am sorry for the loss of such a great man,"

Mari said, bowing her head slightly. "Then I send along the kind wishes to the new chief of the Macleans, who is...?"

"You," Serena said in a near whisper. Mari looked up.

The Maclean turned toward the fire and scanned the small crowd. His face caught the glow of orange light on half of his strong features. The shadows turned his features sharp, predatory, battle hungry. Serena tucked her other hand under Mari's arm.

He half spoke to her and half to the fire. "Nay, Lachlan Maclean is laird." Mari's grip on her arm tightened. Surprise and concern radiated from Mari. Serena never guessed wrong.

The warrior continued to scan the area around the fire. Boisterous laughter came from one of the tables set up on the other side. He reached into his pocket and produced a small bag of coins which he tossed to William.

"For yer trouble," he said and then looked at Serena, "and for yer performance." His eyes searched hers one last time and then turned to Mari. "Yer pardon," he said quickly and bowed. "But I must find my companion."

Mari nodded her thanks.

"Yes," Serena said before she thought better of it. "Find him, he will be in need of you," she said. "I felt death when he touched me."

Keenan Maclean's eyes pivoted towards her. Sharp angles of firelight and moonlight cut across his face. Without a word he turned and jogged toward the laughter on the other edge of the fire.

"William," Ephram, one of the tribe's young men, called near the fire where he waved him over.

"I have work to do." William raised his hand to his friend. "Go inside, Àngelas," he said in his best imitation of King Will. Then he turned to leave them.

"William." Serena stopped him by resting her bare hand on his arm. Her stomach clenched.

"Àngelas?"

She shook her head. "Something feels terribly wrong, dark. I'm afraid for you," she said.

He would take her warning seriously. He knew her powers. Unfortunately he also knew how she often caused more problems by trying to stop fate.

William frowned but then smiled softly at her. "I will be extra careful tonight."

With his promise, Serena hoped the sickening in her belly would mellow, but it didn't. She watched him saunter off toward his friends.

Mari waited until they ducked through the door into the tented room of their covered wagon before the questions began to pop quickly into Serena's head. Mari sat down across from Serena and gave her daughter a tin cup of watered-down wine.

"Keenan Maclean, from Kylkern," Mari said.

Serena nodded, "I know, but only because it came from his lips." She took two gulps of the sweet drink and tried to force the thought of his sensual lips away. She ran her fingers over her forehead, rubbing at the ache she felt coming, and pulled the strand of painted glass jewels off. She looked up into the wise eyes that searched her. "I could not read his thoughts at all."

"How unusual." Mari sipped some of the wine.

"But you could?" Serena asked and Mari nodded slightly.

"Just some. My gift is not like yours, Àngelas."

"Hmmph, my gift abandoned me."

"Only with him?"

Serena nodded in response and took a drink. She turned to look closely at her mother. "Is he dark? Some sort of wizard or demon able to block his thoughts from me?" The thought sent prickles of fear up her neck to her scalp. Could a demon have found her?

Mari considered it but then shook her head. "Perhaps some darkness, but not a demon. He...seemed..." She hesitated and tilted her head to the side. "Sad, I think. I heard the sad skirl of their ancient pipes when I touched him."

Serena took a deep breath, her shoulders relaxing away from panic. "Why couldn't I hear them?"

Serena felt Mari's concern, but the woman kept her voice light. "I don't know. I will meditate on it."

Serena sat back against the bedroll. An itch in her mind tickled at the base of her ears. She rubbed at them and pulled the earrings from her lobes. Goosebumps rose on her bare arms, and she ran her hands down them.

Mari's worry came through her mind, and she leaned forward to rub Serena's arms briskly.

"Pain comes," Serena said. "Betrayal, fear."

"So you feel this darkness too?"

Serena nodded. "But I think it involves the Highlander's companion. The one named Gerard."

Mari laid her weathered hand on Serena's knee. "Reach out to it, child. Gently so as not to open the gates you hold back. A crack to see the darkness."

"You want me to look?" Serena asked. How many times had her duy told her to shut her mind or ignore the warnings, to allow fate's song to play out? And now she asked her to seek out the darkness.

Mari's brow furrowed deeply, and she clenched her calloused hands. "The stars speak to me of treachery." She paused and looked deeply into Serena's eyes. "This darkness stalks us, our family."

"William," Serena said and stood. She grabbed her wool cloak and wrapped it around herself. She ducked out the small door and stood at the top of the steps. The rhythm of the faire was familiar, normal, as were the muted sounds of the forest around their caravan. She didn't see Keenan Maclean or Gerard. Her eyes moved around the fire. No William.

Serena washed a cleansing breath through her chest and closed her eyes. The walls she held around herself were hardly a burden to her now after years of training to control what she allowed herself to see. Mari had guided her, with common sense, a duy's love, and the ancient knowledge passed down through her maternal line.

Serena envisioned a stone wall that reached up to the tallest trees and encircled. The stone was rough granite with stars sprinkled within it. The stars had been in her first wall when she had created it as a young girl, and she had kept it. Using her internal compass, Serena felt for the direction of the darkness. Through the wall she felt its slick presence. She focused on the rocks on the outside of the wall.

A small fissure glowed along a jagged path between the granite stones. Serena narrowed her thoughts into a thread and squeezed through the tiny crack. Out through the cooling night her thread darted into shadows, between trees, past the crackling fires of the tribe, past the merriment in the faire's center. Her mind flew, a single thread intent on only one destination, the darkness that itched.

Through zigs and zags, she came upon the bridge that crossed the creek not far from the faire. "Where are you?" Her mind searched for the cause of her worry, it searched for William. The woods stood silent in the moon-washed darkness, watching, smelling the predator lurking. Serena saw Gerard stumbling, catching himself on the wooden rail. Would he fall in? Was that the darkness? No, it was human darkness, swollen with deceit, full of purpose and perfidy.

Serena's thread hovered over Gerard as the man

gurgled and wretched over the side of the brook. Wiping his frothy mouth, he turned to see another man lunge from the shadows. Serena tried to yell a warning, but Gerard's mind was too befuddled to be receptive. Few could hear her thoughts, and only when they were open to her voice.

The man was larger than Gerard, poorly dressed, a local brute. In one quick movement, he stabbed Gerard through the abdomen. Serena breathed hard, her silent scream useless. She must concentrate to keep her thread. She pulsed against the sight of such blood spreading like dark wine through white linen between his splayed fingers. Gerard sank to his knees. The rough man looked back over his shoulder and nodded. Serena sent her quivering thread to the other end of the bridge.

A man and woman stood in the shadows, their clothes well cut, costly. "Run! Go back!" she mentally yelled to them. Should she break the thread and run for help? The images were so clear that Serena knew that what she observed was happening now. There was no time to run to them.

Serena watched as the couple came forward. Instead of recoiling, the man handed the killer a bag of coins and motioned for him to drop the knife near the body. The thug dropped the knife, grabbed the bag and hurried off into the woods.

Serena watched as the gentleman pulled a rolled paper from Gerard's inner jacket. The petite blond woman tucked it into a small satchel and turned to leave.

Serena breathed, focusing again so as not to scatter her energy. If the thread collapsed, she would plunge back behind her granite wall.

What was happening? Who were they? Serena reached out with her sharpest powers. Anxiety clung to the woman, but purpose held her resolve. The man felt relief.

William burst from the trees, startling the two. The man pulled out a gun.

"No," Serena screamed at William. "No!"

The shot tore through William and shattered Serena's concentration. The scene dissolved and she fell backwards into the arms of Mari. Chiriklò chirped wildly and fluttered around her as she regained her bearings.

"Duy, they've shot Shoshòy," Serena cried and wiped at her tears. "Find King Will, I'm going to help him, he's on the bridge." She jumped down out of the wagon, nearly twisting her foot in the slippery mud.

"Chiriklò, fly to William." The bird shot through the darkness, and Serena ran after him.

Chapter 2

Keenan Maclean knelt over Gerard, loosened the man's cravat and pressed against his neck.

"Bloody hell." He checked Gerard's pockets. Empty. "Bloody, blathering hell," he cursed and stood up. He'd failed to keep the bastard alive, the only Jacobite supporter that had King George's ear. And the damn letter was missing. How could he have failed so terribly? He had allowed the gypsy woman to distract him from his duty.

A bird screeched near the fallen Rom at the other end of the bridge. In the moonlight, Keenan watched the tiny bird hop from one end of the man to the other, tilting its head in the disjointed manner birds do.

Keenan looked up as padded feet slapped across the boards of the bridge. "Now what?" he grumbled. And there she was, the woman from the faire. She ran across the bridge and threw herself on the Rom man. She draped across him, her long hair flowing along his length like a plaid.

Keenan's frown deepened. Was the man her lover? As she turned the man's face upward, Keenan saw that it was the Rom who had called her his sister. What did he have to do with Gerard's death?

Keenan walked over and knelt down next to her. "Serena?"

She looked up at him and wiped her nose against the back of her glove. Tears stained her cheeks. She didn't say anything. She didn't have to.

They worked together to open her brother's jacket. Blood seeped from a hole in his shoulder.

"He's been shot, please help me," she whispered.

The jolt that shot through Keenan was nearly a physical pain, her anguish so raw, her helplessness so devastatingly sincere. All the sorrow in the wretched world seemed reflected in her breathless words. He had felt sorrow before, seen the anguish in the world. But her simple plea tore like sharp teeth into him.

His eyes stared back into hers, promising more than words could pronounce. "I will help ye."

She nodded and looked back down where blood continued to seep from the Rom boy's shoulder.

Several Rom men ran up behind them, speaking low in the Romany language. Keenan finished pulling William's jacket carefully from his shoulders. Serena ripped the scarf that was tied to her waist, balled it up and pushed it gently against the hole. From the small amount of blood, Keenan knew that the shot was lodged in the muscle and dammed much of the bleeding. It must be removed eventually, but right now loss of blood was the first concern.

Serena tied the sash tightly around the wound. She seemed to know what to do. Had she saved many from pistol shots? Her gloved hands shook and slipped as she tied the knots. A dark slickness covered them, and she tried to wipe them on the boards near her.

She swayed slightly on her heels, and Keenan nudged her hands aside. "Let me," he said.

She sat back and pulled off her blood soaked gloves and tucked them in her waistband. When Keenan finished, he grasped her elbow beneath her cloak to help her stand. She flinched at his touch but didn't pull away.

One of the men from her tribe stepped forward. Keenan held her hand out to the man, but he avoided it. Instead, he stiffly pulled her against his side.

Keenan crouched before Serena's brother and glanced at the woman. "Ye called him William?"

She nodded.

"Yer brother?"

She sniffed loudly and nodded again.

Keenan carefully checked William's pockets. A few coins, tinkled together but nothing more. Keenan looked around and spotted Gerard's coin purse next to William along with a bloodied knife. But the papers were nowhere. What would a gypsy want with the letter anyway?

The gun lying near the body must have shot William, but where had Gerard found the gun? It wasn't his. When Gerard had started drinking heavily, Keenan took his firearm from him so he wouldn't shoot anyone or himself. Keenan probably should have let the idiot keep his weapon, another failure on his part.

A pounding crept up the back of his head as Keenan looked between the two men. What an ass he'd been to let his guard down. Without Gerard and his letter, his brother's cause would require months to rebuild. He shook his head in disgust at himself.

"William didn't take his money and didn't kill him," Serena said firmly as she wiped another scarf along her nose.

Keenan threw the purse of coins at her feet as he stood. The loud thump caused a stir amongst the Rom gathered.

Serena spoke to the people around her. "William didn't take the coins. It was the others," she insisted as she waved her hands toward the other end of the bridge and looked back at Keenan. Frantic appeal bled from her eyes. "The man threw your friend's coin purse on William after he shot him. Because William saw him, and his woman paying off Gerard's murderer, some local ruffian." The words flew desperately out of her. Several Rom backed away, disappearing into the shadows.

"What man and woman? What murderer?" Keenan grabbed her arms.

"Out of the way, you filthy Rom," a rotund man huffed across the bridge with two men behind him. They held guns and were sloppily dressed as local authority. The remaining people backed up to allow them into the scene.

The marshal glanced at the bodies. "What crime goes on here?"

"Gerard Grant has been stabbed, killed," Keenan said.

"And my brother has been shot. He is bleeding." Serena pulled away from Keenan to squat back down at William's head. She smoothed his black hair from his face.

The marshal pointed to the weapons each man had. "Looks like the Rom picked his purse and they fought a bit. The gentleman was gutted but got off a shot before he died. Thieving Rom." The marshal spat on the ground near William's foot.

"That's not what happened," Serena shouted.

"And how would you know that, little miss? Or were you in on it?" The marshal leered at her. "I saw you dance with the Rom people. You might not look like them, but you travel with them."

Keenan saw her wide eyes, her trembling hands. She didn't look like someone who would aid her brother in thievery. But times were hard for the poor. Maybe they only meant to take the money, and the boy ended up defending himself. But again, Gerard had nothing to defend himself with. The details didn't make sense. He needed to question Serena about what she saw. But how could she have seen others if she wasn't involved? He had left her back at the wagon moments before coming upon Gerard.

The marshal motioned to the two soldiers with him. "Bring the Rom and his woman."

"No." Serena bent down to cradle William's head.

"She's not involved," Keenan Maclean said above her. Whether she was or not, he didn't want her dragged off by these men.

"And what would you be knowing about this, Scot?" the marshal said with transparent contempt.

Keenan stood to his full height and stared the shoddy man in his black eyes. "I do ken that Gerard Grant is a close friend of the king and was my associate."

The marshal grunted and turned to his two henchmen. "We'll take the Rom boy to Newgate with the other prisoners next week. For now lock him up at Leeds Gaol. Leave the woman."

"But he's still bleeding," Serena protested as the two filthy men walked toward her.

"He'll probably hang or die of gaol fever anyway," the marshal retorted. "Best let him die tonight."

Keenan watched a shudder run through the lass. She was about to say more, when an older Rom man walked across the bridge toward them with a majesty that commanded the others to part. He placed his hand on Serena's shoulder and whispered something to her. She shook her head but he nodded stiffly. Anguish dampened her face. It was as if her spirit crumpled before him. She turned while the elderly man spoke with authority in Romany to the remaining people.

Two men from the Rom group moved past the guards and picked William up gently. They rested him across the marshal's horse. Keenan watched Serena flinch with each movement of her brother, even though her back remained turned against the scene. It was as if she felt his pain.

Keenan had heard of "The Traveling People" and had even seen some at Kylkern. Their ways were so different from the ways of the Scottish people that their differences seemed like magic. The woman before him hardly seemed to control powerful magic. Nor did she look like the sensual creature who had lured him to the fire. Now, she seemed more like a desolate child.

"What should we do with the other one?" the marshal asked him. "If he's a friend of the court, we should send him there."

"I'll take care of the body," Keenan answered briskly and looked over at the sprawled figure of Gerard. He wanted to see if there were any clues on the body. Gerard had no loyal family, and he was too dangerous to have many friends. Keenan had found him tolerable as long as he didn't have to spend too much time with him. King George, on the other hand, found him witty and clever. They had become friends, elevating Gerard to worth. And now he was dead and the letter signed by George describing how he planned to take over Scotland was missing. Lachlan would scream to the rafters in fury.

Keenan wrapped Gerard's body in a fringed blanket he bought hastily from one of the Rom onlookers. His and Gerard's horses were tethered closer to the faire. He watched Serena walk slowly after the marshal's horse. "She's bloody daft," he cursed. She could be attacked and raped, or worse.

From the trees came the older woman, Serena's mother. She looked directly at him as she led his and Gerard's horses from the shadows.

"She will need you." The old woman's eyes glistened. "We can do naught for my boy tonight. But you...Please..." she let the word hang there for a moment and handed the reins to him. She turned away without waiting to see whether he would obey her command.

Keenan watched her limp slowly away as if hopelessness tugged at her feet. The elderly man who had spoken with authority wrapped his arm around her, and they walked back under the trees. The others melted quickly into the forest. Keenan noticed Gerard's bag of coins where he had thrown it at Serena's feet, untouched. Not one of them had touched it.

Keenan rummaged through Gerard's pockets once more, turning him over this way and that. Nothing.

A fierce chirping caught his attention. Now what? The little blue sparrow hopped on the ground before him. It took several hops in the direction Serena had walked and then cocked its head back. Then it fluttered up and around him.

"Odd wee thing." He dodged the winged beast. "Are ye ordering me after her?" He had questions to ask and he wanted to feel her touch him again. He wanted to smell the freshness in her hair. Keenan grunted at the absurdity of his thoughts. "A dead patriot, a missing letter, a ruined mission, and I'm thinking about a lass." The sparrow chirped loudly as it circled his head. "And I'm taking orders from a bird," he said as he hefted Gerard's body over his shoulder and glanced around. Keenan looked down at Gerard. "Ye'll keep," he said and laid Gerard down into a hidden gully beside the bridge. "Ye won't get any worse than ye are now."

Keenan mounted his chestnut charger and wheeled around. "I'll be back for ye." He left Gerard's horse tied nearby. He would return to take the body to one of Gerard's associates to send on to his family.

With a slight pressure of his heel, his horse shot off into the darkness. It didn't take long to spot Serena as she jogged along the dark road. As his horse thundered, she stepped off into the shadows. "At least ye ken enough to hide," he mumbled and slowed to a walk.

"I'll take ye to Leeds," he spoke into the darkness.

He heard pebbles sliding under her feet as she climbed up the small bank out of the shadows. Her glassy, tear-washed eyes turned up to his. Her hair twisted wild around her shoulders, nearly to her hips. She said nothing, just looked up at him.

"I said I would help ye." He put his hand down.

She hesitated before placing a small hand in his. He hoisted her up and pressed his heels into the side of the horse.

They rode along the moon-soaked road. She smelled of sweet spices, cinnamon and autumn apples. Keenan wet his suddenly dry lips. She would taste as delicious as she smelled. Her warmth penetrated into his chest, coiling down into his body. So soft, so lush, her body moved against him with the rhythm of the horse. He grumbled low and shifted in his saddle. When would they reach the blasted jailhouse?

Like most small town jailhouses, Leeds Gaol looked to be only one level. Its crumbling façade of brick squatted heavily on the small plot of grass, its rear pushed up against the woods. The muted glow of torchlight radiated from within the front entrance. All other windows were dark, but Serena could feel the pain and hopelessness bleeding from the structure, emanating from the occupants.

Serena flinched as the men dropped William off the horse, feeling the pain his unconscious body registered. She could detect the emptiness of his mind, only the pain remained. Serena breathed deeply and erected the wall. She must keep her reason in order to help him. The heat emanating from the warrior behind her distracted her enough. *Focus.*

Serena tried to jump down but slipped haltingly

down the side of the horse. Like master, like horse, huge. She ran over to William and brushed back his hair. He was pale, so pale.

"So you decided to join the boy," said the marshal thickly and pulled her up by her bare arm. *I could chain her inside one of the cells, up against the wall, her plump arse bare...*

Serena gagged as the man's thoughts slid along her mind. In practiced defense she erected her most impenetrable barriers to muffle the repulsive images. It left her flushed, breathless.

"It would be wise for ye to take yer hands off the lass," the warrior said behind her.

Even without her senses, Serena heard the thinly veiled threat behind the words.

The marshal snorted and dropped her arm. "No use, girl, your brother is staying the night." The marshal motioned to the men who dragged William along the stone hallway and out of her sight. Keys jingled as the marshal pulled his dirty hand from his pocket. He took a step closer to Serena.

She could smell the foulness of his breath mixed with the odor of old sweat. His voice lowered.

"Now if you want your brother to have a comfortable stay, say with water and food, we may be able to strike a bargain, lovey." He grinned, showing dark teeth.

Serena fought the revulsion that threatened at the base of her throat. She didn't move away.

Keenan Maclean came up behind them.

"Stay back there, Scot, me and the lady is having a private discussion." The marshal reached out to grab her arm again.

Taking a quick breath, Serena stumbled forward into the rank man.

The strong hands of the Highlander pulled her back quickly, just like she'd hoped. But it had been enough time to find the jingle in the marshal's pocket.

"There will be no private discussions with the lady." The Highlander's voice cut through the air with sharp authority.

The marshal shrugged his shoulders. "Too bad for the boy."

The other two men came back out.

She needed a distraction, but what would keep the men outside the small jailhouse? Serena tried to breathe evenly to douse the tingling that had started in her arms. The edge of panic made her mind whirl frantically from one idea to the next. She walked back over to the Highlander's large horse.

He followed. "I will take ye back to the faire." He stepped up close to her.

She needed his help, but could she trust him? A man she couldn't even read? All her life she'd caught glimpses of thoughts and feelings from people. She learned their secrets without trying, their deepest desires, their hushed sins. Darkness lurked in every person. How could she trust someone she couldn't read at all? Even his expression seemed blank. He moved closer to her, and his fresh smell cleansed her of the marshal's foul scent. Serena drank it in.

"I cannot leave William. He will die if I don't get him out of there." She searched his veiled face then sighed softly. "I know you don't believe me, but I know that William did not stab your friend. They made it look like he did."

"Ye saw these people?"

"Yes, no, well in a way I saw them."

"Ye were there; ye were part of the robbery."

"No, no, there was no robbery." She shook her head. Her foot stamped on the cooling dirt. "It was a last minute farce to make it look like one."

"How do ye ken all of this if ye weren't there?"

Serena's eyes dropped to the ground. "It is hard to explain." She looked up. "I know certain things. I can see them from a distance, sometimes before they happen."

His eyes searched hers, but he didn't ask any questions. Without questions she couldn't defend herself so she held silent, waiting for him to weigh her words.

William's pain echoed like a dull ache in her mind. He couldn't read her mind, but she pleaded silently with him anyway. Let him read her desperation in her eyes.

"In return, ye will help me find those who killed Gerard?"

Serena hadn't expected that. She had seen them, the man and woman along with the hired murderer. But what choice did she have? She nodded quickly. "Once my brother is safe, I will help you find them." She wanted to find them, these criminals responsible for nearly killing her brother, ruining his name, ruining his family's name. Finding these people was important to the Highlander too. Perhaps he would truly help.

He gave one quick nod. "A bargain, it is set," he said plainly and looked around.

Serena saw that the three men still stood outside the jailhouse, but how much longer would they? "You need to keep them out here," Serena whispered and produced the keys in the folds of her skirts so that he could see them.

"Yer a pickpocket."

"Only when absolutely necessary." She hid the keys once more in a deep pocket tied around her waist under her petticoat. "I will go in through the back." She hoped that there was in fact a back door and that one of the keys would work in it. "I can find William and bring him out. We will hide in the woods beyond and wait for you."

The Highlander stared. Serena sighed in frustration. What was he thinking? She couldn't tell from his thoughts or from his face. "Will you come for us?"

"Aye, lass, I will come for ye. If ye canna bring him out, hide on yer own. I will find ye."

She nodded and hoped he wasn't lying. It didn't matter for she didn't have a choice.

"So how will you distract..." Serena swallowed a breath with her unspoken words as he pulled her against his solid body. In one swift movement he wound his hands through her long hair and tugged gently to bring her face up to his. His lips descended on hers with such ferocious intent that she thought she'd be consumed by his kiss. Never had she been kissed so thoroughly. At first he had to hold her to him, her body limp with shock. But blood thrummed through her veins, heating, melting her along his length. She pushed back against him. The Highlander's hands cupped her face. He slanted her head so that they fit perfectly against one another.

Serena barely noticed the whoops from the three jailors. She struggled to stay afloat under the onslaught of feelings rushing through her body. Her heart beat against the bone between her breasts as if beating upon the bars of a cell.

He released her mouth and ran lips down the naked column of her neck. A tingling spread goosebumps, causing nipples to harden against her bodice. Liquid heat pooled at the juncture of her legs, making them wobble slightly. The sensations washed away the inner struggle. Like a strong drink it deadened the thoughts and feelings until she drowned in peaceful heat. Without the constant battle to ignore his thoughts and emotions, Serena's other senses pulled in the fullness of the sensations Keenan poured into her.

He branded a path with hot breath back to her face and over to her ear. At the same time, his hands sloped down to her backside, squeezing it, molding it to the evidence that he was just as affected by the kiss as she was.

"Now push me away, slap me and run as if back to the faire." His breath sounded ragged, like her own, and it took several heartbeats for his instructions to register in her bloodless brain. This was the distraction.

William, she thought, shaking off the languid heat. Pinpricks of her brother's fear and pain shot ice through her overheated body. It was a wonder that she didn't see steam billow up.

Serena yanked her head away from him. "Get off me," she shrieked with real anger, anger for losing herself in the farce. Serena shoved against his chest with all the embarrassment she felt, all the shame. The Highlander had befuddled her mind in mere seconds. He released enough to give her access to his face. Serena's slap shattered the hollowness of the night, causing the jailors to double over in raucous laughter. She also kicked the Highlander's shin. He grunted and released her roughly as he rubbed the abused leg.

"Bloody wench," he cursed loudly, and she ran down the road until it turned, her arms pumping.

Serena huffed, feet pounding against the dirt as she ducked off the road. She closed her eyes and breathed deeply of the moist earthy scent around her and waited for her blood to stop rushing. Her face flushed hot in the chilled air, and she touched her lips. It was only a diversion, but she'd dived right in. Like some gypsy tramp. Serena rubbed hands over her face and purposely moved her thoughts to William. There would be time for humiliation later. When her breathing slowed to a more normal pace, she gathered and tied skirts high so they would stay free of the undergrowth. In silence, she circled through the trees back behind the gaol. There she watched the silhouetted clouds glide to obscure the glowing moon and dashed to the rear of the stone building.

Serena heard a single chirp overhead and saw Chiriklò, more with mind and ears than with eyes. He sat above a hinged door in the wall of the building. The bird darted in and out between the bars of a small window in the door. Serena tried to reach the window, but she wasn't tall enough. She stopped struggling and followed the path of the bird with her mind as it moved from cell to cell down the straight inner corridor. Some of the cells were empty. Others were not.

Serena slid her mind past each inhabitant, their resentment, their fear, their pain. One had stolen food for his children and he worried about them now. One was locked inside for a murder. Bleak desperation clung to two others. At last she found William. She focused her thin thread of power over him and through him. He was somewhat conscious. Fear and confusion mingled together, accented by sharp stabs of anger and pain.

"I'm coming, Shoshòy," she whispered and forced the head of one key into the rough lock. She tried to turn it, but it wouldn't budge. She tried another. One had to fit, it just had to fit.

Chiriklò flew back to the window and chirped once. Bawdy laughter from the front of the jailhouse danced back to her on the breeze, twisting her stomach. Finally. The third key turned and the door swung inwards.

The stench of bodily waste and decay slapped against her face. She staggered, catching herself on the slime-molded wall, and then hurried ahead. Ignoring the brush of something against her foot, she slipped down the side of the corridor to William's cell. Her senses open, she felt the wavering hope as one of the inmates watched her go by. Would he betray her? Would any of them betray her? None but the one had seen her so far. She moved to the man's cell and tried one of the keys. The lock clicked open.

"Keep silent if you value your life," she whispered and pointed to the back door that still stood ajar. He nodded and crept toward it.

Chiriklò sat across from the man's cell at another door. His thoughts flitted to her. She should open as many cells as she could. With all the prisoners missing, not just William, the tribe wouldn't take the full brunt of suspicion.

"On the way out," she thought back to her pet. The same key turned easily in William's cell. Serena pulled him off the filthy straw scattered over the stone floor. Rustling and squeaks came from a corner as something bit at her leather shoe. She kicked out at the dark lump, eliciting more squeaks.

"Àngelas?" William asked wearily.

"Shh." She braced him to lie across her shoulder and upper back. "Can you walk?"

"Yes, not well though." He grimaced. "My shoulder…"

"Shhh," she instructed.

"Àngelas, I didn't…"

"Hush, I know."

She held his weight as they shuffled along the corridor, step by step. He was large, a man now. His weight made her clumsy, and she fell against the stone wall several times. As she reached each door that held a prisoner, she jabbed the key into the lock and turned. She'd leave it up to the surprised occupants to find their way out. Serena was almost to the end when she saw the man in the last cell looking at her through his bars. He looked to be the age of King Will.

"How about me, lass?" The thick voice held the rolling brogue of a Scotsman. This man had murdered someone, she was certain. She didn't have time to probe more, for reasons or justifications. But he would probably give her away if she left him. Serena pushed the key in and turned it, stumbling again under William's weight. Her brother had lost consciousness again with the pain and loss of blood. Serena grunted with exertion as she moved closer to the cracked back door. How would she ever make it out into the woods? The other men had staggered past her and out the door, only the murderer remained behind them.

Serena's burden lightened as the stranger transferred William's weight to his own back.

"Ye willna get far that way, lass." He followed her out into the night.

Once they stepped out into the moonlight, Serena turned to the prisoner. His fuzzy beard covered much of his face, giving him a rough look in his torn, ragged clothing. The filth layered onto him made him difficult to see, but his eyes reflected the brightness of the moon. There was kindness in them, kindness in the man's heart. "I will take him, thank you," she said.

The man shook his head. "Ye canna carry his weight." He shifted William across his back. "Ye willna leave him?"

"He's my brother." She touched William's shoulder where her scarf still held the blood. "He's been shot."

The prisoner shifted William again so that he didn't press on his injured shoulder. "I will carry him where ye want me to." He stared into her face, and the side of his bearded mouth went up in a grin. "A kindness repays a kindness."

She hesitated for only a moment and waved him after her as she moved swiftly into the woods. She didn't know where to go. It had to be far enough away from Leeds Gaol, but close enough for Keenan Maclean to find them. She certainly hoped the Highlander knew how to track. If he didn't find them, what would she do? Her heart thumped wildly from the need to run. This was a race, a race to save her brother. Her pulse thrummed so loudly that she could hear it. Its tempo propelled her forward on light feet through the night like a doe caught in the scent of the wolf.

The man behind her bore his burden silently. Only the slight sound of William's toes touching a tree every so often could be heard. The man was taller than she had at first estimated. Even without the sound, she could smell his nearness. The pungent odor of unwashed filth wafted from him. How long had he been in the gaol? Serena didn't have time to discern his thoughts as she continued to scan ahead. She didn't want to run into anyone except Keenan.

After walking for what felt like half a league, she motioned for the man to put William down next to a fallen log. "Let us rest while I see how William fares."

The prisoner put her brother down and sat on the other side of the log. "Would ye have any food, lass?"

"No, I'm sorry," she said and really felt it. "I've known hunger before...I'm sorry. I have nothing with me." The man nodded then leaned back against the log.

Panic hitched in Serena's stomach. She really had nothing, no food, no money, and she had broken the law to save William. Serena breathed deeply to loosen clenched muscles. She bent over William, searching in the darkness. The binding was dry. The shot must be removed and the wound washed and cared for.

Although Serena's eyes had adjusted to the darkness, she still needed light to work. She looked around. Where were they? Would it be safe to light a fire? Where was Keenan Maclean? She knew practically nothing about him yet she had thrown him trust out of desperation. She had learned not to trust promises, when she could read in their hearts what they really felt and thought. Promises were just words and words meant very little to Serena.

The prisoner studied the night sky peeking through the tops of the tall oaks around them. He breathed deeply. "Ahh, the smell of fresh air." He sighed as if savoring a precious meal. He looked at her. "I must smell worse than a carcass." He smiled in the moonlight. His teeth looked white behind the scruff of beard.

Serena grinned slightly. "You could use a bath, sir."

"Robert is the name, Robert Mackay. And I be thankin' ye, lass, for freeing me from that hellhole. Ye are an angel."

An àngelas? But what type of man had she released on the world? The type of man who had helped her, by carrying William farther than she ever could have dragged him. Even without opening herself up to Robert Mackay's mind, she knew his actions were honorable.

"Thank you for carrying my brother for me. I have naught to pay you with, but you may have your freedom. You don't need to stay with us."

"Now, lass, what will ye do out here if I dinna stay to help ye?"

What would she do? Serena ran fingers through her hair to rub at the dull ache. She'd never held such responsibility before. What if they were truly all alone?

Chiriklò's high-pitched chirping pulled her eyes to the right. Hoof beats thudded against the road, a drum beat to the bird's song. Serena reached out to Chiriklò with her mind and concentrated on their location in relation to the bird's song. Chiriklò's chirping grew louder. He flashed her an image of the

Highlander who followed his song through the woods.

"Help is coming, Robert Mackay," she said and felt the beast of worry lift off her chest. "Help is coming, William." She kissed her brother's forehead and a faint smile touched her lips. Serena's head fell forward, letting her hair drape them both. A single tear dripped down onto William's pale skin, and Serena wiped it away with her thumb. Help was coming. Keenan Maclean had kept his promise.

Chapter 3

Luck was a fickle matron, but today she smiled on them. Keenan Maclean stood in the crude doorframe of the warm two-room cottage looking out at the slanting rain. Lazy jailors hated to hunt in the rain, and tracks vanished into mud. He'd been surprised to find a prisoner, Robert Mackay, helping Serena and her brother in the forest last night. But the prisoner had a sister who was generous, accessible, and knew how to remove a pistol shot. Aye, luck smiled on them.

Keenan's gaze shifted to Serena where she lay in exhausted sleep next to William, a brother who looked nothing like her. Who was this ivory-skinned, auburn-haired gypsy woman? Serena Faw was definitely not ordinary. She hadn't complained or pouted as they rode and walked through the forest all night. She hadn't shied away from helping Robert's sister remove the shot. Serena Faw was different.

The lass slept on her back now, one arm flopped over her stomach. He watched the swell of breasts rise and fall, lips relaxed in slumber, partly open. He remembered the kiss at the gaol. It had been a perfect distraction for the jailors and had given him a topic to discuss with the lusty English bastards while she sneaked around back. But the feel of her yielding lips, the press of her warm body against his, haunted him.

Turning, he peered out through the grey sheets of rain. If he were honest, he would admit that he wanted another taste of her, perhaps more than a taste. But what was the point? His life was not his own, nor his heart. The dark prophecy that shaped his every move and strategy owned his life. Keenan ran his hand along an eave, catching the cool rain, letting it run down his bare arm. At present he was too tired to be honest.

Robert Mackay's sister, Gena, placed a hand on his shoulder and whispered, "Go find yer rest. Ye will have to move them once the rain stops." She was a stout, older woman with gentle eyes and steady, strong hands, a solid Yorkshire widow. The concern for their party etched deep lines in her forehead. She sighed long. "It's too easy to find ye here."

"As soon as the rain stops," he said. She nodded and walked to her stool near the fire.

Keenan rotated his shoulders. He stretched out onto his side on the blanket next to Serena. She rolled towards him, and he inhaled. He caught her warm scent in his lungs and held it there until he was forced to release it. He rubbed his fist absently over the ache in his chest. Och, he wanted to touch her doe-like skin, pull her full, soft body to him. The memory of their kiss moved through his mind, and he rubbed a hand over his mouth and jaw, wiping away the feel of her lips. *Mo bhean. My woman.* The thought echoed inside him and he snorted softly. Ridiculous. He had no woman. He had nothing except duty and honor and death.

Her lips were so close that he could imagine the warmth of her breath. Even without the Rom coloring, she was exotic. She had an air of secrets, of magic. Pinpricks of warning ran down Keenan's back, cooling the rush of lust her smell roused in him. Magic already played havoc in his life.

Her blue bird flew in through the window and settled near Serena's shoulder. The strange sight sent a prickle down Keenan's back. What color eyes would Serena have in the sunlight? Keenan rolled away from her and forced himself to rest while listening to the cadence of her sleep.

****

They left Robert's sister when the rain stopped and traveled all night. Close to dawn, they halted at a small abandoned hut near the Scottish border. Serena insisted that William be allowed to lie flat and sleep solidly. She changed his dressing and frowned at the redness around the wound. "He will rage with fever, no doubt," she said and looked up at Keenan in the dim light of the hut. "We need to get him to your home as soon as possible so he can battle it without moving. How long?"

"With good weather, and few stops, four days."

Four days. Serena cringed inside. She brushed the matted hair back from William's forehead and placed a kiss there.

Robert carried chunks of peat cut from the moors nearby and plunked them into the grimy hearth. He peeked up the chimney warily.

"If it doona crumble down on us, we may have a nice fire."

Keenan shook his head. "No fire during the daylight. We'd be too easy to spot. When the sun goes down, we can start a fire to cook some meat right before we leave."

"Aye, of course." Robert walked over to William. He looked at Serena. "How goes the lad?"

"Lucky to have you cradle him so carefully on your mount," she answered sincerely. Robert Mackay had turned out to be a blessing. Upon meeting his sister, Serena had picked up on her relief and guilt. Robert had killed an English taxman who wanted more from his sister than her money. She lived alone and Robert had swooped in during the attack. He now paid the penalty for saving his only surviving kin. Serena had nearly left him in his cell because of her first impression.

Perceptions, even with her powers, could be wrong, she thought humbly and smiled at the man.

"He will rest now, that's all that can be done without supplies," she said.

Robert patted her shoulder and turned toward a corner of the dirty room. "Time to lower these weary bones to the floor, then."

The man's snore whooshed through the room within minutes. Serena's exhaustion lay upon her shoulders. Her head ached with worry. She didn't know much about healing a pistol wound nor a dangerous fever, and she didn't have Duy's herbs.

Serena lowered her body next to William. She threaded out a thought toward Mari, telling her they were alive and as well as could be. Serena didn't know if Mari could hear, but she would try. Her poor duy must be worried, both of her children gone. As the infinite number of hopeless thoughts piled in, Serena felt a heavy blanket drop. She looked up in time to watch Keenan walk back out of the door. She closed her eyes and fell into oblivion.

Her body floated along through dark images of the shooting, the dankness of the jailhouse, the strong arms of the Highland warrior. Just as her mind began to relax and retreat into comfortable blackness, she felt a familiar tug. The tug pulled from the dragonfly birthmark near her bellybutton. It had been pulling at her for years to go northwest. Serena felt it in dreams and sometimes when she was awake, staring off into the woods or sky. Wanderlust, Mari had suggested. It worsened the farther north they'd traveled and changed to a westward pull. The tug barely intruded on Serena when they traveled south of London. But now as they made their way into Scotland, the thread inside her jerked taut as if someone in the west wound it like a rope from the other end.

Serena's body lifted on the breeze and blew past

William and Robert where they lay on the floor. Out the door she moved. Was this real or just a dream? She didn't see Keenan as she walked among the trees, over branches, across a narrow road. She stopped in a clearing of ancient, gnarled trees as if the person who pulled stopped winding.

Serena turned in the circle of trees. She spread arms out wide and tilted her head back. The birthmark tingled against her skin. Sun slanted down through a hole at the top of the dense canopy to fall upon her upturned face. She squinted at its brightness. The smell of fresh earth after a spring rain surrounded her. The stuttered flight of hundreds of dragonflies darted among the trees towering overhead. What an odd sight.

"I am here," a woman's smooth voice came from nowhere and everywhere at once, perhaps inside Serena's head, she couldn't tell. Serena snapped back down out of the trees. The crone stood tall, wispy white hair braided. Her robes looked white, but then translucent and then full of every color imaginable as she moved. The many lines etched into pale skin gave her an ancient and wise look, much like the trees around them. Dragonflies zipped around her head like fairies.

"Who are you?" Serena asked.

The woman smiled. "I know you well," she said, but her lips did not move. She spoke to Serena in her mind. "I am Drakkina, and I knew your mother."

"You know Mari?"

"No child, your birth mother, Gilla. And your father, Druce."

Serena was about to ask more when the crone's thoughts stopped her.

"William will die," she said inside Serena's head. Fear twisted into Serena, and she almost turned to go back to him.

The woman held up a deeply lined hand. It

looked old, yet it seemed to possess so much strength, strength to stop Serena's trembling emotions until she could finish. "William will die unless you give him something now to fight the battle his body has begun. He cannot wait until you reach the Macleans of Kylkern. The poison creeping within his blood will have spread too far by then."

Although Serena was certain that the old woman could read her mind as well, she spoke out loud. "What can I do? Can you help him?"

"I am helping him," she spoke wordlessly, a mysterious smile spreading across her thin lips, "by helping you."

"Then tell me."

The old woman spoke out loud into the clearing. Her voice sounded older than the voice in Serena's head, but it was the same. "You must seek another, one with great powers to heal."

Serena groaned inwardly. "Can't you teach me what to do?"

The woman shook her head. "My powers have faded. You must call upon another. Have patience, Àngelas. I wouldn't have come to you if William's fate was written." The woman winked.

Serena's mouth fell open as the woman used her name. How did this crone know it?

"Close your eyes, child, and ask for the help of a healer," the crone continued. "Call her from your middle, from your mark." Serena felt her birthmark tingle.

Serena wasn't certain if she still dreamed or if she truly stood among the ancient trees in the middle of the sunlit forest. Dream or not, the threat to William was real. She reached out with her mind, past her wall of protection, out into nothingness. "Help please, help from a healer."

A distant voice wavered through her plea. Serena clung to it with the tenacity of a sister clinging to the life of her beloved brother. She focused her thread of energy on the far off voice until she could hear it, almost see it in her mind. The mark on her skin warmed.

The voice was familiar but she didn't know it. It seemed young but succinct, a woman.

"I will help ye," the woman said through the mist that engulfed them. Serena tried to open her eyes to fully see the woman, but as in many dreams, the vision remained fuzzy. "Tell me the nature of the wound."

"My brother has been shot with a pistol. The ball lay embedded in his shoulder for nearly a day before we removed it. Now a fever threatens him and yet we must still journey up into the Highlands before he can fully rest to fight the fever." The unclear vision wavered a moment. "Don't disappear," Serena called.

"I doona understand—piss-tool," came the voice, stronger now.

"He was shot."

"Shot? With an arrow."

Serena shook her head. "It doesn't matter. He has a hole in his shoulder and dirt has tainted him through the wound. We must travel on horseback. What can I do to help him?"

The image cleared briefly, and Serena saw a lovely young woman staring back at her. She looked as confused as Serena felt. She had long flowing hair in a warm shade of brown. Her eyes asked questions that there was no time to put into words. She looked the same age as Serena. A simple dress flowed down her form, and a crown of wildflowers encircled her head. Serena tried to touch on her thoughts, but they were so distant that the words whispered together in translucent cacophony. The woman was confused. They stared at one another for a moment before the woman bent to pull up two plants from the ground through the mist.

One plant had white flowers around a yellow button middle. Serena had seen it before.

"Feverfew," Serena said, and the woman smiled.

"I call it Fever's Foe for it battles away fever. Boil the leaves in fresh water until the water colors with the juices from the plant. Have yer brother drink it, as much as he can."

Serena nodded. The woman tilted her head and studied Serena. Then she held out the other plant, one Serena did not know.

"This is Burdock," the woman said. "Take the roots and boil them down in water until not quite half the water has boiled away. Make him drink it three or four times a day to cleanse his blood." Serena nodded.

"Also, pull off the leaves and cover them in a container with spirits, cover tightly and shake everyday for a fortnight."

"I don't have a fortnight, we move tonight."

The woman rubbed her slender finger along her head as if to ease an ache. She looked back at Serena. "Then grind the leaves into some spirit and make a paste, strain it through cloth. Drip some of the juice onto the wound to help calm the angry flesh. Ye could also take some of the remaining paste and wrap it on the wound under the bandage. But remember to change it daily or the leaves could add to the festering."

"Feverfew and burdock. I need to find them," Serena said.

"And this," the woman said, the plants dissolving from her hands. She held a small rock that shone in the light with an unusual brilliance. "Use this crystal," she said holding it out as if Serena could reach right over and take it from her.

"How?"

"Place it over his pain, his wound. Meditate

upon it, channel your powers through it into him."

"Channel my powers?" Serena whispered.

"Aye, I feel," the woman hesitated. "I feel something in ye, something," the woman's eyes narrowed as if trying to see more clearly, "something like me."

"Thank you," Serena said to the woman.

"I am Merewin of Northumbria. Who are ye?" the woman asked as the mist came up again around her. "I know ye."

"Merewin? Wait," Serena called and waved her hands futilely against the fog. "Don't go," she said and pawed at the white diaphanous clouds. "I need the crystal."

A weight clamped down on her shoulders, fingers pushed firmly into skin. She smelled pine and leather. Keenan. Her eyes still closed, he shook her gently. He took one of his large, rough hands and circled his palm along her cheek. Serena felt a flush run down her neck and through her entire body.

"Wake up, lass."

Serena blinked several times and opened her eyes to stare into stormy gray ones. "Where am I?"

"In the lowlands, still, with me."

The highland burr brought her fully awake, and she glanced around the clearing. The mist and the two women were gone. The ancient oaks still arched knowingly over her, allowing only a little ray of sun to come down through their branches. Several dragonflies flitted around and shot off into the trees. She tilted her face up to the sun and blinked several times.

Keenan pulled her closer, and grasped her chin. He tilted her head so that the rays of light warmed her face. Serena tried to move to block the blinding light, but he wouldn't let her go.

"Lass, yer eyes..." he hesitated. "They are...they are not a natural color."

Serena pulled her chin from his grasp. "They are unusual, but not unnatural," she said and scowled at him. He stood watching like she had grown talons and a tail. "They're mostly blue with some little flecks of red in them," she said waving her hands as if it were trivial. "The colors blend making them look rather, well violet." She was used to the strange looks from people over the color of her eyes. Mari said they were beautiful like blue amethyst, but Serena would give just about anything to have brown eyes instead. Although she withstood the scrutiny from most, somehow she didn't want Keenan to think her unnatural.

Keenan reached out and touched her hair where the sun warmed it. "And yer hair," he said and swallowed hard. "Yer hair, it is as if it flamed with fire."

"It is reddish in the sun," Serena said, yanking her hair from his fingers. She didn't like the strange look on the warrior's face. He looked almost frightened, this mighty man, sword strapped to his broad back.

"Why did ye come to this clearing? Ye seemed to be in a trance," he said suspiciously.

"I was dreaming. I walk in my slumber at times, especially as I travel north." Serena shrugged. "It is one of my," she hesitated. "oddities." It was the word Mari used with love to explain her differences.

Keenan rubbed his hand through his hair, eyes shuttered, lips tight. "It seems ye have many oddities."

Serena was about to start naming some of his oddities, but she couldn't think of any. She glanced down at her feet and gasped. Scattered all around the grove grew clumps of feverfew and burdock. Right in front of her were two bunches in a heap, their exposed roots muddy. The sun sparkled on something among them. Serena bent down and fished out the small crystal. Her heart thumped up into her ears.

"Thank you," she murmured and tucked the rock in her skirt pocket.

"What is that ye have?"

"It is but a rock I found that can help ease William's pain. And these plants, quickly help me harvest some. As many as you can hold."

Serena led a frowning Keenan, arms filled with feverfew and burdock, back toward the cottage. The sun began its descent. Robert had gathered some dry twigs to start a fire. Outside in the remaining light, Serena spoke to herself as she recited the recipes for the cures.

Turning, she caught Robert and Keenan watching. It didn't matter if they thought her peculiar. She had a brother to save.

"Ye can roast these," Keenan said to Robert and handed him two hares. "I'll rest for a few hours before we ride."

Serena looked up at the retreating figure of the warrior. He had remained awake all day to guard them. Would illness seize him with so little rest? Serena went inside to brew the herbs for William in the lapping firelight. Serena mixed the ground burdock with whisky and sieved it through a relatively clean piece of cloth. She placed the poultice on William's wound and bound it in fresh linen.

Serena poured small sips of the feverfew and burdock between William's lips. He seemed to drink it. She turned toward the opposite corner where Keenan rested. He lay with his face to the wall, a mountain of sleeping warrior. Robert turned the skewered rabbits over the flame. No one watched her.

Serena fished out the crystal and laid it on William's cleaned and bandaged wound. She covered it loosely with her hands, closed her eyes, and focused her thoughts into a single thread. Instead of pulling images out, she pushed positive thoughts, her life energy down the strand and into William. The crystal warmed against her palm until it burned. Serena pulled back on her thoughts and the crystal cooled. She concentrated again, this time controlling how much energy she funneled through the stone into the wound. Would it help William?

After long minutes of concentration a pressure began to push into Serena's forehead. Her limbs ached and seemed to weigh more than they should. Channeling magic took effort. A little more sleep would rejuvenate her. She let the flow of magic die away and tucked the stone into her pocket. Serena surrendered to exhaustion as she lay down next to William's pallet, her eyes moving involuntarily to the mountain in the corner.

The fire snapped behind her, shooting red splashes of light across the back wall. The mountain of sleeping warrior had moved. Firelight and shadow sliced across Keenan's face, his eyes open, unblinking, assessing. Serena's breath hitched in her chest as the warrior stared. How long had he been watching?

Chapter 4

Keenan pushed them hard through two more nights, stopping to rest during the day. The Romany lad seemed to be stable. Serena continued to pour drinks down him. Keenan watched closely. Since he'd found her talking to trees in the clearing and seen her violet eyes in sunlight, he had tried to keep his distance. Which had been impossible, since they rode the same horse.

She rode snug up against Keenan over the dark windy moors and through the narrow paths that lead to his homeland. Her head lay back nestled below his shoulder over his heart. She hadn't moved, and her gentle breathing told him she had fallen asleep. His arm tightened to better support her soft body. He breathed in the scent radiating from her and stared out into the starry night as the clouds chased one another across the open sky.

"She must be the one," he whispered. The tightness in his chest made it hard to breathe. She was the witch in the prophecy, and he was bringing her home to his brother. As he should.

When they reached the western Highlands, Keenan bade them sleep the rest of the night in a familiar glade of trees. They would travel the rest of the way by daylight. He purposely settled Serena across the fire from him. Distance, he needed distance to erase the feel of her soft body and alluring smell from his mind.

Keenan woke to the sound of light footsteps on the stone strewn path next to their crude camp. Dawn was just a dim light to wash the east silhouetting the spine of a mountain range. Serena disappeared into the shadows of the trees onto the moors beyond. Perhaps she only sought some privacy. But she could get lost on the moors in the darkness or twist her ankle on the spongy peat.

Keenan rose. William slept across from the gray remains of their small fire. Robert slept propped up against a comfortable boulder. They didn't stir as Keenan moved noiselessly past them, past the boulder, past the copse of trees at the edge of the moor. Serena walked slowly several yards ahead of him.

"Serena, where are ye roaming to? Ye should still be asleep," he called loud enough that she should have heard him easily above the gentle breeze that skidded constantly across the land. She continued without slowing, without a backwards glance.

"Serena lass, stop. Ye could fall," he said louder, his voice sounding like a shout in the quiet so pronounced just before dawn. Still she walked. He looked behind him at the dawn edging the mountain range. She walked west, directly west. She said that she tended to sleepwalk the farther north she traveled. One of her oddities.

In a slow jog across the spongy earth, he caught up to Serena. He stopped in front of her. She walked on. Her eyes, half open, did not register him at all. Her tangled mass of hair caught the glow of sun as it topped the edge of the world behind her. She breathed slowly, her lips parted as if she slumbered.

"Serena." He stood directly in her path, and she walked right into his chest. He gripped her shoulders and stooped to look into her half closed eyes. "She's still asleep," he murmured and shook her softly. No change. He stepped aside and Serena began to walk again.

Stepping along her side, Keenan turned her to

the left. In her sleep, Serena squared herself to the west, and continued. Keenan looked out over the vast moor, west toward the sea. What lay in the direction that pulled at her? Serena of the Faw Romany tribe contained more mystery than clarity.

Keenan caught up and stepped in front only to have her run into his chest once again. There she stood, asleep. He sighed in exasperation, picked her up and carried her back to camp. Robert woke startled as Keenan walked into the clearing with Serena. The older man raised his eyebrows at what must look like two lovers returning from a tryst away from prying eyes and ears.

"She walks west in her sleep," Keenan said without hushing his voice. The explanation sounded doubtful to his own ears so he nodded for emphasis. Robert looked skeptical.

Keenan shrugged and set Serena back on the woolen blanket. After a moment she sat up again. Keenan and Robert watched as she rose silently and began to walk once again.

"See, man," Keenan spread his hands wide, palms up. "West, she goes west."

"Bloody odd that," Robert said. And then after a moment, "are ye going to fetch her again?"

Keenan followed her out of the grove of trees. Bowing his head, he looked straight into her face. "Wake, Serena." She didn't wake. He shook her gently. "Wake, lass," he shouted. "Time to head north." She looked entranced. Keenan frowned. What would wake her?

Keenan placed his hands on her shoulders. He wound a hand in thick tresses and pulled to tilt her face. His eyes studied every detail of her lovely translucent skin, how it lay soft against high cheekbones and a delicate nose, how a sprinkling of freckles dotted the contours. Dark lashes were nearly closed. Parted lips pouted slightly, softly pink just for a man's touch.

So he touched, first with the thumb of his free hand, and then with his mouth. He kissed tentatively at first not wanting to startle. She kissed him back slowly, tilting her face to better meet him. Her response shattered his resolve to keep his distance. He groaned and pulled her against his body, feeling soft curves melt along his length. Perhaps it was he who deepened the kiss, perhaps it was the lass. It didn't matter. The only thing that mattered was the heat igniting between them. The spicy warm smell, the taste, the feel of her lush body pressed against his hardness.

Keenan pulled back and saw violet eyes open. She stared at him, her face flushed. Passion lurked in those brilliant, mythical eyes. Honest passion. He cupped her cheek with his free hand and ran a thumb over her bottom lip. He kissed her again. Serena answered back with as much passion as he gave and molded her body closely. He ran hands down to cup her sweet bottom through the skirts. She reached up on tiptoe and nuzzled intimately against him. Keenan's mind turned wild as he scanned the terrain in his memory. There must be a secluded place nearby.

The loud coughing dragged him back from the edge of madness. Bloody Mackay. He broke off the kiss and set Serena down. She looked totally befuddled.

"I'll just break camp since I see yer about ready to head out," Robert said. "Seems ye found a way to wake the lass." Robert chuckled and turned back toward their camp.

"What? Where?" Serena looked around. "What happened?"

"Ye walk in yer sleep."

"West."

"Aye, west."

"One of my oddities."

"Ye have quite a few," he said.

"So you've pointed out." She frowned. "And kissing someone walking in their sleep?"

Keenan grinned. "I suppose that would be a new oddity for me."

Serena's confusion relaxed into a grin. "Good."

"Good?" He couldn't help but smile back at her mischievous tone.

"Yes, good. You need a few oddities, else you'd be dull."

"Dull?" Keenan ran his hand through his hair. "Oh for a life that is dull." He pulled her hand. "Let's go. Ye'll see Kylkern Castle this day."

As they walked back to camp, Keenan continued to hold her hand as if it were the most natural thing to do. "For future reference, lass, is there any other way to wake ye when ye walk in yer slumber?"

Serena shrugged. "Mari and William used to tie me down until I woke."

Somehow Keenan found that exceedingly funny, and laughter echoed in the small copse of trees. His laughter was infectious, and Serena began to laugh as they swung their hands back and forth.

****

As they broke through the tree line opposite Loch Awe Keenan halted his horse. Rising above the clear waters sat Kylkern Castle. Its three granite towers rose majestically toward the mountain guarding its back. White spots of wool grazed along the mountainside. The castle sat on a peninsula that jutted into the loch with a small village of sturdy cottages before its walls.

He dismounted and lowered Serena. Keenan walked to the edge of the trees and picked some needles from the pine that bordered the water. Breaking the little needles between the nails of his thumb and forefinger he held them up to his face. He inhaled the fresh pine scent and looked out over the water as the sun began to set behind the beinn. Shadows of violet and red orange reflected on the glassy water.

"It is so beautiful," she whispered, sounding awestruck.

She was so beautiful. Her open admiration of his home only enhanced it.

He breathed out long, hoping to expel the pain in his chest and turned back to the scene before them. "Aye, 'tis a thing of beauty," he said and placed his other hand on top of hers.

They stood, side by side, with the trees at their backs and Kylkern Castle before them, the prophecy before them. "Welcome to Kylkern Castle, Serena."

As they approached the castle on the one land route, Serena sighed. "More voices," she whispered so low that Keenan barely heard her words caught by the wind. She rode before him, leaning back into his arms.

Keenan frowned, knowing that he wouldn't be able to cushion her in his arms once they reached Kylkern. The horses plodded over a small wooden bridge and among the houses of the village. The smells of home filled the air; peat smoke from chimneys, tilled earth, sheep dung. The village was modest, but the homes were sturdy and clean, with thatched roofs and mud caked sides to keep the highland winds out. The soft glow of cook fires inside gave the small dwellings a cheery look like a multitude of glowing torches over the surface of land to light their path.

"Hail there, Keenan," Garrett called from beside one cottage.

"Good eve to ye, Garrett," Keenan called back.

Isabell Pritchard came out of the doorway and waved at him. Her two young girls peeked out from her skirts. Keenan nodded at the widow and gave the bashful girls a quick smile. Serena looked behind Keenan's shoulder.

"They follow."

"Aye, they rejoice. Their great protector has returned," he said evenly, in an attempt to keep the edge from his words.

A chirping melody floated on the breeze. "Chiriklò." Serena whispered. The sparrow glided from a barely budding tree. Several people gasped as the bird alighted on her stiff shoulder. Reaching up, Serena let the bird move into the palm of her hand where she cradled it next to her cheek. The bird twittered softly.

"Aren't ye fearful the bird will make a meal for a hawk?" Keenan spoke near her ear as he watched the villagers emerge.

"Chiriklò has been around since I was a little girl. He is not like a normal pet. I would be more afraid for the hawk."

"Another oddity," Keenan murmured. She lowered the bird to her lap and looked back at him.

"I have quite a few." Serena turned back toward the castle.

As she ran her finger down Chiriklò's feathers, Keenan leaned back to her ear. His grin disappeared as he sought for words. He must warn her. "Ye are welcomed to Kylkern Castle, lass. The people are good souls but curious. Doona take offense."

"I am used to curiosity from people. I don't look like a typical Rom."

Keenan brushed his chin against her hair.

"Lass." He hesitated. "There will be more than just normal curiosity." Serena shivered before him, turning, lips open in question.

"Hail, Kennan!" Rus, his first in command, called out and waved.

Serena turned forward again, her question interrupted.

They stopped before the wooden gate guarded by the familiar iron portcullis that rose up to meet the deep azure sky. *Home.* The word settled in his gut, a mixture of anticipation and dread.

His words were low, just above a whisper. "Ye see, lass, ye are the savior of our people, the one who will lead us to peace."

Chapter 5

Keenan tapped his horse into a jog and they plodded across the planked gateway into the torch-lit bailey.

"What do you mean?" Serena asked, but the shouts of warriors rose up as Keenan pulled his horse to a stop before the massive doors to Kylkern Castle.

Men, tall and broad came running out of a low building off to the side. The double doors looked as if they belonged to a giant. They towered up into a peaked arch to point toward the sky. The doors swung outward and a press of more warriors rushed to greet Keenan under the darkening sky. Shouts of "Keenan returns," rang through the air and through Serena's battered mind. Although she was able to block most of the individual thoughts, the hum of emotion washed through her; elation, relief, and something else. Hope.

He's returned. Finally, I'm ready to spill some English blood. He'll lead us to victory!

Before she could contemplate what her senses told, Keenan dismounted amid cheers, and his iron-like hands lifted her down.

"Take the horses and rub them down well, lads," Keenan called to two stable boys who grabbed his reins. Serena could just make out through the crowd of men, Robert Mackay lowering William from his horse.

"The three who journey with me are honored guests. The boy has been hurt and needs to rest." One of the warriors tried to take William from

Robert's arms, but Robert shook his head and marched toward the door with his burden. Serena thought she saw William glance around before closing his eyes again. Concerned, she moved as best she could toward him.

"Let me to him." She spoke out above the low hum and several of the men parted to give her room. She ran up and placed a hand on his head. The fever was nearly gone, but she hadn't touched him to sense a fever. He was frightened and still confused. She bent to his ear.

"All will be well, Shoshòy," she said, speaking in Romany. "Rest easy." Her closeness and the familiar language comforted him. She looked to Robert. "Thank you."

He smiled.

Serena watched him walk up the thick slab steps. It was only then that she noticed the large man standing at the top of the steps, illumed from behind by torchlight. His face hid in shadows but his stance held purpose. She sensed authority around him, an air of importance.

"Aye, come inside," he said to Robert, but continued to watch her. "Ye are all welcome to Kylkern Castle."

Keenan closed his hand around her upper arm and tugged slightly to move forward. "Lachlan, chief to the Macleans of Kylkern, please welcome Serena Faw of the Romany tribe into yer home and protection." Keenan's words rang through the hushed courtyard.

If Serena hadn't felt the push of hundreds of curious minds against her back, she'd have thought them alone in such silence. It was as if the highland wind held its breath as the chief, Keenan's older brother, studied her. The man was not quite as tall or nearly as broad shouldered as Keenan. He had a handsome face surrounded by brown hair pulled back from his straight, unmarred features. His forehead pinched a bit as if he toiled over some complex problem, and his eyes searched her.

Lachlan extended his hand to hers. Serena took a deep breath and prepared to touch him without her gloves. She had left them with the horse. She clasped his fingers timidly to allow him to pull her up the remaining steps.

Soft skin, pure and beautiful. Who is she? Is she Keenan's? Romany? She doesn't look Romany.

His thoughts were normal but something lurked behind them. She sensed fear, fear mixed with great frustration.

"Ye are very welcome here, lass," he said, his soft burr like his brother's. He smiled and led her into the cheery interior of the castle's main hall.

Serena glanced back to see Keenan watching as if pain pulled at him. Their eyes met and he grinned, but the smile did not lessen the intensity of his gaze.

Serena turned. She coughed and pulled her fingers from Lachlan's grasp to cover her mouth. Breaking the contact helped immensely.

Lachlan stepped away. "Do ye have the ague?" he asked, his forehead furrowed.

"No, just a bit of dust from the courtyard." He took her hand and placed it on his arm. He led Serena to a long table laden with food. Most of the men had retreated outdoors leaving only a few talking heartily around the hall. Tapestries covered several of the stone walls, beautifully woven with colorful battle scenes and victories. One of a beautiful woman caught her attention, for the woman had her coloring down to the deep blue violet of her eyes.

"Sit, sit, and fill yer stomachs," Lachlan called out to Keenan, Serena, and Robert who had just descended from where she assumed William lay resting. The fire blazed in a magnificent hearth at the other side of the room, casting warmth throughout. The stone floor was nearly spotless with a few area rugs placed for comfort near sitting areas. The table shone with cleanliness, and the room smelled of dried herbs and flowers. Its cheerfulness did not match the tension around her.

Keenan strolled over to them. He dropped her gloves and turned to talk to his brother. She quickly donned their familiar comfort.

"Tell me brother, what news from Gerard?" Lachlan asked. "Did ye bring the letter?"

"Gerard's dead," Keenan said.

Serena watched cold worry flash across the chief's face. His fear jumped to the surface.

"And the letter revealing King George's plans to rape Scotland?"

"Taken from his corpse."

"And where were ye when our only hope to unite the clans against the English was thieved?"

Guilt sat heavily in Serena's stomach, which made it impossible to pick up the buttered dark bread. Would Keenan place the blame on her or William? Should she speak up? Before she could utter a word Keenan sat down next to her and broke off a piece of bread and began to chew. Serena watched as he shrugged his massive shoulders that looked even bigger since they were now contained indoors.

"Lachlan, ye ken how hard it is to keep a hold of that slimy bastard. He was always trouble. For all we ken, the letter was created as a trap to prove we're Jacobites so the crown could take our lands."

Keenan's brother sat down and rested his head in his hands, rubbing as if that would chase away some ache. "Keenan, what are we to do now?" Lachlan said lowly so that only his brother, Serena and Robert heard. "We need something to bring the clans together."

Keenan nudged Serena's bread closer. She nibbled the herbed bread and let the heady taste swirl around in her mouth. Keenan gulped down some mead before looking at his slumped brother.

"Serena and her brother saw who took the letter, Lachlan. The boy is too weak to travel back, but the lass and I can find them."

This is what Keenan must have meant when he said that she was their savior. The letter must be of incredible value.

Lachlan looked up. Although hope once again brightened his eyes, his brow furrowed deeper. He frowned nearly as much as Keenan did, Serena thought and took another bite of the aromatic bread.

"Keenan!" A woman's high pitched voice echoed through the high rafters of the arched room. "Ye've returned."

A tall, slender woman rushed down the steps, her skirt pulled up in her haste to reach him. Keenan jumped up and caught her as she hurtled into his arms.

Serena watched, the bread turning tasteless in her mouth, as the lovely woman kissed Keenan's cheeks, his forehead, even the tip of his nose.

Keenan wrapped her in a fierce hug and swung her around.

An invisible weight descended upon Serena's shoulders, and the heaviness of ignored tears sat behind her eyes. She turned back and took a drink of the honey mead. She shouldn't care if he had a woman back in the Highlands. He rescued her and William and that was enough. He would help clear William's name, and she could help these people at the same time by finding their letter.

Anger followed the cold path of honey mead down into her stomach. But he had kissed her, kissed her thoroughly, twice. What would the laughing woman behind her think of that?

"Serena." His voice still held his smile. She turned to face the two radiant people, a tangy aftertaste settling in her tight throat. "I wish to introduce ye to the light of my simple life."

Several warriors behind her snorted, and the lady pinched up her nose good-naturedly at them.

Serena stood woodenly.

Keenan continued. "Elenor, daughter to the late Angus Maclean, and my beloved sister. Elenor, please meet Serena Faw of a Romany tribe," he said.

Elenor gripped Serena's fingers in warm greeting. "Rom, the Traveling People," she said, and her eyes glittered brilliantly. "I remember them visiting when I was a lass. Papa would proclaim a festival when they came. I remember dancing to lutes and rattles and drums," she said wistfully.

Serena stood speechless, still gripping the woman's hand. Slowly her stomach began to unknot under the happy stare. Although the glove muted the woman's happiness, it radiated up to her rapidly beating heart. She smiled back.

"I am pleased you share the fond memories of my people. I am glad to meet you," she said and actually meant it. The woman's happiness surrounded her. Elenor seemed to bring out the smiles from all except Lachlan who still brooded in his chair.

Elenor sat and pulled Serena back down. "Continue yer meal, Lady Faw."

"Please call me Serena."

"As long as ye call me Elenor."

Serena nodded and took a bite of a buttery yellow cheese, flavored with dill.

"Delicious," Serena said.

"Aye, I had the cook add the fresh dill to give it a bitterness against the tangy sweetness of the cheese. I think it turned out quite pleasant," Elenor said, and cut off a small chunk from the block in the center of the table.

Serena nodded.

Lachlan punched his fist down on the table making the dishes, and Serena, jump.

"And what the bloody hell will I tell the clan chiefs while yer away finding the blasted letter that ye were supposed to bring back with ye?" Lachlan shouted at Keenan who had taken a seat to his brother's side. Keenan barely registered the outburst.

"Lachlan yells a lot," Elenor whispered to Serena. "He is nervous and impatient by nature, but he calms down eventually.

"There are the three of us, I dinna ken if Keenan told ye about us," Elenor continued.

Serena shook her head.

"Well then, Lachlan is the eldest and therefore laird, I was the second born and last came Keenan."

Serena could feel the love the sister had for Keenan without any of her powers. It dripped from her voice, and Serena wondered if she sounded that way when she spoke of William.

"Call the chiefs together and tell them that I," Keenan said and jabbed his finger into his chest. "I have seen the letter from King George ordering the revocation of their lands, for I have. The English king would give our land to English nobles who have no ties to our homeland because he fears our support of the Jacobite cause. He fears what he cannot control."

Several of the warriors standing nearby muttered obscenely.

"But Keenan, without proof, they willna unite against England. Some even plot secretly with George in order to save their lands. And without the clans united, we willna see James Stuart and his son, the bonnie prince, sit on the throne of all Britain." Lachlan ran his nervous hands through his hair making it stand out around his pale face.

Keenan lowered his voice but Serena could still hear.

"Remember to consider, brother, that Bonnie Prince Charlie maybe should not be the one to lead us."

"Enough," Lachlan said. "That talk is treason, Brother," he said stressing the familial title.

"All talk is treason to one side or another."

Lachlan moved his hand in the air to dismiss Keenan's words. "We support the Jacobite cause, any cause to stop the German miscreant from stealing our lands."

Keenan nodded. "Of course to save our lands, but consider that there may be other ways to secure our lands apart from putting all our trust in the hands of an untried prince who prefers women and drink to battle." Hard words set in a hard face. Serena felt rage emanate from Lachlan.

"Father backed James and his son, and so shall we," Lachlan said.

"Father never met the prince as I have," Keenan countered.

Elenor leaned into Serena. "Old argument. Lachlan willna listen," she said quietly. "Let us away to the hearth, else we get an ache in our heads. Ye have the most unusual colored hair for a Rom," she said. Elenor stood and Serena followed her to the cheery fire lapping up the insides of the huge hearth.

Keenan watched his sister lead Serena away. Had Elenor noticed the lass's hair and eye color yet? His sister had always been obsessed with the legend of his death and the witch that would herald it. Much to their parents' horror, Elenor studied the Wiccan ways over the years so that she would understand her sister-in-law. If Serena were the one, Elenor would discover it. And then what would he do? *I suppose I can die.* He smiled sardonically and tried to pay attention to his brother's ranting.

"And what exactly is so blathering funny that ye smile when I rage?" Lachlan accused. "Do ye mock me, brother? Have ye forgotten yer place in this family?"

"Nay, Lachlan." Keenan forced down the rise of temper, held in check through the years. "I was but contemplating how surprised the clans supporting King George will be when he gifts their lands to English barons," Keenan said smoothly and took a drink of mead while his eyes moved to rest on Serena's back where she stood near the fire.

"Aye," Lachlan said with a grimaced smile. "If they doona join us, we are all doomed to find English dandies stamping before our gates," Lachlan said. "But they'd have a bloody battle to actually broach my walls, eh? What with ye, and yer warriors behind them."

Keenan looked at his brother. Lachlan had just complimented him.

Keenan grinned. "Aye brother, they would indeed," he said and raised his mead in mock cheer. He took a drink and turned back to the room.

Serena's hair fell to her waist. Although dirt still clung to her from their trip north, she was beautiful. Her dancer's grace made every movement fluid. Her gloved hands accentuated words as she spoke. The two women began to laugh. Serena turned and Keenan's breath caught mid inhalation at the magical transformation her jubilant smile created.

In repose the lass was delicately lovely, like a statue, but in laughter, spirit jumped into her features bringing them to life. He took a slow breath and tried to eat more of the venison placed before him, but the food, though of its usual aromatic quality, held little interest to him. The bread stuck to the roof of his mouth so that he had to scrape it off with his tongue. He took a drink, and his eyes studied the gentle sway of Serena's hips as the two ladies walked along the wall. He took another bite of venison and chewed hard.

But if she was truly the witch of the prophecy, she was to be his brother's. Keenan's chest tightened. "Whisky!" he called back over his shoulder.

Lachlan laughed. "Spirits for ye, Keenan? Not yer usual drink. Might open up a crack in that blasted control ye always keep on yerself."

It was true. Keenan always stayed in control. Whisky just reduced reaction time. Bloody hell, the lass was driving him to drink, to lose control.

Keenan grunted and took a swallow of the offered drink. The hot trail of liquor snaked down along his throat and into the hollow of his stomach. Perhaps numbness would help.

"This lass ye brought, Serena Faw," Lachlan said, his mouth seeming to taste her name. Keenan doused the image with another drink of the liquid fire while his brother continued. "She is a luscious looking thing, nothing like the Rom I've seen."

Keenan grunted again and watched his brother's eyes flow over Serena, assessing her, his gaze following the length of hair down her back, the swell of breasts when she turned.

"Aye, very lovely," Lachlan said and wiped the back of his hand across his lip.

Keenan finished his drink in one more gulp. He needed more if he wanted to be numb to his brother's lecherous perusal of Serena.

"Perhaps," Keenan ground out, "ye should go over and acquaint yerself with her, Lachlan."

Lachlan didn't even look at his brother as he rose. "Quite a good idea, Keenan. Always looking out for me," he said and walked over to the two ladies.

Keenan stood, his body humming for battle. He passed two serving lasses who smiled at him, the twin mountains of their breasts nearly spilling from their bodices. Open invitation danced in their eyes.

"I am weary," he lied as he passed them, for every nerve in his taut body buzzed with restless energy. He strode out into the cool Highland night. Within moments he climbed upon his chestnut war horse and rode through the gates past the sleepy village and out onto the dark moor.

Keenan's fierce roars filled the quiet spring night as he flew across the darkness, his sword slicing the air. His foe was not one he could chop and fell. His foe was a dark legend that gave the lovely red headed witch who laughed joyously inside his home, to the leader of his clan.

He spit out a curse born of Scots whisky, regret, and resolve to duty, and loosed his horse to ride at will, wild across the heath. Here alone, just man and beast, he could loosen his control. Here under the cover of darkness, Keenan could rage against his destiny.

Chapter 6

The indoor, hot bath was pure bliss the night before, and now Serena stretched contentedly under the heavy throws on her bed. She thrust hands overhead and cracked her eyes open to see sun shining in past shuttered windowpanes set into the gray walls. It must be late.

Serena sat up and peered at the ivory nightdress that Elenor gave her last night. She noticed a gown draped at the end of the bed. Serena shoved the blankets aside and tugged the soft wool towards her. The shade was of medium blue, bright, a happy color. "Must be one of Elenor's."

Serena washed in the basin on the heavy, carved oak table near the window. She pulled the heavy drapes aside letting the light fall in and looked through the warped glass down the side of the castle tower. She could make out the thatched roofs of the village spreading out beyond the castle walls. People moved about their work.

"It's late," she said. She took off the nightdress and put on a clean shift. She tied her stockings with garters and tied the one pocket around her waist. She draped the blue wool stays over a short white under petticoat.

"Arrgg, how can a girl possibly dress alone," she grumbled and tried the door connecting her room to William's. At first he looked asleep, but when she pushed his door in further, he moved his eyes.

"William, can you help me?" she asked and sat on the edge of his bed.

He smiled when she kissed his forehead. "No

fever," she said. "And your shoulder?"

He moved it slightly. "A bit stiff, but it will heal no doubt to your fine talents."

Should she tell him about the old woman and Merewin? It still felt like a dream. But the burdock and feverfew had been real, as well as the healing stone.

"I didn't know you knew the healing arts," William said as she turned her back to him. Serena heard him press up against the back of the bed.

"Desperation brings out unknown skills," she said and felt him tug on the stay lines. He grunted softly and she turned around. "I'm sorry, William, I'll have someone else do up the stays if it pains you."

Just then a knock came to the door and Serena stood as Elenor stepped inside carrying a tray. Elenor gasped, and the tray teetered.

"Oh my, excuse me. I meant to bring William some broth."

"I hope there's more than just broth in the kitchens," William called from his position on the bed. "A man needs some meat and bread too," he said smiling at his sister's discomfort.

"Elenor," Serena said as she fought the blush.

"Good waking, William," Robert Mackay called as he walked in behind Elenor. Serena's fingers began to turn white as she clutched the undone stays in her fingers. "Excuse me, Serena. I didn't realize ye were unclothed, lass."

"Unclothed?" Where she felt the others' surprise and awkwardness at finding her undone in William's room, Serena heard a hint of anger in the rough burr of Keenan's voice. He pushed in past Robert and Elenor to stand before her.

"I, I," she began.

"Yer undressed," Keenan said looking her over from head to toe.

"Not completely," she said and mustered a bit of

anger. "Have you ever tried to tie stays behind your back?" When he didn't answer she continued, "by yourself."

He stared at her unblinking and then turned to William. Serena heard Elenor's muffled chuckle somewhere near the door.

"Well 'tis near impossible," Serena said defensively and threw out her hand toward William. "He's always been the one to lace them for me at home if Duy was not about."

"See now, Àngelas," William said laughing. "I told you we were too old now for me to be dressing you. Making me act your maid," he shook his head, "it's gotten you into trouble."

"Elenor," Keenan said firmly, "send up a lady's maid for Miss Faw."

"Aye, Keenan," Elenor said, set the tray down near William, and headed back out the door. "And I'll rummage up some meat and bread for our invalid there."

"Invalid?" William grumbled but then called after Elenor, "my thanks, Lady Elenor."

Robert cleared his throat. "Good to see ye feeling better, lad. I best check back later," Robert winked toward Keenan and Serena who still frowned at one another.

"I have many thanks to give to you, sir," William called out to Robert. "You and your sister saved me."

"Nay more than what yer sister did for me, lad. And call me Robert," he said as he waved and walked from the room.

Serena would have replied but she was too busy glaring back at the mountain before her.

Keenan couldn't pull his eyes from her. Her skin, now clean, glowed rosy with embarrassment.

Serena's eyes flashed indignation, while her hair fell in shining waves. He thought the flames incredible during their journey, but now with the road dust stripped away, her mane blazed red with gold highlights shooting through it.

He clenched his fingers so as not to reach for it. Her lips were parted as if waiting to hurl another quip his way, but none came. In her half dressed state, she looked like a woman who had just been tousled. Serena thought of William as a brother, but what did William feel for Serena?

"I would have a word alone with yer brother."

A girl peeked around the corner of the door that led to Serena's room.

"Don't you say anything to upset him," Serena said and looked at William.

"I'm not too frail to talk, Serena," William said with his deep, I'm-a-man-now voice.

"Very well," Serena said and turned to leave. She pulled her hair to one side, and Keenan caught a glimpse of the silky nape of her neck above her shift. It was pale and perfect. What would that spot taste like? He shook himself mentally and turned his attention to the young Rom man. The door clicked shut.

"Are ye in love with her?" Keenan blatantly asked. Full frontal assault was how he usually liked to attack.

"Yes," William said seriously.

Not what Keenan was expecting.

"Ye doona try to hide the fact ye love her?"

"Of course not, she's my phen, my sister. I love her as such." William frowned.

Keenan stared at the proud man, weighing his words. There was truth in them. Keenan dropped into a chair near the bed.

"She was found by yer people?"

"She was found by me," William said. He still looked guarded.

Keenan raised an eyebrow. "By ye?"

"She was little, then," William said, his white

teeth showing in a broad smile. "But she sure made a large splash when she dropped into the middle of the pond."

"Middle?"

William nodded, but didn't say more.

"Where was she before dropping into the pond?"

William frowned. "Why do you want to know so much about my sister?"

Why indeed? Keenan ignored the first answer that popped into his head, the one that he thought he had chased away with whisky and war cries on the moors last night. He needed to discover whether or not Serena was special, special enough to be magic.

Keenan leaned back casually. "It just seems that ye were a little young perhaps and dinna see where she jumped from. Unless she fell from a tree she couldn't drop into the middle of a pond." He shrugged and looked away. "Yer still quite young lad and probably haven't' thought it through."

"Nay, I saw her fall in the middle, right from out of nowhere. I know what I saw," William said defensively. "She fell from the sky into the pond. Like a fallen àngelas, an angel."

Keenan studied William. "She is special, yer sister."

William just stared back.

"She kens the use of magic, William?"

They stared for a long moment.

"What do you think, Highlander?"

Elenor opened the door tentatively. "Meat and bread have come," she said cheerfully at William. "Maddie Grant is with Serena, Keenan." She set the tray near the bed and began to fluff and prop up William to eat.

Keenan stood, noticing the faint flush to his sister's cheeks.

William's eyes caught hers for a moment. What

did that mean? The man couldn't even be a score and ten, and his sister was a year older than he. Keenan frowned. She had never married. Even with her beauty and joyous demeanor, no suitor was confident that the prophecy only applied to sons by blood and not sons in marriage. No one wanted to be the second son. And so his sweet Elenor would also suffer loneliness. If she wanted to blush over the Rom lad, let her.

Keenan mumbled a farewell and left the room, with William's words pounding in his head. "What do you think, Highlander?" Keenan knew. Serena, the angel fallen from the sky. Serena was special. She was the witch.

"Keenan," his sister's whisper followed him, and he turned to see her shutting William's door.

Elenor glanced at Serena's door, and then motioned him to follow her downstairs.

He watched Elenor's delicate hand follow the stones of the wall as they descended. She really was bonny, his sister. She should have been married with three bairns holding to her skirts.

When they reached the bottom, Elenor took his hand and led him to the side behind the stairwell. It was dimmer there but he saw emotions cross her face. Hope warred with worry, questions with the firmness of certainty.

"I saw her eyes this morning, in the light of day," she said. "I nearly dropped William's tray."

Keenan just stared.

"Her eyes are violet, Keenan, and her hair blazes like fire."

"I had noticed."

"Ye had noticed?" Elenor said, her voice going up in pitch at the end.

Keenan waited.

"And I've heard stories of this sparrow that follows her? It sat on her shoulder as she rode through our gates."

"Aye, I've seen the bird. She calls it Chiriklò."

"Chiriklò?"

"Aye, Chiriklò. It means sparrow in Romany"

Elenor stared at him and then whirled around, took two quick paces and pivoted back around and paced back. Her hands fluttered.

"And ye aren't affected by this? Haven't said anything about it, about these, these…"

"Oddities?" Keenan supplied.

"Aye, oddities," Elenor said with a frustrated huff and then raised her small hand to rest on his shoulder. "Keenan, she could be the one, the witch," she whispered the last word.

"At this point, I have little doubt that she is indeed the one," he said matter-of-factly.

Elenor pulled her hand from his shoulder. She tapped her finger against her lips. Keenan liked to watch her think. She wasn't only bonny, but clever as well. And sadly, full of hope for him. Hope when there was no hope.

Elenor lowered her hand. Her small smile worried him. "She dinna seem too taken with our brother last eve," she said.

"Give them a chance," he said gruffly.

"Why?"

Keenan stared at Elenor. He had always known that she loved him fiercely and above Lachlan. She had been trying to discover a way around the prophecy for as long as he could remember. But she had never actually said anything to make him think that he should or could manipulate the prophecy to his favor.

"Why give them a chance," she repeated.

"Why?" he asked back incredulously.

She looked down and began to pace within the small alcove.

"Aye, Keenan. Why?"

"Because that is how the prophecy goes, Elenor. I willna steal my brother's wife to save my life."

"But she loves ye," Elenor said. "It is plain to see if ye look."

"What are ye speaking of, Elenor?" he said. Anger bit into his chest. The hope that Elenor gave him with false words would only slice through him later with more pain. He shook his head. "There is naught between us."

"Well there's certainly more between the two of ye than between she and Lachlan," Elenor said. Frantic hope clung to each word.

"That is because we journeyed together, because I helped her and her brother, Elenor. If Lachlan had done the same, she would be closer to him."

Elenor scoffed. "Lachlan help someone other than himself, not likely."

"Elenor."

"No Keenan, ye ken I speak the truth. I love Lachlan as I must for he is my brother. But he hides himself away, afraid of death. What kind of chief hides away behind his walls, behind his little brother?"

"Enough," Keenan said.

She looked steadily up at him. "I am not the only one who questions his right to be chief when he hides here behind ye and the walls of Kylkern." Challenge laced her words.

Keenan's hands tensed on her upper arms, but then relaxed in resignation. Bullying his sister would not make her stop. "I have always accepted my lot. Ye need to also."

She shook her head slowly, firmly. "No, Keenan I doona have to accept anything. Ye are the courageous chief of this clan. Ye saved the witch and brought her here. Ye protect our people with yer sword and cleverness. We need ye to bring us to peace. Doona abandon us to Lachlan just because our sire named ye the sacrificial lamb."

"Elenor, cease," Keenan said low, his tone of warning evident.

She closed her mouth but looked mutinous.

"I will protect Lachlan and this clan as I always have. I will die honorably knowing that I have done my duty." He said the words he had repeated most of his life, the only words that had brought approval from his parents. It was unthinkable to abandon something he had been raised to believe ever since he could understand what death meant.

Elenor's words were soft. "Keenan, have ye kissed her?"

The question sliced through him. His answer was traitorous, and he would have denied them if the memories did not haunt him constantly.

He looked away from her, and he heard her suck in her breath.

Her voice echoed hope brightly, victoriously. "Ye have. Ye've kissed her."

"Once, to distract the jailors to save her brother, and once to wake her from some sort of trance."

"Trance?"

"Aye, she walks toward the west in her sleep."

"West?"

"Another oddity," he said, and for a brief moment had a hard time keeping his grim expression in place.

Elenor grinned at him. Her eyes shone brightly with youthful enthusiasm. He hadn't seen that for a long time.

"I'm telling ye, Keenan. She's the one, and we will soon see that this prophecy did not name ye to be the one to die, mark my words."

Keenan sighed and shook his head. "Elenor, what am I to do with ye?"

He was about to answer his own question with threats of nunneries and shackles, but a swish of petticoats brushed the stone steps next to them.

"Oh Serena," Elenor said. "Ye look lovely in that gown."

Serena gasped and whirled around, her hand at her chest. Relief relaxed Keenan's chest, she hadn't heard the treasonous conversation. Dear sweet Lord, she was beautiful. Her face flushed, lips parted, the sides of her hair pulled back into a simple braid of blaze to fall among the gentle waves to her waist. The laced stays and petticoats accentuated her narrow waist, and the color of the blue lamb's wool matched the violet blueness of her eyes.

A matching streak of blue shot across the rafters, diving. Elenor gasped and Serena laughed lightly as Chiriklò fluttered to her shoulder. Aye she was the one, and there would be no hiding it today. Once Lachlan…

"Good morrow to ye all," Lachlan called as he clipped across the smooth rock floor toward them.

"Good morrow, Lachlan," Elenor replied softly, her eyes darting between Serena and their fast approaching brother. Keenan nodded in greeting, but Lachlan's eyes had first gone to the bird perched upon Serena's shoulder, then to her gown. Keenan's gut tightened and he forced himself to unclench his fist as he watched his brother scrutinize the gown closely along Serena's full bodice.

"Good morrow, Miss Faw. Ye have quite the unusual pet there," Lachlan said, jovially and then he froze. Keenan couldn't discern even a breath from his brother. Would he die on the spot? Thick tension encompassed the four standing along the points of a square at the edge of the great hall. No one spoke for a moment.

"His name is Chiriklò. His color is quite unusual," Serena said.

Lachlan finally drew in an audible breath. "Aye," he said slowly. "Quite unusual, like yer eyes,

Miss Faw," and then almost to himself, "and yer hair blazes like the flame."

Serena looked at Keenan. He kept his full attention on the raging that strummed through his muscles and tendons. If he didn't start throwing his sword soon, he would explode. It was as if things moved in slow motion, but then all at once. Everyone but Keenan began talking.

"They're really just a violet shade of blue," Serena said defensively as she looked back and forth between Elenor and Lachlan.

"Aye Lachlan, Serena has violet eyes and blazing hair and if I'm correct, a fair number of oddities," Elenor said.

"Oddities?" Serena said frowning, her eyes stopped on Keenan.

"She's the one?" Lachlan said.

"And Keenan brought her safely to us," Elenor said. "As was his duty."

"Brought me to you? Keenan?" Serena said and stared at him.

Keenan released a long breath and shook his head, the same head that now pounded with a need to roar.

"She doesn't ken?" Lachlan asked.

"Nay," Elenor and Keenan said together.

"No!" Serena yelled as Elenor and Lachlan began babbling. Chiriklò flew to perch somewhere up in the rafters. She pressed her palms against her ears and closed her eyes until Lachlan and Elenor paused. When silence sat awkwardly between them all for several long moments, Serena opened her violet eyes and looked straight at Keenan. He saw understanding in those eyes. "Perhaps someone should explain this prophecy to me," she said.

Keenan clenched and unclenched his fists. He breathed evenly belying the passionate need to leave the stifling quarters as soon as possible. "Lass, I told ye as we rode in yesterday," Keenan said somberly. "Ye seem to be the one that our family's prophecy predicts will save our clan and herald in a new era of peace for the Macleans of Kylkern."

"A prophecy of peace?" Serena asked. "Why does fear surround it?" She glanced at Lachlan then back to Keenan. "What aren't you telling me?"

Keenan returned her gaze. "I have no fear regarding the prophecy," he said hollowly. "Elenor will explain it further. I must check on the villagers." He turned to leave.

"Keenan," the plea in her voice stopped him mid step. "I am no witch."

He turned back slowly. She looked betrayed, angry, a bit frightened, and all he wanted was to pull her up against him, run his hand down her hair and promise her that all would be well. And it would be well, after he died.

"Elenor will explain, Serena," he said, and blessedly Elenor chose then to take Serena's gloved hand in hers.

"Come Serena, let us break our fast and I'll show ye to my work room. Ye may find it as fascinating as I do," Elenor said, as they approached the long table. Lachlan hastened to catch up to the two ladies while Keenan turned and briskly exited the hall.

Keenan pulled his sword from the scabbard strapped across his back before he reached the bottom of the stone steps. No foes stood in the bailey, only the ones that plagued his traitorous mind, traitorous in the crack of hope that Elenor had chiseled into him.

Chapter 7

Elenor's amazingly strong arm guided Serena through the corridors.

Serena concentrated on putting one foot in front of the other as fury and fear assailed her. Keenan had known about this prophecy, had realized that she played a part in it, and hadn't mentioned it. Oh, he had tried perhaps in some miniscule way. Serena's chest ached as if out of air, and she forced in a full breath through clenched teeth. She had begun to trust him even though she couldn't read his thoughts. She should have known better. Everyone hid secrets, and she couldn't read his.

Elenor stopped before the entrance to one of the small rooms at the back of the castle. Serena sniffed back the tears and caught the aroma of culled grains and spices.

"Several years ago," Elenor said, "I had the contents moved to set up an herb room."

Inside the tiny room dried leaves and flowers of every botanical species hung from the rafters. Jars of liquid with dark shapes suspended in them sat on shelves. A large iron cook pot hung in a small hearth in the corner. A stout table ran nearly the length of the room. Several books sat open on the table, and more reclined against one another on a small bookcase. Mortar and pestle, knives, bowls and filled bladder sacks sat about on shelves. One small window let in a stream of light where dust fairies floated about. Although crammed full, the room was tidy.

"I call it an herb room to others, but it's really

my magic room," Elenor whispered.

"Your magic room?"

"Aye, I've created it for ye," Elenor said excitedly and started pointing out the many tinctures and dried herbs she had already prepared.

"For me, you say?" A chill ran down Serena's back.

"Aye, for ye if ye are the Maclean witch that the prophecy describes, Serena." Elenor beamed encouragingly at Serena.

"Elenor, I am not a witch." Witches worshipped Satan and sacrificed unbaptized babies.

"Ye have magical powers."

Serena pursed her lips together to stifle a sigh. "Perhaps you should tell me about this prophecy," Serena said.

"The prophecy is a prediction that has come down four generations from a wise woman that my great-great seanmhair, grandmother," Elenor translated, "invited into Kylkern one dark snowy night." Elenor's exuberance dimmed, and she stepped over a bench to sit opposite Serena at the table. "My seanmhair worried about her family and asked the wise woman to scry into the future for her."

"What did she see?"

"She saw many things, like births and deaths, battles and full harvests. And with each part that came true, the final words of the wise woman became more and more real until it became a prophecy."

"Tell me," Serena whispered.

"One day, when the Maclean clan is in its darkest moment, a witch will wed one Maclean son and lead the clan to peace while the other son will defend and die. Lachlan was born seven years before Keenan, so Papa and Ma had already decided it was Lachlan who would live by the time Keenan was born." Elenor nodded. "He has always been told that his place in life is to protect his brother and to die so that his clan will know peace once more."

"Does the prophecy specify a time?"

"Nay, just that the witch," Elenor paused. "Well she has violet eyes," she moved her hand toward Serena's hair, "and red hair." Elenor's voice dropped. "We thought it would be shortly after the witch came."

So Serena wasn't only a burden because of her brother. She also heralded Keenan's death.

They stared at one another and Elenor scooted around the table to sit next to Serena. "This burden, it hasn't been easy for Keenan. Papa and Ma," she sighed. "They didn't seem like they wanted to get attached to Keenan because they kent that he was going to die."

Serena couldn't stop a tear from rolling down her cheek.

Elenor placed her hand over Serena's. "I tried to love him enough for all of us," she shook her head. "But it wasn't from me that he needed acceptance."

"What were the words exactly? Of the prophecy," Serena asked.

This was ludicrous.

How could a whole clan treat one man like this, raising him to defend them, raising him to die for them? Keeping him at arm's length, so they wouldn't get attached. Anger boiled inside Serena.

Elenor nodded briskly and stood, pulling a leather-bound book from a shelf. Its cover was inlaid with a beautiful mosaic made with small polished stones. Serena knew very little of the Gaelic language. She pulled a glove off one hand and ran fingers over the aged page. Dread ran like ants up her arm, and she forced herself not to pull it back. She didn't need to comprehend Gaelic to hear the words, read and thought by so many over the years, but Elenor translated out loud.

"As the century passes to the next, strife with the English king boils over. Yer son's son will join the revolt against the monarch but it will be his son that will carry it through to peace. To yer son's son will be born two sons, handsome and brawn. When a witch of great power comes with hair ablazin' like fire and violet in her eyes, she will wed the brother destined to bring yer clan to peace, a peace to take it into many centuries beyond. The other brother shall defend and die. So say I."

Feelings of hope, worry, and desperate searching rose like waves from the book lying open on the wooden table. The words cut deeply into Serena as if she had read them all these years with all these people.

"Close the book, Elenor," Serena said quietly. "Please."

Elenor clapped the book shut and whisked it off the table. She sat down across from Serena and grabbed Serena's bare hand.

Serena searched deeply into Elenor's pleading eyes. "He's already accepted his death," Serena said, "but you don't."

Elenor gave a brief shake of her head. "Never have."

"Why not?"

Elenor sat back, breaking the bond, but Serena already felt the great love between sister and brother.

"I love him, with all my heart, Serena. We are only one year apart. We grew up together, played together, and fought together. But I was treated much differently." Elenor stood and walked as if inspecting some of the shelves. "Our mother doted on me and Lachlan, withholding nothing. But with Keenan, she was distant. Papa only praised Keenan in his training, so Keenan made sure that he was always the best. He practiced and trained until he couldn't move. I'd convince Lachlan to help me drag him inside to bed."

Elenor sat down again. "It's not just that I felt pity for him, he wouldn't allow that. His is a life of honor, of duty, and he has never complained."

The anger that balled in Serena's stomach tightened at the thought of Keenan as a small, unloved child. "And his parents ended up dying before him," Serena said with a shake of her head.

"Aye and with my parents' deaths, so went Keenan's quest to win their love. He kind of gave up on it, probably well before they died. His great quest was to gain respect."

"He wanted respect?"

"He grew from a child craving love which never came into a warrior that wanted respect, respect from his clan, from his men. And probably from Lachlan, too."

"And what of Lachlan? Did he try to help?"

Elenor spoke carefully. "I love Lachlan too, as a sister must." She lowered her voice. "But I have never respected someone who allows unfairness to preside without voicing fault." Elenor kept her face even, but Serena felt the bitterness pour out of her. Serena nodded in understanding. "Let us get some fresh air," Elenor said and rose.

The two stepped out into the bright sunlight. The wind skittered across the ground to run past the edge of Serena's blue gown. She drew in a cleansing breath, filling her chest and pushing out the remnants of musty air. Her mind replayed the information about Keenan and Lachlan. What darkness dwelled inside Keenan to have been raised under such pressure?

"So Lachlan does not practice the art of battle as Keenan does?" Serena asked.

"No. He kens how to hold a sword, not how to

swing one," Elenor said as they walked around the edge of the stone wall far from anybody who might overhear.

"And he is the leader of your people?"

Elenor nodded. "Through title, aye, he is the chief, but it is to Keenan that the warriors look for leadership. It is Keenan who trained them, bled with them, healed with them. They swear fealty with words to Lachlan, but they swear fealty with their swords to Keenan."

"Perhaps Lachlan's strength lies in his cleverness?"

"Aye, my brother is smart, but he only carries on what my papa started. He doesn't consider new ideas."

Chiriklò dove down off the bailey wall to land on Serena's shoulder as a group of Macleans escorted in a man and a boy. An image of a woman, her hands tied behind her back, left in the back of a dim cave, flashed from the mind of the bird into Serena's.

"Chiriklò? Who is the woman I see in the cave?" Serena said to the bird and then turned to Elenor. "Who is that man, that boy?"

Keenan stood beside them, his hand resting on his sword as he spoke with the man. The boy stared at the steps under his feet. Every once in awhile, he nodded.

"I doona ken the man, but he wears a tartan with a weave unlike those around here. The boy looks familiar. There are several farmers and shepherds living on the other side of na beanntan," Elenor said pointing to the mountains rising behind them.

Panic rolled along the thread that Serena focused on the boy. "His name is Jacob, and he's terrified that man will kill his mother who lies bound in a cave nearby."

Elenor gasped. "And the man?" Elenor asked.

Serena moved the fine invisible thread of telepathy from the boy, past Keenan who was still a void, to the man who now clasped Keenan's hand and smiled.

Death, hate, vengeance. It twisted into a fuming ball at the center of the man, behind his calm smile, behind the proper words of greeting and story of saving the lad. And it lay coiled to spring as soon as he had a clear shot at, at Lachlan.

"He wants to kill Lachlan."

"Good Lord, and Keenan will try to get in the way," Elenor said and broke into a run.

"I can help, Elenor, please slow down. Trust me," Serena whispered. Elenor nodded and the two of them walked up the steps.

Serena went to the boy. "Hello, lad, this is Elenor, lady of the house. Why don't you step back away from all these gruff looking warriors with her."

"That lad is in my care. His mother was killed and I have brought him here to ask the Maclean of Kylkern for the warriors to avenge his mother's death. Until then, he is under my protection."

"Yes, Fergus Campbell, I know why you've come," Serena said. "And I know the boy's mother is alive and kept captive."

"Ehh? I doona ken ye?" he sputtered and looked around him. "I'm no Campbell, I tell ye."

Keenan looked back and forth between them, his eyes narrowing.

They stood in the growing wind at the top of the stone slab steps, before the giant double doors. Lachlan appeared in the doorway.

"I hear that this good man has saved an innocent child? Come inside and let us speak of this injustice," Lachlan said and stepped out to face the man.

Serena carefully prodded at the Campbell's mind, his plan of attack. He held two long bladed dirks tipped with poison. One sang of rage for Lachlan, the other tasted a necessary bloodletting for Keenan. He would strike Keenan first. Serena's stomach twisted and her smile faltered.

I won't let it happen. Serena caught her toe on the edge of the step and tripped forward against the Campbell. Two seconds, could she but steal two seconds?

Her hand snaked under the plaid over the man's shoulders. Careful to grab the handle and not the deadly blade, Serena pulled the dirk out and threw it down the steps.

"Beware," she yelled, her eyes locking with the Campbell as she pushed away with all her senses. "The blade is coated with poison." In a heartbeat, the monster pulled her up against his chest, his other blade pointed into her back as he jostled them over to the side of the outside alcove. Lachlan disappeared. The tip of Keenan's sword stood balanced in the air mere inches from the Campbell's throbbing jugular, just above Serena's head.

"One move, Keenan Maclean, and this poisoned blade slides through her back," he said. "It was meant for a man full-grown, so the poison is strong. She'll die painfully before yer blade could reach me."

"Who are ye?" Keenan asked, his voice solid as twelve-inch ice.

The man jostled Serena with him closer to the wall. The direct contact with such open panic and rage tore at her defenses. He smelled of hatred and fear verging on crazed viciousness. His foulness enveloped her body and her mind. Standing there locked in his arms, she could hardly feel or sense anything but him.

"I am Fergus Campbell, and I'm here to kill the chief that supports the Great Pretender, the Bonnie Prince."

Serena knew all his motives, all his pain. She

saw the death of Fergus's mother by his abusive father. She witnessed the crippling of his sister, Jane, and the guilt he felt at having shoved her so hard that she fell in front of the charging horse. Serena saw it all. His twisted mind, given the seed of hatred and blame from Campbell rumblings, focused on a mission, to right his wrongs, to give his life meaning.

Serena stared into Keenan's deadly eyes. Fergus would die. She didn't need to read Keenan's thoughts to know it. Fergus knew it too, but he planned to take her with him.

Perhaps her death would break the prophecy? Serena focused on Keenan's face, the scar running down his cheek that she longed to touch again, the pulse in his neck she wanted to feel beneath her lips. In that moment, she was able to sort through all the jumbled feelings she had about Keenan and his secret. In the space of a heartbeat, Serena knew that despite it all, she still wanted to feel another kiss from him, feel his hard body pressed against her. She wanted to live.

Serena sent an image to her pet. From high above the silent bailey filled with armed Macleans, an angry cry rent the heavy air. Chiriklò dove, an arrow from the clouds straight for Fergus Campbell. Before the man could press the blade against her neck, the sparrow's sharp beak stabbed him directly in his wide open eye. He screamed wildly, the pain crashed into Serena. She closed her eyes and let her legs buckle. Before she hit the stone step, an iron like arm pulled her to the right and up against her peaceful void.

The muscles in his chest moved effortlessly to pull his sword back out of Fergus's throat. Her eyes still closed, Serena felt the tortured mind of Fergus Campbell dim with his life.

"God forgive me...failed..." His last thoughts

faded into the ether.

The clang of metal against granite rang through the bailey, and then she felt both of Keenan's arms engulf her in warmth and safety. Her body shook on a silent sob.

"Serena," his low voice vibrated through, warming her. He pulled back and bent to peer into her face. "Are ye with me, lass?"

"The boy's mother is alive. Fergus was using Jacob to get close to Lachlan." She swallowed hard. "If the boy didn't cooperate, he'd kill his mother. She's tied up at the back of a cave." Serena turned in his arms and scanned the mountain range surrounding them. Using the thread, she closed her eyes and let it roam searching for emotion, for dread and pain. She pointed at one small mountain.

"There, she is there, in a cave. She's hurt." Serena's limbs felt weak and her head pounded.

"Thomas, be quick. Gather a rescue party," Keenan said to the men staring wide-eyed at Serena.

"Serena, are more Campbells out there?"

She shook her head just slightly causing the scene to sway. She sensed her sparrow washing in the nearby loch. But no others. "Not that I've sensed." She took a deep breath.

Keenan nodded. "Thomas, a party of six."

Chiriklò glided in and landed on Serena's shoulder. He fluttered his wings, spraying her with droplets of water.

"Can yer bird lead them to the cave?"

Serena closed her eyes and sent the image to Chiriklò. "He will lead your men."

Keenan nodded. "Thomas, follow that blue sparrow to the cave."

"Aye, Keenan," Thomas said, his voice slow, but he turned quickly. Horses trotted out and six strong men departed minutes later, Chiriklò a blue dart before them.

Keenan drew Serena with him as he stalked into the keep. "Where is my brother?" Keenan asked. Keenan looked down at her. "Ye must rest."

Serena leaned further into him, relaxing and trying to rid herself of the taint.

"Lachlan, get out here," Keenan called. The only sound that answered him was the surprised gasp of a kitchen maid as weapon brandishing Macleans filed inside. Keenan beckoned Elenor over to him. Jacob followed her.

Serena took the mug Keenan offered and drank.

"The Campbell planned to kill," Keenan said.

"Fergus Campbell lived a miserable life," Serena explained. "His one wish was to do something honorable. The Campbells think Lachlan's support of Prince Charles Edward Stewart will bring in more supporters. They'll rally and possibly win, giving the prince govern over their lands. The Campbells would rather stick with King George, a ruler they know. They think Prince Charles would lead Scotland into more bloody war with England. Fergus had decided to take it upon himself to wipe out one of the rallying points."

"He had two blades," Keenan said.

"One was for you. You first, so you couldn't save your brother. The second was for Lachlan."

"And ye kent his plan," Keenan's calm voice belied the tenseness she saw in his clenched jaw line. He wasn't as calm as he tried to present. Maybe she was learning how to decipher some emotions from his face, like normal people had to do. She studied him as he continued. "So ye sought the poisoned blades and used yerself as a shield."

"Not exactly." Serena held up her fingers and waved them. "I sought the blades, but only to pick them from his pocket."

"Ye were only able to pick one blade," he said. "Ye knew that ye couldn't grab them both." She watched his jaw line begin to tick. Amazing what one could discern from another without using magic. He was angry, perhaps furious inside.

"I had to do something," Serena said.

"I can protect my brother. I have since I could walk," Keenan replied flatly.

Serena looked up at him, her eyes narrowed. "I didn't grab the blade meant for Lachlan," she said and looked back at the cup in her hands. Her hands shook slightly as she held it to her parted lips and sipped the broth.

Serena nearly jumped when she felt his thumb touch her cheek. "Ye protected me." His words sounded calm, intrigued, so she looked back to him. But his eyes held fury, as if all of the emotion had drained from his words into them. "Doona do it again."

Chapter 8

Serena swayed with the gentle roll of the horse's gait as they clopped along the misty path against the green mountain. They rode south to find the letter and the true murderer. She traveled with Keenan and four other Maclean warriors. They were polite but made certain not to touch her.

Brodick, a burly man with reddish hair and small fuzzy beard, seemed the kindest. He answered her questions about some of the local foliage. Ewan had a handsome face and quick smile, but didn't really want to talk to her. Thomas was suspicious of everything she did or said, his blue eyes always darting between Keenan and her. Gavin usually led the way. He preferred to ride fast, his shoulder length brown hair flapping behind him as he scouted ahead. They all were fiercely loyal to Keenan.

Their small group had four days journey back to Leeds and then south to Leicester where King George held court at a manor house. Serena hoped that the two courtly dressed conspirators would be near the moving court. If they had ducked out of royal society, they would be very difficult to find.

Serena sighed as she watched the dawn sparkle across the dewy grass. Her thoughts flipped between Keenan's secrets and William's health. Serena sighed again.

"So many sighs," Keenan said. He pulled his horse back as the path widened into a narrow cut road. "Are ye bored of our journey already?"

Was he teasing her? Serena still wasn't always sure how to read the slight changes of tone to know if he was serious or not. She looked at his handsome face, made even more masculine by the scar. There was a sparkle in his eyes, as if he smiled at her without the smile appearing on his lips. He was teasing her.

Serena grinned. "Perhaps the company," she said so that the others riding near them could hear. "No one talks out here. I miss your sister."

Keenan did smile then. "Aye, I miss her too. She is a whirlwind, but she makes me laugh." He reached over and plucked off a small flower petal that had settled in her hair. He let the length run slowly through his fingers. Serena held her breath, savoring the feel.

Thomas snorted. "And that is quite a feat considering how ye brood so much, Keenan. The man's smiling more out here as we travel than I've ever seen him," he said and turned in his saddle to look at Serena.

Serena didn't need to see the faint tightening of his lips to hear his unspoken suspicions. Thomas, just like the other three Macleans, believed Serena to be Lachlan's soon-to-be wife. Their discomfort every time Keenan paid her attention felt almost like a physical obstacle that she needed to avoid.

One day gone, five to go, Serena thought dismally as Keenan moved back up to the front of the line. What did he think of their disapproval? She watched Keenan's broad back and shoulders. She would never love Lachlan. After reading the prophecy it did seem probable that she was the witch. But marry Lachlan? Not willingly.

They traveled for two more days along the spring roads into England. The trees and bushes were flowering and the woods were alive with the songs of birds and animals awakening. Chiriklò came to Serena after the first day and shared images from above to stave off the torturous silence and boredom. Serena even caught a comforting thought from Mari during her long hours of silence. The Faw Tribe moved through eastern England and would head back north of Leeds by the next full moon, about two weeks time. She tried to send an image of William healed to Mari but wasn't certain she would pick it up.

It was the fourth night on the journey. They set up camp just north of Leeds in a grove of old oaks and birch. A creek ran nearby, and a cave sat empty. Gavin, who worried overmuch about most things including Keenan's lighter mood around Lachlan's bride, laid Serena's pallet out in the cave. The five Maclean warriors set up their pallets near the entryway. They would take turns staying awake to guard against enemies and to guard Serena from walking too far west.

Moss grew along the rough walls of the cave. Moisture glistened on the contours of the exposed stone. Serena shivered and wrapped the wool blanket, crisscrossed in Maclean red, around her shoulders.

Keenan's head ducked under the low entry. "Not asleep?"

Serena shook her head. "Soon to be. You're not asleep either?"

"Soon to be," he said mimicking her words. "After ye're settled." Serena shivered slightly. "Are ye cold, lass?" Keenan asked. He squatted down, pulled his cape from around his shoulders, and placed it over hers. The warmth penetrated immediately, and the masculine smell of pine and leather surrounded her.

"Thank you," she said, and looked down at the layers draping her body. Keenan leaned so close that she could hear his breath moving between his lips.

"Won't you be cold without this?" Serena asked.

"Nay." Again silence sat like a wall between

them. But he didn't move to leave. He looked around. "There's a natural smoke hole toward the back of the cave. I could start a fire for ye."

"I will be warm enough. Although," she said as casually as she could. "If you sleep in here with me we will both be warmer." Serena didn't know what she hoped would happen if he slept near her, but she would feel warmer.

Keenan seemed to consider her words. "My men, Serena," he hesitated. "They believe ye are Lachlan's witch and soon to be his wife."

"I know what they think, Keenan."

"Ye can read their thoughts?"

"Yes," she said and stared into his eyes.

"But ye haven't touched them."

Serena shook her head. "When the thoughts are strong or when I focus on a person, I can read their thoughts and emotions without touching them."

Keenan sat back on his heels. Had she said too much? Would he label her evil, too?

"But not me, ye canna read my thoughts or emotions, can ye?"

"No."

"Why not?"

"I don't know, but you are the only person I've ever met who has been hidden to me."

"That is why I startled ye at the fair," he said as if wanting confirmation.

She nodded.

"So if ye can read all these thoughts, why did ye not ken the prophecy when ye met my family?"

Serena scooted back up against the wall of the cave, trying to find a comfortable spot where a rock wouldn't grind its way into her spine. "I separate myself from most of the thoughts around me, else I'd probably go insane. My duy guided me in setting up a wall to protect myself. Behind the wall, the constant chatter is dulled until I barely notice it.

Then only strong or threatening emotions catch my attention."

She shrugged. "And I don't like to pry into people, partly out of respect for their privacy and partly because I've seen enough inside people to know that it is better not to know. Thoughts and feelings are raw, without civilized boundaries." She looked him straight in the eye. "And I didn't know there was some secret I should be looking for, a secret involving me, a secret that you could have easily told me before we arrived." There, it was out, and she had managed to keep her voice even as if she hadn't been deeply hurt.

Keenan sat down and leaned back against the wall to her right. "I wasn't certain," he hesitated, and crossed his arms in front of his chest. "Lachlan had looked so long, it dinna seem real that the witch of the prophecy could find me in England."

Serena frowned over the word witch. She didn't think of herself as a witch. Her duy had never called her a witch.

Keenan's eyes followed the length of her hair until it ran under the blankets. "When I saw yer hair and eyes in the daylight, I still wasn't convinced. Even when I watched ye perform some ritual over yer brother with that crystal." He shook his head. "Perhaps I dinna want to believe it," he said and shrugged.

"But when we rode up to Kylkern?"

"Yer bird flew to ye and I heard the gasps of the people. There was no denying that ye were different. I tried to say something then, but there wasn't time." His eyes searched hers. "I would have prepared ye more but what was there to say?"

"You could have started with, Serena, I think you are the witch in a prophecy that says you will marry my brother and lead my clan to peace."

"While I die."

Her jaw ached from clenching and she purposefully relaxed it.

"Would that have helped?" he asked. "Having me say those words before we arrived? Would that have given ye comfort or made the trip easier?" He shook his head.

"Either way, Keenan, I don't believe in your prophecy."

Serena breathed deeply, the musty smell of the cave catching in her throat. She coughed a little. Keenan leaned forward and pulled the plaid up higher until only her head stuck out. Keenan touched the red waves as they cascaded down the plaid.

"It ripples like fire," he said.

Serena held still, caught in the tingle of the soft touch. "Duy says it flows like red lava from a volcano."

"She's visited a volcano?" he said with the hint of a grin.

"Only in the stories from her father's ancient texts."

Keenan sat back. "A witch of great power comes with hair ablazin' like fire," he quoted.

Serena frowned at him. "Your prophecy may have some ring of truth, but that doesn't prove it will all come to pass."

"Do ye scry then into the future, too? Is that how ye saw Gerard's murder? Have ye seen a different outcome for my clan?"

"I don't have far sight, but sometimes I can tell when bad things will happen to someone. It's not exactly the future, because the future can change. It is not set. And that's why I don't believe in your prophecy."

"God sets the future," Keenan stated flatly.

"Some aspects of the future can change," she stated just as firmly. "When I see something that will happen in the future, it is very hazy and sometimes I see multiple outcomes. I've learned that sometimes when I try to warn away the disaster, I end up making it happen." Keenan just stared at her. "Anyway, I felt death on Gerard when he grabbed my arm. A darkness seemed to envelop William when I touched him. Mari encouraged me to concentrate on the darkness."

"Mari, yer mother, she is a," he hesitated. "She can read people, too?" Serena shook her head. "She has some powers of perception, but not like mine. My real mother was a great priestess with immense powers. I suppose one could call her a witch, but she was good, not evil. She gave me her clairvoyance and sent me away."

"Sent ye away?"

"Yes, to hide me," Serena said slowly as flashes of memory surfaced. "My sisters and I," she said quietly looking down at the blankets but not really seeing them. "Yes, I have sisters, and they're hidden away too." She frowned.

"Who are ye hiding from, Serena?"

"I...I am not certain. Something evil."

Silence sat between them like a third person.

Brodick stuck his head in the entrance of the cave. "Wondering what was taking ye so long in here," he said, his eyes moving between the two of them.

"We're having a conversation," Keenan said.

"A pretty quiet conversation," Brodick quipped.

"I'll be out before long. Who's on first watch?"

"I am."

"Then go watch." The command was evident in Keenan's voice.

Brodick ducked back out into the darkness.

"So ye focused?" Keenan asked as if not sure of the correct word. "Ye focused on yer brother and ye saw in," he pointed to his head, "yer mind Gerard's murder and William being shot?"

"Yes, and then I ran to him."

"And yer bird arrived first."

"I sent him."

"So what exactly is yer bird?" Keenan said and looked around the cave to see if Chiriklò perched nearby.

"He's a blue sparrow, and he's not here right now."

"Of course it's a blue little bird, but what is it to ye?"

"A friend."

Keenan's eyes narrowed a bit. "A friend," he said and ran his hand over the shadow of beard along his jaw. "Ye can think to it, and it understands ye?"

Serena nodded. "He's a gift from my real mother. She didn't want me to be alone."

Keenan took a deep breath and let it out.

"Anything else you want to know about me?" Serena asked. The man looked a little besieged, which was almost humorous considering Keenan Maclean looked like a man who wouldn't be overwhelmed by a lethal band of ten battle-ready warriors.

"Not right now, lass. It's a lot to understand in one sitting."

Serena nodded. She'd never shared so much of herself with anyone other than her duy before. It was vast. "So about you sleeping in here to keep both of us warm…"

"Lass," Keenan interrupted, and stood up, "since ye canna read my thoughts I best tell ye then that I believe the prophecy is truth and that ye are the witch to lead my clan to peace."

His lips seemed to tighten as the stillness invaded again. It would be so much easier if she could read his thoughts. The strained silences would at least tell her something.

"I agree that I do fit the description," she said hoping to relax him. He didn't relax.

"If ye are the one in the prophecy, then ye will be my brother's wife, Serena."

Serena shook her head hard and fast. "Not likely."

Keenan straightened abruptly and hit his head on the jagged ceiling. "Bloody hell," he cursed, rubbing his scalp. "Serena, can ye read possibilities of yer own future, too?"

"No, I can't read my own future."

"Then how do ye ken that ye willna wed Lachlan?"

Serena paused. Should she tell him the truth and risk insulting his family? She wanted Keenan to know what was in her heart.

"Because I don't respect him, I don't really even like him, and I can't imagine kissing him, let alone loving him."

A mixture of bewilderment and outrage played across Keenan's strained face as he stood.

"Ye will learn to love him," he said.

"No." She crossed her arms under the blankets.

"Aye, ye will," he retorted, his voice rising slightly as if he commanded an errant squire.

Serena presented her fiercest scowl. "You can tell me what I will and will not do, Keenan Maclean, but I know enough," she said, thumping her chest, "to know that I will never love someone who hides behind his brother instead of standing to help defend his clan."

"I was born to protect him, Serena. It is my lot, my destiny."

"What if the fates have something else in mind for you, Keenan? Ever consider that?"

A frustrated noise, somewhere between a snort and a growl, came from Keenan. "Ye've spent too much time with Elenor."

"She's a bright woman."

Keenan turned around and walked out of the cave.

"Good night to you too," Serena called into the darkness. "Hmmph." She closed her eyes for only a moment when a bright light glowed red against the inside of her eyelids.

"You need to kiss that man," a woman's voice said in the stillness. Serena gasped and struggled into a sitting position. The woman from the meadow, Drakkina, sat cross-legged on the floor beside her. Her body glowed, filling the small cave with warm light. Several dragonflies flitted around the low ceiling.

"What?" Serena said.

"I said that you have to kiss him again, that's what you have to do child. He wants to kiss you, but his stubborn honor won't let him. It's up to you to," the woman fluttered her fingers outward, "encourage him some."

"He wants me to kiss him?"

"Certainly, all men want a beautiful woman to kiss them."

"No, I mean, you can read his thoughts, and you know that he wants me to kiss him?"

"Not exactly," the woman said as if frustrated. "But I've studied him, and I'm certain he wants you to kiss him."

"Who are you exactly? How did you get here?" Serena asked and wondered briefly if the Maclean warriors would come running inside any moment.

"They won't bother us," the woman said reading her concern. "And you know who I am, I'm Drakkina."

"You just read my thoughts?"

"Yes, yes, I can read yours somewhat. What powers I have left are linked to you and your sisters through the mark of your parents."

"My sisters? My mark?"

"Your birthmark, child. The dragonfly," she said and opened her palm up to the ceiling where dragonflies circled.

Serena glanced back from the luminescent insects to the woman. Her lined face held a sheen of youthful vibrancy. She sat with her legs akimbo as if a child. "Yes, I remember that your name is Drakkina, but who are you exactly?"

"I trained your mother and father in the Wiccan ways. They were masters by the end, but not strong enough to conquer the demons that hunted them."

Serena swallowed past a sudden tightness in her throat.

"I was once a master Wiccan priestess until my mortal body finally withered to dust. What you see is a shadow of my energy held together by what remains of my power."

"A shadow?"

"Yes, yes," Drakkina said briskly. "Try to touch me."

Serena reached her hand out toward the woman. Serena's hand moved through her as if she were mist. The only indication that she had touched Drakkina was a hot tingling.

"I can't read your mind either," Serena said and moved closer to the apparition.

Drakkina smiled. "That's because I can block you. Perhaps it would be quicker if I didn't." Drakkina closed her silvery blue eyes.

The end of the ordered world. Tomorrow and yesterday bleeding into today. Times crushing in upon one another. Demons, misshapen winged creatures with fangs and talons. Enslaving millions to perform their evil whims under their reconstruction of a timeless existence. Children slaughtered in their innocence for amusement.

Serena paled visibly. "What hell do you show

me?"

Drakkina smiled sadly. "The great oracle in my realm warns me of this outcome. The demons you saw were the same ones who killed your true parents. To create that hell, they need the powers of both of your parents. They were only able to take Druce's. He sacrificed his life so that Gilla could save you and your sisters. And give each of you one of her powers. "

"Are the demons coming for me then?"

Several dragonflies alighted on Drakkina's silvery spun hair. "If they knew you were here, but they don't and probably wouldn't waste too much time looking for you anyway."

Serena didn't understand.

"You see," Drakkina continued as if instructing a child, "they know you and your sisters will eventually come to them."

"I don't understand."

"I know. For now it is crucial that you find your soul mate."

"And you believe that Keenan Maclean is my soul mate."

"What a bright girl. You have Gilla's intelligence, I think. If only Druce had been so wise, he wouldn't have attempted to subdue the demons alone."

"My father confronted the demons?"

Drakkina nodded, a frown securely set on her lips. "Thought he could lead them away from your family and defeat them on his own."

"You warned him that his magic was not strong enough?"

"No, he never asked me. Probably thought I was dead."

Serena stared. "Aren't you?"

Drakkina snorted and rolled her eyes. "My body might be dead, but my spirit is not. And for some crazy reason," she said sarcastically, "I'm determined to save this chaotic world. Which is why I'm telling you," she said pointing at Serena with a long crooked finger, "to convince that Highlander that you are his soul mate."

"But he doesn't want me. He thinks I should marry his brother." How much did the priestess know? "There is a prophecy."

Drakkina waved her ringed hand in the air causing several of the dragonflies to buzz up into the ceiling of the cave. "Prophecies are often misinterpreted."

"But he believes it is true. He was raised to protect and die for his brother and clan. He knows only that, and I don't think I can persuade him otherwise."

Drakkina floated to her feet, her diaphanous body shortening proportionally. "Giving up so soon? Very unlike your parents," the woman criticized.

"I'm just," Serena started, "well, I don't know much about convincing a man to kiss me."

"I could give you some instruction."

"No! I will try on my own. I just need to get him to kiss me?"

"That should do it," Drakkina said. "Then he'll realize he loves you and this part of my mission will be done."

Drakkina held up her hands. Serena opened her mouth.

"No time girl. Do what you must do."

Serena looked around at the glowing cave filled with dragonflies. "What if I'm just dreaming you?"

"I am real, Serena, and you can feel it. I'm as real as your siblings out there. As real as Merewin, giving you that crystal to heal William."

"Merewin," Serena said. The name was familiar, like the taste of a sweet treat that she craved.

"Yes, she is the eldest after you." Drakkina

studied her as if contemplating her next move. The woman sighed. "Touch my mind, child, and remember her."

Heart pounding, Serena opened carefully to Drakkina's thoughts. She saw herself as a child running hand in hand with a girl with brown hair. The two laughed as they wove between huge stone megaliths around a beautiful thatch-roofed cottage.

Serena's eyes blurred. "I remember," she said softly. "My home." She looked at Drakkina. "I need to find her, find them all."

Drakkina closed the door. "Not now. In time I will help you find them. Right now," Drakkina said, "you have to kiss that man."

Serena worried at her bottom lip. "The guards won't let him alone, and I will not throw myself at him with four other men watching." Serena caught Drakkina's narrowed gaze. "I'm not giving up, and I'm not being difficult, I'm being realistic."

Drakkina tapped her long finger against her lip. "Hmm, I will come up with something. I'll keep those men busy tonight. I'll have a storm brewing. With a little prompting, those men will find shelter in caves some way from here."

"And I kiss Keenan and the rest falls into place," Serena said with a hint of mockery.

Drakkina ignored her sarcasm. "Very good then, child. Why don't you freshen up a bit."

Serena ran fingers through her tangled mass. She pulled it to one side and tied a green ribbon in it.

"Better," Drakkina said. "Now get some rest before the storm starts." Drakkina peered at Serena. "And pinch your cheeks."

"If you are trying to build up my confidence to seduce a kiss out of this man," Serena said caustically, "you are failing."

"He's your soul mate, Serena. You could have a

rat living in that fiery mass and dung on your face, and he'd still fall in love with you."

"Better I suppose, but not much," Serena grumbled and leaned back up against the wall suddenly exhausted.

"Child, rest," Drakkina's words floated.

Was the woman able to dull her mind into sleep? Serena yawned.

Rest. She would rest for a bit. Serena snuggled deeper into the warm blankets. Perhaps when she woke, it would be morning and she would know it was all a dream.

"I'm not a dream," Serena heard the voice in her mind. "Kiss him, child, for the greater good."

"Kiss him," Serena mumbled.

Keenan balled the rough horse blanket under his head. The cool, firm ground felt good against his back and the stars watched overhead. It was a perfect night to sleep outside. Why then did the musty confines of the obnoxiously small cave pull at him?

Never before had Keenan felt so tempted by a woman. It must be because she was untouchable, unattainable. Serena Faw was the witch of the prophecy; he had no doubt about that. And therefore, she would belong to Lachlan. Never before had Keenan envied his brother in his duty to wed a witch. Though death followed Keenan through his life, he had been happy to concede the bonding to a witch to his older brother. But that was before her hair had skimmed his hands, before she had slept nuzzled against his chest and then stood awestruck by the sight of his Highlands. That was before she had returned his kiss on the moor and risked her life to protect his. Before she had asked him to sleep next to her in the cave. Aye, Keenan had actually pitied Lachlan before, but now his purpose filled life was changing.

Crack! A bolt of lightning cleaved through the storm-lit clouds above. Keenan jumped up and took two long purposeful steps toward Serena's cave. Her still, slumbering form rested on its side within the folds of the blankets. Her face, lit up by the storm, frowned while she mumbled and turned away from the wind that shrieked around the edges of the rocky hillside. He almost smiled. The lass could sleep through a battle.

Tingles ran along his arms and legs, all the hairs standing up. Boom! A bolt of white light shot down from the sky, splintering a white birch across the clearing. The ground rocked with the force of the explosion and threw Keenan back against the rock wall. His men scattered, yelling, but the ringing in Keenan's ears blocked their words. Crack, crack, creek!

"Watch out," Gavin mouthed the warning as the birch's weight launched its flaming body down toward the cave. It seemed to fall in slow motion as if giving him time to react, but suddenly the branches clawed toward him.

Keenan hurled himself into the cave just as the top of the massive tree crashed in front of him, its flaming branches scratching against the stone on either side of the cave entrance. Greedy fire licked into the opening. Behind him, he heard Serena yell out. He grabbed one of her blankets to smother the flames threatening to invade the cramped space.

With a howl, the clouds opened, and sheaths of rain slanted down outside the cave. The flames flickered as the water battled it from outside and Keenan battled it from inside. Small balls of ice danced inside on the rock floor, sizzling as they rolled into the char. As the last snake of flame flickered out, Keenan backed up into darkness knocking his head on the low ceiling.

"Bloody hell."

"Watch your head."

"Too late, where are ye?" The brightness of lightning had made it impossible to see in the darkness.

"Over here, Keenan." Her soft voice beckoned him. His name on her tongue brought back flashes of a dream.

Lightning lit the cave suddenly, and he glimpsed her sitting, the blankets pooled around her waist.

Crouching down, he moved carefully in her direction. He felt almost predatory as he bent and listened for her movement. Every few seconds the cave lit up followed by a deafening blast of thunder. He lowered himself against the wall.

"It's best we stay in here," Keenan said.

"I don't think we have a choice." Her voice seemed small against the gale outside. The next illumination showed the blackened tree branches fully blocking the small entrance.

"Can ye bring on storms, lass?"

Her hair slid against his arm as she shook her head. "No."

"It seems almost unnatural. The suddenness and strength."

"It's not me, Keenan. I don't have that ability, plus I was asleep when it began."

She hadn't lied about her abilities, as far as he knew. The storm scattered light around them for several seconds. She had wanted him to sleep in the cave.

"Where are my men?" Keenan crawled over to look around the branches out into the darkness. No souls moved about, only violent tree branches slashing against the hail and rain.

"I will try to find them." The next flash showed her face, eyes closed. As the white light blinked out again, Keenan waited impatiently for another view of her. She was using the power. What was it like to travel into peoples' minds? To have to protect yourself against their darkness? He needed to see her. Keenan felt the limbs of the old birch and broke off the tiny twigs. He still had some peat and flint in his sporran. They would have a small fire near the back where remnants of past fires scorched the rock wall. The warmth from the rock would radiate heat throughout the cave. The wind would carry the smoke off into all directions.

"They've found shelter," Serena said as Keenan scratched against the flint. "Gavin and Thomas are together in one cave and Ewan and Brodick are in another." A spark caught against the dry peat under the small dead branches. Keenan blew on the flicker that battled against the dampness until it grew. He sat back on his heels.

"They're safe, tired and wet, but safe," she said reassuringly. "It seems they will just stay there the night." The fire glowed against her as it had the first night he'd seen her dancing, a twin to the flame. But instead of half closed eyes, hers were wide open. She seemed especially small and vulnerable with the blankets wrapped around her hips, trapped in the small space with him.

Keenan nodded.

Serena tried to brush her hair aside and caught her hand in the ribbon that held it against her shoulder. "Oh." Serena jerked her hand from the ribbon.

"It's but a ribbon."

"Yes, it is, isn't it. I forgot I tied it in."

Keenan added more branches to the small fire until a steady flame filled the cave with orange light. He sat down closer to the fire against another wall.

Serena's eyes still reflected worry. Perhaps if he got her talking.

"Does yer tribe move all the time or do ye stay in certain places for awhile?"

Serena wrapped a strand of hair around one of her fingers, absently twisting it into a tight coil. "We winter north of London usually. But when it's warm, we move from town to town, running faires and selling tin wares and worked leather."

"And ye dance?"

Serena nodded. "And I tell fortunes of course."

"Of course. Ye must be very good at it."

"When I happened to be too good, well, then we moved on sooner."

"Moved sooner?"

"I used to try to warn people about their upcoming misfortune. Despite what King Will told me."

"He dinna want ye to tell people everything ye saw?"

"No. When my predictions came true, it raised questions. Inevitably someone would blame us for the misfortune. Some accused us of causing what I saw. Some just accused me of being in league with Satan."

"Ye are a witch," he tried to tease, but Serena didn't smile. Maybe he should stop talking.

She glanced at him, a small grin on her lips. "I suppose I am, but I'll only admit that to a Maclean of Kylkern because there's nothing in your prophecy about needing to burn your witch." Serena turned back to the fire. "Either way, I am trouble for the tribe." Her voice softened, as if sadness muffled her spirit. "With me gone now, I wonder if," she started and then looked down at the blanket. She ran bare fingers over the crisscross pattern. "Well they may have less problems, anyway."

He couldn't tell if the tears he thought he heard in her voice were also in her eyes. To hell with staying away. Keenan knelt to shuffle the fire and add more twigs. He then settled down next to her, his long leg pressed up against hers through the blanket. Without a word, he stole her hand from its course along the plaid lines and held it in his large one.

"Yer mother misses ye, Serena. I know that without yer powers."

He held her small hand against his palm. At first it felt like a lifeless little bird, unmoving, fragile. Keenan began to rub his thumb along the delicate bones of each digit.

She cleared her throat. "So what of your life, Keenan?"

"My life?"

"It must be difficult thinking you will die to save your clan, your brother."

"Actually," Keenan released her hand and stood, his head bent against the low ceiling. "My life was probably easier than most."

"Easier?"

"I've always known exactly what to do in life. Unlike the men who flounder around wondering what mark they will make on the world, what purpose their existence is meant to fulfill. I've always known my purpose." He watched her face. "It has been taught to me through word and expression since the day I was born."

Pity? Did pity just cross her face? His jaw tightened. "I'm na some sacrificial lamb to be pitied for its meaningless slaughter, Serena, so doona look at me as such."

"I don't pity you, Keenan. I was just thinking how alike we are."

He threw another branch on top of the crackling fire. "As night and day."

Serena shook her head, causing the green ribbon to fall among the blankets. Her hair broke free over her shoulders to veil her in fiery silk. Unbound curls that were made to wrap around a man's hand, coiled gently but purposely to trap her. She could be trapped easily.

"Trapped," Serena said.

"What?" Had he said the word aloud? Could she suddenly read his thoughts?

"We're both trapped. Me in my constant battle to control my power, and you behind the bars of your prophecy."

He must concentrate on something other than trapping her against him. He looked out at the wet, miserable night. The lightning had finally moved off, leaving a relentless dousing of cold rain. He huffed quietly. Trapped indeed. In this small cave with a beautiful siren.

"Has your family ever considered that, Keenan? That the prophecy is wrong?"

He sat back against the front wall putting space between them. "The seer saw many things, alliances, failed crops and plentiful seasons. She saw remarkable births and bizarre sickness." Keenan spoke slowly to emphasize his point. "Every single predication that the crone foretold has come true. All of them. And this is the last. Her words are true, my fate is to die."

"Perhaps you are the brother to live."

"I believe we've been over that."

"Elenor read me the prophecy. It doesn't specify which brother."

"Lachlan has never defended a soul, Serena. He made it a point not to learn how to defend. He knows that the brother who defends will die." He shook his head. "Nay, I am the defender. I've been raised as such, and I will fulfill my destiny."

Her gaze retreated to the fire. Did she begin to understand or did she tire of arguing the point? She wore the blue gown he had left in her room back at Kylkern. The neckline swooped low, low enough to see the swell of her breasts pushed up by her stays. Her softly translucent skin lay across the contours of her collarbone. He imagined his fingers skimming along that lovely flesh to dip low under the boundaries of her bodice.

Keenan groaned inwardly. He was a man after all, and therefore, not immune to the charms of a lovely lass. She had responded out on the moors on their journey north. Perhaps she would respond if he kissed her again.

The gown curved inward at her waist, a perfect resting place for his hands. She pulled her hair back to one side and re-tied it with the ribbon. She bent her head low to unlace the garters under her knees. The nape of her neck caught Keenan's gaze, that very spot he had glimpsed when she fled William's room, the very spot he longed to touch. Och, this was insanity. Keenan glanced at the blocked entrance. It would take his men to free them unless he started hacking away with his sword.

"Enough of this dark talk," Serena said with a forced smile. "Let's talk of happier times. Have you kissed many girls?"

Kissed many girls? Knowing that he would die he'd wasted no time with the pretty lasses. "Aye," he said, amazed at her switch in topics.

Her lips tensed into a false smile that looked more like a grimace on a carnival mask. "How many?"

"Dozens," he said nonchalantly. Her teeth still showing, the corners of her smile faltered, and a hint of anger sparked in her eyes. He could melt that tension in her face, and if encouraged, ignite that spark into a firestorm.

"And ye?"

"Me?"

"Aye, how many men have ye kissed, Serena?" Keenan threw some more twigs on the fire even though it didn't need it. Had she noticed his movements around the small space, like that of a caged animal?

"For women it is different. If I were to kiss dozens," she emphasized his word, "I would be considered unclean, a whore perhaps."

"Have ye been kissed by other than me?" he asked softly as if he caressed her rosy skin with his words. He watched her slender neck as she swallowed.

She nodded. She nodded to say yes, she had been kissed. By who, when? Keenan's hand clenched along his side.

"I was to be married when I was thirteen, and Mari wanted me to know him better before the vows. He kissed me and," she stopped. "And I knew I couldn't marry him."

Keenan crouched before her and tossed more twigs on the flames. "Why?" He leaned across to adjust the blanket around her. They were so close, nearly nose-to-nose.

"I could read his thoughts." She paused and looked back into the fire.

"And his lustful thoughts scared ye," Keenan said. Thank the heavens she couldn't read his or she'd be the one hacking through the branches to get out of the cave.

"Yes, his thoughts worried me, but Mari had warned me what boys and men thought about with a woman. But that's not what stopped me from wedding him."

Keenan placed his finger under her chin.

"Why did ye na wed, Serena?"

Tears shone, brightening the violet hue. "He only wanted me because of my powers. Otherwise, I was an embarrassment to him."

"The bastard told ye this?"

"He didn't have to, I felt it in his touch." The tear slipped out. His finger caught it near her temple. His hand cupped the side of her face and his thumb traced her cheek.

"He was a foolish boy," he said. Keenan ached to wipe away that pain on her face, the loneliness. "Ye need a man, Serena. A man who reveres ye for who ye are, na for yer powers."

She leaned into his hand. "Keenan, will you kiss me?"

His body and blood surged forward. His hand burrowed into the hair cradling her head. His lips met hers as his other arm wrapped around and cocooned her. She hesitated, timid in her virginity, but as he slanted against her lips, subtly caressing, she relaxed. A small moan escaped on her breath. Both of Keenan's hands combed through her hair, brushing the ribbon to the ground.

A loud pop in the fire startled her and she tensed.

"It's just the fire, relax, lass." Keenan traced her face again with his hand.

She closed her eyes, her lips parted. They were just too perfectly pink to abandon. Keenan leaned in again. This time she returned the pressure from the start. Slowly, Keenan unwound the blankets from her body and lowered her backwards to the ground. He leaned over her on his forearms. Drawing back, his gaze raked over her angelic features and passion filled eyes. Serena's quick breaths swelled her breasts upward to strain at the blue fabric.

"Keenan." The passion in her voice pushed his conscience aside.

Keenan spread long hair out around her face. She looked like a sun angel fallen to earth. Bloody hell, he should stop.

Her eyes were half closed, sultry, bewitching. She was to marry Lachlan, but she refused. She wanted him, Keenan, not his cowardly brother.

"Kiss me, Keenan," she said. Her hand wound around the back of his neck, her fingers spreading through his hair.

He descended, his intent filled with raw passion fueled by rage against the future. The smell of earth and fire penetrated Keenan's senses. He pulled back, his sight taking in the mud and ash around them. He couldn't take Serena here in the dirt. He shouldn't be taking Serena at all.

Keenan tucked Serena's head below his chin as he pulled her up against him. "Sleep now, lass or I'll have to go sleep in the storm."

Serena tried to push away but he wouldn't let her. "All I can do is hold ye, lass. Let me hold ye."

As the fire slowly turned to embers, Keenan listened to her steady breathing. Even her breathing sounded soft and feminine. Her smell infused him. It was the most uncomfortably long night of Keenan's life.

****

"In here," Keenan called back to Thomas's hail.

It took all four Maclean warriors to heave the huge birch tree from the mouth of the cave.

Serena awoke and sat up, dazed.

"Bloody hell," Keenan grumbled. The lass looked like she'd been tupped.

As soon as the others unbarred their entrance, he plunged out into the morning, free from the cage. "Where the hell have ye all been?" Keenan roared at his men.

"We slept in some caves through the storm," Ewan supplied as he motioned over his shoulder. "We dinna ken ye were trapped."

"Is the witch well?" Thomas asked looking toward the cave entrance.

"Her name is Serena or Lady Faw, not witch," Keenan growled and walked off to find some privacy.

The men had the small, wet campsite packed by the time he returned.

Brodick indicated the cave. "She's still in there

preening."

Keenan turned abruptly toward the cave. Better to get this over with in a little privacy. Keenan took a deep breath and stepped into the dark hole.

"Oh," Serena said as she bumped into his chest. "I was just on my way out."

"What's taking ye so long in here?"

Serena frowned at him. "I said I was just on my way out." She stepped closer to him.

He stood up abruptly, grazed his head on the cave ceiling and cursed. She laid a hand on his arm causing him to jerk and run his elbow into the jagged granite wall.

"Keenan, last night," she began. "The kiss—"

"Should never have happened, Serena."

"What?"

"Ye are to be my brother's wife. I took liberties, I…"

"Didn't do anything I didn't want, Keenan."

He continued to berate himself silently. "It shouldn't have happened. Ye will be my sister."

"Not in this lifetime," Serena huffed.

"Ye are the witch."

"Agreed, but the kiss, Keenan?" Serena blushed.

Keenan stared stonily for a moment and then rubbed the front of his skull. He closed his eyes. "I will never forget yer sweet taste, but lass, it will never happen again."

"Never again?"

Keenan shook his head.

"But, but," she stammered. "Drakkina said, she said that all would fall into place if we kissed."

"Who?" Keenan glanced about the cave.

"Drakkina, a crone, or a spirit of one. She came to me. She knew my parents, my real parents. And I have sisters and she knows them, she knows so much." Serena's words tumbled over one another in their rush. "You can't say you'll never kiss me again."

"When did ye talk to the crone?"

"Last night, she appeared in here before the storm."

Keenan's lips tightened together. "The unnatural storm." He'd been tricked.

"She said that we must kiss and that we are soul mates and meant to be together. I asked her of your prophecy and she didn't believe it. Keenan, she's very wise. She helped me heal William," Serena gestured with her hands and shrugged. "She linked me to a healer, my sister I think." She stopped and waved her hands. "That doesn't matter, but I'm telling you, she knows things. She's magic and she says that we must be together. For the greater good, she said."

Keenan stared, his face transforming. "She told ye to kiss me last night?" Serena had asked him to kiss her, not because she wanted him to, but because this spirit told her to.

"Yes, she said that if I kissed you that we'd be together as is meant to be."

"So ye kissed me because she told ye to do it, for the greater good."

Serena swallowed. "This isn't coming out at all right. I wanted to kiss you, Keenan. I'm just not one to ask. Her words helped me be bold enough to ask you."

Her confession rolled a boulder into his chest.

"Keenan, last night…"

"Was done for the greater good." Where had he heard that before?

"No," Serena's voice rose.

"It sounds like ye have yer own prophecy controlling ye, Serena. I suppose we do have much in common."

Serena just stared, her eyes wide, pleading.

He was in no mood to listen. "Aye, much in

common. We both are performing a role in our own stories. Performing our role for the sake of the greater good."

Keenan turned on his heel and strode out of the cave. "Find yer horse. We have a mission to complete."

Chapter 9

They arrived the next night at the Red Cloak Inn, in Leicester. Keenan procured two rooms. Serena retired immediately, requesting food and a bath to be sent upstairs. Keenan sat at a table in the corner of the common room with his men and took a long pull off his tankard. He hadn't spoken more than a handful of words to Serena. He was furious with himself for wanting her kiss. The witch would wed Lachlan.

"What's the plan?" Gavin asked Keenan as he leaned forward, his elbows planted on the rough table.

"King George is visiting Frampton Manor nearby," Keenan said casually, his gaze washing over the busy room. "Word in town is that he is entertaining his latest mistress there on holiday, but I think he's meeting with Scottish supporters."

"Bastards," Ewan swore.

"I've requested an audience with the king to explain Gerard's death. If I see the excuse, I will play the part of traitorous brother."

"What's that?" Thomas asked and coughed, his eyes glancing toward the stairs leading to Serena. "Traitorous in what way?"

Keenan ignored the glance. "I'll say that I support him, not Lachlan and the Bonnie Prince. If he's meeting with Scottish supporters, I'll just be another."

"Without an army?" Gavin asked with one eyebrow raised.

"Nay," Keenan said. "George kens that the

Maclean warriors from Kylkern support me." Keenan looked at his men, the men he had trained and fought with. All four of them nodded easily. "I can convince him that ye follow me, na' Lachlan."

"What then?" Ewan said and pinched a serving maid who had wandered nearby. She smiled coyly and sauntered over toward the kitchens. His eyes followed her.

Brodick punched his arm. "Yer neck may depend on this, pay attention."

Keenan sat back in his chair. "Perhaps he'll confide his plans to me. Perhaps I'll find some other battle plans or overhear some important information."

Thomas motioned toward the stairs. "What of the witch?"

"She is a lovely lass," Ewan said glancing at the stairs. "Hard to believe she's a witch."

"Her name is Serena," Keenan corrected brusquely.

"Then what of Serena?" Thomas asked undaunted.

"She will come to court with me, a distant cousin who supports me in the break from Lachlan. In reality she will try to identify the thieves who killed Gerard and took the letter. If they are following the court, I need to retrieve the letter."

"But what if the murderers are there and reveal that Gerard was a Jacobite?" Gavin asked.

Keenan leaned back considering. "Giving Gerard's name would only call suspicion on themselves. Suspicion is something everyone avoids these days. But if they do, I willna refute it," Keenan said.

Brodick wrapped his fingers around his tankard, his other hand tugging at his beard. "He could have ye locked up, as a Jacobite."

Keenan shrugged. "Unlikely, but Serena can

warn me if she picks up on any ill thoughts of dungeons and gallows." He grinned darkly. Keenan knew the lass scared them a bit.

The kitchen maid brought another round of ale and neatly avoided Ewan's hand this time, though her smile held promise.

Thomas leaned over to Keenan. "Why bother, Keenan? Chances are, the letter is gone. What good is it really to get into court? What, with the risk?"

The thought of Serena bent over William on the bridge sat heavy in Keenan's mind. She had promised to help him identify and possibly recover the incriminating letter, and he had promised to help save her brother. Keenan led him out of Leeds and to relative safety, but William still had a price on his head for the murder of a prestigious man. Serena herself may even be wanted in association with William's disappearance.

"I made a bargain to help Serena's brother, William. If there's a chance to expose those who plotted and hired Gerard's murderer, I need to expose it. Otherwise, William Faw will run his entire life."

Gavin nodded. "No honor in running and hiding yer entire life, now is there." The other three quickly agreed. Gavin silently raised his cup in salute.

Perhaps the farce about controlling his brother's army was not that far off from the truth.

****

The pretty kitchen maid smiled at Serena as she turned in a circle.

"Milady, you do look lovely in that gown. You'll fit right in with the court at Frampton Manor, if you don't mind me saying."

Serena smiled reassuringly. "I owe it to you, Winifred. And you certainly know how to weave hair." Serena peered into the small glass mirror above the dressing table in the cramped room above stairs at the inn. Winifred had coiled and woven her hair with ribbon to match the emerald court gown Keenan had commissioned upon arriving in town.

Ewan had ridden down to Leicester with bolts of the silk mockado velvet tied tightly to the back of his horse. It had taken three seamstresses two full days to cut, pin and stitch it together in record time. They had just finished in time for Serena and Keenan's audience with King George that evening followed by a small reception feast and dancing.

Winifred stopped in front of Serena, hands on hips, and stared at Serena's bare neckline. "Hmm, I hope you aren't chilled this eve, Milady. The neckline is quite low."

Serena looked down at the tops of her round breasts held up by the tight stays.

"I should wear a handkerchief to cover the neckline."

Winifred shook her head. "Not in the evening at court. All the ladies wear their costume without covering up. It seems they would likely fall out if they bend down." The maid smiled at Serena's concerned look. She patted her sleeve. "Don't fret, you'll do just fine."

Winifred's kind eyes eased Serena.

"Just in case, Milady, you should stay as upright as possible," she added and demonstrated a curtsey while staying in a vertical position.

Serena mimicked her moves. If she didn't stay down too long, she could hold the pose. "Lovely, Milady. You'll do just fine."

Serena wasn't so sure, but she didn't have a choice. She was on a mission to find the murderers to clear William's name. How she would do that, she hadn't a clue. Even if she found the man and woman, why would anyone believe her? Serena took two more deep breaths. On the last one she looked down at her breasts. No deep breathing either, she thought, as the flesh seemed to swell dangerously over the velvet edging.

A sharp rap trembled the thin wood door. Winifred opened it timidly and then threw it wide to let Keenan and Brodick enter. "Isn't she a lovely sight?" she said with sincere enthusiasm.

Serena turned around to face the two sour faced men. She took a deep breath without thinking. Brodick's eyes dropped to her ample display, and then his face turned several shades of red. No deep breathing. Keenan's eyes rested on her chest as well, but instead of looking embarrassed, he looked irritated, even angry.

"They say it's the latest fashion," Serena offered.

Brodick cleared his throat and tugged on his beard. "Ye look very courtly, Milady."

"Call me Serena, Brodick."

"Not at court," Keenan said briskly. "At court ye are Milady."

Serena nodded. He still hadn't said anything about how she looked. She held arms out to her sides and turned in a circle. "The fabric is beautiful. Thank you for bringing it down with us. I had no idea Ewan carried it all this way. I'll have to thank him."

"I'll tell Ewan. Doona ye bother him about it," Keenan said briskly.

Keenan continued to stare, his eyes traveling up and down until she too began to blush. He looked stern, serious, as if ready for battle. Did he expect battle this eve? Serena reminded herself not to breathe deeply. She would just have to let her heart race.

"Do ye have a cloak?" Keenan asked abruptly. Winifred brought a soft lamb's wool coat from the bed. "Good," he said and turned.

Whisked through the inn at a breathless speed, Serena's heart beat rapidly as she stepped up into a hired carriage. The door clicked shut behind Keenan as he followed. He settled himself across from Serena in the tight cabin. Thomas rode above with the driver. Ewan and Brodick rode their horses alongside. The carriage bumped and pitched along the pitted road. Serena concentrated on keeping her seat else she would end up in a pile of velvet and fluff on the gritty floor.

Keenan watched out the window. The moon reflected against his face, accentuating the scar and his rugged masculinity. He wore English court clothes, perfectly cut to show off his strong body in elegant style. Every part of his grooming, down to his neatly queued hair, made him look the courtly gentleman, proud and serious. Serena sighed quietly. She preferred her Scottish warrior, who smelled of pine and highland wind. She preferred the man that used to trust her.

"Keenan. I'd like the chance to explain about Drakkina and the cave."

Keenan turned to her. "What else is there to ken," he said nonchalantly. "A spirit woman told ye to kiss me and that it was meant to be for the greater good." He stared.

The moon flashed through the trees to flicker across her eyes, making it difficult to see his expression. Serena's chest clenched. The man was impossibly stubborn. How would she ever be able to convince him that his perceptions were skewed? "I didn't kiss you because she told me to," she said, silently adding "you big oaf." "I kissed you because I've wanted to since you caught me at the fair."

Keenan didn't move. Serena caught sight of the lights of Frampton Manor sparkling against the darkness outside his window.

"When you kissed me on the moors," she hesitated thankful for the dark interior, "I...I wanted more." His black eyes watched. Oh, she wanted to look away, to hide the embarrassment her admittance brought, but she didn't. He had to see it in her eyes. "But then we were at Kylkern and you," she took a deep breath. "You gave me up, up to the prophecy, up to Lachlan. It was as if you had just begun to see me and then you shut the door."

He didn't say anything, just continued his silent stare.

"Drakkina had only just told me that you were my soul mate before you woke me in the cave. At first I thought she had been a dream." She paused. "And then when I began to think that maybe she was more real than dream, it was, well I," she turned her head away. "I had decided, Drakkina or not, I wanted to kiss you again. And I thought that it might be my only chance."

Still he said nothing. "I seem to remember," she continued, as anger began to well back inside, "that you, too, felt you had no time to tell me something you should have."

Keenan peered through the darkness, his blank stare seemed to weigh her words. Shouts beyond the windows heralded the gates of Frampton Manor.

She folded her arms and leaned back into the seat.

"In battle," his muted voice filled the small cabin, "I must trust each of my warriors completely." His mellow tone couldn't conceal the stark undercurrent. "They disclose everything, and I use all their information to best calculate my strategy so we all can survive."

"I speak of my heart and you lecture me on the tactics of war?"

"Life is war, Serena."

They passed through the lit gates into the bailey of the fortified manor house. "And I'm one of your warriors," she mocked quietly.

"The prophecy declares ye as such."

Serena snorted softly. "You trust that bloody prophecy more than you trust your own instincts, Keenan." Torchlight flashed across his face as they jarred to a halt.

Keenan spoke softly.

"There is danger here this eve, Serena. I need ye to be a warrior."

"I know the plan. You've gone over and over it."

"Aye, but can I trust ye?"

Serena leaned forward. "I've bared my soul to you, and I have absolutely no idea what you think about what I said or about me. I think the better question is, can I trust you, Keenan?"

Brodick clicked the latch up on the outside and whipped the door open.

Keenan escorted Serena up the many steps to the entrance of Frampton Manor. As they entered, he spoke to one of the pages over the quartet playing in a small ballroom. "Keenan Maclean of Kylkern, and my cousin Serena Mackay of York. We have come to announce the death of a friend to His Majesty." Keenan pulled out the summons that he had received upon his request. The page took the letter and Serena's cloak, revealing her deeply dipping neckline.

Keenan almost demanded the cloak back, but etiquette and performance were as essential to court as water to human life. Another glance assured him that the rose hued areolas encircling her nipples were still trapped within the clinging fabric.

Keenan took a deep breath and forced his eyes to roam the landscape of the gilded rooms. What was wrong with him? He had never been so distracted on a mission before, and distractions could be lethal.

The servant ushered them into the dazzling lit cage of decadence and etiquette. Several familiar lords and ladies stood about the room in whispering groups. It was a veritable wolves' den of powdered wigs and pompously stuffed costumes. The aroma of stale lamp oil mixed with fragrance to hide body odor filled his nose. He hated the court. Why indeed would he purposely lower himself into this belly of sweet smiling assassins and proper looking miscreants? Duty, honor, all the same reasons that propelled him from his pallet each morning.

Keenan glanced at the statuesque Serena as they approached the makeshift throne where George sat expectantly. Elizabeth Darlington, the king's latest mistress, sat in a high backed chair next to him. After his wife Catherine died years before, George swore that he would never marry another. He would only take mistresses from then on.

Serena dipped low into a formal curtsey displaying her cleavage before the monarch's keen eye. Aye, Keenan thought dismally, he should be here, but he shouldn't have brought Serena. It was too dangerous. It didn't feel right. He bowed low.

"Your Majesty," the page said formally to their right. "I present Keenan Maclean of Kylkern and his cousin Serena Mackay of York."

"Rise, rise," George said smiling like a cat about to indulge in fresh cream. He all but licked his puffed up royal lips. Keenan helped Serena rise and placed her hand on his arm. "Come forward, fair lady. I don't believe we have met before." Without looking at Keenan, "I've met your sword-throwing cousin, but didn't know he had kin so fair."

"Hello, Keenan," Elizabeth said coyly from her seat. "We didn't know you had relations in England."

Keenan ignored the subtle invitation he read in Elizabeth's voice. A chill of suspicion tore along Keenan's muscles, the weight of his dirks ready to be unleashed. Something wasn't as it seemed. Was Serena sensing anything apart from Elizabeth's sexually explicit thoughts? Keenan had danced with Elizabeth at a party in London last year. It was before her entanglement with George and he had flirted with her, but nothing had come of it.

"Serena is a distant cousin on my mother's side," he said stiffly.

George rose and walked down the two steps. He took Serena's other hand in his. "What a pleasure to have a new face at our little court." He indicated the room. Serena had her gloves on, but Keenan knew she could still touch the king's thoughts and emotions. Hell, Keenan could sense them.

Benjamin Frampton stepped out from a tall double door and nearly trotted to their side so as not to be left out of the introductions. He was a little man, full of overstuffed pride and self-glory. He blended well with the usual courtiers. Frampton's sly eyes slid along Serena's neckline. Keenan's jaw began to ache.

Frampton turned to him. "So Keenan Maclean, what brings you onto English soil?"

Time to enact the plan. "I've come to bring news of foul play."

"Eh?" Frampton said. George barely took his eyes off Serena to glance at Keenan.

"I regret to inform Yer Majesty that yer friend, Gerard Grant was murdered near Leeds a little over a fortnight ago."

Silence. George tucked Serena's hand into the crook of his arm. Had he touched her skin? Keenan wasn't sure. Frampton was saying something again, probably important.

"What was that, Frampton?" Keenan said steering his mind back to the plan, the mission.

"I said, it's a shame." Frampton tsked loudly. "I heard a Romany man stabbed him for his money."

"So ye've heard?"

"Yes, we had news several days ago," King George said. "Terrible tragedy."

Keenan caught sight of Thomas and Brodick

near the door. When his gaze turned back to Serena, she looked flushed, almost dazed. Keenan watched as George's hand ran up the side of her neck near her ear. Fury roiled up within Keenan, and he took a step toward them before reining himself in physically. *Think, think.* This was no battlefield where he could lay his enemy open with his blade. This was the court and the enemy was the King of England and nearly all of Britain.

"Miss Mackay and I also bring happy tidings of our own," Keenan heard himself saying. George looked at him, one puffy eyebrow slightly raised in question. Good, his hand had lowered upon Keenan's words. "Miss Mackay willna go by her maiden name much longer. We have wed in the Highland tradition by handfasting."

Serena's glassy eyes blinked several times as she stared back into his own. *Handfasting?*

Keenan walked over and pulled her into his side as George casually disentangled himself from her. "Aye lass, that is what we call it," he smiled and kissed her forehead before turning back to George and Frampton. "We will make it official with the kirk as soon as we return to Kylkern."

Frampton laughed. "I thought you had sworn off the bonds of marriage Maclean. Something terribly romantic, about a dark curse or other."

Keenan laughed back. "I suppose I was cursed until I found my dear cousin."

Elizabeth sauntered over and placed her hand on George's arm. "What happy news."

Keenan felt Serena's weight increase on his arm. He looked over and her pale face seemed to flicker shut a second before she slumped under the heavy weight of her gown.

"Good Lord, I think she's fainting," Elizabeth said.

Keenan picked up Serena as the twittering

crowd drew closer. Frampton's wife, Olivia rushed over issuing orders for a guest room to be readied. Keenan glimpsed Brodick and Thomas flanking them slightly behind. Through twists and turns and up stairs, Keenan only watched Serena's face, her dark lashes against her milk white skin. She was perfectly chiseled from marble, so cold, so deathlike.

As they entered a room, Keenan laid Serena on a large bed surrounded by heavy curtains. Thomas moved quickly to the hearth to encourage a fire while Brodick shooed the servant out of the room.

"Lass," Keenan whispered near Serena's ear. "Lass, are ye in there?" Had she taken in too much venom surrounded by vipers? Had she peered into too much darkness and lost herself? "Brodick, get over here," Keenan roared.

Brodick stepped up to the bed, his eyes worried.

"Think of the happiest time of yer life."

"Like when I slaughtered that MacCallum from Inverness?"

"Aye, I mean nay," Keenan said, his eyes still searching Serena's face. "Something happy like that, but nothing bloody, only happy. Like when yer nephew was born and yer sister was happy and healthy."

"Fine, aye, I'm thinking of it."

"Now touch her skin."

"Her skin?" he asked and ran his large hand over his beard.

"Aye, think the happy thought and touch her," Keenan pulled off Serena's glove so Brodick could take her hand. "And mind ye, if ye slip and start thinking evil or foul thoughts," Keenan looked Brodick in the eye with deadly seriousness. "I think ye could kill her." *And I will kill you.* He thought the words because they hummed through his body like his pulse. But he wouldn't say them. He didn't have to.

"Aye, happy thoughts." Brodick swallowed hard, and then breathed slowly. A grin came across his face, and Keenan put Serena's hand in his large paw.

Keenan bent back down to her ear. "Open up to Brodick's happiness, Serena. Let it in."

Serena's eyes moved behind the delicate veil of her lids. Her lashes flickered against the creaminess of her skin as she opened her eyes. "That's it lass," Keenan said and motioned to Brodick to break contact.

"Did my thoughts wake her?" he asked curiously.

"Yes, they helped," Serena said and tried to sit up.

Keenan pulled her into a sitting position and sat down. She leaned into him and looked up at Brodick. "What a beautiful little boy your sister has."

Brodick smiled proudly. "He's na' so wee anymore. He's going on ten now."

"I will have to meet him when we return to Kylkern."

"That ye will, I promise," Brodick said, his smile genuine.

Keenan watched the intimate exchange and frowned. He had always considered it a strange advantage that Serena couldn't read his thoughts and feelings. However, the same advantage also refused him a connection to her, a connection that every other man could form with her. Keenan's hands balled into fists at his side.

"Brodick, see if we were followed," Keenan indicated the door. "And send word that my wife is fine but needs to rest. I will return soon."

"Yer wife?" Gavin asked, his bushy eyebrows raising over wide eyes.

"Dinna ye hear Keenan in the hall," Brodick said walking to the door. "Clever too, to keep those royal

English claws off her. Probably what knocked her out." Brodick opened the heavy door and inclined his head to a guard a bit down the corridor.

Serena pushed upright against the soft tick of goose down. "Keenan," she gasped her eyes wide. "I need to tell you." She grabbed his fist with both her hands. The concern in the contact warmed through his gut. "King George, he knows that Gerard was a Jacobite. He knows that he stole the letter. Keenan, George hired the two I saw to kill Gerard." She moved his hand back and forth in her excitement. Gavin came over to the bed. Serena looked between them both and squeezed Keenan's hand. "He's setting you up to fall into a trap so he can arrest you, Keenan."

Keenan's mind chewed on the information as he stroked her grip with his loose hand.

"Was it George's treachery against us that made ye faint?" Gavin asked peering at her. It was the closest the man had ever allowed himself to be to Serena.

"Yes, and no," Serena looked down and blushed. "When I tried to read the king. His thoughts were," she hesitated, "carnal, so full of lust, I...I lost my concentration and all the other voices in the room began to flood me." Serena wouldn't look at them. "I heard so many things." She glanced at Keenan. "Elizabeth Darlington may be on the king's arm, but she'd rather be in your bed."

Keenan thought he heard a spark of jealousy in her voice. "I danced with Elizabeth last year, nothing more." Why did he need to defend his actions? "What about the two on the bridge? Did ye sense them in the room?"

Serena nodded. "Yes, I think they were there. I only had a glimpse of their thoughts, and they were tangled with the rest, but yes, I think they were there."

"Did they recognize ye," Keenan said softly.

She shook her head. "No. I only saw them that night through my mind, not my eyes. They've never seen me before."

"So when the king was touching ye," Gavin said, "he was imagining all sorts of perverted things with ye?"

Serena nodded.

"And with his mistress standing right behind him," Gavin said.

"And when Keenan announced that we were handfasted," Serena said and squeezed his hand tightly. "The king's thoughts moved toward eliminating you, Keenan. That's when I really understood his plan to trap you."

Keenan nodded. His impulsive thrust to get the king's hands off Serena had brought forth his dark plans. Spontaneous strategy sometimes worked in ones favor.

"Good thing ye said what ye said," Gavin slapped Keenan's shoulder. "So what do we do now?"

Keenan walked over toward the fire. His mind maneuvered through scenarios, rejecting and building plans.

Strategy.

He felt his blood hum with energy.

To outwit a king, and his council. He looked back to Serena. There were definite advantages to having a witch in the family. His forehead tensed. He turned to the two watching him. "I'll announce to the king that Gerard was in fact a traitor and Jacobite. That I discovered his treachery but before I could bring charges against him, someone murdered him."

"Not William," Serena said.

"I will say there was speculation that others may have been involved, loyal to England. But until we find out more about the two ye saw on the bridge,

I willna say more."

Serena nodded.

"I think then I must name Lachlan an incompetent leader in his indecision about the Bonnie Prince," Keenan said.

"Ye willna call him a Jacobite?" Gavin asked.

Keenan shook his head. "Better to show him indecisive which is weaker. I will claim support of George's right to rule all of Britain and convince him that Lachlan's army is mine to control. The rest of the plan will continue as before."

Gavin nodded. "Best be convincing, Keenan."

It wouldn't be too difficult. Apart from Keenan hating George for his lustful desires for Serena, the man had better sense than what he'd witnessed in the untried Prince Charles. Keenan really didn't support either when it came down to it. He supported peace for his clan and freedom to be Scottish. And he preferred to proclaim fidelity to a ruler whom he respected. Right now George, with all his pompous ways, was still the lesser of the two evils.

Brodick rapped on the door and walked in. "They await yer return with all the speculation ye would see at a cock fight."

"The two of ye, stay with Serena. Make certain no one tries to take her anywhere. If they seize me, get her out of here." He knew his words scared her, but she didn't say anything. Very brave. Serena would make any highland warrior proud.

Keenan walked back and engulfed her icy hand in his hot one. "Thank ye, Serena, for unveiling the trap. I will endeavor to step around it."

"You better," her eyes sparked with mock irritation. "We have our own business to finish."

He squeezed her hand and walked out the door.

Serena listened as his boots clipped down the corridor, fading into silence. Brodick and Gavin looked between each other and then both turned to her. She folded hands in her lap. The ordeal in the ballroom still weighed against her limbs along with the heaviness of the court dress. It was well over an hour before the official start to the king's reception so she had time to rest. She smoothed the gown in the awkward silence and glanced at the two Macleans. They still stared at her.

"Have I suddenly grown horns or a wart?"

"Nay," Brodick said. "It's just," he hesitated, "ye could really read my thoughts about my nephew and sister?"

She nodded. His words held no judgment, just curiosity. She had traveled for six days with these men as almost constant companions and spent two more days cooped up in the inn with them. And this was the closest they had ever approached her, physically and personally.

"Yes, I could, because I opened myself up to your thoughts. But I don't do that normally," she added quickly. "It is rude to eavesdrop in normal circumstances."

"So ye doona ken what I'm thinking right now?" Gavin asked stepping a bit closer and staring into her eyes, his own eyes buggy like a toad.

"I can tell you are thinking something quite loudly, but unless I open the door to your words, I don't hear them clearly."

"What about that Campbell?"

"I felt pain coming from him and darkness, so I opened myself up to his thoughts because I sensed danger."

Brodick stepped to the edge of the bed. His leg leaned along her dress. "But what if I touch yer skin, can ye block that?" He pointed to her gloves in her lap. "Ye wear those all the time."

Serena nodded. "They protect me when I accidentally touch someone. It's hard to shield myself when I touch someone skin to skin. And scars are even worse."

"Have ye touched Keenan's scar?" Gavin asked. He too, leaned in.

"I touched his scar the first time we met because I couldn't read anything about him. I'd never met anyone like that before. Even when I try to read his thoughts and emotions, I can't sense anything. Even his scar remains silent."

Brodick unlaced the ties at his throat and pulled down his shirt partway revealing the puckered line of a scar. "Ye could read this."

"But I don't want to," she said quickly. "I don't want to see the slaughter that you survived."

Gavin punched his arm and Brodick retied the collar. "It wasn't much of anything," guilt laced his words.

Silence fell over them and she began to worry about Keenan. Serena took a deep breath and tried to think of something other than what was going on in the ballroom.

"Let's play a game," she said cheerfully.

The two men looked wary. "What type of game, lass?" Gavin asked.

"Gavin, you think of something," she held up her hand, "nothing bad and no," she cleared her throat, "no intimate thoughts please. And I'll tell you what I see." She smiled. "Make it hard, something I couldn't possibly know."

Gavin smiled hesitantly. Brodick waved him away from her and whispered in his ear. His smile grew. He walked back over to her. "Here's something that only Brodick and I ken, none other could have told ye."

Gavin put out his hand, palm up. Serena cupped his hand in hers. Whatever it was he was slightly embarrassed about it. Serena focused a strand of power into Gavin's rough skin, up under the fur covering his arm, along the muscles, tendons, and vessels running up the back of his neck and into the very core of his brain. All this she covered in the space of two heart beats without even contemplating how. It was as natural to her as breathing.

And there it was, hidden amongst the questions and slight fear about her abilities. Serena could almost taste the tang of the berries, the flakiness of the crust, just the right amount of spices swirling together into one glorious bite, a bite made even better by the danger. Her mouth began to water and she swallowed. Her stomach growled audibly through the room. Gavin and Brodick looked at one another and then back at Serena.

"Excuse me," she apologized, "but I'm near to starving for Nelly's wild strawberry pie."

Gavin pulled his hand back.

Serena tsked. "Really you two, stealing the poor lady's pie right off her window sill."

Brodick smiled and rubbed his stomach. "It's been nearly a score of years, but I can still taste it."

"Made better by the thrill," she said trying to frown despite the quivering corners of her mouth.

"We were but boys," Gavin defended.

Serena just shook her head. They looked between each other in silence, their grins growing until all three erupted in laughter.

Gavin hushed them and pointed toward the door. "Unseen ears may start rumors about our mirth." Serena put her hand over her mouth. Brodick nodded but his deep chuckle still punctuated the sudden stillness.

"Brodick, stuff something in that hole of yers," Gavin said.

"If we only had pie!" Serena said and fell back on the bed in a fit of giggles as Brodick guffawed loudly. She felt so light, so at ease with these two men. She shifted back up on her elbows. Gavin grinned at her and shook his head.

"My turn," Brodick said and grabbed Serena's bare hand to pull her back into a sitting position. As his fingers wrapped around hers, Serena felt his mirth and acceptance wash through her. Her eyes blinked shut as tears welled. She took a long even breath, savoring the feel, the feel of a friend, or at least the beginning of one.

Brodick dropped her hand. "I am so sorry, lass. I dinna think. I just grabbed yer hand and..."

Serena held up her hand to stop him and opened her eyes. Both Gavin and Brodick peered at her worried. She smiled. "Thank you, Brodick." He frowned and looked at Gavin. Gavin shrugged.

"Are ye having a spell again, lass?" Gavin whispered and moved his face just inches from her. "Did Brodick think something evil into ye?"

"I dinna do any such thing!" Brodick defended.

Serena laughed and swung her legs over the edge of the bed. The weight of her exhaustion had melted away with Brodick's touch. "Nay lass, ye should stay in bed," Gavin urged.

"I'm fine, Gavin, even better now that I know," and she looked at Brodick, "that Brodick actually likes me."

Gavin's eyes narrowed and he turned to Brodick. "Ye like her? What's that mean?"

Brodick's astonished face turned red to match the flames dancing in the hearth. He opened his mouth to protest but couldn't seem to find the words. Serena patted the stunned man's arm.

"I mean, that when Brodick grabbed my hand without thinking first about my powers," she looked at Brodick, "it meant that you trusted me." She shook her head, her smile fading slightly like brightly colored curtains left too long in the path of the sun. "I've never had someone just touch me without fearing me in some way, except for my duy and William."

The two men looked at her. Brodick spoke first. "Ye mean ye've never had a friend?" Serena shook her head and walked over to the fire.

"My tribe has always seen me as strange. I'm pretty certain they're glad I'm gone." She kept the self-pity out of her voice. Serena despised self-pity in others. It was so useless, did nothing to alter their circumstances. She turned away, embarrassed.

She heard them walking over to her. Hands on her arms turned her around into a bear-like embrace. She knew it was Brodick even before she looked up. "Well I'm yer friend, lass. Ye've already saved Lachlan and Keenan from the Campbell, and ye've already saved us here in England. Of course I trust ye."

Not to be out done, Gavin's large hands on her shoulders pulled Serena around and into his chest. "Touch my skin and tell for yerself, Serena. I'm yer friend too." His hug was awkward but Serena felt his sincerity. She laughed into his barrel chest. "What, ye doona believe me?" Gavin said. "I'm telling ye, Serena, touch me."

"Touch ye! What in bloody hell is going on in here!" Keenan's voice was punctuated by the door ricocheting off the wall. It cut through the pleasant waves of trust coming from the two Maclean warriors. Gavin dropped his arms and jumped back from Serena, which nearly knocked her down with the sudden absence of physical support. "What the hell are ye asking her to do?" Keenan stopped and moved his hand about, "I ordered ye to guard her, not touch her!" Keenan picked her up, strode past an open mouthed Thomas who stood in the doorway. Keenan lowered her back into the bed. Both men began defending themselves, each other, and Serena all at once.

"All is well, Keenan," she said cutting through

the noise. "Gavin just wanted to show me that he trusts me now. He knows I would feel his sincerity if I touched his hand."

"His hand, huh," Keenan grumbled and frowned at the two furiously nodding warriors. Serena almost laughed for they looked like two innocent boys swearing they weren't stealing a pie from the window sill.

"While the two of ye were hugging Serena," Thomas said and shut the door behind him, "Keenan was weaving one hell of a believable lie about his hatred for the Bonnie Prince." All eyes turned to Thomas. "Keenan even said that he had been about to kill Gerard himself when he found him dead."

"What about the letter?" Gavin asked.

"The King asked Keenan if a letter had been found on Gerard and Keenan said that Gerard had bragged about it which was how Keenan discovered that Gerard was a Jacobite. But after Keenan found Gerard dead, there hadn't been anything in his pockets," Thomas smiled. "Brilliant."

"Why brilliant?" Brodick asked.

Keenan's weight sank into the soft tick causing Serena to roll into him. "It gave me a plausible way of discovering Gerard's loyalties, and it was partly the truth so the true murderers and King George would ken I wasn't lying."

"And then," Thomas joined in, "King George said that the letter had been retrieved."

"So it still exists?" Brodick looked hopeful and Thomas nodded.

Serena climbed back out of the Keenan induced gully. "So the king admitted that William hadn't killed Gerard?"

Keenan shook his head slightly and looked down. "When I suggested that someone else may have killed Gerard for the letter, Frampton joined in to say that someone may have taken it from Gerard's pocket after the Romany man had killed him for his purse."

Disappointment stabbed through Serena. It must have shown on her face for both Gavin and Brodick stepped to the end of the bed.

"We're na' done here yet, Serena," Brodick said with encouragement.

"Aye," Gavin joined in, "once we identify the true murderers, perhaps they will admit it."

Serena tried to roll past Keenan to rise, but he wouldn't move. "Why? Why would they when they know the king protects them? William is the perfect innocent to blame." Serena's eyes blurred with tears that she fought to hold in place.

Keenan ordered his men out to scout the halls. He sat next to her, his weight once again pulling her to him. He took the gloves she had just picked up and tossed them aside to take her hands in his large ones.

"Serena," his words, soft, but commanding, made her look up. "We will do what we can."

"But we have no plan."

"Aye we do. We will try to find the letter, and we will try to get the murderers to admit their foul play."

"But it won't matter if they admit it. The king commanded it."

Keenan smirked slightly. "Aye, he may have commanded it behind closed doors, but if they admit it in public, the king willna support them."

"And what possibly could make them admit such a thing when doing so would mean abandonment by their society and possible imprisonment?"

Keenan shrugged. "Perhaps we can convince them that it would benefit them to show publicly that they are willing to commit murder to help the king's cause?"

A snapping in the fire sparked fiercely until it

became a familiar voice.

"What a stupid plan." Drakkina stepped from the hot air in the hearth. Serena sucked in a breath at the wild tingling along her birthmark. Drakkina advanced. Keenan jumped up from the bed and brandished a dirk he drew from his thigh.

Drakkina waved her hand at his short sword. "Put that away, Keenan Maclean. You can't stab me. I'm but made of air."

"You can see her?" Serena asked him even though the answer was obvious.

"Aye," he said guardedly while lowering the dirk to his side. "Is she the one who visited ye in the cave?"

Serena nodded. "Yes."

"What do ye want, spirit?"

She winked one sharp blue eye at him. "You can call me Drakkina or Master if you prefer." She smiled a small mouthful of perfect white teeth. "Although I don't think you have it in you to call anyone master, Keenan Maclean, warrior chief of Kylkern."

"I am na' chief of Kylkern."

"No? Who controls the honed army of warriors from Kylkern? Lachlan?" She laughed darkly. "I think even with your head clouded by duty, you still see that they follow you, not him."

Serena stood up beside Keenan. "Why do you come here?"

"Ah Serena, you are angry with me," Drakkina said softly.

Was she angry with the crone? More so with herself. "You know the answers before I speak so why ask?"

Drakkina inclined her head. "I concede the point, young Wiccan." She turned to look pointedly at Keenan. "To answer the tumbling questions behind that blank façade of yours, I did tell her to kiss you, but she responded to your touch out of love for you, not out of duty or purpose."

"Drakkina," Serena said, but the old woman held up a hand to silence her.

"She loves you even if she hasn't identified it yet. And if you'd set aside your imprecise perceptions of what is right and wrong, then you'd realize that you love her, too." She looked between them and frowned. "You are both bumbling fools in your ignorance." She sighed deeply and then waved her hands in dismissal.

"Did ye come to tell us this?" Keenan asked as he glanced to see Serena at his side.

"Not mostly," Drakkina answered. "I've come to help." She smiled cryptically.

"Help?" Keenan asked dryly.

"Yes, first I wanted to introduce myself to you, Keenan Maclean. And then I wanted to tell you that I will help."

"With what?" Serena's hand crept up the back of Keenan until she had a piece of his tunic twisting in her hand. She couldn't pull at her hair, but she needed to work at something in her nervous state.

Drakkina shrugged. "Where I can. Help to find the letter, help to clear your Romany brother's name."

"Thank ye, but we doona need yer help."

She let out one loud "Ha". "We'll see," she said as her body began to mist away like a wisp of wood smoke swirled by a light breeze.

Chapter 10

A light reel moved the courtly dancers about the ballroom as Keenan and Serena stepped under the arched entry flanked by Thomas, Brodick and Gavin. Ewan remained with the servants and investigated the kitchens and stables. Although the spirited notes cast a guileless mood amidst the dainty smiles and appreciative glances between guests, Keenan knew the minds behind the façades often slithered with deception and darkness. Which was why he had commanded Serena to keep up her wall, or whatever she used to keep out thoughts. Through the evening she would be able to identify the murderers by sight.

Keenan steered them toward the king. "We need to pay homage first."

"You are sound and back on your feet," George said in response to Serena's curtsey. "Good, good. Lady Serena, please rise. I would not be responsible for a repeated fainting spell."

Serena straightened. "Pray, please excuse my earlier fragility. It has been a long journey and the excitement of meeting Your Majesty, well I think it was too much for me." Serena blushed to add to the excuse.

Keenan mentally added actor to Serena's attributes, which already included witch and warrior.

"Yes, you do seem a bit frail, dear," Elizabeth Darlington drawled out. "Those Highland winters just might do you in."

Olivia Frampton tittered nervously and took Serena's arm. "I'm sure you will fair quite well up north, Lady Serena. The court can be quite overwhelming when one has not been raised within it. Take a turn with me," Olivia said indicating the perimeter of the room. "And tell me about your upbringing. I hear you hail from York?"

Keenan watched them weave a path through the gossipy courtiers. He and Serena had discussed her contrived background earlier.

"I say, she's quite a lovely woman," King George's words snapped Keenan's mind back to the moment.

"Aye, Yer Majesty. It was what first caught my eye."

"And now that you've handfasted with her, will you follow up with a church wedding or has your lust been sated enough that you'll abandon her?" George glanced at Keenan. "I understand that you can leave a handfasted woman after a year and a day if you're not satisfied with her. What a wonderfully barbaric custom."

Frampton hovered nearby, chuckling. The condescending snorts raked against Keenan's temper, making the muscles in his arms begin to bunch. Years of practice hiding his emotions kept his tone level.

"We will have the clergy bless the union upon return to Kylkern." George's eyes followed Serena, but Keenan caught the haughty eyes of Frampton. "Serena is under my protection and I gladly give her the Maclean name. We are tied together until death."

George smiled slyly. "With God's will that will last longer than the year."

"And a day," Frampton added.

George laughed.

Keenan forced a grin and tried to switch the topic to arms and strategic alliances.

George sighed. "Let us talk of lighter things this

eve, Maclean. You have a beautiful woman soon to be on your arm again. The food and spirits are a delight."

Frampton puffed up visually on the compliment.

"Let us talk of Jacobite plots on the morrow and leave tonight open for delights," George finished as Elizabeth moved against his side and linked her arm in his. After long moments of ridiculous, polite banter, Olivia brought Serena back around. Serena came directly over to Keenan, and he took her arm.

"Perhaps we will talk on the morrow," Keenan said. "It is only that we canna tarry long here in Leicester."

"Oh?" George asked.

"We have vows to say," Keenan said and pulled Serena within the confines of his frame.

Frampton stepped up. "We can easily procure a priest and have a grand celebration right here."

Keenan felt Serena's body stiffen against him. "We appreciate the generous offer, but must decline," he replied with a slight bow of his head.

Olivia pouted audibly while Elizabeth delivered a look of skeptical elation while tapping her fan shut.

Keenan looked only to King George. "I have failed yet to present my wife to my brother and chief, Lachlan. As it is, I shouldn't have handfasted without speaking my intent with him first. I wouldn't show further disrespect by wedding officially without his knowledge and consent."

The king raised an eyebrow as if he would argue, but Keenan continued with ease. "I would also appreciate the opportunity to give Lachlan one more chance to join ye in yer quest to unite Britain before I dethrone him." He shrugged slightly and tucked Serena's hand in his arm. "After all, he is my brother."

George pursed his pudgy lips. "He has a strong

argument, Lady Frampton," he said as he addressed the sulking woman across from him.

Olivia's pout broadened into a smile. "Then I will gift you with a wedding costume," she said to Serena.

"Your generosity is too much," Serena murmured.

Olivia waved her free hand. "It will be my pleasure, fun actually. We will clothe you as befitting a friend of the royal court."

Serena nodded politely. "Your graciousness, Lady Frampton, is without bounds. I thank you." Serena curtsied.

"I will come with my seamstresses to your room on the morrow," Olivia continued.

"At the inn?" Serena asked.

"Heavens, no. You and your lord will stay in your room here at Frampton Manor of course. I'm sure the King would want you close."

Keenan stepped in. "Doona fret, wife, I have had our bags brought to our room." Aye, he would have to share a room with her, but he would deal with that later.

A tinkling bell announced dinner.

Hours later, the last course of sugared fruit was tasted and the same bell signaled the end of the feast. The string instruments began a slow waltz to draw the guests back to the ballroom. Keenan pulled Serena to the dance floor amidst several other couples.

He bent low to her ear. "Do ye ken the steps, lass? I doona wish to embarrass ye."

She smiled at him. "Thank you, but yes, I know the steps. I have been dancing a long time, and not just around a campfire."

Keenan frowned slightly. "But this dance is a bit," he paused, "intimate. Ye've danced it before?"

"I think William would purge his supper if you

told him that this dance is intimate, since he was the only man who would dare dance with me, or touch me, for that matter."

Serena closed her eyes and tried to control her blush. Had those words actually rolled from her mouth? Such pitiful words. Keenan whisked her into a turn and her dress flared out to the side. Keenan said nothing through several rounds. They twirled and stepped, bowed and slid.

As they stepped together once more at the end of one round, Keenan lowered his voice. "Those who were too afraid to touch yer softness, they were cowards." He shook his head once, a slight movement almost unperceivable. "I am glad though that they never felt the silk in yer hair or the movement of yer form against their body." He slid his hand along her waist. "I am no coward."

Serena could scarcely breathe. She took several shallow breaths without breaking the contact between them. Her heart danced wildly inside causing her chest to swell upwards with each inhale. Keenan glanced down along her neckline and then back up to her face. His eyes fiercely intense, his tongue touched his bottom lip causing a shudder to run through Serena. Keenan's thumb grazed her jaw where it rose up into her hairline.

"Keenan," Brodick stepped to their side, shattering the moment. She had felt something from Keenan, something in his words had tugged at her mind. Had she connected in some way with him? It hadn't been words she had heard, but the echo of emotion.

"Keenan, Ewan heard from a maid who overheard from Frampton's valet that George keeps his letters and papers in Frampton's study off the library on the east side of the manor."

Keenan blinked, his eyes moving from Serena around the room. "The letter could be there." Serena followed his gaze.

Serena's eyes locked onto a couple with the king. She sucked in her breath so quickly she coughed. "That's them, with the king right now," she whispered. Casually Keenan turned. The man and woman laughed with King George before his makeshift throne.

"Gerard's murderers?" Brodick asked.

"Are ye certain?" Keenan asked at the same time.

"Yes and yes."

"Ye haven't touched them," Keenan continued.

Serena shook her head. "Their faces have haunted my mind since William was shot."

"Cumberland," Keenan said. "Let's find the library." Keenan placed Serena back on his arm. "Brodick, keep an eye out in here."

"Do ye intend to take the letter tonight?" Brodick asked.

"If I can find it."

"Then I'll alert the others to prepare in case we must depart abruptly," he said, his eyes twinkling as if he anticipated a good fight.

"But then we won't be able to make the true murderers confess," Serena pointed out.

"One step at a time, Serena. Let's first see if the letter actually exists," Keenan said, and turned to her. "Trust me. I've sworn to help William."

"But what if your duty to your brother and your clan is stronger than your word to me?" He didn't answer her but led her out on the balcony.

"Quickly, around to the far entrance," he said. They stepped back inside near several potted trees and walked slowly out of the ballroom and down the empty hall.

Keenan opened several doors before he found the one leading into the library. Serena smelled the tang of ink and the mildew of old pages even before she saw the rows of aged tomes in the glow of a small fire. Keenan left her to find a taper near the hearth and lit it. They walked silently through the room to another door in the back corner. "Can ye tell? Is there anyone in there?" Keenan asked.

Serena focused her power through the door but heard nothing. She shook her head.

They slipped inside. Another hearth fire chased shadows around the snug study. Two windows flanked the massive wood desk. A map of Britain lay unrolled on a second table near the desk. Keenan moved over to it, studying the lines and numbers.

Serena lit another taper from the fire and padded to the desk. Several piles of papers sat along its perimeter. One semi-rolled letter sat before the chair as if someone had left it half read. She scanned it quickly down to the signature. George's elegant script marked the bottom.

Mari had taught Serena to read in Romany.

Serena had taught herself some English, but George's handwriting was long and fluid, more beautiful than informative.

"Keenan," her whisper carried in the still room. "There's a letter here from George. I can't make out his handwriting, but it has the feel of something important."

Keenan moved with stealth and pulled his taper close to the unrolled parchment. "This is it, the letter outlining his plans to gift land in Scotland to his English Barons." He smiled broadly. "It's found." He handed Serena his taper and began to roll it.

Keenan stopped. A frown wrinkled across his forehead. "It's too effortless," his words tickled a path down the back of Serena's neck. Keenan peered around the room, into dark corners. "This whole thing," he said. "It was too simple to find. It doesn't feel right."

Serena nodded. "What shall we do?"

A loud voice from the outer room threw her heart into her throat, and she jumped into Keenan's arms. As the study door opened, Keenan's lips descended upon hers. Firmness and purpose melted quickly into a rapid pounding of heat as it flooded through her. Fear mixed with excitement as danger enveloped Serena inside and out.

"Aha, we've found Maclean."

Serena recognized Frampton's victorious voice through her haze of sensations. She felt dizzy but also full of energy all at once.

"He's not alone," a woman's voice said.

Serena stiffened. It was the woman from the bridge.

Keenan pulled back slowly and smoothed Serena's cascading curls along her collarbone. He seemed to be taking all the time in the world. The touch raced through her, battling against the shock of seeing five pairs of eyes on them at the doorway, one pair belonging to the king.

"Pardon us, Yer Majesty," Keenan drawled. "We found this cozy room tucked away and but succumbed to a quick dalliance."

"You were given a room for that, Maclean," Frampton said sharply. George walked into the study and stopped in front of them. Frampton, Gerard's murderers, and Elizabeth Darlington followed him into the room.

George studied Keenan. "Just found this study to sate your lust a bit, huh?" George asked. He then yanked aside Keenan's coat and pulled the rolled scroll from a side pocket. "Did this just happen to fall into your coat while you were frolicking?" George unrolled the letter but his look showed that he already knew what it was.

"The letter, aye, I saw it just sitting on yer desk," Keenan said calmly. "I fear for the security in this house, Frampton." His eyes moved to the fidgety man.

"What?" Frampton said raising his already pinched nose in the air.

"This letter is gold to the Jacobite cause, yet it is left just lying here for any to take." Keenan said.

"Which is what you were doing, wasn't it?" the man next to Frampton said.

"Stealing the letter, Cumberland?" Keenan asked the man. "Thievery is not one of my vices. Is it one of yers?"

"Nay, Maclean. I am no thief, but you seem to have been caught red handed." Cumberland said with conviction. The tension saturated the room and seemed to suck at the momentum of time itself.

Serena dared not open even a crack in her protective wall. Already the anger, the dark elation, the hunt for blood, beat against her mind.

"Aye," Keenan admitted easily. "I was taking the letter." Keenan pulled the letter back out of George's hand and strode to the fire. Before any could utter a word he tossed the parchment into the flames. The fire caught quickly on the brittle roll, and long shadows flickered as the fire gorged on the sudden fuel. Keenan turned back to the stunned audience. "I was taking the letter to destroy it before a damn Jacobite could get his hands on it again." Keenan frowned. "I doona mean to criticize Yer Majesty, but having such a thing lying around unguarded. Well it could be disaster to yer campaign."

Everyone stood still, watching the parchment blacken and shrivel.

Elizabeth was the first to break into the stillness. "I'd say that proves Keenan Maclean is loyal to you, Sire. He just destroyed the very letter he could have stolen."

"What use would it have been to me?" Keenan asked.

"We weren't certain of your loyalties, Maclean,

not with your brother being such a supporter of the Stewart prince." Frampton said.

"Oh my," Serena said faintly. "What an awful thought." She smiled timidly at Lord Frampton. "If my husband was to steal the letter and make us leave tonight, I would never have my wedding costume." She shook her head as if she were one of the silly courtiers. "I would never have allowed that."

George chuckled low. "I suppose you've escaped the dungeons for now, Maclean."

The dragonfly birthmark on her belly began to warm, and Serena's gaze flicked about the room. As George began to talk with Keenan, Serena watched a misty haze expand in the corner. Drakkina glided along the floor toward the Duke's mistress. What was she doing?

"I'm helping." Serena heard Drakkina's voice clearly in her mind. By the Earth Mother! Serena held her breath while Lady Amberley spoke quietly to Elizabeth about her cousin's wedding costume from the previous season. The men stared at the unrolled map.

Drakkina's cloud-like body hovered next to the Duke's mistress. Drakkina looked at Serena and winked just before the dry mist of her body melted into the unsuspecting body of Lady Amberley.

The pain in her chest reminded Serena to suck in a breath, and she reached out a thin thread to the woman's mind. Serena instantly felt a tightness throughout Lady Amberley, a stunned consciousness shoved aside and muted as if someone literally held her tongue. Serena blinked several times as Drakkina's pale eyes stared out from behind Lady Amberley's dark green orbs. Drakkina had completely invaded the woman.

"I must say," Lady Amberley's voice filled the room. It was the woman's own voice, but unnatural power pulsed behind the words. "I must say that it is wonderful to be surrounded by those loyal to the crown. The duke and I are just as loyal to the king as you and your husband are." Serena just nodded, unsure of what else to do. Cumberland looked curiously over his shoulder toward his mistress.

"Yes, William is so loyal, Lady Serena, that he paid a local peasant to gut that bastard Jacobite, Gerard Grant, and took back the king's letter in the first place. We were both there to make sure the letter did not move north into enemy hands."

Everyone turned toward the woman. Cumberland's mouth tightened into a grim line while Frampton's mouth jerked open in amazement.

Keenan was the first to speak. "Did ye just say that the Duke of Cumberland killed Gerard Grant, Lady Amberley, out of loyalty to the crown?"

"I certainly did," Lady Amberley bragged. "We are proud to serve the court."

"I never ordered such an act," King George said.

"Of course not," Elizabeth Darlington jumped in.

"Of course not," Frampton agreed.

Cumberland turned such a dark shade of purple that Serena wondered if he would have an attack and fall on the floor in convulsions.

"So the young Romany man, William Faw, dinna commit the crime?" Keenan said evenly as he eyed the courtly lady suspiciously.

Lady Amberley clasped her hands in front of her and looked remorseful. "No," she shook her head. "No, the Romany man came upon us while we paid the assassin. My darling William reacted without thinking. I'm afraid he shot the boy."

"William Augustus, Duke of Cumberland shot an innocent man?" Frampton asked.

Lady Amberley nodded.

"That will be enough, Judith!" Cumberland shouted, causing Serena to jump at the impact. The man's panic flew through the air like an arrow, piercing her wall. Serena took two steadying breaths. What would this man do to his mistress once Drakkina left her?

"He was a Rom," Cumberland said with a slight sneer. "He was most likely going to rob us anyway. I but shot him in self defense."

Serena's mouth opened as a nauseating sweep of anger washed through her belly up into her chest. Would she protest the bigoted man's ignorance or merely vomit on the spot? A quick wave of patience slid across her body, calming her. Serena's eyes were drawn to Keenan's. He stood staring at her, his eyes seeming to will her silence. Serena swallowed down her fury and shut her mouth even as she shouted in her head.

Keenan turned back toward Cumberland. "Rom or not, William Faw did not stab Gerard Grant."

"Correct," Lady Amberley called from her place by the gaping and furiously fanning Elizabeth.

"Keep your silence, Lady Amberley," Cumberland ground out between his pristine, evenly spaced teeth.

King George looked at Keenan. "You knew this William Faw?"

"I traded with the leader of his tribe who is his father. The lad is on the run since he's been wrongly accused of the crime."

"We must do something about that," Judith Amberley said and looked expectantly at Cumberland.

"Judith, stop speaking," Cumberland's words sliced across the room.

George nodded contemplatively and then looked to Frampton. "Have word sent to Leeds and surrounding townships that William Faw is cleared of the murder of Gerard Grant. He shall not, nor his relations, be held accountable." King George regarded Keenan. "Do you know his whereabouts?"

Keenan kept his answer guarded. "I can carry a letter of innocence to his family. They will most likely ken his whereabouts if he still lives."

King George nodded. "That should take care of this mess then."

Serena couldn't keep the bubble of anger down in her stomach any longer. It boiled up to the top. "And the punishment for the Duke, for shooting, and nearly killing an innocent man?"

Silence filled the room, but Serena could barely hear it with the cacophony of emotional noise bombarding her defenses. Suspicion, hatred, unveiled bigotry. Yet there was an undercurrent of worry, worry for her, compassion. Where was it coming from?

King George cleared his throat. "First I would like to commend Lady Amberley for bringing up this injustice. It showed amazing courage. Second I would say that I appreciate Cumberland's concern over Gerard Grant's betrayal and his courage to act on it." Lady Amberley curtseyed and Cumberland bowed stiffly.

King George then turned to Serena. "Cumberland shot William Faw in defense of an attack, imagined or real." The king looked back at Cumberland. "I suggest that you be much more careful in the future."

"I heed your council, Sire," the Duke replied smugly. Serena nearly bit her tongue.

King George continued. "However, a man's life has nearly been lost and he and his family have lived in fear for these past weeks. I believe you owe them a recompense of two hundred pounds to be paid to Keenan Maclean to take to the family."

"Two hundred?" Cumberland asked in a flat tone. "I do not know if I have that with me at this time."

"I will loan you the amount. Maclean will be leaving soon," George said. "Does that satisfy Lady Maclean?"

The amount was huge and would be celebrated. But was it enough to pay for a man's life? No. But Serena knew the answer that was required. "Yes, Your Majesty. Quite a generous settlement for the injury, and accusation." She curtsied slightly and inclined her head.

King George clapped his hands twice, the sound echoing in the room. "Good then, let us go back to the reception. Cumberland, be sure to speak with Frampton on the morrow to arrange your payments to me."

The Duke of Cumberland did not say anything but nodded and stalked over to take his mistress's arm. Serena watched with fascinated horror as a dry mist wafted its way out of Judith Amberley's body. The woman lost her stride and nearly collapsed.

"Oh my, what's happened to me?"

"You've about lost your bloody mind," Serena heard Cumberland sneer. Louder he said, "I think it is time for you to retire for the evening."

"Yes, yes, I think that might be best," she said simply and let him draw her out of the room. "I feel as if I've been holding my breath." She patted at her chest and coughed a bit.

Serena looked at the thin vapor of Drakkina and willed her concern to the crone about Judith Amberley's welfare. Drakkina frowned slightly and her image wavered. But then she nodded and disappeared.

Keenan took Serena's hand and placed it on his arm. His warm words brushed against her ear as he leaned in. "Ye frown? Everything has worked its way out."

Serena kept her eyes forward and whispered. "Not on its own. Drakkina helped."

Keenan's breath left her ear as he looked around the room. "She's here?"

"Not anymore."

There was no time to explain more as Serena and Keenan joined back in with the courtly conversations about nothing specific or interesting. It was several hours more of standing, curtseying and dancing before Serena and Keenan were finally allowed to leave the ballroom. As they walked across the threshold of their room with Brodick, Thomas, and Gavin in tow, Serena let out a groan. She yanked off her torturous shoes and dropped them to thud on the floor.

Serena pointed at the offending articles. "Try dancing and walking in those for hours and see if you don't throw them in the fire." She tried to reach her aching foot, but couldn't find it under all the layers of dress. Brodick's muffled laugh made her give up, and she sat back on the bed.

She listened while Keenan gave the men orders to find warm beds or sleep in the stables with Ewan.

"And ye will be sleeping where?" Thomas asked with his usual dose of guarded suspicion.

"I need to stay in the room for awhile so that it looks like we're truly married. I will join ye soon or if the corridor is watched, I will bunk down near the fire. It's not as soft as lying on earth, but it will do."

The three Macleans began shuffling out the door.

"Good sleep, Serena," Brodick called.

"Good sleep to you too, Brodick."

"Good sleep to ye, Serena," Gavin called.

Serena raised her hand to wave. "And to you, Gavin."

Thomas grumbled something of a good sleep, and Serena waved back. Then the door shut, and Keenan lowered a bracing bar to lock it. He walked to the fire to add more kindling. His footsteps clipped over to the bed and he sat down on the soft tick making Serena roll toward the gully.

"Is she here now?" Keenan's deep timbre pulled tightly at Serena's stomach. Not quite nausea, more like nervous flipping.

"Who?" Serena managed to answer.

"Drakkina, ye said she was in the study but I couldna' see her."

Serena sat up on elbows and looked around the room. "I don't think so. I can sense her now, now that I know her better. Plus she seemed pretty weak after invading Judith Amberley's body and making her talk."

"Drakkina confessed to the murder."

Serena nodded and scooted back into a sitting position against the headboard, which brought her battered feet against Keenan's thigh. "I only hope she helps Judith Amberley now that the woman will have to deal with Cumberland's wrath."

"But the crone isna' here now, ye're sure?"

Serena looked around again, and even reached out a bit with her senses. No Drakkina. "I don't feel her presence at all. I would tingle."

"Tingle?" He looked her body over as if he might catch a glimpse of her tingling.

Serena flushed a bit as she moved a hand to her stomach. "I have a birthmark, strangely shaped like a dragonfly. I've noticed that it warms or tingles whenever Drakkina's around."

Keenan looked at her stomach as if he could see through the heavy material to her skin. "I suppose we can add that to the list of yer oddities, lass."

When he looked up, Serena couldn't help but smile at his grin. "I suppose so."

"So," he looked again at her stomach, "nary a bit of tingling there right now?"

Oh there was tingling going on in Serena and she blushed even deeper, but not on her birthmark.

"No, no tingling," she said.

Keenan picked up one of Serena's feet still clad in silky stockings. She gasped and tried to pull it away. He held on and began to rub it gently between his two large hands. He ran his knuckle up the middle, giving even pressure along her instep and then to the balls of her foot. Serena pulled back a little at the immense sensation.

"Hold still, lass, I'm only trying to help these mistreated feet."

While cupping her heel in one hand, and circling it slowly, his other fingers massaged each of her toes. A cross between a sigh and a groan seeped out of Serena and she closed her eyes at the sensations of achy pleasure rolling up her leg.

"I wouldn't think that one used to dancing would hurt so badly after a night at court."

Serena snorted as she relaxed back into the soft feather down pillows. "Around the fire, I dance in soft leather shoes that are flat, not those hard, pinching contraptions."

Keenan continued up her calf to her knee and then took up its abused twin.

"Mmm." Her eyes flitted back open and found Keenan studying her. Her throat clenched, preventing another breath.

Serena felt the blush creep up into her face. She touched the tip of her tongue to her upper lip. "So," she began and swallowed. She tried to push back up into a more upright position. "Where did you learn to rub legs like that?"

Keenan grinned. "Mostly on mares after long rides."

Serena pulled her leg back a bit and frowned. He laughed. "But also on Elenor, when we were alone, I would massage her feet."

"She had sore feet?"

Keenan's grin broke into a full smile. It reached

his eyes, making their gray depths sparkle. He was the most handsome man she had ever known. And he even rubbed his dear sister's feet.

"My poor sister had sore feet from chasing after me."

"You ran a lot?" Serena said on a laugh.

"All over Maclean lands, inside and out."

"And Elenor followed you?"

"Aye, 'twas her job." Keenan's smile weakened back down into a mild grin. He kept rubbing and circling her foot.

"Had you no nanny?"

"Nay, the woman responsible for watching us had to keep a constant eye on Lachlan, so nothing would befall him."

"Oh," Serena said, her own smile going flat. "And your parents?"

Keenan bent forward to run the flat of his hand up her shin. "They dinna have time to watch after me."

"So they ordered Elenor to do it."

"She volunteered." He smiled warmly. "She loved me, raised me really. Taught me the ways of my world, about the prophecy."

Serena watched him, his head bowed slightly as he worked. "No one else told you about it?"

"Nay, they left it to her. And I wanted to understand why I was treated differently from Lachlan."

"How were you treated differently?"

Keenan stopped rubbing her legs. Serena held her breath as he moved up close to where she sat. Keenan circled his finger in the air. "Turn around and I will endeavor to pull the ribbons and pins from yer hair, else ye may never sleep." Serena let her breath out and turned around as best she could in the heavy court dress.

With her back to him, Serena could feel his

gentle tugs as he began to undo Winifred's beautiful weave. The touch of his fingers in her hair sent chills along the nape of Serena's neck. As each curl came down around her waist, he ran his fingers from her scalp to the end to relax the bound curl.

"Once when Lachlan was sixteen, he decided that he had had enough of playing life safe. At least for the day." His fingers trailed down her shoulder to fan out her hair. "I was nine summers and had been training with the young warriors, eager to show that I could complete my duty for my clan." Keenan pulled a clip from the top of her head and a mountain of hair cascaded down. "Lachlan just wanted to venture outside the walls of Kylkern having ne'er been allowed to leave the surrounding village. I offered to help him. I pitied his existence more so than mine. His shackles were obvious even to a nine-year-old."

Keenan reached up under her hair and sieved his fingers through the waves to her scalp. He began to massage the roots of the heavy tresses. Serena closed her eyes to the wonderful feel, but her mind held tightly to his story.

"So I helped him sneak past the guards, and we ran down to the loch. He dinna ken the way of keeping afloat and dinna tell me until he was past his head. At nine I wasn't as big as he, but I still managed to pull him to shore, thrashing and wailing." Keenan left her scalp and ran his fingers down the length of her hair, untangling little snarls as he went.

"Brodick's father found us stretched out in the mud like fish and gave us a ride back to the Keep." Keenan breathed deeply behind her. His voice lowered to a sultry whisper. "Lass yer hair smells of sweet spices and highland wind." Serena didn't move, didn't know what to say. Keenan remained silent for several moments.

Serena's words were so quiet, it was hard to hear them. "What happened when you returned to the Keep?"

Keenan's hands began to move through her hair again. "Lachlan was scolded and sent to bed. A guard followed him for some time after that."

"And you?"

"I was flogged and sent to heal in the stables."

His words were devoid of emotion, no self-pity, no resentment, just words. Tears stung Serena's eyes, and she closed them. Pain, she felt a low pulse of pain and then it was gone, snuffed out. She opened her eyes. From where had the feeling come?

"Elenor tended me and as ye see, I recovered."

"On the outside."

Keenan ignored her comment. "I learned much that day. I learned my place in the world, the rules of my existence. I learned how lucky I was to have Elenor."

They were quiet for a while, her back still towards him. When his hands stopped stroking her hair, Serena turned around.

"So this prophecy chained Lachlan to the Keep and forced you out to defend yourself and the clan against the world."

Keenan's grin did nothing to chase away the muted sadness in his eyes. "It certainly affected our lives."

"Cursed your lives."

Keenan looked down at his hands. And then back up at her. "It seems to be dooming our Maclean line. Lachlan waits for his witch. And Elenor has become an old maid."

"And what of you, Keenan? Will you not wed and have children?"

Keenan shook his head, pushed off the bed and walked to the hearth. "I ne'er thought I would. I dinna want to sire children only to leave them to be raised without a father."

Serena followed. "But you don't know when you are supposed to die. Maybe it will be when you're old and gray and ready for a natural death, Keenan."

Keenan frowned at her. "I doona wish for that."

"Why?"

"Because this life is hard enough." He bent to add dry peat to the fire. "To go on alone for so long only to realize at the end that I could have had a life, had children and watched them grow." He shook his head.

Serena rubbed her hands along her cheeks in frustration. "Then do something about it now, Keenan. Find a woman to love. Give her your children. Watch them grow and love them well."

He looked over his shoulder at her as if considering her words. "And where would this woman be, lass?" He asked the question, but his gaze told her he knew an answer, an answer that stood before him, her hair fanned out around her waist. It was as if she felt his desire. Was it in his gaze? Or could she actually feel something from him?

The fire sparked behind him, and he turned to kick some embers back into the hearth.

"So what of ye, Serena? If ye could find a man that respects ye as ye are, would ye marry?"

Serena stepped closer to the fire. "He must accept my powers and not feel ashamed of me. But also, I must feel love for him."

"Love can grow after ye marry."

He spoke of Lachlan. She knew it and frowned. "We talk in circles, Keenan." Serena turned and walked to the washing pitcher and poured some water in the basin. "And I am weary. Let us sleep."

When she turned back to him, he stood before the fire, his feet braced apart and his fists next to his sides. Battle lurked in his eyes.

"I canna sleep here, Serena."

"The King and court think we are married, at least in the highland way."

"But my men ken that we are not. And they ken that ye are the witch of the prophecy. I need to bed down with them."

Serena pointed toward the door. "But what if someone sees you leave? Would a newly wed man stray already from his wife?"

Keenan handed her a short dagger from his boot. "If someone is about, I will come back in. Otherwise, bolt the door after I leave. I will come back before dawn." He turned away and strode quickly toward the door. "Keep the dagger near ye."

"Keenan," Serena called, but he was already shutting the door. "Good sleep," she whispered to the empty room. She sighed slowly. She would give him a minute or two and then get undressed for bed. She looked down at her court dress and groaned. How would she wrestle the garment off of her alone?

Keenan heard her call his name, but he closed the door anyway. He stopped and willed his blood to slow.

"Leaving your new wife so soon," a voice came from the shadows. Frampton stepped out with a small candle in hand.

"She but needs a drink of sweet wine from the kitchens," Keenan answered smoothly and walked away from the door.

"I'll show you the way, Maclean. My manor house can be quite the labyrinth."

Keenan acknowledged him and shortened his step to match the shorter man. "I'm surprised to find ye still roaming yer halls, Frampton. 'Tis the dead of night."

"One learns more about ones occupants in the dead of night than during the brightness of day." The wily man smiled knowingly at Keenan.

Keenan forced his well-practiced, non-caring smile. "Like the fact that my timid little wife needs some wine to relax herself before a night with her rather new husband."

Frampton laughed quietly and nodded. "Perhaps. But I will keep that in confidence. Wouldn't want to embarrass the lady."

Keenan inclined his head in gratitude. They continued to the kitchen in mild conversation about the success of the reception. Frampton didn't bring up any of King George's plans, and Keenan was in no mood to play spy after his near escape from Serena's chambers. Unfortunately, Frampton continued to follow Keenan from the kitchens.

As they rounded a bend in the stone corridor, Keenan caught a glimpse of Thomas watching from around a bend. Thomas would see that Keenan had no choice but to return to Serena's chambers.

Keenan continued on to her door. "Thank ye for accompanying me, but from here, I think I can make it on my own."

"Of course, good eve to you," Frampton said and bowed before rotating on his heel. Keenan watched him turn the corner, but wondered if the man actually went farther or stood in the dark listening for him to enter the room. Keenan had no doubt that the man would love to report to King George that the lady Serena was being neglected by her husband. The letch would probably visit her during the night. That thought twisted in his mind and he pressed against the door. It slid open effortlessly. The foolish lass hadn't yet bolted it.

Keenan stepped into the dim room lit only by the hearth fire. A fresh breeze blew in from an open window. The door clicked closed quietly behind him.

A flutter at the window caught his eyes as they adjusted quickly to the dark room. Serena's pet bird sat on the ledge chirping.

"What, Chiriklò?" Serena's muffled question brought Keenan's attention to the fire where she stood, her head covered with the white fabric of her shift as she pulled it up over her head. The bluebird chirped one last time and flew off the ledge out into the night. "Chiriklò, where are you going?" Once she struggled the shift over her head, it slid off her long hair and puddled onto the floor. Serena stood facing the window away from him, completely naked. Keenan didn't move from his position by the door. His breath lay dormant on an inhalation.

"Thank you for pulling the knots from my stays," she called toward the window, walked to it and pulled it closed. Keenan's eyes traveled up her shapely legs and the gentle slope of her backside, perfectly rounded for a man's hands to splay and knead. Blood rushed through him and he felt himself harden.

Serena turned back toward the fire and stopped. She gasped, clenched her legs together and threw her hands over her luscious round breasts. "Keenan!"

He didn't say a word, just followed the landscape of her beautiful form with his eyes. Taking in every exposed hill and valley, studying, memorizing. The fire glow splashed shadows along her where her hair fell in waves about her hips, hips that curved gently outward from a trim waist. Dark curls hid the core of her femininity at the vee of her thighs. His eyes slipped from the silk tresses he had run through not twenty minutes ago, to the tips of her tiny toes he had also just explored. She took two steps forward to stand next to the waning fire.

"Keenan," her voice was lower. "I didn't expect you to return."

Each breath seemed as if he pulled it from under a heavy stone. He moved his hand below to adjust himself. Serena's eyes followed and then widened. "Ye dinna bar the door, lass. I told ye to bar the door."

They stared at one another. Keenan's eyes stung and he blinked quickly not wanting to miss even a second of the masterpiece standing before him. This was likened to a stand off in battle.

Slowly, Serena's fingers released their death grip on her arms. She lowered them to her sides, and the soft round globes of her breasts lifted slightly with each of her breaths.

Keenan's jaw began to ache and he made himself part his lips. They were so dry. He wet his bottom lip with the tip of his tongue. The ache in his thighs told him just how hard he pushed back against the door where he stood. And the ache in his groin robbed him of coherent thought. He just stared at her.

She wanted him, desired him, needed him in a way she had never felt before. How did he know this? He wasn't sure, but he knew it for a certainty as if he lived for a moment within her heart. There was some connection between them. Her intense passion rooted her naked and unashamed before him. Without taking his eyes off her, he shook his head slightly. How was it possible that he knew what she was feeling? Or was he imagining it?

"You want me, Keenan Maclean, don't deny it." Her words were small in the silence, but their impact tore through him. She frowned slightly and closed her eyes and then opened them again. "I," she started, "I can feel that you want me? I don't know how, but I do." She took a small step towards him, and he pressed his head back against the door. "Do you feel something from me?" she asked.

"I feel yer desire, lass." Keenan swallowed hard.

"How?" she asked.

"I doona ken the way of it," he swallowed again. "But I feel it." He breathed deeply, his hand again adjusting the enormous ache building below.

She was close enough now that he could see her rapid breathing, the flush rising up her collar bone along the soft lines of her neck. He looked back down at her ample breasts, the nipples peaked and rosy. Och! How he wanted to touch them.

Serena touched one of her breasts. Keenan groaned. Passion flared beneath her lashes. The tension in Keenan's body ripped through him. Never before, even in battle, had he felt this energy bunch his muscles. He felt as if he could rip a hole clear through the wall.

His fists clenched until his fingers ached. But he couldn't look away as she hefted her other breast too. What was she doing to him? Serena was the witch of the prophecy. How could he touch her? How could he make her his if she was supposed to belong to his brother? Was he possible of such treachery, such betrayal?

Aye, he thought as his hand moved on its own over his hard erection. He was capable. But was it treachery? She had sworn she would never wed Lachlan. What if Serena was right and the prophecy was wrong? But none of the old seer's words had ever been wrong before.

Somehow he continued to breathe as the thoughts, the justifications tangled through his mind. What if he was meant to love her before he died? And then after, she could wed Lachlan? What if he was supposed to father the next generation of Macleans through Serena before he died for his duty? Perhaps this was how the prophecy would work. Perhaps he could touch her, could love her.

Keenan took a step away from the wall. Serena's breasts rose and fell on a muted gasp. She lowered her hands and focused on his gaze. She waited.

He took another step towards her, his hands unfisting. "I doona ken how it is that we feel each other's desire, but we do." He stopped and she nodded. "But I'm done denying it." He shook his head. "I canna deny it." With one more step, Keenan stood before her and inhaled the spicy sweet scent that enveloped her form. He reached one open palm to skim the softness of her hair. Gently he moved his hand down its length to where it fell against the curve of her hip. His hand cupped the soft bone beneath her silky skin. He pulled her against him, her breasts pressing up against his tunic. His lips were so close to hers that he breathed her own sweet breath. "Ye're mine, lass." The words rang through him and hope broke open inside his chest.

Pounding on the door. Serena gasped and pulled away. She flew to the bed as the door opened.

Keenan turned around, his dirk out in a flash ready to strike.

Thomas stood there, his eyes scanning the room. "Keenan, quickly. Ewan has taken ill in the stables. Ye need to tend him."

"Bloody hell, he's taken ill," Keenan roared.

Thomas neither advanced nor retreated. "I swear Keenan." Thomas lowered his voice. "And this gives ye a good reason to leave yer wife," he said emphasizing the improvised role.

Keenan looked over to Serena who sat in the bed with the sheet up to her ears. The passion had fled her wide eyes. He shook his head in frustration. Why hadn't he barred the door?

"I'll return." She nodded and he strode after Thomas to the door. He looked back at her. "As soon as I leave this room, bar the door. I will call to ye through it when I return. Doona open the door unless it is I."

She nodded again and he left. He motioned to Thomas to wait until he heard the bolt slip in place. Keenan rested his hand on the door and breathed deeply. The connection he had felt with her was gone. But he had felt it and so had she. There was a connection, something powerful enough to make him rethink his call to duty. Something powerful enough to make him claim her. And he had, if not with his body, then with his words. Keenan spun on his heel and headed toward the stables. Thomas kept well behind him.

****

Serena woke groggily from a familiar dream of a cottage surrounded by a circle of tall stones. The smell of fresh baked bread dissipated from her mind as a tight rapping penetrated the dream-induced peace. As she climbed out of the oversized bed, she realized she was still naked. Memory flooded, and her chest clenched. Keenan hadn't returned.

"Who is it?" she asked as she slipped into a chamber robe left in the room by a maid the day before.

"Your hostess, Lady Maclean," Olivia Frampton laughed. "And a regiment of seamstresses I fear."

Serena quickly pulled the bedding askew on the other side to make it look like she had slept with a bed partner.

She ran to the door and unbolted it. Olivia Frampton stood there, grandly dressed in a lovely organdy morning gown, her mousy brown hair piled high on her tiny head. Serena moved aside as the lady's four maids followed her inside with baskets of sewing supplies.

"Sleeping late?" Olivia tittered. She began to order the maids around the room. "It seems we have no time to waste, Serena," Olivia said. "Your husband is eager to be on his way." She lowered her voice to a conspirator level. "I think he's anxious to present you to his brother for his blessing and marry you before God." Olivia smiled at her. "He wants you bound to him until death, not just a year and a day. I can see it in him when he looks at you."

The woman's sincerity made Serena smile back. Benjamin Frampton may be a pompous windbag, but his wife was genuine.

"We are to leave today then?"

"Yes, yes, which is why I've brought this gown," Olivia waved her hand towards one maid who promptly held up the nearly finished dress. "It was to be Miss Wimberley's wedding costume, but the sage green suits your coloring more I think, plus it is almost finished. We will just mold it to your lovely young curves, and it will be yours."

Serena was speechless. The gown of green velvet was richly embroidered with seed pearls and gold thread. Birds and butterflies flew along the bell of the skirt. Serena even saw several dragonflies glittering amongst the folds.

"It is," she sat down numbly on the edge of the bed, "exquisite."

Olivia smiled at Serena's appreciation. "Good, let us get it on you." The woman clapped her hands, which signaled the two women to advance upon Serena with a silky shift.

The two sturdy ladies pulled the robe from Serena and threw the shift over her head and down over her body. Serena ran her hands down the softness of the expensive material, too expensive for under clothing.

"I had a few other womanly items to add to your wardrobe." Olivia indicated the shift. "I hope you don't mind that they were originally intended for another, but there really isn't time to outfit you from bolts of material."

Serena shook her head. "Your graciousness is overwhelming." Serena's words huffed out as another maid wrapped her in stays and pulled the strings behind.

"Please call me Olivia," the woman said squeezing one of Serena's hands. The jolt of giddiness from the woman flipped through Serena's stomach. "Now let us have fun."

Over the course of two hours, Serena was fed, washed, prodded, and pinned while Olivia had fun watching and fussing. While the flitting woman chattered away with her hoard of seamstresses, Serena played the events of last night over and over again. She analyzed each word, each touch, each look until her head ached.

Keenan Maclean had stared at her naked and had claimed her as his. Even if he didn't stay to physically claim her, as he no doubt would have if Thomas hadn't barged in. A flutter of nervous energy tickled inside Serena's stomach at the thought of what would have happened if only...if only they had been left alone, if only he had returned.

Serena frowned. He hadn't returned, and for a brief moment Serena worried over Ewan. Maybe the man was in peril. The exchange with Thomas had happened so quickly, and she had been so disoriented that she hadn't thought to read Thomas's intent at all.

Serena's mind continued to whirl. But now it was daylight, the passion of the night dissolving with the dawn. What if Keenan acted as if nothing had happened, that he'd never said the words? But he had. *You're mine, lass.* She heard it, could still hear it.

There had also been a strange connection between them last night. She hadn't read his thoughts, but rather felt his sensations, wore his emotions as if they were her own. Serena shuddered slightly as she remembered his need to cup her breasts, to feel their weight, to roll her peaked nipples. His deep desire mirrored her own, fine tuning it as if they resonated in harmony. Serena felt the pulsing ache deep down under the layers of fabric as the maids tucked and pinned.

"Oh, it must be getting hot in here. Poor dear, you're flushed as can be," Olivia said and opened the window. "Someone break down that fire in the hearth." Serena forced her mind onto the mundane task of choosing decorative buttons for a long lamb's wool cloak.

A large, shined looking-glass was brought in for her to see herself. The dress fit perfectly along the contours of her breasts and waist, and then flared out in the full skirts that fell in a wide bell around her legs. Serena turned before the glass and enjoyed the swish of fabric around her ankles. She smiled at Olivia who still prattled happily, completely enthralled with all the details of creating her wedding costume. A costume, Serena thought sadly for a moment, she may never wear.

"There now, Serena, you look lovely," Olivia crooned. "I'm so happy I decided to give the green costume to you. Your hair stands out even brighter against it." The tiny woman came up to stroke Serena's curls. "Such a brilliant shade of auburn with gold spun within it. Just beautiful. I can see why you don't powder it or wear a wig."

The four maids all nodded their agreement just before the door to the room flew open causing all four to gasp.

"I told ye to bolt this door," Keenan strode into the chaos of thread, scraps and pins. All eyes turned to him, his towering shoulders making him a giant in the suddenly cramped room. He stopped, his eyes resting on Serena as she turned toward him.

"Pardon me. I," he stammered, "I dinna ken ye had visitors."

"Come, Lord Maclean, this is your room after all." Olivia waved him over as the nervous maids giggled and stepped back to give him room. Keenan walked closer to Serena where she stood before the glass.

"Turn around for your Highland lord to see you," Olivia urged and Serena turned her body away from the glass.

Serena curtseyed; a tentative smile curved her lips.

"She will make a lovely bride, don't you agree?"

Serena watched Keenan's eyes, but she couldn't read them. She tried to reach out to him, but the connection had disappeared. As usual, he was a void to her. Panic pulled at her chest and she retreated behind a haughty look. If she hid her heart and convinced herself that it didn't matter what he thought, then she would be just fine. She would still breathe and live. If she could only build a wall around her heart like she did around her mind.

"Say something," Olivia teased him.

"Aye."

"Aye?" Olivia asked. "That's it." She smiled mischievously. "Why Serena, have you married a blind man?"

Keenan shook his head and looked toward the woman and then back to Serena. "Aye, I mean Nay. Aye, she will make a lovely bride."

"There now," Olivia clapped her hands together. "You will want to get her properly wed before some other fine young man comes along to steal her."

"Aye," Keenan mumbled, his eyes back on Serena. It was too difficult to return his stare. Serena smoothed invisible lines in the petticoats. Her finger traced a dragonfly as she tried to ignore the heat of his gaze. It was suddenly hard to breathe in the tight stays.

"Did you want to tell Serena anything, or were you just coming by because you can't be away from her for long?"

Serena listened to her hostess and peeked from under lowered lashes to see if Keenan still stared at her. He did, and he caught her eye.

"I came to tell Serena that we leave within the hour."

"So soon?" Olivia asked, but already began to issue orders softly to the maids.

Keenan turned back to Serena. "We've had a report of the Faw tribe of Romany moving just north of here."

Mari was close. A wave of excitement washed over Serena.

"I'd like to intercept them to give them the recompense from Cumberland and let them know that William Faw is no longer a fugitive."

"Well yes, that makes sense." Olivia clapped her hands again and the platoon of maids began to strip Serena.

Keenan turned on his heel and headed for the door. "I will be back in less than an hour for ye."

Serena hadn't said a word the entire visit. "And how is Ewan?" she asked to his back. "He is able to travel?"

Keenan stopped at the door, but did not turn around. "Bad ale perhaps. He will live."

Serena listened as his footfalls grew distant. While the maids pulled pins and untied laces, Serena fought within herself. She wanted to cry, wanted to scream. What had just happened? His cold emotionless stare. Where was the man who had rubbed her feet and stroked her hair last night? Where was the man who had claimed her as she stood naked and vulnerable before him? Anger welled up inside Serena, a protection against the worry and sorrowful pain she couldn't quite admit.

Chapter 11

The tangy scent of rain clung to the unfurled spring leaves as they rode along the narrow path near the gypsy camp. Serena rode her mare silently in the blue gown she had found on her bed the first morning at Kylkern. She sighed. So much had changed, yet it had only been just over a fortnight since she fled with William. The prophecy, Drakkina, and then there was the elusive connection with Keenan Maclean.

He rode beside her or in the front, his men surrounding Serena. Several times his eyes had locked with hers, assessing, studying. What thoughts swirled in his head, what evidence did he weigh, what memories did he dwell upon or ignore? Serena screamed her frustration inside, which came out as a sigh.

"What ails ye, Serena?" Brodick asked. "Ye should be happy that ye'll see yer clan again this day."

Serena smiled at the kind man. They had all seemed a bit grumpy today. She felt some guilt from Brodick and Gavin as well and a bit of victory from Thomas. Ewan did look pale, so he had been ill. From the others, though, Serena could easily conclude that Ewan's illness had not kept Keenan away all night. Rather the attitudes of his men had bound him to the stables. Had they also talked him into refusing his claim upon her? Did they even know? She rubbed absently at the back of her head and neck.

"Forgive me. I have come down with an ache in

my head."

As they caught the familiar sounds of a small camp, Serena's stomach rolled. So much had changed in such a short time. The old worries over what her people would think coiled around her like an evil serpent. She took a steadying breath and mentally checked her protective wall. Just before revealing themselves within the circle of firelight, Keenan pulled his horse back and stopped. He motioned for his men to move on ahead and reached over to squeeze her gloved hand. His voice rolled low in the darkness.

"We've had only silence between us this day. And silence can create strife when none exists."

Serena looked up into his face. It was softer than it had been before, but his eyes were still distant, devoid of the passion she had witnessed last night.

"You didn't return last night."

His face hardened. "I couldn't."

"Keenan," Thomas called from the shadows before them.

"We have to go," Keenan said. Serena nodded.

They walked their horses into the firelight together. A wildly chirping Chiriklò swooped through the camp and landed on Serena's shoulder.

"Angelas," Mari yelled and ran toward Serena's horse. Serena jumped down while Chiriklò flitted to a nearby branch. Mari wrapped arms around her. Serena laughed, tears stinging as she squeezed the woman.

"You've returned, my child," Mari pulled away and touched Serena's cheek. Relief, exhilaration, celebration raced along the contact. But there was an undercurrent of concern too.

Serena kissed her cheek. "William is alive, and well, Duy. We are both alive, and well."

Mari laughed and hugged Serena again, and

then held her at arms length.

"Let me see you, Àngelas." She tilted her head. "It's been not even a month, but," the older woman paused, "you are different, grown suddenly."

Serena smiled. King Will stepped forward, a kind expression on his usually stoic face. He was happy to see her. Serena turned and smiled at the stares, ignoring the questions rolling through everyone's' minds.

Keenan stepped next to Serena, and addressed King Will and Mari at once. "Serena has saved William Faw. He is alive and well at Kylkern Castle in the West of Scotland." A murmur rose within the gathered group. "We have been to King George's court," he said indicating his men and Serena. "Serena risked her life to masquerade as a gentlewoman to prove William's innocence in the death of Gerard Grant." Keenan pulled out a rolled parchment, and motioned to Gavin to bring forth the small wooden chest off the back of his horse. Keenan unrolled the parchment, and read for several minutes.

"And in conclusion, William Faw of the Faw Romany Tribe, is held as innocent in the death of Gerard Grant in the year 1746. Signed King George II, King of all Britain."

Keenan handed the letter to King Will and motioned to Gavin. "The man responsible for Gerard Grant's death has been fined two hundred pounds for inflicting worry and grief on the Faw tribe and for endangering William Faw's life and freedom." Keenan transferred the heavy chest from Gavin to King Will's arms.

Hushed elation rippled through the people.

"Serena's courage and cleverness before the King and his court saved William and cleared his name. The Faw Tribe owes her the respect of a warrior, for she is one."

Mari squeezed her arm and Serena blinked several times to stop her watery eyes from ruining her calm, courageous façade.

Keenan wasn't merely repaying the debt from the Duke, he was fostering respect for her, respect from her tribe. Something she had never been able to do before. Again Serena nearly lost the battle with tears as the first waves of pride emanated from her adopted father.

King Will bowed slightly to Keenan with the chest in his hands. "We accept this retribution and will use it to benefit the entire tribe, as my daughter would want." King Will looked to Serena and she nodded quickly. The old man quirked his lips into a smile showing the tips of his teeth. She had never seen him smile enough to see his teeth before, at least not in her direction.

King Will handed the chest to Ephram who hovered nearby. Even William's cocky friend smiled shyly towards her. King Will clapped his hands. "Let us celebrate tonight!" A cheer rose from the tribe as they jumped about suddenly. "Raise the fire, raise the music." King Will looked to Serena. "Will you dance tonight, before the fire?"

A tear of joy slipped from Serena's eye. "Yes, I will dance." King Will nodded his approval and turned toward the gathering fire.

Mari touched Keenan's arm. "Thank you, Highlander. You gave yourself little credit, but I know you kept my children safe."

Keenan nodded at her. "It is my duty to protect."

A bit of Serena's joy seeped away at his words. She had become his duty too, as soon as he had discovered her link to the prophecy. Serena looked at Keenan and glanced at the other Macleans who had been given drink and seasoned food. "We will stay for awhile, here?" she asked.

Keenan nodded. "Aye."

Mari looked between them. "Of course, you will stay, child. You've come home. You've cleared William's name."

Panic clenched tight in her stomach. Was this then the end of her journey? Would Keenan and his men ride away tomorrow and never be seen again? No, she thought darkly, he wouldn't walk away from her as long as she was tied to his prophecy.

"Come Ångelas, time to change," Mari said aloud. And time to talk, her duy said within her mind.

Serena bent over to enter the small space inside the wagon. It had never felt cramped before. But after living under the open sky and in spacious rooms, its tight walls were no longer a comfort. Serena jostled past the table and bed rolls along the sides of the wagon. She bent her head to miss the lantern and sat on her bunk. Mari pulled out one of Serena's dancing gowns, shaking the slightly wrinkled material.

"I didn't have time to prepare it," Mari said shaking the dress harder. "No matter, they look at you not your gown, when you dance."

"Did you not receive my thoughts that we were near?"

She nodded and laid the garment across one bunk. "I hoped that I wasn't imagining it. Then I heard your bird nearby. I knew." Mari unbuttoned the bodice over Serena's stays and then smiled broadly, nearly bouncing in excitement.

"What is it?" Serena smiled.

"Oh Ångelas, I am so happy that you are alive and returned to us. I have news that should please you very much."

Serena nodded, her eyebrows raised in surprise.

"We've received news of a young man, Damin Yallow," she said and smiled coyly. "He is Petra's sister's cousin by marriage."

Serena frowned in confusion. What did this have to do with her homecoming?

Mari patted her hand. "King Will has negotiated with his family and with him for your hand in marriage."

"What?" Serena stood up, hitting her head on the lamp, and flopped back down. "Duy, you know that I can't marry someone. I mean, I won't marry someone who can't accept my powers."

Mari smiled enthusiastically. "Of course you can't, but he will accept them."

Serena held her breath, trying to keep the alarm at bay while she pulsed a thread through Mari's mind. It was taking too long for her duy to get it all out. Serena had to know what her mother was talking about.

"Damin Yallow was raised by his grandmother, a well known seer in the Yallow tribe. She was greatly revered," Mari said and grabbed Serena's clenched hands. "Don't you see, Àngelas? He knows of magic, has lived with it, has loved it in his grandmother. He will respect yours." Mari nodded sharply to punctuate her point, then sat back with a smug smile. "We didn't know when or even if you would return, but I urged King Will to move forward once I heard about his background. Damin will be so pleased to know you are safe with us again."

Serena's probe of Mari's mind confirmed all she said and all the details. The Faw tribe would receive two young milk cows and a bull from the Yallow tribe for Serena. Damin Yallow was reputed to be a bit rash but in very good standing in their community. He was also said to be handsome and was on his way to discuss the marriage compact with King Will.

Serena let out a little groan and buried her face in her open palms.

"Àngelas?"

"No, no," Serena's words were muffled. She felt sweaty and chilled at the same time. She looked up. "I can't marry Damin Yallow. Keenan Maclean has already claimed me."

Mari's eyes widened. "Claimed you? In what way?"

Serena sat up. "Not with his body," she looked into her mother's eyes. "But with his words." Over the next ten minutes, Serena rattled off every detail that she remembered of the last three weeks, eluding to, but keeping out the details of the intimate ones. Mari just sat, her hands folded in her lap, silently watching and listening.

Finally Serena came to their arrival. "So you see, Duy, he claimed me last eve."

Mari nodded. "This Drakkina sounds very powerful."

Serena nodded. "Yes, and she says that Keenan and I are soul mates, that we should be together for some greater good, to fight a battle in the future."

Mari frowned and lowered her voice. "She could be evil, Serena. Deceiving you."

"But she knows of my parents. She told me of my family, of my sisters."

Mari shook her head slowly. "What if it is to manipulate you? All of it."

"But for what purpose?"

Mari shrugged. "Who knows the purpose behind evil?"

Serena thought back on her interactions with the spirit of the great Wiccan. "But she helped me save William. I know he would have died from fever without her interference."

Mari sat for a moment and then huffed loudly. "I don't know how the future is supposed to work out, Àngelas. But I do know that Damin Yallow is handsome and strong and would respect your magic, child." She shook her head. "You would be foolish to reject his offer before meeting him, before touching him to see if his actions are honorable."

"You would have me compare him to Keenan, yet I cannot read if Keenan's actions are honorable?"

Mari grabbed Serena's hands in hers. "Àngelas, I want only happiness for you." Her eyes pleaded as well as the flood of hope and worry washing through the contact. "This match with Damin, it sounds like a good one, one that will make you happy through your life. One that will give you children." Her duy knew how to pull at her heart, but Serena could feel that she manipulated out of true love for her.

Serena still shook her head. "But I am unclean."

"You said that he claimed you only with his words." Mari sat back.

"Yes and no. He's also," Serena stopped and took a deep breath. "He's seen me completely unclothed." Mari sat up straighter. "And he's touched me, my legs, my breasts, my neck, my..."

Mari held up a hand. "Stop."

Serena couldn't help but overhear Mari's mind working through possibilities. Her mother's thoughts nearly screamed at her. Disappointment, sadness for the loss of such a chance at happiness, worry. What would become of her daughter? No children, no one to love her as a woman should be loved. Serena bowed her head and tried to block the sad thoughts.

"Don't tell anyone, Àngelas. Only you and I will know."

"And Keenan."

"Yes, he knows, but he doesn't know the ways of our people."

Serena shook her head. The Romany culture was very strict with regards to seeing and touching women who were not your wife. In some tribes, if a man touched the skirt of a woman who was not his wife, then he was considered unclean and must seek pardon from a council of elders. Serena's encounters with Keenan Maclean would be as damning as if she had given him her maidenhead.

"He does not consider himself linked to you," Mari said.

Serena felt her face heat. "He may honor his words."

Mari squeezed her hand. "Think daughter, were his words given while desire numbed his mind? Would he have said just about anything to touch you?"

Serena looked down at her lap, her face so hot it should have melted. All she could do was nod.

"A man in such a state can barely remember his words let alone intend to honor them," Mari said gently. Her duy ran a hand down her hair, and Serena tried hard to forget the feel of Keenan's fingers working the tangles out.

"Àngelas, just consider Damin Yallow. Meet him. Give him a chance." Mari cupped her cheek and Serena looked up into her duy's bright eyes. "I want you to be loved. I want you to have a life next to a man who is worthy of you and your gift, who can give you children of your own to love. That is all a mother wants for her child."

Serena's words were so soft she almost couldn't hear them herself. "Keenan could give me those things."

"Your Highlander speaks of curses and death, not love and children."

Her duy's words were true, painfully so. When had she heard words of love from Keenan? When had he ever talked of a future? He didn't even think he would father children of his own. He actually believed that she should marry his brother.

Serena sniffed back the tears that wet her vision and nodded. "I will consider, Duy."

****

"Here Keenan," Brodick said, handing him a

tankard of ale. "It's a celebration after all." Brodick ran his hand down his beard, pulling slightly as he eyed the small clusters of Rom.

"If ye keep tugging on that thing, it will fall off," Gavin said to him and also turned to scout the area.

The Faw tribe celebrated the news of William and Serena and the gift of gold. King Will sat near a lantern counting the contents of the chest. He was on his third count when Keenan sent Gavin over to make sure the man didn't see a problem.

Gavin walked back over to Keenan moments later, shaking his head slightly. "Na' a problem. I just doona think the man's held so much gold before." Gavin turned towards a boisterous knife throwing game.

"He should put that out of sight," Thomas said cynically, looking around.

"I think the people here are all Faw," Ewan murmured, "not likely to steal their own money." Ewan smiled at one of the young Faw women. "Perhaps I should mingle with the natives a bit, to better understand their customs," he said with a wink, and sauntered off in the direction of the colorfully dressed woman.

Thomas walked over from the knife toss game. "Where's Ewan off to?"

"To find a Romany wench to warm his pallet tonight," Brodick grumbled and looked around. "Not many of them out now, mostly just the men. Where did they take Serena?"

Keenan didn't move his eyes from the fire as he took a long pull off his drink. "She's still in that wagon over there," he pointed toward the wagon he had seen Mari pull her into an hour ago.

Several musicians came forward on the outskirts of the fire glow and began to play a familiar rhythm. Keenan's eyes moved to the wagon door. Would she dance then? King Will had asked her to. Keenan's body grew taut at the thought of watching Serena's body moving around the bonfire just like that first night weeks ago.

"That's a fine melody they're playing," Brodick said. "Perhaps a show is about to begin."

The door remained shut. Would she come out? Keenan's eyes stared into the shadows. Out of the corner of his eye, he saw two riders approach King Will.

"Who's that?" Brodick asked suspiciously.

"I ken that old man should put his coins away," Gavin said and moved his hand to the hilt of his sword.

Keenan watched two men dismount and greet King Will with formal bows. One quick glance told him Serena's door was still closed. He turned back to watch King Will motion them to sit down. Both visitors were dark of complexion, much like the entire Faw tribe, except Serena. They must be Romany, perhaps from a neighboring tribe.

The older man did most of the talking while the younger man surveyed the area. He looked strong, could possibly make a good warrior. His eyes were piercing, searching. As he moved from one end of the lit camp to another, he finally came to Keenan. The two men locked gazes. Keenan felt the man weigh him, judge his capabilities. Keenan shifted his weight into a battle stance, legs apart, arms at his side, ready to move toward his weapons. He moved with the natural reaction of a warrior. Something had triggered it. Was the visiting Rom a threat?

The man spoke without looking away, and King Will glanced over at Keenan. Keenan nodded once to the Faw patriarch. King Will nodded back and then went on talking to the visitors.

"Thomas," Keenan said evenly, "find out who they are. Quietly." Thomas moved off into the opposite direction. He would skirt the area and try to hear the conversation.

The constant murmur of the small crowd changed, hushed, as the rhythm of the music turned more hypnotic, like undulating waves.

"Bloody, look at that," Gavin said in awe, and Keenan turned to see Serena break into the circle of firelight. She wore the same type of gypsy dress she had worn the night he'd met her, but this one shimmered in a shade of blue turned nearly purple by the red glare of the fire. She stretched her arms over her head, bare except for her gloves. The blue silk wrapped around her waist accentuating her trimness and the womanly flare of her hips. The bodice was cut low enough to see her collarbone but not her cleavage. The way the material hugged her breasts was even more enticing than the low necklines that were in courtly fashion.

Her red hair hung in waves, free to dance around her hips as she moved with the waves of music. Her eyes were half closed like the other time he had watched her. Without conscious thought, Keenan moved forward to stand with the others around the perimeter. Would she feel his presence, the void she had felt the first time? The outline of his scar tightened slightly as he remembered how she had run her fingers down it to read him. He rubbed his jaw.

Keenan watched her move, her hips and arms, her torso, her feet dressed in leather slippers. Serena mimicked the waves of flame in time to the melody that surrounded them. He heard the tinkling of the small bells tied to a scarf around her tilting hips. As she disappeared on the other side of the fire, Keenan noticed that Gavin and Brodick stood next to him, their mouths open like fish thrown ashore. Thomas stood across the fire with much the same expression.

"Sweet Lord Almighty, our Serena can dance,"

Brodick said.

"Uh huh," Gavin answered, the same dim-witted expression marking his face. Keenan frowned as he noticed the appreciative looks of the men around him. Keenan's hands clenched into tight fists. They were watching Keenan's woman. He wet his lips remembering the kiss in the cave while the unnatural storm raged.

The younger Rom visitor stepped forward and caught her hand. No one stopped him. Fury, from watching the men ogle Serena, fed into his need to protect her. Keenan shouldered his way quickly through the onlookers. With one quick grasp of the man's hand, Keenan flipped his arm off of Serena.

"Doona touch her," Keenan warned.

The man looked mildly amused but Keenan saw the restrained anger in his eyes. Despite his coloring, he would fit in nicely with the snakes at court.

"I was introducing myself to King Will's daughter."

"She was in the middle of her dance."

The man smiled. "I could hardly help myself." Then the man said something in Romany, something that made Serena look down at her shoes. Had he offended her?

"I doona speak yer tongue." Keenan began to pull his long sword from the scabbard across his back until the soft touch of Serena's hand on his arm stopped him.

"He didn't offend me, Keenan."

Mari and King Will stepped up next to the visitor. Keenan noticed that Brodick and Gavin flanked him. Thomas stood across, his hand on his sword as well. No one spoke for a long moment as everyone assessed one another.

Finally Serena spoke. "Keenan Maclean of Kylkern, this is Damin Yallow of the Yallow Romany tribe. He is here," she stopped as everyone looked at her. "He's here on family business."

"Ye ken this man?" Keenan wanted to run the man through, wanted to face him across a bloody moor, wanted to run him into the ground.

Damin Yallow's voice was smooth as he spoke in the lyrical Romany language.

"In my land, it is rude to speak in a language that isna' understood by everyone present."

Damin turned his gaze away from Serena to lock with Keenan. Controlled annoyance lurked there. "Forgive me. My native language flows more easily from me."

"So what are you?" Damin asked Keenan and smiled. "I mean, I know who you are, Keenan Maclean of Kylkern, but what are you to the Faw tribe?" He inclined his head to Serena. "What are you to Serena Faw?"

Bloody hell, what was he? Keenan's eyes rose directly to Thomas's pinched face. What could he say? What was he to Serena? Was he her lover or her soon to be brother? The last one turned his stomach so he threw it out immediately. Was he her soul mate then? Time stood still as he warred with the words in his mind.

"I," he began strong and hesitated. "I helped to save William Faw from the false accusation of murderer."

"Serena's brother," Mari supplied to Damin.

Damin nodded. "So you are a friend," he said stressing the title. "A friend to the Faw Tribe. A friend to Serena."

He was so much more than that. But what could he say here in front of his men, in front of her family? Did they know that he had claimed her? Keenan looked at Serena. She watched him, her eyes glassed over with some emotion he couldn't quite understand. She almost seemed to plead with him.

But what did she want him to do?

Keenan felt himself nod. "Aye, I am a friend and protector."

Mari seemed to release her breath as she took Serena's arm. "Yes, and a very fine protector at that. He's brought my daughter home to us and has my son safely up in his brother's castle."

"My thanks to you, then," Damin Yallow said. His eyes followed Serena as Mari turned her toward the wagons.

"Good eve, men," Mari called out. Serena looked back at Keenan over her bare shoulder. Were those tears in her eyes? Keenan's chest clenched so tight he thought he might double over. What had just happened? All the Romany filtered away leaving him with his men.

Ewan walked over from the wagons, a scowl on his face.

"Rom women only let their husbands touch them," Ewan grumbled at the dumbstruck Macleans. "What's going on here?"

Thomas spoke first. "They only spoke in Rom over there. I couldn't understand a word. They may have been discussing a couple of milk cows if I understood anything."

"I doona like this," Brodick said low.

Gavin frowned fiercely. "Why do I feel like we were just in a battle?"

Keenan slammed his fist into his other palm. *Crack*. "Because we bloody hell were. And I'm fairly certain that I just lost."

****

Serena felt the hollowness that a shadow must feel if it had its own consciousness. Her will left her as Mari pulled her along behind her toward a new wagon.

"Angelas, you will sleep here tonight." She indicated the door and smiled. "It is nice inside, comfortable. Look," Mari said indicating the edges along the wagon, "good sturdy holds for garden boxes. You can have your own."

Serena nodded and ran her hand over the side of the wagon. "My own gardens," she trailed off then turned to Mari. "Wouldn't it be nice, though, to plant seeds in the ground?" Serena indicated the ground around them. Mari looked confused. "There is so much more space."

"But you would leave them behind when the camp moved."

Serena smiled slightly. "Wouldn't it be nice not to have to move, but to settle and raise vegetables on the land where you live?"

Mari shook her head. "Àngelas, that's not our way. We move on and take what's ours with us."

Serena couldn't explain to her duy her newly recognized feelings. She was only beginning to realize them herself. Perhaps it was all the travel in the last weeks, perhaps it was the nights of luxury in soft, large beds. But the thought of moving on once again with her tribe or any tribe, made Serena's head ache.

"Of course," Serena said and turned back to the wagon. "It looks sturdy enough to hold many garden boxes."

Silence sat between them until Mari's voice broke into Serena's thoughts. "You will be happy."

Serena turned to her, realizing that her duy had tears in her eyes despite the smile. Serena had been so wrapped up in her own torment that she almost missed the deep sadness of loss underscoring Mari's hope for her future. Her duy had just found her again, and now she was urging her to move away.

Serena looked at her. "It is still my decision."

Mari nodded and let go of Serena's arm. "Of course. But please, consider your future." Mari smoothed one of Serena's curls that lay along her shoulder. "He's quite handsome."

Serena nodded. "I will consider." Mari seemed satisfied and left Serena standing there in the darkness, its fresh spring smell calming her. Calming her until she heard the sharp snap of a stick somewhere off to the right behind the wagon. Keenan?

Damin Yallow stepped from behind a tree. His hands were in the pockets of his coat, his broad shoulders seemed stiff up around his neck. She sensed his nervousness. Luckily he couldn't sense her disappointment for it was so strong she could taste its bitterness on her tongue.

"Good Eve, Serena." His words came out calm.

The anger, infused by her disappointment, turned on him. "Were you eavesdropping?"

His eyes opened a bit wider. "No," he stammered. "I saw you talking over here near the new wagon, and I came this way as your duy left. I just wished to speak alone with you." He pulled a hand from his pocket and gestured back toward the fire. "Our introduction was strange, uncomfortable. I meant only to start fresh." With that he bowed gallantly. Upon standing he found her hands in the folds of her gown and cupped them.

"I am honored to meet you, Serena Faw of the Faw Tribe. I am the eldest son of John Yallow, leader of the Yallow Tribe." He spoke in the comfortable smooth flow of the Romany language.

Serena nodded and leaned against the brightly colored side of the wagon. Damin moved closer. "You know why I have come to visit the Faw tribe?"

"Yes," Serena said plainly, without encouragement. She was tired, tired of pleading in her mind for Keenan to claim her publicly. Tired of searching for some sign from him that she should risk her heart and go against what her family had clearly laid out for her future.

Damin pulled a long strand of her hair gently between his thumb and forefinger. "I will officially ask King Will for you in marriage. I will ask him tonight."

Serena breathed out slowly and looked up at the handsome, hopeful man. "You don't know what you are asking for." Serena touched Damin's bare arm, closed her eyes, and wove a fine thread through him, seeking, discovering who he was. Details that only he would know.

"If you speak of your magic, Serena, I know about it. My grandmother could scry the future and had an unnatural ability to judge people. I loved her and our tribe revered her wisdom. The Yallows will welcome you."

Strong confident words. Serena nodded.

"But do you understand the extent of my magic?"

He looked confused for a moment but then smiled. "I will learn."

Time for his first lesson. Serena smiled back. "Good. I know you speak the truth for I've read it in you."

He raised an eyebrow but smiled encouragingly. Did he believe her when she said she'd read him, or did he think she just played the witch to scare suitors? She sensed it was more the latter, just from his face. When had she begun to read faces, expressions? She never had before. Her chest tightened, Keenan appeared in her mind, but she quickly squelched the image.

Serena touched Damin's arms again and could feel his tamped down desire for her. But he was honorable and would hold onto his patience.

"Yes, you are honorable, Damin." She smiled. "And an excellent judge of horseflesh." He raised both eyebrows, but Serena heard his thoughts through the contact and nodded. "Yes, I could have heard that from King Will I suppose, but could my father really know about the foal you brought into the world when you were eight. You were all alone and scared and knew you should find help. But you wanted to be the one to bring the foal into the world. Your pride kept you there even when the mare screamed."

Damin's smile turned stony. "That was a long time ago," he whispered.

"Yes, a very long time ago, but it still haunts you. Rides in your mind whenever you see a mare heavy and about to foal, like the one you rode by on your journey here yesterday."

Damin just stared at her as if she had grown a hideous wart on her cheek. Serena almost lost her nerve. "I also know that you are excited about this union for it will elevate you in your father's tribe, once you have a wife and children. You intend to get me pregnant as soon as possible."

Damin's face began to harden. Had she pushed too far? "Do not be angry with me for stating the truth."

Damin forced a smile that almost looked real. "Serena, I am not ang..." he began and stopped. "You would know if I was angry inside, if I lied to protect your feelings."

"Yes." Serena nodded. "You are beginning to understand, understand that I have more than just a feeling about things. I know things, Damin. I could know all about you, your thoughts, your secret desires, your past, those feelings you keep deep down inside. I could know them all."

He looked at her, tilting his dark head slightly. "You say, could know?"

Serena glanced down. "I can block your thoughts and emotions from coming to me. It is harder when I touch you skin to skin." He looked at the gloves tied to her side. "I wear them to mute the images I see when I inadvertently touch someone."

"Is it just your hands that are sensitive?"

"No, my entire body."

"So," he stopped. "So, if we touch skin to skin," he raised an eyebrow, "you won't be able to help but read me, read everything I want to," he hesitated again and cleared his throat a bit. "Everything I want to do to you."

Serena took a deep breath in and nodded.

He raised both eyebrows and grinned. "That has its advantages."

Serena couldn't help but smile at his reaction. "I suppose it could."

Damin put his hand out to her. "Here, take my hand. I give you permission to walk your way through me. See me for who I am. I have nothing to hide."

Serena laid her hand in his palm. Feelings of worry tangled with excitement. Damin held nothing back. He felt no embarrassment toward her, about her. Only wonder at what Serena could do. Brief images of alliances formed by using her powers, knowing the plans of certain enemies, keeping his tribe safe from trickery and bigotry. These all came along her thread mixed with ideas of dark haired children running around her skirts.

It was so much that Serena leaned backwards letting the wagon support her. He offered her an honorable life, filled with children and respect, with the potential for love. As Serena opened her eyes, she realized that Damin had moved much closer in the darkness, so close that his lips hovered near hers.

"That's it. Open your eyes." His words sang soft and deep in the chilled air. "I want you to see me, Serena Faw, when I first kiss you." His lilting Romany words were a luring song promising her a future of happiness.

Damin's lips brushed against hers and a course of desire rushed from him. She felt it in her mind, images of how he could make love to her. He would be erotic, gentle, teasing. He tilted her head with his hand so that he could easily slant his mouth against her, deepening the kiss.

Serena felt the hard planks of wood against her back as he leaned into her slightly. She felt the chill of the air around her legs. She felt the pressure of his body. She heard Chiriklò chirping somewhere high above her. Serena could hear the woods breathing around them as Damin kissed her. Her mind roamed to the scene at the fire and then the lovely wagon she leaned against. What did it look like inside?

She kissed him back. It was pleasant. He seemed quite the expert at kissing. Serena dove into his mind. There were other pretty girls there, lurking in his memory, one in particular still sat heavy near his heart. Kristina.

Serena waited for the stab of jealousy to hit her as Kristina's face surfaced briefly during the kiss. Instead she just felt curiosity. As Damin touched the tip of his tongue to hers, Serena waited for her mind to give way to tumbling heat, but instead she just wondered when she could fit in a breath of air. She must have pulled back slightly because Damin pulled away and smiled at her.

Serena realized that she must have looked stunned because Damin's smile turned cocky. "Forgive me, Serena for taking such liberties. I lose control around you."

Serena smiled blankly as she worked through the strange kiss. It had been pleasant enough, not forced or awkward. But something was missing, something important. Her smile faltered as she realized that the something missing was Keenan Maclean.

She closed her eyes to hide the emotion. Damin Yallow had everything to offer her, but her heart didn't want it. No fire burned in the kiss, nothing hot and rushing to melt her insides, no throbbing desire in the pit of her stomach and below at her core. Serena's stomach tightened into nausea, a sickly feeling.

Damin put his finger under her chin to tilt her face up. "Serena, I did not mean to upset you."

Concern flowed through the touch. She smiled sadly and opened her eyes.

"I am fine, Damin. Just overwhelmed."

He thought her overwhelmed by the feelings he thought he had produced in her. Male confidence, anticipation.

Serena felt the first stabbings of guilt. "Damin, I have much to consider before accepting your offer of marriage. You are a fine man from a fine family. You do me much honor by your interest. But I have long since decided not to wed." Serena shook her head. "I have much to consider."

Damin was undaunted. "I understand, Serena." He stopped and backed up a bit, giving her space. "I know you could read my mind and figure out what my life is like, but let me tell you some things about my tribe, about where you will live. Let us pretend that I must paint a picture instead of you viewing it." He teased her, trying to break the tension. Serena nodded.

Damin stayed close to her as he spoke. Serena let his words flit by her. He had a need to talk to her as if she were a normal woman. And she had a need to sort through her emotions. As Serena replayed the kiss and lack of response on her behalf, she found herself comparing it to her response to Keenan. The difference was vast. Each time she tried to imagine her life with Damin something turned in her stomach.

The children she imagined didn't have dark hair and deep brown eyes. They had blue eyes and light hair. They carried little wooden broadswords and chased sheep on the shores of Loch Awe.

Off to the left, Serena saw a movement of mist among the trees and her birthmark began to itch. She continued to nod appropriately while keeping her peripheral focus on the white image as it coalesced into a ghostly figure. Drakkina. Her diaphanous image floated close until Serena could make out her face pinched in a deep scowl.

The thoughts of the crone stabbed at her lightly through the air. "What are you doing? Who is this man? Where is the Highlander?"

Serena fortified her wall and sent a quick series of thoughts back to the witch. Thoughts of disappointment at Keenan's refusal to claim her, angry thoughts of appreciation for Damin, mutinous thoughts against Drakkina's interference.

The hovering image crossed her arms over her chest. The shimmering cloud dissipated and then pulled back together.

You are weak, Serena thought.

Images came to her from Drakkina. Images of the Duke of Cumberland yelling at his mistress, images of Drakkina forming in the room, and scaring the man, images of Drakkina entering him and making him confess publicly so that he couldn't blame Lady Amberley. Serena's eyes opened wide.

"Yes, I know the waters in the south can be quite exciting. If you'd like we can stay there for some time," Damin said.

"That would be very nice," Serena said, trying to keep her voice normal and interested. "Tell me of the last time you ventured there, Damin. I like to hear the sound of your voice."

He smiled and Serena ignored the guilt stabbing at her as she reconnected with Drakkina. The woman was so angry she nearly stamped her obscured feet.

You are encouraging him! Drakkina's accusation crackled silently through the air.

I must hear him out, Serena defended. *He wants to marry me.*

Drakkina threw up her hands in disgust and turned half way in a circle before centering back on Serena. *You are meant for Keenan Maclean.*

Serena snorted. *You need to be telling Keenan Maclean that, not me.*

"I know. It is terrible how the English gengas treat us," Damin said, and Serena realized she had snorted out loud.

Drakkina continued to fume so intensely that Serena could actually see her powers waving in and out. What was she doing?

I'm trying to summon enough power to get that ass away from you. Drakkina's thoughts huffed with her frustration. Drakkina's interference to save Lady Amberley must have weakened her immensely. She barely had enough strength to appear.

As Damin fell into a comfortable monologue, Drakkina stomped around behind him. She moved her arms this way and that trying to pull any power she could from the surrounding earth. It was almost comical, and Serena had to watch so that she didn't smile at an inappropriate time.

"And then we travel up into the Lake Country. It is beautiful there." Damin stopped. "Has the Faw tribe traveled there?"

Serena moved her eyes back to Damin's and repeated his question in her head. "Um, why yes, we have traveled near the Lake Country, but did not stay long. It would be nice to live there for awhile."

Damin continued on that note. The man seemed to be able to talk forever, how annoying. So unlike Keenan, who barely said more than a few sentences in a single sitting.

Drakkina stopped waving, a smile crinkling her eyes. Serena squinted into the dark toward a buzzing sound near the bush next to where Drakkina stood. A bee, perhaps a wasp, and it was furious. As Drakkina waved her misty hand around it, the little insect tumbled about, poked, infuriated. Serena leaned away from the buzzing insect.

Drakkina continued to tumble the little creature toward Damin.

"Damin," Serena interrupted. "I think that wasp may try to harm you."

Drakkina frowned at her and continued to disrupt and antagonize the insect. The wasp tried to sting Drakkina, but couldn't contact with her form. Damin looked at the insect and shooed it a bit with his hand. "Never mind. It's just a little insect." He turned back to Serena, oblivious to the woman bent on attacking him in the only way available to her.

The wasp picked up Damin's scent as he waved his hand near it. It had a new target. Drakkina smiled broadly as the angry insect zipped around Damin. Serena backed away as it buzzed loudly. Damin turned quickly and slapped at the undaunted wasp. It had been agitated to the point of obsessive fury.

"Damin, you best leave. I think it's out to sting you."

"Aaa!" Damin yelled as the wasp delivered its first sting on his hand. And then it dove in toward his face. "Blasted bee!" he swiped in the air as the wasp stung his cheek.

Serena cringed and hoped that he did not have a bad reaction to wasp stings. Drakkina threw back her head and laughed, but the only auditable sound was a gust of wind.

"Damin, I'm going inside the wagon now. I don't want it to come after me."

"Go, go, Serena. It's bent on blood," he said, swatting at the intent creature. Serena looked back just as she was ducking into the wagon. Damin ran toward the fire, his arms circling in wide arcs of defense.

Serena watched Drakkina's image waver. "Good night, Drakkina," she said into the darkness.

"Dream of the Highlander, child." The woman's words floated to her on the gusting wind as the misty form dissolved.

Chapter 12

"Good, I see you're awake," Mari said as she entered the bridal wagon.

Serena looked up from the pile of green ruffles and silk. "Yes, but all that is here is this beautiful court dress."

"I brought it in for you." Mari moved her finger in a circle. "Turn and I will pull the stays tight. Ah, what a slender waist you have, just like me when I was a bride."

Mari didn't see Serena's frown. Her duy finished the ties and moved on to the heavy petticoats. As Mari's fingers brushed against her back, Serena felt her duy's excitement.

"Damin's been to talk to King Will hasn't he?"

"Yes, he has," Mari could barely contain her happiness. "He says that you and he seem perfect for each other."

Serena nodded but didn't smile.

"What is it?" Mari asked, concern coursing through her touch.

Serena pulled the white fichu off and draped it around her neck to cover her swelling neckline. "It's, well," Serena sat down on the edge of the rumpled bed. "I don't think I can marry Damin Yallow." Serena stopped. "No, what I mean to say is that, I will not marry Damin Yallow."

Mari flopped down on the chair and dropped her hands on the table top. "But why?"

Serena took a deep breath. "I love Keenan Maclean. And I cannot marry someone else when I love another. It would shame Damin." Mari didn't move. "And I would be miserable." Serena's eyes begged her duy to understand. She was afraid to try and read her, afraid that she wouldn't find the understanding she craved. Instead Serena studied her duy's face. They stared at one another for some time before Mari finally stood. She came over and kissed Serena on the forehead.

"I cannot tell you to marry Damin, Àngelas. But I fear that you are headed for heartbreak my child. Keenan Maclean is," she hesitated, "he's so different from us, and you can't tell what he's thinking or feeling. You can't be sure of his motives. How could you put your faith in someone when you can't be sure of them?"

"Blind courage?" Serena asked and smiled timidly. She could feel Mari's reluctance.

Mari patted her shoulder and sighed. "But Damin is perfect for you."

"Damin kissed me last night."

"And?"

"And I felt nothing, Duy. How can I marry someone who makes me feel nothing?"

"Love can grow in time."

Irritation surged through Serena at the words that so mimicked Keenan's lectures regarding his brother. Her eyes narrowed. "How can love grow when I love another? Unless my love for Keenan dies, love for another cannot grow." Her angry words caused Mari to sit back from her. Serena had never raised her voice to her duy before. "Forgive me, Duy," Serena sighed. "I am just so tired of people telling me to love someone that I don't. I want to love who I love." Serena's eyes lowered to her hands.

She felt her duy's hand touch her hair. "There is more to your journey than you've told me. Who else don't you love, Àngelas?"

"There is a prophecy," Serena shook her head. "Which I don't believe. It's…it's too much to say."

Mari leaned in again. Serena felt her mother loop a strand of her hair behind her ear. "Ever since William brought you home to us and you became my daughter, I've longed for your happiness, Àngelas. That's all I've ever wanted for you." Serena looked up at the tears resting in her duy's eyes. Mari nodded slowly. "And if you think your happiness lies with Keenan Maclean, then I support that."

Serena threw her arms around her mother. "I love you so much," she squeezed the woman until Mari laughed. When Serena released her, Mari pulled out the fichu exposing Serena's cleavage.

"If you're out to catch a Highlander, you better start showing off the prize." Mari laughed and stood up in the quaint wagon. "Too bad, it was such a lovely wagon." She looked back at Serena. "Hurry now, and fortify yourself. King Will has requested you to come to him."

"Did he want me to wear this?"

Mari nodded. "He said you should look your best."

Serena buttoned the snug matching jacket bodice embroidered with dragonflies, butterflies and flowers over her stays. Luckily there were no bees anywhere on it. Serena tried to slow the nervous thumping of her heart as she stepped from the wagon out into the bright spring sunshine.

The wagons seemed oddly quiet as people moved about their business in hushed tones. They nodded and smiled at her in her gown, practically bowing. Inside their minds, they had as many questions about the subdued atmosphere as Serena.

Chiriklò chirped from a tall birch, and then glided down to flutter daintily on Serena's gloved hand. She trailed her finger down the sleek blue feathers and flashed the question to her pet. What did her sparrow know? Images of Damin Yallow talking with his father and King Will came to her in the fragmented bird version Chiriklò used to communicate. All the images were clear to the finest detail, but only viewed rapidly before flitting to other images. Her bird had seen Keenan ride away with Gavin at dawn. One glance around the camp told Serena he hadn't returned, but the other three Macleans stood talking near some trees across the clearing.

Would Keenan return soon? Where had he gone? Chiriklò didn't know the answers.

She stroked his feathers as he hopped up her wrist. King Will saw Serena from across the camp and beckoned her. Chiriklò shot off into the trees. As she walked, most of her tribe set down their tasks and followed until they made a semi-circle behind her as she stood before King Will, John Yallow and Damin. Serena looked over at Damin and gasped softly at the swollen side of his face.

"Damin?"

"Bengikanò bee," Damin swore. He called it the devil's bee, but Serena knew who was responsible for the poor man's stings, not a devil but a witch.

"Oh Damin, I'm so sorry," Serena pulled her glove off and laid her hand against the side of his face gingerly. His thoughts slid quickly along her touch. She stroked the side of his face, staring into his bloodshot eyes.

Damin Yallow hadn't slept well last night. He'd been up late planning, strategizing with his father, realizing the amazing power he would possess in Serena. Thoughts of her beauty and a happy future as father and husband had given way to thoughts of power and possible riches. He would never lose a negotiation again once Serena could move inside his opponent's mind. He still desired her, but the more he understood her powers the more he realized that he must have her.

Serena stepped back. Out of the corner of her

eye, she saw the Macleans gather close as King Will spoke in Romany. The whole exchange so far had been in her tribe's native tongue. Serena saw frowns on all three warriors. What must they think of her touching Damin? She purposely kept her wall up. She couldn't become distracted now.

"Serena, my daughter, Damin Yallow of the honorable Yallow tribe, requests to marry you." King Will smiled slowly and turned to the rest of the tribe. "He gives two milk cows and a bull to us for a bride price." The tribe clapped and murmurings ran amongst them.

Serena waited until the chatter quieted. She curtsied. With a deep breath, she pronounced her words in firm English. "I am honored that Damin Yallow wishes to wed with me." She saw Damin's father smile. "However, I cannot marry him." A hushed gasp hovered behind her. She lowered her eyes submissively.

"What is this?" King Will said.

"I respectfully decline his proposal of marriage."

"Serena, last night you kissed me," Damin Yallow said in English.

"Damin, you kissed me," she corrected and felt her face flash heat. Maybe it was a good thing Keenan wasn't here. "I am sorry, but I have decided that I cannot marry you." Serena was polite but firm.

"Bring him," King Will raised his voice over the crowd and Ephram led a man into the circle. It was an Anglican priest. King Will turned to Serena. "I have already accepted Damin Yallow's offer on your behalf, and he has paid the fines to Father Banning for a hasty marriage, today, right now."

Bile rose in Serena's throat. She tried to pull in air, but panic gripped her like a noose. She shook her head. "No, I will not marry Damin Yallow, not now, not ever."

Serena felt Maclean presence behind her. She looked to see Brodick and Ewan, legs braced as if about to battle. Their hands rested upon the hilts of their swords. Thomas ran for his horse. Brodick's thick burr rose up in a threatening growl. "If the lass says she willna marry, then she willna marry."

"This is none of your business, gurbeti," Damin said. His black eyes, swollen from the bee, glared at Brodick.

"Damin, I tell you I cannot marry you." Serena looked at King Will where he stood in silent fury. "I have already been claimed by another."

The gasp she heard echoed through her tribe's thoughts.

In the sudden silence, Mari's panic pounded against Serena's wall. Her mother begged her to elaborate, to defend herself. When Serena remained silent, Mari's voice filled the clearing. She spoke in English.

"Claimed with words, just words. My daughter is still a virgin."

Serena felt her cheeks flame. King Will finally controlled his rage enough to speak. "Claimed by whom?" he said in English and looked to the two scowling Macleans.

Serena raised her eyes to her father's level. "Keenan Maclean claimed me two nights ago." She held her gaze steady, refusing to look toward Damin, while King Will snorted skeptically. He held out his arms wide.

"Your Highlander is not even present to support you."

"He didn't know that you had my wedding planned for this morning," Serena said with quiet defiance. King Will's eyes snapped. He was not used to defiance. In the Romany culture, the patriarch of the tribe ruled and could only be questioned by another man. Women had no authority, and the fact that his own daughter disobeyed him in public was a grave insult.

Disdain, well controlled fury. "That he would leave you at all shows that he does not hold to this claim, a claim based on words alone."

Brodick stepped forward. "Keenan is on an errand to cleanse yer son's name. He rides to the surrounding authority to show the king's letter freeing William from blame in the murder of Gerard Grant. It is an honorable errand, done to help the Faw family. He left his trusted men to safeguard Serena. He felt she would be safe amongst her own family." Although the last was a statement, Brodick's expression questioned its validity.

King Will regarded the huge warrior with narrowed eyes. Without a word he turned back to Serena. "Come here," he said in Romany.

Serena took two steps closer until the edge of her petticoat nearly touched the toes of King Will's leather boots.

"Àngelas, you will marry Damin Yallow. You will marry him now."

Serena looked to the left, at Damin, his swollen face distorted more by his muted anger. "Forgive me, Damin, but I cannot marry you." The silence that followed was so thick with tension that Serena could barely swallow the packed air.

King Will's face turned a blotchy red. She wondered absently if her father would break out in hives over her defiance. With swift power unexpected in one his age, Serena's father grabbed her arm roughly and shook her. Serena heard steel slide free behind her, as she tried to keep her head from snapping back and forth.

"Wait! Stop! I say I've been claimed," she hesitated only briefly before plunging ahead. "He's claimed me with more than words alone." King Will pushed her from his grasp as if she were dirty.

Serena caught herself and turned to face him. "He's seen me naked, he's," she stopped to take a quick breath, "he's touched me, with his hands, with his mouth." Serena saw Mari shake her head and close her eyes as if Serena's shame was too much for her to bear. Serena looked away from Mari to Damin. "I may yet be a virgin, but I am not pure, not pure to wed with you, Damin. Again I am sorry."

Names like "whore" and "libnì" mixed with pity and fear for her. Serena turned slowly to face the semi-circle. "I am no whore," she said looking directly at those with the name in their minds and watched their eyes grow wide. "I love Keenan Maclean. I will wed no one, unless it is he."

"Taynè!" King Will yelled and pulled her around to face him, his hand raised high to strike her face. Ewan's large hand engulfed King Will's fist, forcing it to his side while Brodick shielded Serena behind his massive body.

Serena heard the deadly cocking of flint pistols. She watched Ephram center one on Ewan and another of William's old friends aimed his weapon at Brodick. Brodick turned slightly to better shield her, obstructing her view of the gun.

Please no! Please no! Serena desperately peeked out from under Brodick's raised sword arm. She reached under her skirts and pulled free her own dagger, not that it would do much against pistols.

Chaos erupted. Ewan cursed loudly in Gaelic. Mari wailed in maternal terror. The clergyman dove into the tent while beseeching God. The women screamed and grabbed their children, running toward the safety of the wagons.

Serena turned her back up against Brodick, her own dagger raised. Her eyes moved across the scattering people of her tribe and came to rest on the woods.

The leaves quivered along the north path.

Chiriklò darted out of the trees, beak closed like an arrow bent on a target. Following out of the dense trees and bushes thundered Keenan's lathered horse. Keenan's face boiled with war rage. He steered the horse with his legs alone while loosing two drawn daggers into the air. They hit their marks splintering the shafts of both pistols, scattering their fragments around the two men. A shower of gunpowder covered them like fine ash as they covered their heads in defense.

Without fully stopping his horse, Keenan swung down into a run before the last piece of metal thumped to the ground. His long sword sang for blood as he pulled it out before him ready to strike. Before Serena could move, he sandwiched her between him and Brodick, shielding her from any possible threat.

Two more horses thunder into the clearing. Before she could take two breaths Thomas and Gavin flanked her sides, blocking her view completely. Her face was smashed up against Keenan's back, his shoulders so broad above her, his hair loose and falling down his back. She buried her face in the fresh pine smell that clung to him and tried to calm her heart.

"Keenan they may try to shoot you," panic pitched her voice higher. He didn't respond. "Keenan, I told them I wouldn't marry Damin because you claimed me," she paused, "intimately." She knew the other men could hear her since they stood so close. But she had to warn him. "If they shoot, you will be the target."

"My death doesn't frighten me," he said softly.

"Well it scares the bloody hell out of me," she retorted and thumped his back.

"Ewan," Keenan yelled. Ewan jogged over and replaced Keenan in front of Serena. She was still surrounded by human shields. She wiggled in the tight space until she turned toward where Damin and King Will had stood before. She peered out under Brodick's armpit.

Mari was pleading with her father, but King Will didn't seem to be listening to her. He only stared at Keenan. Turning her eyes slightly, Serena caught sight of Damin who gripped his bleeding arm where Chiriklò had pecked him with his beak. Her pet now sat poised in a branch over the man. Damin's eyes watched him warily.

The clearing was once again silent. Keenan's voice nearly shook the trees with its anger, yet the volume remained controlled. "I leave to clear a Faw's name of murder, only to return to find members of the Faw Romany tribe ready to murder my men."

"You have dishonored my daughter, Highlander." King Will stood proud, defiant. "I have matched her with a respected man, but she is unclean and cannot wed him."

The clergyman peeked out of the tent cautiously.

"Brodick, tell me what's gone on here," Keenan said. "Talk fast."

"Serena's father demands she marry Damin Yallow, now, this day. She refused." He stopped and took a breath that he let out in a huff. "She says you claimed her, with your words. When her father said your words didn't matter, Serena told everyone that ye've seen her naked, that," he hesitated. Serena felt him shift his weight from foot to foot. "That ye've touched her. Her father was about to strike her when Ewan and I stepped in."

Could she blush any more? At least she was hidden, if only the ground would fall away beneath her feet and suck her down. At least Brodick had omitted her declaration of love.

Damin's voice rang out. "I will wed her anyway."

Despite her shock, Serena threaded her power out towards the man. And there it was. He was desperate to hang on to her, desperate now that he had spent the night developing uses for her magic. But under that desperation was anger. He would punish her. Serena grasped the dagger tighter, determined to use it if necessary.

King Will looked over at the fortress of Macleans. "I would have my daughter before me."

Keenan nodded slightly and Brodick stepped aside. Serena straightened to her full height and forced her face into calm seriousness. She continued to hold the dagger along her side.

King Will took a deep breath. As he released it, Serena felt some of the anger flow out of him and his eyes softened. He spoke in quiet Romany. "Àngelas, I took you into our tribe when you were a young girl. I've raised you to be Romany and have found an honorable man who will care for you despite your strangeness. You would throw that back in my face?"

Serena's eyes turned glassy, but she refused to let the tears escape. How could she make him understand, when she had trouble understanding her feelings herself? She spoke in Romany. "Father, you honor me greatly with this proposal. And I am very thankful to you for the years of protection you gave me, the wisdom you taught me, the care you have shown me." She shook her head sadly. "But I cannot wed someone I do not love. And I cannot love someone when I love another."

King Will lowered his voice even more. "What if he cannot love you?"

And there was the question that kept Serena's stomach knotted. What if Keenan Maclean couldn't love her, wouldn't allow himself to love her? Was she dooming herself to a loveless life? Courage, she thought. Warriors took risks, didn't they?

Serena spoke in Romany. "Father, even if he cannot love me, I still love Keenan Maclean. I will wed no other." Serena kept her focus on her father.

Keenan stood unmoving next to her. Did he think her rude for not speaking English? She blushed. Could he have picked up enough Romany to understand her words?

Damin stepped forward, still not ready to give up. "What does he have to offer for her? I offer two milk cows and a bull as a bride price."

Serena lowered her eyes. What if Keenan offered nothing?

"I give the Faw tribe my sword," he said and with one powerful toss, flipped the long sword high in the air to land, point down in the dirt beside King Will. Her father didn't even flinch. His eyes moved over the intricate designs etched into the steel and the small jewels embedded at the ends of the well worn hilt.

"Keenan, that is yer grandda's sword," Thomas warned behind them.

"It is my sword now and freely given. King Will, I believe that the jewels alone will buy your tribe several milk cows."

Damin's hands fisted at his sides. "I give the Faw tribe the bridal wagon I brought for Serena."

King Will turned from Damin back to Keenan to see if he would raise the stakes.

"My sword also carries the allegiance of Clan Maclean. Your tribe would always be welcome on our lands and you would have our protection."

"The Yallow tribe is just as powerful. An alliance with us far surpasses protection from a tribe leagues away," Damin threw out.

King Will looked back to Keenan. Keenan's voice stayed deadly calm, his eyes cold, calculating. "I could continue to match you object for object, but I'd rather jump to the end. King Will, in return for Serena, I gift you back yer son, William."

King Will looked confused. "William is no prisoner."

Keenan's words held all the threat of a man determined to win. "With one word from me, yer son is dead. And if I must hold him as ransom for Serena, I will."

It was a bluff, Serena thought. A good one, but Keenan couldn't order William's death. Actually he could, but he wouldn't. She knew that without reading his mind.

Mari gasped, her hand touched King Will's arm. King Will studied Keenan for several long moments. Damin opened his mouth to speak, but King Will held up his hand to stop him.

"Keenan Maclean, I accept your terms. I will take your sword and the promise of William's safe return for my daughter."

Keenan nodded, and King Will looked over his shoulder. "Father Banning."

"Ah, yes, yes, I am here." The nervous priest stepped forward and wiped his hands along the sides of his long vestments.

"There will be a wedding today." King Will said evenly. "For although I accept Keenan Maclean's terms, I will not let my daughter leave with him without his vow before God."

"Father!"

King Will continued to stare at Keenan. Serena felt her father's stubbornness like a massive boulder. Blood would spill before he budged on this point. Her father's pride had already taken such a hit. She could feel him mentally digging in his heels.

But she had to try. "Father, you can't expect him to marry me today."

"I expect a lot from the man who takes my daughter," he replied evenly without moving his eyes from Keenan. Serena didn't even think that her father blinked. It was a staring contest, like two wolves. "Would you demand any less if she was your daughter, Maclean?"

Keenan's expression didn't change. Serena tried to thread her way into his mind, but it was as if she threaded it through a dark room. She released the thread and just opened her heart up and cleared her mind. Faint shades of emotion pricked her consciousness. Stubbornness, subdued anger for being trapped, then something calmer, perhaps acquiescence. Serena blinked. Was she really picking up on his feelings or had she grown very adept at reading expressions and body language?

Keenan turned to her. His face still looked like a beautifully carved rendition of an ancient warrior as his hair fell haphazardly around his broad shoulders. But something was different, the ice in his eyes melted as he looked into her own. Was there admiration in the gaze, perhaps encouragement? She wasn't sure, but whatever it was, it was not rejection nor pity.

Keenan turned back to King Will. "I would kill any man who tried to steal my daughter without vows between them. I accept yer terms."

Mari gave a little shriek and wiped at her eyes.

"I but ask for an hour to bathe and talk with my men."

King Will nodded majestically. "Agreed."

Damin Yallow threw up his hands in disgust, turned and stalked off toward the bridal wagon, his father following.

Mari engulfed Serena in her warm arms. Her duy's lips brushed against her ear. "Oh Àngelas, you wed today." Her duy pulled back to gather the hair from Serena's face and smiled brightly. "My daughter, a wife, married to the man she loves." Mari pulled her back into a hug. Serena leaned into her mother and watched numbly as Keenan walked off toward the stream where her tribe washed. The other Macleans looked between one another, shock marked their faces. Only Brodick turned to her and winked. Then they all followed after their leader.

Mari ushered Serena through a quick bath in a tub of cool water. Serena was too numb to respond much to her duy's chattering. After Serena was dried and dressed once more in the bridal gown, Mari stopped talking. She looked into Serena's blank face and mentally asked, "what is it, child?"

Serena let out a breath she hadn't realized she held. "What if Keenan can't love me?"

Mari looked at her. "But you love him."

"But what if my love is not enough? What if I spend the rest of my life loving someone who doesn't love me in return?"

Mari squeezed her fingers and smiled grimly as Serena shook her head slowly. "Love, Àngelas, is a leap of faith." Serena looked blankly at her. "You have to trust in it for real love to grow. If you think about it, if you loved anyone else, someone you could read, well then it would be cheating, wouldn't it? You'd know for sure if they loved you and there would be no risk, no trust, you would just know."

Serena nodded slowly, trying to take in Mari's wise words. She looked down at her hands. "What if he chooses the prophecy over me?" Serena jumped when someone rapped on the wagon door. Mari swung the little door outward. Thomas and Brodick waited to escort Serena to the priest. Thomas wore his normal frown while Brodick smiled encouragingly at her.

"Ye look beautiful, Serena," Brodick said as she stepped down and Mari fussed at the ribbons she'd woven in her hair.

"Thank you," she whispered. Thomas said nothing. Did she really want to know what he thought? Yes. Leap of faith or not, she needed to know what she was walking into. Serena walked between the two men, listening to their thoughts as they reviewed Keenan's words when he spoke to them at the stream. Keenan didn't want bloodshed, that this was the best strategy. Then Keenan's words came to Serena. "I can marry her here and still die while she fulfills the prophecy by marrying Lachlan after my death. The prophecy never states that the witch must be pure, never married before."

Hurt coursed through her causing her to stifle a sob. Instant tears stabbed behind her eyes. Brodick turned his head to look at her.

"What's wrong, lass?"

Serena shook her head unable to speak. What was there to say? She was about to marry a man who planned to die.

As she approached the small tent erected for the ceremony, her legs grew numb. Keenan stood there proud and brooding, watching her as she stepped up alongside him. She turned toward Father Banning and concentrated on his droning voice. Behind her the busy minds of her tribe whirled about as they watched in stunned silence. Serena could hear Damin Yallow's horse dragging away the bridal wagon. Keenan's deep timbre pulled her attention back as he recited his wedding vows. Then she repeated her vows. "Through happiness and sorrow, until death do we part." The words caught in her throat. Until death do we part. And just when would that be?

Chapter 13

Keenan watched Serena impatiently as she hugged her mother. His new bride seemed melancholy to be leaving despite her fight earlier to claim him. Brodick came over and thumped him on the back.

"Meala-naidheachd ort, Keenan! No bonnier lass lives that I have seen."

Brodick always had a way of lightening the tensest atmosphere with his good humor. Keenan grinned slightly. "I have to agree with ye there, but I will take offense if ye continue to notice her so intensely." Brodick laughed.

"Aye, good tidings are in order, Keenan," Gavin said as he walked up. Keenan nodded to him. "Any thoughts of how ye'll explain this to Lachlan?"

Brodick punched Gavin's arm.

"I was just asking," he said rubbing the bruised limb.

Keenan looked at Thomas and Ewan who walked up in time to hear the question. "Nay, na' yet."

He turned toward Serena where she stood near Mari. She didn't smile.

"What did ye say to Serena?" Keenan looked to Thomas. "When ye walked her to the ceremony."

Thomas frowned even more. "Nothing.

"I told her she looked bonny," Brodick said.

Keenan nodded but continued to watch Thomas. "Did she touch ye?"

Thomas shook his head.

"Aye she did, Thomas. Remember, she stumbled

a bit on one of those roots and caught herself on yer arm. Ye let her hold yer arm the whole way over."

Keenan scrubbed his hands over his face, closed his eyes briefly and glanced back at Serena. He lowered his arms and crossed them over his chest. "Rather then, Thomas, what were ye thinking when ye walked her over to the ceremony?"

"What?" Thomas stammered. "Ye doona think she kent my thoughts, do ye?"

"Of course she kent yer thoughts, ye idiot," Brodick said glowering at Thomas. "She said she could hear strong thoughts sometimes without trying." He nodded, his bushy eyebrows raised, to emphasize his words.

"I, I doona ken what I was thinking at the time, probably about traveling home." Thomas turned red through his hasty explanation.

Keenan watched Serena where she sat just inside the wedding tent while her parents moved about collecting her few things in a roll of fabric. She was beautiful as usual, her hair woven with ribbons cascading like red gold over her shoulders and breasts. Her delicate features held the mask of serenity, but Keenan knew better. Somehow he knew. It was more than the subdued spirit lurking behind those telling violet eyes that warned him. It was as if he felt the weight of her sadness pressing in on him.

"I want ye all to think happy thoughts, right now," he commanded.

"What?" Ewan and Gavin asked in humorous synchronicity.

"Now."

"What do we think about?" Brodick asked.

"Think about how happy ye are that Serena is my bride." Keenan watched Serena's face and Brodick followed his gaze. "Think about how beautiful the moors around Kylkern are. Think about the wonderful Macleans ye will see again soon, whatever. Just think of happy thoughts."

"Ye doona think she's trying to read our minds right now, do ye?" Gavin asked in a whisper.

Keenan almost laughed. "Ye doona need to whisper, man. She can hear ye loud and clear when she concentrates."

Gavin's anxious look spread to each of his men.

"Think of happy things," Keenan said again. Keenan saw Serena frown and knew his men were failing.

"But she said she tries to block the thoughts of others," Thomas said.

His men had no idea who Serena was. Keenan shook his head at them. His words came slowly as if educating a group of young lads. "Serena was raised among people who mistrust her. The only comfort she had, came from her mother whom she is now leaving, again. She knows ye all think she should marry Lachlan, not me. And therefore, once again she is encircled with mistrust."

Keenan looked back at the lovely woman seeming to catch her breath amidst the chaos of packing. "Her only protection lies in her gift." Keenan's eyes warmed with admiration for the beautiful, strong lass he'd just wed. "She may na' wield a sword or shoot a bow, but doona doubt that Serena Maclean is a warrior. She risked her life to save her brother. She saved Lachlan, the boy and his mother from the Campbell. She masqueraded in court to cleanse her brother's name. She defended herself here this morning. Serena has courage that could match any of ye." Keenan stared his men in their eyes, challenging them to refute his words.

None did.

"So she will use the only weapon she has when she is threatened. Just as ye would. Just as any warrior would." Keenan nodded to emphasize his point. "Serena Faw is worthy of the Maclean name."

As the point he was making sunk into his men, Keenan watched Serena's face. A slight frown still haunted her lips, but when she opened her gorgeous eyes, there was a light in them, a hint of the spirit that made her so incredibly desirable. She shifted in the seat so that she sat taller. Aye, she had heard his words of her courage through the minds of his men. His wife still couldn't read his thoughts, but she could read the interpretations, and unfortunately misinterpretations, of his thoughts through them. Keenan's jaw tightened. For the first time he wished that she could spy into his mind instead of depending on those around him to supply her with information.

Thomas turned to him, his face tinged pink again, but he looked straight into his leader's eyes. "I may have thought about her marrying Lachlan once ye die, like ye said to us at the creek."

Keenan had already guessed as much. He clapped his hand on Thomas's shoulder and walked past him toward the tent. "Next time try na' to dwell on my death. It seems to upset the lass." Thomas nodded as he hastened past him. "Ready the horses," Keenan said.

Keenan strode across to Serena. She stood as soon as he began to approach.

"Wife, we must leave for Kylkern." Serena's cheeks reddened at the new title. "Make yer farewells," he said as he hefted her rolled bundle over his shoulder. Keenan turned to King Will and Mari and gave them a nod. "The Faw tribe will always be welcome on Maclean land."

King Will bowed his head in reply. "We will travel up into your Highlands this summer. That should give William enough time to recover and continue on with us." King Will's eyes moved to Serena. "And I will want to see that my daughter is happy with her choice." The hint of threat tinged the old man's voice as his eyes glanced to Keenan and then back to his daughter. King Will walked over to Serena. She stood tall before him. He placed his hands on her shoulders and leaned forward to kiss her forehead. The old man cupped her face in his wrinkled hands and they touched foreheads. "You are very brave, my Àngelas. I am proud of you." When he released Serena, she smiled fully despite the tears in her eyes.

Mari came over and wrapped her arms around Keenan's torso in a hug. "Care well for my daughter, Highlander," she said smiling. Tears brightened her knowing eyes. She lowered her voice. "Be true to your heart, and don't give into death too easily." She poked him in the chest. "I want grandbabies."

Keenan's eyes mirrored his amazement at the Romany woman's nature. He smiled at her. "I will try na' to die."

"Good, good," Mari said then lowered her voice to the wisp of a whisper as she turned from him. "Because she will never marry your brother." But Keenan still heard her. The woman walked back toward Serena.

Nodding once more to King Will, Keenan went to Serena's mare to tie her bundle across its rump.

His men led their mounts toward him. Keenan pulled out two of the four scrolls clearing William's name of murder. One he had left with King Will, another he kept to give to William. He handed the third one to Brodick and fourth one to Thomas.

"Brodick, ye will ride with Gavin to the north and west. Thomas, ye will ride with Ewan to the north and east." His men looked confused.

"We doona travel to Kylkern?" Ewan asked.

"Serena and I travel to Kylkern," Keenan answered. "Ye," he indicated the men as he'd paired them, "ye will travel to every town on yer way to

Kylkern to show the local magistrate that William is innocent." He saw the question in their faces. "The Romany travel, and it would be best for them to have us spread the word before they encounter accusations. That is why King George sent me with four original parchments with his signature."

This excuse was authentic enough that Keenan did not have to supplement it with the real reason he wanted his men away from Serena. His new bride needed to learn what was in his mind through him, not through the skewed perceptions of their traveling companions.

He turned briskly toward his horse. "We will greet ye at Kylkern. Doona tarry. King George is making plans."

Thomas and Ewan took off at once. Brodick and Gavin walked over to Serena. Keenan tensed as he watched Brodick engulf her in a large hug, his massive body eclipsing her frame. The sight of another man wrapped around Serena brought every muscle in Keenan's body alert. With great restraint, Keenan stood his ground. Lucky for Brodick, he released her quickly. But then Gavin put his arms around her. Keenan strode over before he realized where he was headed. Gavin saw him and dropped his arms. "Only a farewell gesture," Gavin said a bit too quickly.

Keenan stopped, relaxing his hands that were fisted at his sides.

Brodick pulled a sword from his scabbard, flipped it and handed it to Keenan. "Since yers is gone, use mine to guard yer bride." Brodick looked to Serena. "She may be a warrior too, but her sword is puny."

Serena laughed. "I will miss you, Brodick," she looked to Gavin, "and you too. I look forward to greeting you at Kylkern."

Gavin and Brodick departed to the northwest.

Keenan led them along hills and narrow paths. Serena rode behind him when the path remained too narrow. They traveled in silence, broken only by her bird's chirping and an occasional sigh that escaped her.

Keenan looked toward the deepening sky. A granite boulder sat at the base of each tree.

"The gloaming is upon us. I ken a place to shelter for the night." Serena's large violet eyes shone with fear, but she nodded. A maiden's fear, perhaps? He would find out soon enough, as soon as he could find the clearing he knew hid among these trees. Where exactly was it?

Keenan led them off the narrow path into a woods budding with the warmth of the spring evening. "Aye, blackberry bushes, in full flower as usual," Keenan said to himself.

"What do you say up there?"

"Follow me, Serena. Let yer horse find her way through."

Keenan disappeared through a curtain of shrubs and trees. The blackberry blossoms flitted up into the air as a funnel of wind whipped them into a dance. They hovered before scattering around the perimeter of the ring of bramble, ash trees and ancient oaks. The trees reached upward into the deepening blue sky, swaying, their branches filled with newborn leaves, so green and eager.

"Isn't it too early for blackberry blossoms?" Serena called from behind.

"Just follow me," he said, as he pushed through the dense shrubs and grasses.

"Oh," she called and Keenan heard her pull on her skirts. "These thorns are catching me. They will harm the dress."

"Elenor will repair it. Just come through."

Keenan broke through the thick foliage into the clearing he knew was there, hidden in the small unpopulated forest. The first time he'd come across the odd clearing, he had wondered if it held magic. It certainly looked like a fairy ring the bards liked to sing about when visiting Kylkern. Tall oaks bent gnarled limbs up into the sky. They formed a nearly perfect circle around the clearing. Low ash trees spread their screening leaves at the height of a man riding a horse. Blackberry bushes billowed up out of the earth blocking entrance to all but the rabbits that grew fat on the berries, berries that grew year round. Moss pillowed the soft ground so one could lie back comfortably and stare at the stars as they moved across the open circle of sky overhead.

Keenan inhaled a full breath of clear air. Aye, the ring had to be enchanted. He'd stayed many nights in its sanctuary, nights when enemies hunted him, nights when he had no one to guard his sleep, but he had to succumb to slumber else lose his mind. He had never brought another person to this place. It had always been his alone, a sanctuary where he could sit and ask the stars about his fate. But tonight he brought Serena into its quiet refuge.

Serena dismounted in the cumbersome costume and smoothed her skirts before turning toward him. A gentle wind blew through the clearing encircling her with blossoms.

"Oh," she said in a hushed tone and raised her arms to allow the fragrant flowers to drift about her as if investigating a new arrival. Serena blinked several times and let her eyes wander around the darkening area. "By the Earth Mother," she whispered.

"Ye feel it."

Serena nodded. "What is it?"

"I thought ye might know." For he certainly didn't.

"It's like a hum, a hum of energy."

"Are there spirits here then? Anyone speaking to

ye, lass?"

Serena shook her head and walked around the mossy ground as the wind gentled. "No real voices, no real consciousness. It feels like it's warded." Serena turned back to him. "I think magic was practiced here at one time, long ago perhaps. Protective magic. Only the residue remains."

"Nothing dark then?"

"No," she closed her eyes and opened her arms to the sides as if opening herself up to the air around her. "It feels more like a cloak of protection."

Keenan nodded. "It's saved me before."

A small smile tipped her lips upward casting a playful look along the planes of her face as the last color of twilight vanished. "Perhaps we should stay here in this glade forever then. For we're in definite need of saving," she mused.

Keenan turned to the small ring of stones still at the center of the clearing where he'd left them last fall. "Hmmph, and hide away like a rabbit." He let out a quick snort as he gathered some sticks and crouched down to pull some dry peat from his satchel. "Nay, I am not Lachlan," he mumbled and cracked the flint and stone together. As night flooded the clearing with darkness, the fire's glow reached out to illume Serena where she still stood. Keenan leaned back on his heels. She stared at him, the smile gone.

"Nay," she said staring at him. "You are not Lachlan." His brother's name sounded bitter on her breath.

Keenan stood, sensing battle. "Serena, I..."

She held up her hand to stop him. "You don't need to explain your reasons, Keenan."

"Reasons?"

"Yes, your reasons for marrying me. I know you were as desperate as I was to get me away from Damin."

That much was true. "Aye," he said cautiously.

She frowned. Had he given the wrong answer? Serena moved closer to the growing fire and splayed her palms out to catch the first waves of warmth. Her eyes watched the flames. She spoke to the fire. "You married me to keep me from marrying another."

Also true. "Aye."

"You intend to take me up to your brother so that when you die, I will have to marry him."

"Serena…"

She turned abruptly toward him, her eyes sharp. "Don't deny it, Keenan. I read your plans through your men."

"Through my men."

She didn't answer, just glared at him, her arms crossing under her luscious breasts, plumping them upward. He couldn't deny it so he nodded instead.

"I suppose I said something about that to convince my men to accept my plan quickly. It was a tactical choice that made sense at the time. I had no intention of ye knowing about it."

Her eyes widened at his confirmation.

"A mistake on my part," he admitted. "I kent that ye couldna' read my thoughts, but the skewed thoughts of my men were easy to sense."

"So you admit saying that you are bringing me up to Lachlan, so that when you die, I can marry him?"

"Nay, I dinna say all of that. That is what my men inferred. I but said that if we wanted to bring you up to Kylkern it would be as my wife. The prophecy couldna' come true with ye married to Damin Yallow."

"You never mentioned your death?"

Keenan thought for a moment. He wouldn't start their marriage on lies. He spoke slowly. "I did say that the prophecy never specified if the witch had been married before and that if I died, the prophecy could still be fulfilled."

Serena's shoulders sagged. "So you still intend to die. You intend to leave me."

Keenan took two steps and caught her shoulders in his hands. He stared down at her until Serena slowly raised her gaze back to his.

"Before I met ye, all I thought about was staying alive to die." She tried to look down but he caught her chin with a finger beneath it. "But now that ye've entered my life, all I've been thinking about is staying alive to live my life, no matter how long or short it is." Keenan lowered his voice to a rough whisper in the still circle. "I want to live, Serena. I want to father children, I want to be more than a sacrifice for my clan, more than a wall of defense around my brother, more than a noble death as part of a long recited prophecy."

Serena's lips parted as her face remained upturned to him. Her warmth penetrated the linen of his shirt. "Forgive me, Serena, if I pulled ye away from yer life out of selfishness. But understand, I dinna do it for my clan, and definitely na' for my brother. I married ye for me." Keenan placed one hand against her chest where he felt the rapid pounding of her heart. He leaned in so that their hands lay trapped between their bodies. When she leaned in too, he smiled feeling his whole body relax. "Aye, I will die one day, Serena. But God willing, I will die after a good dose of living, with ye beside me." His lips brushed hers. "Let us start this eve. Let me love ye, Serena."

Her nod was almost unperceivable, but it was there. Permission granted, a truce given freely. Keenan's lips descended on her parted mouth. So warm, so soft, he nearly melted into her sweet, moist breath. The heat in her mouth surged through him as his mind moved to another part of her tender anatomy that he anticipated would be just as moist and hot. A lightning flash of masculine power surged down through him, hardening him. He tilted her head, twining his fingers through the ribbons still tied loosely in her hair. His tongue touched her lower lip timidly, testing while his hand moved down her back to cup her buttocks through heavy skirts.

Serena moaned and touched her own tongue to his. Again Keenan's muscles tensed in frustration at the costume that locked her supple body away from his touch. Without breaking the kiss, Keenan slid his hands in front and unbuttoned her jacket bodice, sliding it off her shoulders. His fingers shook with the exertion not to rip the gown from her.

He released her rigid stays. The peaks of Serena's breasts pushed upward as he hugged her, cradling her upper body. Next came her heavy skirts. The ties caught, the tight knots mocking him.

"Cut them," Serena breathed.

He severed the restricting ties with his dagger. A billow of cloth settled around Serena as the petticoats landed on the moss beneath their feet.

Serena stood in her silky shift, the thin white fabric lying seductively along the hills and valleys of her breasts, waist and hips. Keenan held his breath as Serena pulled the ties of her sleeves so that they fell in the voluminous cloud of green silk at her feet, leaving her slender shoulders bare except for the thin strap of lace at each shoulder. He stepped back to better view the landscape of her body where the silk ebbed and flowed like a sea of milk across her skin. She breathed deeply, her full breasts rising and falling, their erect peaks rubbing teasingly against the confines of the shift.

"Ye are so beautiful," Keenan murmured as he combed his fingers through her hair, freeing one of the ribbons. He watched the slender, milky column of her throat as she swallowed, his gaze moving back up to her wide eyes. Desire lurked there, but also fear. He cupped her cheek in his rough palm. He traced his thumb below her eye and looked deep.

"Ye ken the way a man makes love to a woman," he said and she nodded slowly.

"I've," she said and swallowed as if her throat were dry. "I've seen the minds of men before."

No wonder fear warred with desire. The minds of men could be violent in their lust. He pulled her close into the warmth of his arms and rested his chin on the softness of her hair. Keenan breathed deeply to calm the rush of his blood. "The minds of men, lass, are not always accurate and often lack the gentleness and respect that guides desire." He felt her tremble, from cold or fear?

"Stay here while I raise the fire."

"Isn't that dangerous?" She looked about the clearing.

Keenan found several dry branches under an old saddle blanket that he had left the last time he had visited. He threw them on the fire looking back over his shoulder at Serena's soft form reflecting the glow of firelight. "Not in this clearing." He indicated the thick bushes around them. "It seems to hide anyone it allows in." He stood up. "And tonight lass, we are its guests."

The fire caught greedily on the dry wood, and Keenan fed some fresher branches as well. It drove back the chill, and light bathed the clearing in cheery glow. Serena stared into the flames. She pulled off the other glove and held both hands out to the warmth. Keenan stood close but didn't touch her. Fear lurked in her face. She seemed so fragile, like a glass angel in her shimmering cocoon of silk.

As she moved her arms before the fire, catching the heat, Keenan remembered her dance. Even amongst the roughness of drunken men, Serena had found peace in the movements around the Romany bonfire.

"Dance Serena. Dance around the fire, into the calm oblivion that ye find around the flames."

She stared at him, her fear turning to confusion, and then to unease as she glanced between him and the waving flames.

He stepped back. "I willna touch ye while ye dance. It is yers alone, lass." He turned her by the shoulders, careful not to caress the skin that slid under his fingers. He let go and spoke low near her ear. "Close yer eyes, listen to the crackle of the wood, hear the flute and drum in yer mind. Find yer peace, lass."

He stepped back. The large oaks and ash trees swayed around them. The dark cool breath of night crept inward. Serena stood motionless.

Keenan took a deep breath and ran his hands over his face. *Foolish idea.* But then she stepped closer to the flame. Serena's head rolled to the side and back along her shoulders, her hair cascading down to her knees. As she leveled her gaze again on the flames, Keenan watched her naked arms rise up and over her head, her wrists mimicking the twists in the fire that licked upward into the crisp, clear night. He could see her profile flushed with fire heat. Her eyes were half closed.

Serena's hips moved slowly with her arms and she took a step, then another as she began to dance around the perimeter of the fire. As her body turned and canted, twisted and bowed in near perfect match to the dance of the flame, Keenan watched. She was a moonlit wood nymph bathed in fire glow, dancing in union with the scorching flame, taming it, worshipping it, becoming it.

In that magic-filled clearing with night falling around, Keenan felt something working within him as he watched the beautiful woman, his wife, dance. He began to hear the flute, the drum, the fiddle of her tribe playing a timeless tune, as timeless as the movement of flame, as timeless as the movement of a woman's body. The rhythm of nature and the magic that flows up from the earth itself.

Keenan felt bewitched, caught in Serena's spell. She held his breath hostage. Her body pulled but he forced himself to stand still, distant. He waited on the perimeter as she passed. Turning, her hair brushed against his arm. The pain in his groin rose higher into his chest as lust gave way to something stronger, deeper.

On she danced, around and around, her arms graceful, her steps floating as she skimmed the earth on her toes. The silk shift flared and twisted tight as she swiveled in arcs full of beauty and spirit.

Twice Keenan took a step out into her path, and twice he forced himself to recede. His breathing became more ragged as he followed her every turn, hoping with each circle that she would stop before him. As she passed him again, Keenan groaned low and turned his back to the heat to set his eyes on the sharp darkness that had descended around them. He sucked in the cool air, trying to force it down through his burning body. The fire blazed against his back, urging him to turn around again, enticing him to take her.

Keenan turned abruptly and stopped still. Serena stood there directly before him, her arms resting at her sides. He took a step toward her, his fists balled. Her eyes were open, without fear. Keenan raised his hand to touch her face, but stopped. She must come to him.

Serena stepped forward guiding her flushed cheek into his palm. He cupped it gingerly and rubbed his thumb across its smoothness.

"So warm, so soft," he murmured with an undercurrent of longing he could no longer hide. "So beautiful."

Serena closed her eyes and stepped into him, her form pressing into the contours of his hard body. She looked up at him. "Love me, Keenan Maclean. Wipe out the lies of other men's minds. Teach me the truth. Teach me about the pleasure I feel in your touch."

Time froze as Keenan stared down through her violet eyes into her heart. She trusted him, she loved him. He felt it as if they were his own emotions. Instead of shying away from the intensity, his chest released, filling his body with power. His blood raced, his heart battered against his chest. Keenan controlled the tremor in his hand as he moved it to the back of Serena's head and wound her hair, slowly, reverently. His other drew her even tighter against him, melding, making them one. Her softness in brilliant starkness against his own hardness.

Keenan's lips met hers and she opened under him. He groaned and tilted her head to gain better access to her sweet taste. He felt her small plea against his mouth and pulled back. Passion glazed her eyes.

"Keenan," she breathed.

He picked her up and carried her to the pallet he had laid beside the fire on a soft mound of moss. Several blankets lay nearby to chase the chill once the fire died down in the night. He lowered her and pulled his linen shirt from over his head.

Serena's eyes washed over his muscles and down his chest. Keenan leaned forward, his arms coming down on either side as he supported his weight above her. She was trapped, captured within his circle of strength. Keenan kissed her, tasted her, explored her until Serena groaned against his mouth. Her hands roamed his skin, lower still until she reached his hardness. The timid touch through his trews culled a roar from deep down out of

Keenan, and he rolled to his side to strip quickly out of the rest of his clothing.

He knelt beside her, naked and fully male in the warm glow of firelight. He watched her cover him with her eyes, lingering on him for a moment. Her perusal fueled his own desire. Keenan touched the edge of her shift ready to pull it up, when a glint of fear dampened the desire in her eyes.

"Och, lass. Doona fear me." He bent down over her for a sweet kiss then moved over to her ear, touching it teasingly with his hot breath. "Let yerself go."

Keenan felt her breaths quicken, and he kissed her again before teasing a hot trail along the delicate lines of her neck. His hand cupped her breast, and he began to roll her nipple through the silk. Serena moaned and he worked his mouth down to the searching peak, sucking it tight through the damp fabric.

"Keenan," she murmured and then gasped as he grazed his teeth against the sensitive flesh. His hand rubbed and massaged along her leg under her shift, pushing the fabric higher until he reached her hip.

His hand smoothed over the soft roundness of her abdomen, pausing to dip into her navel. Keenan continued to raise the shift until the thin fabric pulled over Serena's head breaking the kiss. The shift caught Serena's hands for a moment, holding them hostage extended above her. The flickering flames glowed against her flawless skin.

Serena's round breasts stood full and erect, rising and falling with her breaths. Keenan's eyes traveled down along the slope of her torso to the soft amber curls at the juncture of her legs. His gaze came back up to the birthmark on Serena's stomach. He released her hands and touched the unique mark.

"The dragonfly." He kissed it tenderly. Serena shivered and he lay back next to her, his hands stroking her exposed skin. She stared back into his eyes and nodded. "Na' tingling along it right now?" he asked in reference to the spirit crone.

"No tingling there." A small smile crept onto Serena's lips. "Perhaps there is some tingling elsewhere."

"Lass," he drawled out in his deep burr. "When I'm loving ye, ye will tingle everywhere." He kissed her forehead. "From the top of yer sweet hair," he ran his parted lips along her throat, down between her breasts until he crouched, placing feathery kisses on her stomach. He looked up. "To the soft skin over yer womb." He ran his finger from her naval down to the soft curls at the vee of her legs. "To yer sweet, slick lips," he said and watched her as his fingers gained entrance to her heat. Her eyes fluttered nearly closed, and she moaned softly. "To the tips of yer curled toes, ye will tingle." He began to work his fingers, moving between the wet folds against her nub and then inside to a most sensitive spot. She moaned louder and closed her eyes.

"Nay, Serena, keep yer eyes open. I want to see yer passion."

Serena's eyes, dark and sultry, opened to watch. Keenan's muscles bunched within him. She was ready and he could no longer wait to feel himself within her.

Without stopping the purposeful stokes below, Keenan laid on his side next to her. His thumb rubbed rhythmically against her sensitive nub and he bent his head to catch a peak between his lips. She gasped, arching up against him.

"Keenan, please...please." She was lost in the storm brewing within her body. Her skin flushed and dewy, warm and soft yet seemed strung as tight as Keenan felt.

"Aye, wife, let it come." His ragged breath moved back up to her ear. "Let me hear yer pleasure."

Serena's eyes closed as she threw her head toward the blankets. A deep, resonating sound, somewhere between a moan and a scream came up through her to fill the clearing. Keenan's fingers continued to move in the flooded folds while her body pulsed. Before it completely ebbed, he moved above her.

In one swift motion, Keenan pushed himself inside her at the same time his lips met hers. His tongue moved intimately inside her as he drove through her maiden's barrier, fully claiming her as his own. She tensed for a moment and he stilled, fully embedded within her sensuous frame.

Keenan kissed her, his hands stroking through her hair, waiting until she grew accustomed to his intrusion. His forehead beaded with sweat as he fought to remain still within her tight passage. Slowly he felt her relax as he kissed the side of her long, smooth neck.

"Does it feel better now, Serena?" he asked as he pulled back to see her eyes.

"Aye, it does," she said mimicking his brogue and pressed her hips gently upward. "Except that ye arena' movin'."

Her teasing lilt was also reflected in her eyes. It was all the permission Keenan needed. Serena rose upward again.

"Prepare to tingle, lass," he said, his own teasing tone all but ruined by the rough need rushing within him. A need to move within her, to sweep her up with him. Breathing rapidly, he captured her mouth again and moved. Slow at first, but as Serena increased her rhythm, he took over. She moaned under his weight, meeting him with unexpected strength. Keenan felt her body begin to clench as his own body neared the precipice.

"Open yer eyes, Serena lass," he ground out while grabbing a length of Maclean plaid lying next to them. He slowed their rhythm as he wound her hand and his together in the wool. Glazed and liquid, her eyes stared back to him.

"Before the stars, within this enchanted place, I claim ye, Serena. I bind ye to me, I bind ye with my body," he growled, circling his hips and grinding into her. She moaned, her eyes closing and then opening. He stopped until she focused again on him. He leaned down to her lips. "And I bind ye with my heart." His breath mingled with hers. "Do ye claim me lass?" he asked still not moving despite her attempts to continue.

She nodded. "Keenan, please."

"Say it, lass, the words," he gritted out, his last bit of strength obstructing the tide within his straining body.

"I claim you, Keenan Maclean, I claim you with my body," she said and Keenan thrust deeply, ripping a scream from her. She grabbed the back of his hair, her nails biting into the sides of his head, and pulled his lips down toward hers. She pierced him with her eyes as her climax began to crest. "I claim you, Keenan Maclean, with my heart," she yelled. All her passion erupted, pouring through her, pulling along his shaft.

Keenan pounded into her, all control gone, lost to the crashing wave of ecstasy that now toppled over him. His roar thundered through the clearing as he filled her, following her into bliss.

****

The blaze behind Keenan relaxed into that of a normal fire, and Serena curled contentedly in his arms. Keenan cocooned them in the blanket on a pallet of moss. Serena nuzzled into the side of him, exhausted. He kissed her forehead and she sighed in her sleep.

His one free arm pillowed his head as he stared up at the clear night sky ringed by the trees. Stars glittered in the inky blackness, unblocked by clouds. One star shot across the circle. Keenan followed its wide arc until it disappeared. A shooting star.

Elenor had told him as a child that he must wish upon every shooting star he witnessed. She said that they were magic and would grant him his wish. For decades he had watched stars trail across the wide skies of Britain, but had never once wished upon one. For Keenan Maclean didn't know what his wish should be.

Should he wish to defend and die quickly, without prolonged agony? It didn't seem right to wish for death, it went against the warrior in him that battled. Should he wish to live a long life? A life full of missed opportunities because he refused to fully live knowing that he was meant to die. That would be a torture much worse than death. So instead, he just followed them with his eyes as they shot across the night, watching him, listening perhaps for his wish, a wish that never came. Until tonight.

Serena murmured contentedly in her sleep, rubbing her leg across his thighs. Keenan pulled her closer and caressed her hair, while his eyes searched the circle above. There, off to the right, another one. His hand stopped in a soft tangle as he watched. The star blazed a trail across his view, its tail so bright it seemed to etch the darkness. Keenan's breath caught as he watched the pinprick of light begin to fade. For the first time in his life, there in that magic-filled clearing, Keenan Maclean, second son of the Macleans of Kylkern, wished upon a shooting star.

Chapter 14

"Caoch!" Drakkina cursed as she hurled a flash of energy at the brass basin of swirling water, causing it to pitch off the granite slab at the center of ten stone monoliths. The water soaked into the tall grass. Drakkina kicked her hazy foot at a clump of yellow wildflowers. The flowers waved as her foot passed through them.

"Caoch! Where are they?" she yelled into the wind whipping through the circle where once Gilla and Druce's house had stood near the western shore of Scotland's Highlands. All that remained was the hearthstone and the stone altar. The altar had once served as their table at the center of their cottage. It was a table built for purpose, built with magic. Drakkina collapsed upon it, resting her cheek against its cool solid structure. At least the magic alter held her form.

Self pity rolled through her, mixed with frustration. "They married, that should be enough," she growled up at the passing clouds. "And now they've disappeared," she grumbled and looked back down at the tumbled brass scrying bowl. She tapped her gnarled finger on her full lip. "Where could Serena and her mate have disappeared to? The demons?" Drakkina frowned, but then shook her head. "They have no idea in what time she's hidden." Drakkina shook her head again, slipping her loose indigo veil off her gray hair to fall around her shoulders. "Serena and Keenan are still here somewhere, just hidden right now. Hidden by some other power, not Serena's. The child doesn't know enough yet to hide from me. There's magic all over this world that she could have slipped within." Drakkina frowned. "My pull on her has also been severed."

The sun grew heavy and began to drop toward the horizon. If she listened deeply, Drakkina could just make out the roar of waves hitting the beaches beyond the stones and pines. She sighed. "If I can't look to find them, perhaps I can scry a bit into their future." Drakkina focused a thread of energy out of the center of her wrinkled palm toward the abused basin. The bowl teetered in the tall grass, slowly rising up to sit once again on the stone table. She closed her eyes, imagining the small brook not too far from the circle. Once again Drakkina threaded her power to the brook, gathering a fistful of water, pulling it through the trees, past the stones and back to hover over the basin. As she released the water into the bowl, she leaned against the table. "Don't be so quick this time to knock it over," she chastised herself. "This is no time to waste energy."

She covered her hair once again with the thin shawl and peered past the small pool reflecting the deepening sky above. "Once again then, but a little different to search for what is to come," she murmured and threaded her power in an intricate weave above the water. Once the colors lay in a perfect pattern hovering in the air, Drakkina lowered her hand and the woven magic lowered onto the surface of the water in the brass basin. The colors swirled across the slick surface, bending and mixing. Drakkina watched, her breath shallow as she waited for the images to coalesce into something meaningful. "Speak to me of Serena and her mate," she whispered, her breath reaching the shadowy surface. "Show me what is to come of them."

Images began to collect on the surface. Serena and Keenan kissing. Drakkina smiled. Then Keenan charging off into a battle, gun smoke, blood curling around his figure as he grimaced in pain. Serena's image appeared, sobbing.

"No, no." Drakkina yelled at the water. "This can't be their future. They are wed now, bound to one another. She loves him, I heard her confess it."

The images swirled apart melding into others. Serena and Keenan smiled at three grown children who rushed into their arms. Bountiful orchards, fluffy fat sheep. Then the image changed. Serena held a wee baby against her while she cried, clinging to a grave marker. Lachlan appeared, spitting angry words, then hiding, then charging.

Drakkina shook her head silently. Keenan's image appeared again, throwing himself before his brother. Keenan turning from the battlefield, fear changing his face to stone. Serena laying in a pool of blood as it gushed from her belly.

On and on the images swirled under Drakkina's tense stare. When the images began to repeat, she took a deep breath in and closed her eyes, releasing the scrying spell. "It's no use. The future's still not firmly set. No matter how hard I look, I only see possibilities."

Drakkina leaned back. "Caoch," she whispered. "What more can I do to force this love between them? I threw them together by sending William toward the bridge when Grant was killed. I trapped them in the cave. I cleared up their problem with William. I chased away that gypsy man before he could take more than kisses from her. I even altered time so Keenan could reach Serena before her idiot father forced her to marry the other." Drakkina tilted her head to the side. "Which was very tricky by the way."

She floated off the table. "But does anyone care or appreciate my help? No," she said dramatically to the surrounding stones.

"Love, it should be easy enough to orchestrate," she flapped her hands through the air as she frowned. "Get each daughter to find their mates and fall in love," she shrugged. "That's all I have to do." She began to pace through the tall waving grasses. "That and get them here," she glanced around at the calm clearing. Drakkina tied her cowl under her chin. "Before the demons rip the threads that hold each time in its proper place." She looked out past the stones again and sighed dramatically. "Get them to love one another?" Drakkina snorted. "I can't even find them."

****

Serena woke to the heavenly smell of roasting rabbit mixed with campfire and sweet spring air. Her stomach growled, bringing her fully awake. She rolled onto her back and stretched before opening her eyes to blue sky above her encircled by large oaks. Memories of the night before ran from her mind down into her body. Her hand moved under the Maclean blanket. She was still naked and a bit tender. Without moving further, Serena turned her head toward the fire and smiled.

Keenan wore only his boots and trews as he crouched down turning the hare over a low smoldering flame. Through the fog of wood smoke, Serena could see his eyes. They held mischief, and yes, happiness.

"Ye're awake finally, lass." Keenan stood up, and Serena swallowed hard as her eyes traveled across his naked torso and chest.

She rose up on one elbow as she held the blanket against her breasts.

"In time to break yer fast on roast hare and blackberries."

He kicked at some of the blackened branches to scatter the flame and walked over to her. Serena glanced around for her clothes but didn't see them.

Keenan reached under her arms and lifted her up to stand. Serena yelped, trying to grab the blanket before it fell away. Keenan chuckled deep and wrapped Serena in his warm hug while his free hand tucked the blanket. He stepped back but kept his hands on her bare shoulders, his thumb massaging the tense muscles stretching from shoulder to neck.

Serena couldn't stop her blush. It was one thing to be naked with him in the muted glow of firelight. Serena had never thought herself shy, but after what they'd shared last night, she had trouble meeting his gaze. So she stared at the hollow at the base of his strong neck where she could make out the faint beat of his heart.

"I overslept, I suppose."

Keenan used his finger to lift her chin, his eyes sparkling with mischief. "Mmmm, ye were up late last eve." He ran his hand across her cheek and into her tangled hair. "Ye have the look of a lass properly tupped."

Before she could frown at him he bent to kiss her. Serena's stiffness melted as soon as his lips covered hers. It was a slow kiss, unhurried, gentle. He pulled his face away as if they had all the time in the world to just taste one another, breathe in one another.

A gentle breeze cooled Serena's bare backside. She gasped, looking down. The blanket crumpled at her ankles. Before she could bend to pick it back up, Keenan pulled her up, his hands stroking down her back, her breasts pushed up branding his hot naked skin. She felt his length press along her belly and her nipples hardened as his fingers cupped together under her round backside. The bright light and the twittering birds around them began to fade away in Serena's mind. Warmth pooled in her abdomen. Desire wrapped around her limbs, filling her with languid heat. When he lifted to mold her tingling body against him, she moaned.

He pulled away from her lips and rested his forehead against hers. "Och Serena, I want ye."

"You have me," she whispered.

His hand moved between them to cup one of her breasts. His gaze narrowed with a fierce heat as he stared. Then he lowered his eyes and gave a frustrated sigh before bending down to pull the blanket up to wrap her tightly.

"It would hurt ye so soon after last night."

Serena frowned. "You mean we can't…" she indicated the mossy pallet that had been their bed last night.

Keenan smiled broadly. "Doona fash yerself, lass. I'll be loving ye soon enough." He adjusted himself in the tight trews and went to pull the hare off the spit. "We are getting a late start this morning, and I have a waterfall I'd like to show ye by this evening."

Serena sat down to pull apart some of the tender meat. Keenan handed her a cup full of fresh blackberries.

"Blackberries, this early? They don't fruit until summer," she questioned as she popped one of the plump berries into her mouth.

Keenan sat down next to her. "It's a mystery." He shook his head as he studied the little bumps on the outside of the fruit. "No matter what time of year I come here, there are always plump purple blackberries." Keenan popped the thoroughly inspected berry into his mouth and chewed. He leaned back on his wrists, the muscles in his shoulders cording under his weight. Serena took a steadying breath and looked out at the trees.

"Huh," she said several minutes later.

"What is it?"

She tilted her head at him. "I don't feel the pull I usually have, the one that pulls me West."

"Ye dinna walk in yer sleep last night, but I thought that was because ye were a wee bit exhausted." Keenan chuckled when Serena's face reddened. "Wife, I foresee many long nights. Perhaps we need to work in a nap time for ye."

Serena threw a blackberry at him and it broke against his forehead leaving a purple juice mark. She laughed at his shocked expression and then squealed when a volley of plump berries came her way. She jumped up, clutching the blanket and ran around to the other side of the clearing to catch another handful of berries from the bursting bush. Within minutes the two of them were covered with the sticky sweet juice.

Keenan raised his hands in surrender. "I'm unarmed, lass."

Laughing, Serena dropped the few remaining berries she had in her now purple hand. She tucked the end of the blanket into the valley of her breasts and walked into his open arms. She stuck her tongue out and licked a purple blotch on the inside of Keenan's bicep. It was sweet and tangy and mixed with the fresh pine and leather smell that was Keenan.

Keenan's deep laughter stopped abruptly as her tongue continued down his arm licking at the little purple marks. She saw another one out of the corner of her eye on his chest and moved her mouth over to it. Her lips closed over the sticky juice while her tongue swirled around his smooth skin. She closed her eyes. His skin felt hot and stretched as if over granite. As she moved over to the purple splotch on one of his nipples, she felt his body jerk. His hands closed around her shoulders. The sweet juice lay sticky against his skin. Serena swirled her tongue around his nipple until she couldn't taste any remains of blackberry.

"Serena," he gritted out. "Ye doona ken what ye

are doing to me."

She trailed licks across to his other nipple, her hands stroking up the sides of Keenan's naked torso. "Perhaps I know exactly what I'm doing." Her words came out mumbled as she spoke against him. Keenan's large hands released her shoulders and moved to gently grasp her head. He groaned low in his throat, so low that she could feel its vibrations through his chest.

"Serena lass, a man can only stand so much of that before," his words turned into another groan as she trailed her tongue down his chest.

Serena couldn't help the smile that turned up the corners of her lips as she laved at another purple splotch under the fine sprinkling of hair in the center of his tight chest. He was enjoying this. She could hear it in the rush of his breath and feel it in the rigid length of his body. He was enjoying this greatly, and she was in control. What wonderful power she had over him, she thought and leaned up on her toes to kiss a blackberry mark in the beating hollow of his throat. His pulse pounded beneath her tongue as she dragged it across the valley.

Keenan's arms circled, pulling her up against the strength that lay beneath his hot skin. She felt his hardness seek the juncture of her thighs through the Maclean blanket. She relaxed her arms, letting the fabric slide down to her hips where it remained pinned between them.

Keenan reached both his hands to hold her face and tilt it up to meet his lips. Serena opened her eyes. What she saw sent a bolt of hot giddiness through her. Untamed heat glazed Keenan's eyes. His hard jaw flexed as if his strong will alone kept him from devouring her in one bite.

As he slanted across her already wet sweet mouth, Serena's last coherent thought was that she had been so wrong. She was not in control of this powerful man. The fire she had kindled began to blaze out of control.

Keenan's lips seared her as he tangled hands through her hair. She had just baited a lion and she was about to be consumed. Keenan loosed the rest of the blanket while leaving her lips to run his hot mouth down the side of her neck. Serena panted softly into the soft waves of his dark hair as his mouth claimed one of her breasts. His desire rolled through, bringing her own senses to a boil. Whether through some magic connection or through touch alone, she felt his passion as her own climbed to meet it, to embrace it, to build upon it. Yes, she had baited a lion and he was ready to swallow her, she thought as she sank to her knees before him. Never before had prey looked so forward to being eaten alive.

****

Lachlan Maclean paced before the dying flames in the great hearth. He watched the shadows play against the stone walls hung with polished shields, axes and swords. His father's broadsword, his grand da's shield. They hung there, a place of honor after days of battle. They hung there waiting, waiting for him to take them up. He sighed heartily and took another gulp of the fine mulled wine Elenor had brought him after the messenger had ridden away.

Lachlan glanced back at the table where several Maclean warriors stood, where the missive lay curled exactly where he'd left it. He saw Elenor where she still watched him. His beautiful sister, so lovely and yet none was brave enough to marry her. He turned his stare to the tapestries overhead, their threads woven and needled to depict great scenes of Macleans defending Kylkern, Macleans knee deep in battle defending their family, their people.

Would anyone ever take month after month to needle a depiction of him, Chief Lachlan, son of

Angus, into a tapestry? What would it look like? Would it be of him hiding behind the locked doors to his rooms, or him fleeing down one of the secret passageways saved to evacuate the women and children? Perhaps there would be a magnificent tapestry woven to depict him clutching behind his beautiful sister's skirts.

Lachlan rested his forehead against the back of his hand on the mantel. He looked down into the brittle logs, licked black with flame. More likely there would be a tapestry of his brother, Keenan, standing in front of him, his sword raised to protect him, as his duty demanded.

Hamish, his friend from childhood, came to stand beside him at the hearth. "What answer do we send, Lachlan?"

Keeping his forehead against his hand, Lachlan turned his gaze to his friend. "Do we ken where my brother is?"

"Nay, but I've sent a scout down our usual route toward England."

"One scout?"

"Aye, I dinna dare send more in case we need to ride quickly."

Lachlan nodded, rubbing the top of his hair against his hand. He turned his head again so his eyes could study Hamish. "What say the men," he said glancing toward the standing warriors on the other side of the room.

"They are ready to chase the English from our soil and raise Prince Charles to his rightful place. They but wait for word from ye and for Keenan to return."

Lachlan shifted away from the mantel. "Keenan, they but wait for Keenan." Lachlan held his voice down, but softness could not cloak the sharp edge in his tone.

"And yer word, Lachlan. Ye are our chief."

"Chief in name only," Lachlan forced out from clenched teeth.

Hamish did not answer for a long moment. "Chief Maclean, we wait yer word."

Lachlan turned to the bowing man and then looked out toward the rest of the room. "Send word that we arm ourselves to join the call to Drumossie Moor." His voice filled the rafters with its force.

"To Culloden!" the men echoed, raising their swords to stab high into the air.

Lachlan turned to Hamish. "Send the answer to the MacDonalds that we ride in three days to meet them at Culloden. We will lay camp on the fifteenth."

"And Keenan?" Hamish asked.

"Keenan can come along if he makes it in time. Otherwise, I will lead this clan into battle."

Hamish hesitated just long enough for Lachlan to narrow his eyes. A challenge.

"Aye, Lachlan," Hamish answered. He turned on his heal and headed for the door, his men behind him.

Lachlan turned back to the fire as Elenor walked over to stand beside him. She placed her soft hand on his rigid shoulder, but didn't say anything at first.

Lachlan kicked at the logs and several sparks shot out, crackling in the thick silence.

"Very brave, brother," she said. "Perhaps foolish, but very brave."

Lachlan lurched and kicked the stone hearth. Elenor jumped back. "Doona pass judgment on my actions, sister," he hissed before throwing himself into one of the two chairs flanking the fire.

Elenor didn't retreat, but remained standing. Lachlan looked at the palms of his hands. They were supple. He rubbed them together. "They are like hands of a woman," he said softly.

Elenor sat down next to him and took his hand in hers. She didn't say anything, just ran her fingers along his palm. He looked up to her. "They should be rough, calloused, Elenor. Not soft like a maid's." He pulled it back and put his face in his hands, leaning forward with his elbows on his knees.

"Dear God, Elenor, what have I been doing with my life?" The fire cracked and wheezed.

"Hiding," she said simply.

Anger surged through him only to crash down as he recognized the truth in her word.

"Hiding," he repeated and scrubbed at his face. "Aye, that I have."

He looked up to Elenor and straightened in the chair. "But I've finally found the witch. Perhaps I can stop hiding."

Elenor frowned. "Serena's not here."

"But she was, and she will return."

"With Keenan?"

"Aye, of course," he began and hesitated, wondering at her question. "Keenan will bring her back." Lachlan's frown increased. "My brother kens his duty."

"Just as ye ken yer duty to hide, Lachlan?"

"What do ye hint at, Elenor. I grow weary of reading behind words."

"Just this, how would we all act, who would we all be, if we weren't ruled by the prophecy? Would ye hide here watching yer friends grow in valor and strength? Nay. Would I wither away as an old maid?" She tipped her head to the side and smiled. "Perhaps," she teased. "But perhaps ye would have wed me off long ago so I wouldn't plague ye so, brother."

Lachlan clapped his hand down over hers but did not release his frown.

She continued more seriously. "Would Keenan spend his whole life obsessed with protecting ye, only to die without having ever lived?"

Lachlan caught his breath at the tear swelling the rim of Elenor's eye. He watched it grow until it broke free to race down her cheek. Leaning forward, he caught it on his finger.

"Or," she continued ignoring her tear. "Or would there be bairns filling the nursery and young lads and lasses laughing through these grand halls, playing out the stories of bravery, stories about two great brothers, strong and cunning." She sat back to look into the dying fire. "Aye, Lachlan," she sighed. "I wonder how different things would be if we had never heard a single word of our prophecy."

Lachlan let her hand go and looked up again at his father's sword. He had raised it upon the wall at his da's death. Keenan already had his own sword, from his seanair. That sword on the wall was meant for him, Lachlan.

Lachlan jumped up from the chair. He felt Elenor's eyes as he picked up a stool from against the wall to move it under the sword. Climbing up, he placed his two hands under it, careful not to slice them on the blade. It took a little force to wrench the weapon from its slumber in the hooks. He curled his hands around the smooth leather wrapped hilt and stepped down.

Lachlan turned, sword pointed upward. Elenor stood by the chair, her smile at odds with the tears running freely down her cheeks.

"It looks good in yer hands, Lachlan," she said and sniffed.

Lachlan swung it slowly in a low arc. "Three days, Elenor. I have three days to learn to swing Da's sword."

She came up to lay her hand on his arm. "Yer a Maclean, Lachlan. The feel for it runs in yer blood."

He nodded and turned the weapon slowly catching the firelight along the polished steel.

"Da is smiling down from heaven, Lachlan. I know he is." She was crying again.

Lachlan lowered the sword, tip to the floor and put his arm around her shoulders. "Da smiling? Da never smiled. When he was happy, he just bellowed softer."

Elenor laughed through her tears and hugged Lachlan. "I love ye, Brother."

He hugged her again, and then took the sword up again. "And I love ye, Elenor." The heaviness of the sword ripped through him, causing all the hairs in his body to come alive. He gave a shout, a battle cry in the sleepy hall.

Elenor laughed and shushed him.

"Na' quiet this eve, Sister. I am off to ride."

"It's dark, Lachlan."

"Aye, and a fine night for a ride with my sword."

Lachlan left her as he strode to the door. For once no one stood behind him with words of caution. He was done hiding, done being the Maclean coward. Lachlan Maclean had three days. And he planned to live every minute to its fullest.

****

Keenan walked his horse over to Serena's and mounted. "Doona look so sad, wife. We'll return someday," he said, as he too looked around the soft, mossy ground. His words held hope for their future, but something in his tone made it sound more like a goodbye. He turned his eyes on her.

"It's a special place, Keenan. Thank you for sharing it with me."

He smiled. "It's our special place now." He reached out and squeezed her hand before nudging his horse forward out through the thorny bramble.

As they rode out of the dense clearing Serena noticed a shift in the wind. She shivered against it and pulled the blanket closer around her. She sucked in her breath so quickly that Keenan turned in his seat.

"What is it?"

"The pull," she said holding tight to the mane of her horse. "The pull to the west is so great it nearly yanked me from my horse." Serena looked directly west, feeling the tight thread pull sharply from her birthmark. She rubbed her hand across it through the layers of her shift, stays, bodice, and the blanket.

Keenan reigned in so that he sat next to her. She looked at him. "I feel that we must both go west," she said, staring into his eyes, trying to convince him of something she didn't even understand. "Like it is the most important thing in the world for us to go," she paused. "Together."

Keenan's frown turned in that direction. "I'm not sure, but I think I feel something also."

"You do?"

"Aye, like a tug telling me exactly which way west lies."

"What do we do?"

Keenan looked out through the tree line that broke onto rolling hills that would eventually lead them to the sea. He slowly shook his head. "After we return to Kylkern, then we will see what lies to the west."

Serena's stomach turned, and she took some steadying breaths to focus her shields against the tug. Something or someone was pulling with all their might to bring her, to bring them, west. Keenan's hand grasped her upper arm, and she opened her eyes.

"Are ye well, lass? Do ye need to ride with me?"

Once she fortified the wall around her, Serena felt better. She smiled timidly. "It takes a bit more concentration to prevent me from galloping off in that direction," she tipped her head west. "But I am well."

Keenan didn't like that answer and swiftly

pulled her onto his horse. He leaned back to tether Serena's mount to follow his. "We'll ride together, then. I have no time to be chasing ye across Britain."

Serena's head bumped his chin slightly as she settled against his hard chest. "So you would chase me?" she teased.

His arms came around hers like warm iron. "Yer mine, in the eyes of the church, and with our vows in the clearing, yer mine before the stars and before God, lass. Aye, I'd chase ye."

Serena smiled up into his serious eyes. "Then you best chain me to your side tonight else I walk all the way to the sea."

She turned and felt his breath hot against her head as he chuckled into her hair. Then he leaned down to her ear, his lips just skimming the tender ridge. "I'll be sure to tire ye out then, lass, so exhaustion will hold ye in place by my side."

His threat, spoken so intimately caused a ripple of giddy excitement to run down her neck and into her body. Serena leaned back into him and enjoyed the ride. She closed her eyes to rest, a smile played across her face as she thought of the long night ahead in his arms.

****

Icy mountain water rushed into a pool below, raising a mist of colors within the secluded glade. Sharp, thin slices of ice jutted out from the high peak where the water crested to fall. Serena shivered, looking at the freezing majesty of water nature before her. She leaned back into the warmth of Keenan's chest as they stared at the beauty. She felt him move, his arms tightening around her, his breath hot at her ear.

"Ready for a swim?"

Serena twisted in his grasp until she caught his gaze and saw the teasing glint that revealed his jest. "To swim in that would be a wish for death," she retorted with a sarcastic smile.

Keenan's arm extended past her to point at a flat rock on the other side of the pool. "There, the rock bakes with the sun in the summer. A perfect place for a nap." He kissed her ear lightly causing Serena to tilt her head at the ticklish sensations. "Secluded, warm, rushing water to hide yer lusty screams."

She twisted again to look at him. "My lusty screams? I remember some ferocious roars that left my ears ringing," she teased back but her fierce blush didn't back up her boldness.

Keenan laughed out loud. "Aye, ye bring it out of me, lass," he said kissing her upturned mouth. He turned her slowly in his arms without breaking contact. After a few minutes he broke the kiss and looked at her.

Serena saw joy lurking in his eyes, joy to match her own. Over the last four days, she had watched Keenan transform as they loved one another thoroughly through their journey. Serena had kissed out every last bit of sadness and hopelessness she had seen before in him. In their place she now found an easy laughter and genuine smile that crinkled the little lines at the corner of his gray eyes. They were beautiful eyes, sparked with life. She stared into them and smiled.

"What goes through yer beautiful head, lass?"

"I hope our children have your eyes."

For a moment, Keenan's teasing smile faltered, and a slow one of warmth and contentedness replaced it. He spoke low and cupped her cheek with his palm. "Our children will be beautiful." He kissed her lightly and pulled back. "Our sons will have my strength and cunning." Serena laughed at his boast. "Our daughters will have yer beauty."

"And perhaps my magic?"

Keenan frowned briefly before nodding. "Aye, if

they do ye will teach them to protect themselves. To use it for good and to not let it rule their lives. "

Serena's eyes blurred a bit with her tears as she smiled up at Keenan. Here was the man who accepted her for all that she was. Even when they were surrounded by intrigue in the middle of English court, he never asked her to use her powers to discover plots or make mischief to better himself. He'd never tried to manipulate her or anyone else. In fact, he'd never once asked her to read anyone, only to alert them to danger. Keenan Maclean was a good man, the man she loved with all her being.

Keenan dismounted and lifted her to the ground. He pulled the blanket from the rolled pallet and spread it for them to eat their evening meal upon. Serena watched the muscles in his back stretch beneath the thin weave of his shirt. She blushed remembering how she had come up behind him to run her tongue between his shoulder blades that morning before they left their latest camp. Her sneak attack had delayed them two more hours. Although, he didn't seem to mind overmuch.

Serena sighed. Would Kylkern welcome them? What would Keenan say to Lachlan? How should she act? Several times the conversation had come around to their homecoming, for she thought of Kylkern as her home now. Each time the subject came up, silence fell between them. Neither one was willing to break the spell of happiness that had begun in the magical clearing.

As if sensing the change in her mood, or perhaps reading the tone in her sigh, Keenan looked over his shoulder from where he sat on the blanket. He patted the spot near him and leaned back on his wrists as Serena kneeled down in the spot.

"I've been thinking, Serena, about where we will live."

"Not at Kylkern?"

Keenan crossed his ankles in a gesture of ease, but Serena could see a small furrow across his brow. "I was thinking that we might want a bit more privacy." He smiled wickedly at her, but Serena was not fooled.

"Do you think we won't be welcome at Kylkern?"

Keenan shrugged slightly, his smile faltering at her words. "It's a possibility, Serena. The whole clan thinks ye are for Lachlan, except Elenor."

Somehow the reminder that Keenan's sweet sister would not hate her and Keenan for wedding, felt like a warm balm through Serena. Serena lowered her voice so that it was almost inaudible over the rush of falling water.

"And do you still believe that I'm meant for Lachlan, Keenan?"

Keenan looked deep into her eyes. She dared not blink for fear of missing some unspoken communication. After a moment, Keenan shook his head slowly. "Nay lass, I feel ye in my bones, Serena." He touched her cheek lightly while she held her breath. "I burn for ye from my loins all the way to my heart." He let out a long sigh, as if he'd been holding his breath all his life. "I doona understand the way of the prophecy, but I ken that I would kill Lachlan myself if he were to try and take ye from me now. Tha gaol agam ort, Serena," he said in thick Gaelic. "I love ye, Serena."

Serena had felt his love in every caress, every kiss, every touch of her hair, but he had not said the words. Until now. Tears poured as she leaned forward to kiss him.

"I love you too, Keenan."

Keenan quirked a grin on his face. "So I've heard."

Serena laughed lightly. "Brodick?"

"Aye, and Ewan."

She blushed. "It's true," she said falling forward

into him, knowing that he would catch her. After many long kisses, Keenan leaned back on his elbow as they lay before the small fire he had built near the edge of the blanket.

Serena watched Keenan quickly clean and spit another hare for their dinner. Her voice broke the silence. "So we will live outside Kylkern then?"

Keenan glanced at her and then back to the fire as he rigged the hare over it. "There is a vacant cottage on the edge of the village before the castle. It is sound, and I could build onto it."

Serena felt her pulse pick up speed. "A house? Where I could raise a small vegetable garden?"

He smiled over his shoulder. "If we are welcome at Kylkern, aye, then we will live there. I wouldn't want to stay in the castle, welcome or not. No privacy and the tension may be tiring until Lachlan gets used to the idea of ye being married to me. It took a lifetime for him to find ye, it may take him the rest of his lifetime to give ye up. I wouldn't have us live under that."

Serena turned back around. "I married a wise man."

Keenan snorted and stood up. "For someone so wise, I've never been so unsure of the future in all my life."

"We'll figure it out together." She sighed happily. "And to think, I will have a house, my very own house, without wheels."

Keenan's laughter rumbled and he sat back down with her on the blanket.

"I will grow herbs in one section," Serena grabbed a small stick and knelt at the edge of the blanket to draw in the dirt. "Cabbages too." Serena talked on of vegetable gardens and little fences and a hearth. The fear that had plagued her turned to excitement as they talked about setting up their home.

Keenan nodded and listened while giving advice. As they laughed and talked of their future, Serena felt such relief. They would be happy, they would live and love one another. As long as they were together, joy would weave itself through each day of her life. Together, they would face the words and thoughts of betrayal. Together they would survive, and love, and live. Together.

Chapter 15

Serena rode her own horse as they skirted the perimeter of Loch Awe. Keenan's warhorse chomped and stamped, longing for his stable. High above them, Serena heard Chiriklò chirp as his bright blue body darted from one branch to another. Her pet had been absent during most of their journey, only showing up after they left the waterfall. Serena was thankful for his sense of privacy, leaving them truly alone after their wedding. Chiriklò's bird eye view told her that all four of Keenan's men had returned to Kylkern earlier that morning. As they neared the village, Serena longed to reach out mentally to them, and to Lachlan, but she forced herself to erect walls.

The wind blew cool as spring's sun tried to thaw the earth. Sheep called to one another over the fields, and the glassy surface of Loch Awe reflected the waking land. The world hummed, ready to burst with life. Somehow it was oblivious to humanity's fears, anger, and wars.

Serena had learned about Prince Charles Stuart from Keenan on their journey. Keenan completely supported Scotland in its war for independence, but he despised the prince. Keenan had spent some time with him in France. The Young Pretender, as he was called by loyalists, knew nothing about Scotland and her traditions. He drank hard and wenched hard, sometimes too hard. Keenan had softened the details of one story where he saved a woman from the princes' drunken wrath. Although charismatic with his men, the young prince knew nothing of war, nothing of strategy. Aye, Keenan would support his brother's cause out of loyalty to his clan and to Scotland, but he put no faith in the leadership of Prince Charles Stuart.

Before entering the village, Keenan reined in beside Serena, keeping his horse under control with firm but gentle words. He turned to her, his look serious. "Have ye walled yer senses off?" She nodded. "No need to hear the ugliness in peoples' perceptions. They ken nothing of us, only the prophecy."

She reached for his fisted hand against his leg. She had put her gloves on as they neared, but she pulled one off so she could feel the warmth of him in the contact.

"Keenan, you have done nothing wrong. Even if I had never met you, I would not marry Lachlan. I love only a man of strength and courage." Her eyes filled with tears she refused to shed, not now, not when he needed her strength. "No matter what greets us, know that I am only yours."

He reached back, bringing her knuckles to his lips and kissing them.

"Keenan," someone from the village yelled. "Keenan's returned and he's brought her."

Keenan dropped her hand, and she pulled on her glove. She nudged her horse up alongside his. They would walk into Kylkern together.

Smiles and greetings surrounded them as they rode to the gates of the castle. Serena didn't see the four Macleans who'd reached Kylkern before them. She focused ahead as they approached Kylkern Keep, step by step, her horse's hooves squishing in the mud along the road. Chiriklò landed on the blanket tied behind her, tilting his head this way and that. As before people gathered behind them and whispers of their thoughts seeped through minute cracks in Serena's walls. None that she could fully hear, it was more like a soft hum, a tone of voice and not the words themselves.

There was unease in the hum of the village, a waiting tension among these good people. But as they stepped from their homes to see their arrival, the tension transmuted into anticipation, an ease to their shoulders and their worries. As if they all took a collective sigh of relief. The happy relief of seeing their leader return, of seeing the witch they thought would lead them to peace.

"Keenan, they do not know yet," Serena said next to him.

He frowned at her. "Ye're supposed to be protecting yerself from their thoughts."

"I am. But I still feel their underlying emotion."

The wind whipped around Serena's hair swirling red tendrils up in dance. A murmur rose through the onlookers. She pulled it close to her head, twisting it to behave. The hum of awe and excitement grew. Serena's stomach flipped about. These people believed in her, believed that she was their savior to bring peace to Kylkern. They were about to learn that she was not living up to their prophecy.

Would it have been easier to feel their disdain from the very start? Serena swallowed hard and tamped her guilt down into the pit of her belly where she resolved to keep it. Keenan didn't need her guilt on top of his own to bear.

"Ready?" she heard him say as he stared straight ahead, lifting his hand in greeting to the guards along the walkway above them. They stopped before the tall arching gates, the doors open.

"Together, then," Serena answered, and they nudged their horses forward in unison, under the walkway, under the arch, into the bailey crowded with warriors.

Serena's eyes scanned the armed men looking for Brodick, Gavin, perhaps William or Elenor. She didn't see any of them in the gathering. As she continued to look across the faces, it took her a moment to realize what she actually saw. Blood? Dark stains wavered in and out over their cloaks. The tangy stench of sweat and fresh wounds filled her nose. She coughed against it. The piercing caw of carrion crows made her gasp. She tilted her head back to search the blue, empty skies above them. Smoke, she smelled gun smoke.

"Serena?" Keenan said from his horse, reaching his hand out to steady her on her mount.

She looked back out across the men. "What battle has befallen them," she whispered at the sight of broken and torn limbs, gnarled bones twisted out of their ragged skin. Most of the warriors around her seemed like they should be buried in the ground, not standing before her, hailing Keenan in greeting. They even smiled, their broken faces twisted and pale. Her stomach curled against the sight, and she looked to Keenan. Thankfully he looked normal, but then her powers didn't work on him. If they did, would he match the others? A shudder rippled through her, and she swayed.

Keenan nudged his horse up alongside her until their horses touched. "What do ye see, Serena?"

"They're," she hesitated before looking at him, pleading him with her eyes to believe her. "They look dead, Keenan, most of them anyway. Dead as if slaughtered by sword and shot."

Keenan's eyes scanned the crowd. He held his hand up to stop them from advancing around them, giving them a moment.

"All of them?"

His voice held no doubt, no worry about her sanity. He trusted her sight, even though he might not understand it any better than she did. She looked out past him again. For a moment they looked normal, but in a blink, they turned back to grim specters, smashed, bloodied, bashed and crusted with dark blood and smears of battle. Several women were among them. They looked normal, just curious as they watched them. Several older men looked whole and as hardy as they could in their advanced age. Here and there, Serena was able to pick out a man or two that didn't look to have a fatal wound, only a scratch or two.

"Not all, not the women, nor the old men. Some warriors don't look dead, just battered." Serena rubbed her eyes. "Keenan," she mumbled against her hand. "What am I seeing?"

With powerful arms, he lifted her off her mount in front of him and shouldered through the crowd to the stone steps of Kylkern Keep. "I doona know, lass, but we'll get ye inside. Try to focus yer power on blocking the images."

"Make way," he called out. "Serena feels unwell. Make way."

He bent to pick her up into his arms.

"Please, Keenan," Serena said. "Let me walk. I want to walk inside beside you."

He halted a long moment, and then released her to the stone steps. A warrior stood at the door, holding it open. She knew him from her first visit. Rus was his name, and his wife worked in the kitchens. Serena let her breath out slowly thankful that he looked whole, worried but whole. She smiled timidly at him and he smiled back.

"Welcome back, Milady," he said bowing slightly. He reached out to help her up the steps.

"Doona touch her," Keenan's sharp command was too late as Rus grabbed her arm near her elbow.

As he stood, snatching his hand back, Serena saw the spear tip protruding from his belly, bloodied flesh and muscle caught along the jagged shaft. He warped into a corpse before her eyes, the rancid smell of bile and stomach juices assailed her. She coughed, covering her mouth with her hand and rushed inside. In the darkened entry Serena pressed herself against the cool solid stone wall. Keenan came up before her.

"Rus, too?"

All she could do was nod. Words may have brought up her meal. Serena sucked in shallow breaths.

"Deeper breaths, Serena, or ye will end up heaped on the floor." She forced herself to slow. "That's it, one step at a time. Rebuild that wall of yers to keep them out. I willna let anyone touch ye." He frowned at her. "We need to find a way to strengthen yer defenses."

"Drakkina said she could show me, teach me," she said between deep breaths.

"Then we will find her after this mess is cleared up."

Serena nodded and stepped away from the wall. "I'm ready."

They walked into the great hall. The fire blazed hot across the room in the hearth. The tapestries, chairs and tables all looked as they had left it. A group of men stood near the far wall under where a sword and shield had hung before. Serena breathed in the warm smell of fresh bread that hung in the air. She closed her eyes and imagined her breath moving down into her. As she exhaled, the breath seeped out of her nose into a long thread of power that wrapped around her in circles from head to toe. She drew deeply on an inner core of strength that stemmed from her stomach. Her dragonfly mark began to warm, branding her with tingling heat, hot but not hot enough to burn.

Opening her eyes, she surveyed the men as they came forward. Serena smiled broadly.

"Brodick, Gavin, so good to see you here," she said stepping forward as the two men came close. Brodick opened his arms to embrace her as Keenan stepped between them. Serena nearly ran into his broad back.

"She is not well," Keenan said.

Brodick peered around Keenan. "She looks healthy enough."

"Aye, she does, but if ye touch her, she may think ye look very unhealthy."

Brodick frowned in confusion.

"What do ye mean?" Gavin asked.

"Not sure yet," Keenan said cryptically as he watched Lachlan walk over with Thomas and Ewan. "I'll explain later, just she shouldn't be touched right now."

"It's good to see ye lass," Brodick said around Keenan. Gavin also smiled at her.

"Does he know?" Keenan asked before his brother could yet hear them. Thomas talked close to his ear as they walked slowly.

Gavin shook his head. "Nay."

"Don't forget me, Keenan. We tell him together remember."

"I doona remember that part, lass," he said with a frown. "This is between me and my brother."

"But I am part of it, part of your prophecy."

Lachlan had reached them and stopped. Serena turned away from Keenan's frown to look at his brother. Something was different about the man. True, his hair was still shoulder length brown, his build still tall but not filled out like the warriors around them. But there was an air about him, a confidence that hadn't been there when they'd left. And something caught her eye, a sword, strapped to his back. That definitely hadn't been there before.

"Welcome home, Brother," Lachlan said and clapped Keenan on the shoulder. "I see ye've brought the lovely Serena home with ye." He turned an awkward smile toward Serena, a smile that seemed at odds with the deep furrows of his brow and circles beneath his eyes.

"Aye, I've brought Serena. Lachlan, we have much to discuss."

"Talk fast, we have much to do before we leave on the morrow for Culloden Moor."

"Culloden?" Serena gasped.

"Ye plan to go to battle, Lachlan?" Keenan's eyes moved to the sword strapped to Lachlan's back. "With Da's sword?"

"Aye, I do," Lachlan answered and turned bright eyes to Serena. "It's about time I come out of hiding?" He looked back at Keenan. "And we've been called to join the Prince, a final blow to drive those English dogs back down into their country."

Keenan shook his head the smallest amount. "Lachlan, I've seen King George's plans for Culloden." Lachlan's eyes grew round. "We," Keenan looked first at Serena, and then back to his brother, "saw them at Frampton Manor where George sojourned."

Lachlan's face fell into a frown reminding Serena of the man they'd left behind. "Ye were close to him and yet he breathes?"

Keenan ignored his bait. "He has near nine thousand troops moving that way under the Duke of Cumberland. And there are also some Scots that plan to join him in return for their lands."

Lachlan's face grew red, mottled. "Baa, bloody bastards! It's their betrayal that will defeat us."

Lachlan's words thundered through Serena's ears. That he spoke of Scotsmen and not she and Keenan, didn't matter much. She watched Keenan's face, but he gave nothing away.

Keenan kept his voice level, unimpassioned. "Even without the Scots, he has nine thousand troops, well trained troops. We are no match to that, Brother."

"Prince Charles Stuart will outmaneuver

Cumberland."

"Ye doona ken the prince. I do. He is a grand speaker, a grand talker of dreams and glorious victories. He can rally a group and boil their blood against any army. But nay, Lachlan, he canna outmaneuver Cumberland and his nine thousand soldiers."

Lachlan didn't look at all convinced. "But we have the advantage of prophecy, Keenan. We ken that we will come out of this in peace." Lachlan glanced back at Serena. "Ye are the witch of our prophecy, Serena, ye ken that. Ye herald the tide of peace for the Macleans at Kylkern."

Serena felt her heart beat hard in her chest. "So I've been told, Laird Maclean."

He laughed. "Laird Maclean? Ye have no need to bow to formalities here, Milady. As ye will be part of this family before long. In fact, here before everyone," he began, raising his voice so that the handful of men in the room all could hear.

"Nay, Brother," Keenan said low, but Lachlan talked over him.

Serena spotted Elenor as she rounded the corner into the great hall. Serena kept her eyes locked on Keenan's sister, as if she were a floating branch to hold onto in a rapid river.

"Before God and my family and friends, I make it official and ask Lady Serena to wed with me." Lachlan bowed low and moved to his knee before her. Serena couldn't pull in a full breath. She had to look down at him and away from Elenor. "Send me to war with yer kiss and yer vow. Lead this clan to victory against England."

Time seemed to slow down as Serena stared at Lachlan bent down before her. She had no idea what to say. For a moment she felt like she sat outside of herself watching the horror unfold, wondering what would happen next, what she would say next. Serena wished she could see ahead so she would know what words to force now out of her frozen lips. If it were but a play, and she could see her next line. What would it be?

She must have paused too long for she heard Keenan start to say something, but she couldn't let him stand alone before his brother, before his clan. If she let him answer for her it would seem that he manipulated all the events in his favor. No, she had to say something.

Serena held up her hand to Keenan to stop him as her words came forth, loud in the absolute silence of the hall. "Laird Lachlan Maclean, you do me great honor with your request." Serena glanced at the other occupants of the room. The four Macleans who had journeyed with them stood, their legs braced apart, arms crossed. Elenor stood unmoving by the stair with William who had descended. Five or six other Maclean warriors, including Rus, had come inside. They all seemed to hold their breaths, waiting on her words. As if those words would decide the fate of their clan. Serena swallowed and looked back down to Lachlan.

"Please rise, Milord." Lachlan stood and she began again. "It is a great honor you bestow upon me, but I cannot accept."

Lachlan frowned slightly at her as if humoring her. "On what grounds, Milady?"

"On the grounds that I cannot marry where I do not love."

Lachlan smiled. "How young and fresh," he said. "Do not fear that, Serena. Love can grow once we are wed. Ye can consider it for the night. It is a good match."

For a brief moment, escape lurked in Serena's mind. She could lie. She could say that she would consider and stop this terrible scene. She could meet with him later, send him a message. Have Keenan talk to him without the eyes of his clan stripping them for all to see.

Serena sighed inside as the weak plan dissolved into an ache at the back of her head. She couldn't retreat, lie out of cowardice. For no matter how she justified the lie, it would still be said out of fear. Serena shook her head. "I cannot love you," she whispered, and then stopped. She wouldn't confess her love for Keenan quietly, she would proclaim it. Serena took a deep breath. "I cannot love you because I love another, I have wed another."

Several shocked grunts came from across the room, but she ignored them. Elenor's feminine gasp came from the stairs.

"But," Lachlan's voice shook on the word before he forced enough breath to make the words strong again. "But ye are the witch, the one to bring us to peace. Ye cannot have wed another."

Keenan stepped up next to Serena and took her hand in his. He squeezed it gently, but continued to stare at his brother.

"Serena and I were married six days ago at the Faw Romany camp near Leicester."

"Ye married her?" the question hissed from Lachlan, as much an accusation as it was a question.

Thomas stepped forward with the other three warriors. "He had na' choice. They were going to marry her to a Romany man from another tribe."

Gavin spoke as Thomas paused. "Keenan had to marry her else she would not have returned with us."

Ewan jumped in. "Nothing in the prophecy says that she needs to be a maid. Once Keenan dies, ye can marry her."

"Enough!" Keenan's voice bellowed over Serena's fierce denial, smothering it. "Enough," he said again.

Lachlan stared at Keenan, his face made of stone. "If ye married her to bring her to me, let us find a man of the kirk to annul the vows, Brother." His words were soft but firm. "Do yer duty, Keenan, and give her to me." Desperation lurked behind his words.

Serena's shock turned to internal fury. He spoke of her as if she were property, an object to be used, taken and given. A cloak of protection and nothing more.

Emotion fled Keenan's face as he stared into Lachlan's eyes. Calm, incredible calm, almost bored. Serena only felt the slight clenching of the fist that wrapped around her hand.

"I did more than wed her, Lachlan, I bound her to me in handfasting. I claimed her with my body." The slight edge of challenge sharpened his words, deadly calm challenge. "She is mine." Keenan used his grasp on Serena's hand to tug her to the side, slightly behind him, as if he used his body as her shield.

A long pause ensued as each brother weighed the other. No one moved. Serena's heart beat so hard that it hurt with the weight of the air in the room. The ache at the base of her skull throbbed.

Lachlan's words were low. "Then ye have killed me, Brother," he flung the last word as if it were a curse.

"Prophecies are often misinterpreted, I have been told," Keenan said. His words remained low.

In a burst that made Serena jump, Lachlan whirled around and strode to the hearth. He took a goblet of wine from the mantel and slammed it into the flames. Wine sputtered within the fire, hissing, dissolving quickly in the heat.

The outburst moved each warrior's hand to their hilts. Brodick, Gavin, Thomas and Ewan formed a close circle around her, guarding her and Keenan's back. Would civil war break out in this hall, a war between brothers over her? She couldn't let it happen.

"No," she yelled out and pushed past Keenan toward Lachlan. "He has not killed you, Lachlan. The love that grew between Keenan and me, it was meant to be. Our bond formed on its own, not to spite you, and definitely not to harm you in any way. Your prophecy…"

"Ye ken naught of our prophecy, Witch!" Lachlan roared. Serena heard steel slide free behind her.

She continued, undaunted, her heart pounding with her need to end this. "I know you don't want to die, none of us do, but we all do eventually. No prophecy will cause it as none can prevent it." Lachlan stared at her with a mixture of fury and condemnation. What could she do to stop this? What could she use to squelch the smoldering emotions of betrayal and resentment?

"Use me," she said to Lachlan. "Use my powers to avoid death, death for both of you."

"Serena," Keenan said, but she continued.

"No Keenan, even married to you, I can still read the minds of enemies. I can see probable outcomes. If you two but listen to me, you can both live long lives."

"And continue to hide," Lachlan said, the edge dulled from his voice. He shook his head, and looked past Serena to Keenan. "I am through hiding. I have lived more in these last three days than I have my whole life." He glanced back at her. "I willna hide behind yer skirts." He scoffed. "Let my brother hide behind them."

"I doona hide, Lachlan, I never have. I only warn ye of a disaster ye are about to walk into."

"I am going to Culloden, with or without ye," Lachlan said with a wave of dismissal. Keenan walked close to him.

"Serena is seeing things with her magic," he

lowered his voice so it wouldn't carry. "She's seeing the slaughter of our men. If ye lead them to Culloden, ye lead them to death, Lachlan."

Lachlan turned toward Serena. In two steps he was before her. Lachlan grabbed her head in his two large hands, one on either side of her face. She gasped at the contact as it crashed through her defenses.

She saw Lachlan's eyes bulging, his lips pulled back in a snarl. But more than the sight of his face, she saw his emotions. His anger, the pain of betrayal, resentment that he'd wasted thirty-seven years not living. "Then see me, Serena Maclean," he spat. "See my future, tell me of my death, a death brought on by ye and my brother."

His face blurred before her, changing. Lachlan's face turned gray, gun smoke char smeared cross his brow. Red spread out from his tunic along his chest. The aroma of death filled Serena's nose, and slaked against her tongue as if she had licked him.

The scream rose up out of her like a frightened bird taking flight, as if she could escape upon it. Lachlan was ripped from her as angry Gaelic curses bellowed up. Serena's gaze wobbled, and then steadied as she tried to center on the moving room. The men shouted and some shoved. Serena watched Elenor run to her, William behind her.

"Serena, come with me. Away from this," Elenor's soft voice beckoned. Serena tried to focus on her words. She nodded dumbly without looking behind. She took Elenor's outstretched hands and looked down at them. Red, warm blood covered Elenor's hands. So hot, so slippery.

Serena's breath huffed from her like she'd been punched in the stomach. The throbbing at the base of her skull pounded into her as if she were being pummeled from behind. "Elenor, blood, on your hands, so much blood."

"Serena, whose blood?"

"I don't know, but there's so much." Elenor's concerned face swam before her.

"Àngelas!" Serena heard William call her from what seemed far away.

The throbbing rose, pounding in time with her aching heart, with each rapid intake of breath. The floor gave way beneath her, and Serena knew she was falling. Falling into blessed darkness, away from the madness. Would he catch her? Before the question could solidify into fear, Serena felt a net of strength envelope her. No thoughts, no anger, no bloody premonitions, just blessed peace wrapped around her limp body. Keenan had caught her. She could let go.

It wasn't until later, when she felt a large, warm body next to her that she was able to stay afloat. Serena flicked her eyes open, blinking at the piercing glow of the hearth fire. She rolled to her side until her face pressed against a bare, warm chest. With one indrawn breath of pine and leather and musky man, Serena knew it was Keenan. She sighed into his skin. Safety, love, happiness, acceptance. All that she so wanted in life. She wiggled closer.

"Mmmm, ye feel good, lass," Keenan's words rumbled up from the very spot she lay her cheek. He sat up on an elbow and rolled her flat so he could peer down into her face, searching. Deep lines marked his forehead. "Serena," he touched her forehead at the hairline, tenderly running his fingers across her temple and down along the bone of her jaw. "How do ye feel?"

She smiled gently. "A kiss would help."

He looked confused for a brief moment before a grin grew, easing away the lines of worry. Keenan bowed his head and kissed her as if she were a delicate flower he could crush. Even though she still could not read Keenan's thoughts or feelings, he left an impression on her heart. A sadness lay below his tenderness. He pulled back way too soon.

Without opening her eyes Serena said, "nice, but I'd like more." She heard him chuckle, at odds with the impression. She should ask about it, ask what had happened below, but she didn't want to, not yet. Serena felt him roll from the bed, and her eyes snapped open. She pushed her heavy body up onto an elbow. Keenan walked over to add more peat to the fire. He wore a Maclean plaid draped low over his hips, and she watched the shadows play across the muscles of his bare back.

Her hand moved under her hair to massage the nape of her neck. The pounding had relented but it still felt tender.

She should ask. He must be expecting it.

"Is it the middle of the night?" she asked glancing toward the covered windows. No light peeked through.

"Aye, near midnight. Ye slept through supper," he said and picked up a bowl to bring over to her.

So they had actually eaten. Perhaps the clash of bitter betrayal and resentment had settled down after she had swooned. She really should ask, but then Keenan turned back and her eyes watched the teasing lines of his chest. He sat back down, his hands pushing her hair from her face.

"Really lass, ye are well?"

She nodded as best she could with his two large hands incasing her head.

"Ye screamed downstairs and fainted."

She nodded again. "The images, the smells, they broke through my defense," she hesitated, "when Lachlan touched me." Keenan released her face, his one hand fisting as he planted it on the bed next to them.

"He willna touch ye again, Serena. We," he

paused, "discussed it, and he willna harm ye in any way again."

Oh, she really should ask what had happened. Keenan took her hand and rubbed the palm.

"But yer well now? No images of corpses."

"I don't know. I've never been able to read you." She blinked and looked down at his hands rubbing hers. "Except through our strange connection sometimes."

His voice was low, not asking, but still asking. "Ye said there was blood on Elenor."

Serena took a deep breath. "Yes, on her hands, but she looked whole to me."

"And others did not?"

Was he asking about Lachlan?

"No, some did not. But Elenor did, just her hands were covered. Perhaps she will help the wounded?"

Keenan stared at her a moment and nodded. "Aye, perhaps." He stood up and began to pace. She sat cross-legged in the center of the large, curtained bed and watched him. He stopped, turning eyes deep with emotion to her. Was it in his eyes, or did she feel the hesitation within him? And something else, guilt.

"Ye ken I doona ask lightly for ye to remember such terrible things, nor have I asked ye to use yer powers to my advantage. But the fate of my clan, Serena, the fate of my family," he trailed off. "If there is anything ye could tell me, that ye saw or kent that could help them survive," he paused. "Tell me." From such a large, imposing man whose presence seemed to steal the air from the room, those last words should have sounded like an order. But spoken from his heart, spoken despite the guilt she could feel within him, Keenan did not demand. Although he would never plead for his own life, he would for the lives of his clan. And she would do no less for William or Mari or King Will, or any of the Faw tribe, because they were family.

Serena dropped her chin and closed her eyes while nodding slightly. "Of course, Keenan. I will help you." In bodily detail, she began to describe what she saw, from the ashen faces to the spear through Rus, to Lachlan's bleeding chest. Sometime during the recounting, Keenan moved to sit next to her, stroking her hand, adding his strength to her.

"And then I saw the blood on Elenor's hands, and you caught me." He nodded. Serena leaned closer to him. "I knew you would catch me." He brushed his lips against hers and pulled back. The sadness weighed again on Serena's heart, but she ignored it. She told herself that it was the guilt he suffered from having asked her to go through the bloody details.

"Serena, I need to talk with ye."

Panic curdled up through her stomach like sour milk. Not yet, she didn't want to know anything yet. Her brain was just too tired to take in any more. "Keenan, it is the middle of the night after a very long day. Come to bed, husband. Help me wash the blood from my mind."

Keenan's protest melted on his lips as Serena rose up on her knees to kiss him fully. She ran hands across the firm skin of his chest, brushing her fingertips back and forth against his nipples hidden in the soft hair. After a week loving him, she had discovered subtle ways of making Keenan lose his stringent control. Serena moved her kiss to the edge of his ear, letting her hot breath whisper against him. "Love me, Keenan. I need you tonight." Her lips closed teasingly around his earlobe, her tongue tickling the skin.

For the briefest of moments, she thought he would deny her. Serena threaded fingers through his light brown hair that had fallen loose across his shoulder. Keenan closed his eyes and she ran the tips of her fingers along his temple, following his scar down across his rough jaw. He seemed to hold his breath as she continued to trail down his neck to his chest.

When she followed the planes of his body down his muscled stomach to tease along the top of his plaid, Keenan sucked in a full breath and buried his face in her hair. He held her tightly to him as her fingers worked to loosen the material. Serena squeezed her hand within the gap she'd made, into the warmth. She found him easily and wrapped her hand around his hard length. Keenan growled low against her neck and pulled her hair to the side so he could kiss the nape of her neck, sending streaks of heat racing downward.

"Ye play with fire, lass," he said, his thick brogue muffled against her skin. Serena didn't catch each word, but she caught the warning. In answer she slid her hand up and down along his shaft, running her thumb along the soft skin of the tip.

Keenan growled deeper and pressed her back into the mounds of furs and pillows on the bed. His lips descended on hers, full of purpose, full of desperate passion. Serena poured herself into the kiss, all her worry, her denial, her trust in him.

She felt him pry her fingers away from him and pull back enough to strip the plaid, leaving him completely bare. The glow of the fire brushed him gold, the shadows outlining every dip and hill of muscle running across the warrior. His eyes locked with hers, intent eyes, hungry eyes, as he pulled the shift up her body, releasing her breasts, and then over her head. The silk floated to the floor somewhere next to the bed.

Her breasts felt heavy, the nipples chilled, waiting. Serena moved her hands slowly to cup them, lifting them upward so they looked even fuller. She saw his eyes drop to them and she rolled her nipples between thumb and forefinger. She moved her legs against his where he kneeled between them. Between his hungry stare, the bare arousal of his body and the rolling of her own nipples, Serena's body ignited. The flame spread. She tried to keep her eyes open, but they flickered closed as she moaned softly, her fingers still playing with her breasts.

"Och lass, I love to watch ye touch yerself."

And she loved to touch herself, knowing that he watched. He shifted, and she opened her eyes. He watched her as if she were his prey. A tremor of excitement mixed with the flame inside.

Keenan's lips came back to bathe her flushed neck in more heat. His hand replaced her own on her breast, lifting, teasing. The rough contrast of his hand against her skin poured more sensation into her. His lips followed and the feel of his hot, wet mouth brought her off the bed.

"Keenan," she breathed, her hands running along the broad muscles of his shoulders. "I want to feel you inside me," she said and trailed her fingers down her body to the juncture of her legs. She touched herself, feeling the dampness and heat there.

Keenan groaned as he watched her. His large hand spanned the skin across her gently rounded belly, moving lower in long caresses. Keenan met her hand and pushed past it into her channel. Serena grabbed the handfuls of fur on either side of her body as he worked his fingers expertly within her. He rubbed his thumb against her most sensitive spot. "Do ye trust me, Serena?" Her eyes closed. Her breathing rushed out in a pant as she nodded, her head thrown back into the pillow.

"Look at me," he said stopping. Serena opened her eyes. "Do ye trust me, Serena?" Serena stared into his face. Vulnerability played with the warrior before her. Did she trust him? Of all the people in the world, he was the one she could not fully read. They had a connection sometimes, forged by some mystery, but she couldn't read his thoughts, couldn't peer at his future, couldn't read his past. Did she trust him? Mari had said that love was a leap of faith. To trust someone whom she could not and may never be able to read, that was love.

Serena focused on the stormy gray of his steely orbs. "Keenan, I love you. I could not love without trust."

No single part of his visage changed, but somehow his entire expression did, subtly. The vulnerability turned back to strength, unease turned to conviction. He moved back up her body, his face centering on her own as he lowered his lips back to hers. His kiss held all the promise of love, of life together, of sincere happiness. Serena felt the tears of joy gathering at the back of her eyes.

He pulled back but still hovered over her face. She felt his breath warm against her lips. "Aye, I love ye too," he said.

She smiled but still a tear slipped out the edge of her lashes. Keenan caught it with one finger and touched it between his lips.

"I would catch all yer tears, lass, and keep them." She laughed lightly as more tears trickled out. Keenan ran his hands down her cheeks wiping them all. He kissed her. "No more tears now, lass," he said with a deeply seductive grin. "Since I have yer trust," he said sliding back down her body until he knelt between her thighs. "Trust me to teach ye something ye may like." He grabbed one of her ankles and lifted it up to lay it against his shoulder.

Serena gasped as he grabbed her other ankle and slid it upward against his other shoulder. "What are you doing?"

Keenan moved his hand back to her curls and entered her slick folds. Serena moaned while he shifted to position himself before her. He lifted her backside up so that he slid inside her with her legs still up in the air on either side of his head. "Something ye may like, lass," he groaned as he completely sheathed himself in her wetness.

Serena's eyes widened and she huffed through the intense pleasure that rolled along her limbs. The comical look of her toes curling around his ears was forgotten as Keenan began to move within her, hitting parts of her core that sent streaks of sensations ricocheting toward her womb.

"Yes, Keenan, that," she swallowed between quick breaths as he moved, "that spot."

"Aye," he rasped, "it is a good spot." Keenan rubbed his length back and forth within Serena against the most sensitive ridge inside. Serena's mind whirled into numbness as her entire being focused on the sensations below. The enormous energy ached inside her, building. Her moans became ragged as she drove toward him to meet each of his thrusts. Faster, he rubbed faster within her.

Serena forced her eyes to stay open so she could watch his powerful warrior's body straining over her, against her. Flesh slapped against damp flesh. Heat enveloped her and Serena slid her hands up and pulled at her aching breasts. Keenan growled above her as he watched. He reached down to the vee between her legs to rub his callused thumb against her. The incredible friction built the ache within Serena, higher and higher.

"Keenan," she screamed as the eruption shattered through her. The rolling waves of ecstasy pulsed through and around Serena, gripping her, splitting through her. Keenan's roar echoed her own as he poured himself into her quivering body.

He continued to pound into her until the last shudders of sensation began to ebb. Keenan turned his shoulders so her feet could fall to either side of him. He stayed within her as he pulled Serena against him on the bed.

Serena's heart still hammered inside her chest. She lay her hand against his heart and felt the same rhythm pulsing in him. She rubbed her cheek against the thudding. She was so close, so close to his heart. Keenan's arms surrounded her, his heart beat against her cheek, his legs lay entwined with her own. She couldn't be closer to him. She breathed in his scent, pine and man mixed with the scent of their love.

"Mmmm," she said against his skin. "I definitely like."

For a moment he was silent, but then a deep chuckle rumbled up from his chest. Keenan laughed out loud. He pulled back and kissed her soundly on the mouth. "And I definitely love ye, lass."

Serena laughed too. Keenan pulled the covers over her cooling body and wrapped her in his arms again. She fell asleep totally ensconced in his love.

****

"Serena, lass, wake up." Keenan's voice rippled the dark warm pool of exhausted sleep. Serena rolled away and back toward the warmth of the blankets. "Come now, lass, I must go. I willna leave without kissing ye."

Serena's eyes flew open, and she rolled toward Keenan. One look showed that he was fully dressed, dressed in the rugged clothes of a warrior as he sat beside her on the large bed.

"Where?" she asked, pushing up and hugging the blankets over her naked breasts. "Where are you going?" She asked the question, but the rolling in her stomach told her the answer. "No, no, Keenan," she said shaking her head. "You can't go with them to Culloden." Fear rushed tears behind her eyes.

"Serena," he soothed, "I must. How could I stay behind when my entire clan goes to fight for their freedom?"

"But you don't support Prince Charles."

"Nay, but I support Lachlan and my clan. If he is foolish enough to go, I must go too."

"To defend him," the words spat from her mouth as she threw her legs over the side of the bed. Serena ignored the wobbling in her muscles as she wrapped the blanket around her body.

"If I must," Keenan answered. "But I also go to lead my men." He came around and took her hands. "Serena," his words were gentle but firm. "I trained those men. I canna abandon them now to my brother's strategies, he has none. They truly will be slaughtered if I doona guide them through this."

"But," she glanced around desperately. "But there are others who could lead, others you have trained."

He shook his head, adjusting a strap that crisscrossed against his chest.

Serena grabbed at his hands, anger poured with her tears from her eyes. She shook her head, her eyes blurred.

"Keenan, I saw so much of that slaughter yesterday. Please," she pulled on his hands, "do not go. We are supposed to be together, the house in the village, the vegetable garden, the years of living and loving. Keenan I trusted you to stay with me."

Keenan's face hardened. "Would ye have me stay here, hiding while my clan goes off to war? Could ye love a coward?"

"You would not be a coward."

"To my clan I would. To myself, I would," Keenan led her back over to the bed and pressed her gently to sit down on it. "Serena, every one of my men is leaving a wife or their family. I am just one of them, one husband who must do my job in keeping this clan safe."

She shook her head and brushed the tears off her cheeks. "You are not one of them." Serena tried to steady her quivering voice. "The prophecy marks you for death, Keenan."

"Yer sight marks most of them for death, Love," he pointed out.

Serena jumped up. "But they don't know that. I will go down there and tell them all what I see, then they'll stay home."

Keenan pushed her back down. "Nay," his voice warned. "Doona put the fear of death in them. It will crumble their will."

"But it will stop them from going."

Keenan shook his head. "It willna. They will still go, for not to would make them cowards, afraid of death like Lachlan has been his whole life. For those ye scare into staying, ye will dishonor. For those who still go, ye will kill their confidence. It is what feeds their strength. Confidence and courage will carry them through this battle. Without it, ye will kill them."

Serena flashed watery eyes at him. She stayed seated. Keenan knelt down before her. "Lass, every wife must wish her husband farewell to battles."

"Not every husband has lived for his death," she whispered in the cold room.

He shook his head and tilted her chin up to meet his gaze. "I no longer live for my death," he said. "My life changed when I realized that I loved ye, Serena. I wished, back in our clearing under the stars. I wished to live my life with ye, a long life. That wish willna change no matter what enemy I face." He squeezed her hands as if willing her to understand. "Before, I never cared if I returned from a battle. Now I ken that I must."

Keenan pulled a soft cloth from his belt and

wiped the tears washing her cheeks. The anger drained out and her shoulders sagged. Serena took a long deep breath past the ache in her chest. Keenan saw her resignation. He stood, wrapping his strong arms around her. Serena clung, rubbed her face into him, and breathed his scent. She felt his hands play through her hair.

"I will not be left up here while you ride away," she said. "I will not play the coward, either." Serena felt his chin graze her head as he nodded.

"You could never play the coward, my lovely warrior." He kissed her hair, then pulled away slightly. He pulled a dagger from his boot. The light caught the glint of the sharp blade. Intricate knots twined together along the silver length up into the cross hilt. "It was my mother's, gifted to me to help me defend, to help me to fulfill my obligations." He looked at it and turned its hilt to Serena. "Keep it with ye." He said as she slid it from his hand. "Ye'll be safe here, but I want ye to keep it with ye."

A quarter hour later, Serena's wobbly legs flew down the winding stairs into the great hall, its silence profound like that in a tomb. She shuddered and wrapped her wool cloak tightly as she pushed out through the oaken doors. Elenor stood next to Robert MacKay and William.

William, she hadn't even greeted him yet. One look from him, one touch of his arms around her, and she knew that he understood. She pulled away and turned barely concealed tears up to his eyes. "I love him, William."

William touched her forehead with his. "I know, Àngelas, I know," he said pulling her to his side. "But he must go."

Serena looked out across the Maclean warriors standing in orderly groups within the bailey. Keenan walked amongst them, issuing orders, inspecting weapons, horses and supplies.

Elenor looped her arm through hers. "He's made sure that the Macleans have their own supplies. He doesn't trust the Prince to bring enough food for his troops." Serena nodded numbly as she focused on Keenan, his tall figure walking with confidence and strength among his men.

Perhaps with his decision to go they wouldn't look so bloody to her. Serena turned her attention to some of the troops and little by little lowered her defenses, spying as if through her fingers to see their futures. She spotted Rus, the spear still poked out gruesomely from his gut. Serena caught her breath, her legs losing their strength. Elenor pulled her up against her.

"No, no, I'm fine," Serena lied as she slammed the layer of protection back in place. She had to be strong, as strong as the men before her and the women and children huddled within the walls placing bits of ribbon and early spring flowers in the tunics of their husbands, brothers, sons, and fathers.

Keenan spotted her and walked through the soldiers towards her. Serena formed a stiff smile on her lips. Shoulders back, chin held even, eyes clear of tears. Keenan walked up the steps, and she pulled the green ribbon holding her hair. She tied the ribbon tightly to a strap that ran above his heart.

"Fare thee well, Keenan," her voice rang out in the hushed air. "Come home to me." He stepped up and pulled her into his embrace. His warm lips moved against hers for an intimate moment before he pulled away. The angry cries of crows overhead fell across the bailey as a brisk morning wind whipped hair around her head, sending its ends flapping like a flag. Keenan captured the errant strands in his leather-clad hand.

"Trust me, Serena. I will be with ye again."

Despite her will, tears threatened, but she sniffed, refusing to let them come. Keenan turned away, and she watched her warrior jog back down the steps toward Thomas and Ewan.

Lachlan sat mounted near the gates. His eyes met Serena's and he nodded. She nodded back. Fury no longer contorted his face.

"Serena," Brodick's voice caught her attention from where he stood below on a step. Gavin stood beside him. They were suited like the others.

"Brodick, Gavin, find your mounts," she said softly.

"Keenan just asked us to secure yer safety, Milady," Gavin said.

"So we will stay behind to guard ye," Brodick finished.

Panic gripped the inside of Serena's stomach. "No, no," her frantic whispers rushed out of her as she grasped Brodick's tunic. She stepped down so that she was level with his face. "You are going today."

"Lass?"

Serena touched Brodick's face with her fingertips. Yes, there it was, reluctance to stay behind. Disappointment, impotence. The panic in her stomach relaxed slightly. "You have to go, Brodick, you and Gavin," she looked at her other friend. "William and Robert will watch Elenor and me. But you must go."

"Keenan worries about ye," Gavin said.

Serena looked past the two warriors and watched Keenan's back as he rode out of the bailey, out onto the road leading through the village. In orderly fashion the Maclean warriors followed, some on horseback, some on foot. Wagons of supplies lumbered through the gates.

"Nay lass," Brodick said. "We will stay to guard ye."

Serena looked back into Brodick's eyes. "Brodick," desperation seeped into her voice. "Who will guard Keenan?" The two warriors looked at one another, and then back to her. "With your prophecy, no one will guard Keenan's back. They will all guard Lachlan thinking that he is the one to survive, not Keenan. Who will guard Keenan's back?"

Brodick looked at her for a long moment. He frowned deeply, and then slowly nodded. He kissed her hand and turned on the stairs.

"Brodick, what are ye doing?" Gavin asked.

Brodick looked back at Serena. "I'm going to aid the Maclean who has wed the witch, who with him will bring peace to our clan."

Serena nodded at him.

Gavin looked between them and let out a loud huff, his breath puffing white in the chill.

"They left us but one horse," Gavin groaned. Minutes later the two warriors sat on Brodick's large horse.

"Fare thee well," Serena called as she and Elenor waved to the two men. The horse snorted and turned in a run through the gate after the army of Maclean warriors.

As the gateman rotated the gears to lower the heavy iron bars, Serena pushed her hand into her pocket where Merewin's healing crystal sat with a bit of the Maclean plaid. The scrap of fabric was part of the blanket Keenan had used to handfast them in the clearing. In the privacy of her pocket she wound it around her fingers.

Elenor hugged Serena's shoulders. "Trust in him, Serena. Ye will be together again."

Serena nodded. "Yes we will." She turned to go inside, her next words caught within a gust of wind. "In this life or in death. We will be together again."

Chapter 16

Drakkina stood in a pentagon scratched into the layer of meadow, her arms stretched out above her head. Her voice throbbed through the sun filled circle within the soaring rocks.

"I call out to the wind, to the sky, to the fire of the sun." She tilted her face up to catch the heat of the glowing orb directly above her. She spread her feet apart in a V where she stood among the wildflowers that stood still, absolutely still as if listening to her words. "I call out to the earth that circles life through its layers, to the rocks that support us upon their shoulders." She moved her arms, rotating them, her aged fingers pointed toward the western shore. "I call to the water that gives life to this world." Drakkina closed her eyes and raised her hands upward until they pointed in line with the fierce sun overhead. "I need your strength, the power from each element. Fill me up, gift me with your power as I gift you with a sacrifice of my blood." Drakkina drew her nail across her palm, her magic easily cutting into her own misty flesh. Black red blood swelled along the line, and she held it over the center of the pentagon. Drops of her blood, misty, half-real blood dripped onto the scuffed dirt and scattered flowers.

A howl resonated through Drakkina's ears as a hot wind whipped up and through the tall stones. The heads of each wildflower bowed down flat as if in worship. Drakkina held her arms open wide. Her long white hair whipped around with her flowing robes. The heat branded her skin, scorching with its power.

Drakkina smiled, her eyes closed to the onslaught of power. She knew, she heard. The stones. The tones vibrated, swirling with wild magic, bouncing off each of the ten stones where they stood guarding the sacred circle. The power poured into Drakkina, fighting against her indrawn breath, squeezing her as if there was no room left in the circle for her ephemeral body.

Drakkina forced a breath down into her aching chest. "Yes," she screamed above the cacophony of swirling, vibrating chords of sound. "Yes, bring me your power. Death stalks Serena and her mate. I need your power to bring her here to safety. It must be done."

With her last word, Drakkina opened her eyes to the blinding light of magic glowing in the circle. The white light swirled around the inside of the stones. She moved her arms to mimic the swirl, and the glow began to move in harmony with her arms as if it picked up the rhythm of an ancient dance.

Drakkina pulled the power into a tight ball above the center of the pentagon. It was not physical, but mental strength, strength that came with centuries of training and honing her skill that wound the thread of elemental magic into her.

The light hit the center of her palms first, the burning tight against her skin. She pulled then, from her center. Slowly the hot light bore down through Drakkina, sliding between her ribs and spine, flicking along the vessels and arteries, pumping the magic through her entire body.

As the last of the energy disappeared inside Drakkina's body, she lowered her arms and breathed deeply. The space was once more empty air, the tightness released, now running through the spaces of her body.

Drakkina smiled and bent down to study her

misty body. It looked solid, to the point that her legs almost blocked the sight of the wildflowers behind them.

"Thank you," she whispered and wrapped arms around her once tired body that now resonated with youth and energy. "I will use your gift wisely." The breeze swayed the flower heads and rippled through the trees outside the circle. A swarm of dragonflies moved above the trees and zipped down as one body to engulf Drakkina. She turned toward the east with determination.

"Deny me now, Serena. I dare you." Drakkina held her hands out to that direction and felt currents of power gathering through her. "Come to me, Serena. Come. And bring your Highlander with you."

****

It was nearly noon. The hot, clear sun beat down as Serena walked the edges of the bailey, speaking in soothing tones to the women and children of the departed warriors. It had been a day and a half since the men had left. Even though the threat to Kylkern was minimal, many of the families had come to stay within its walls. Serena and Elenor opened the castle to all who could fit as if they were under siege. The close proximity of the nervous, anxious people pummeled Serena with emotional energy. She was becoming mentally exhausted at holding the voices and unease at bay.

Serena ducked through the doorway and stepped past several playing children on her way into the great hall. She sat down next to Elenor and William at the long table. Robert Mackay stood across from her.

"I'm off to make the rounds," he said and stood.

"Thank you, Robert," she smiled weakly as he nodded and turned toward the door.

"I am tired," Serena said softly.

William took a drink of mead and looked at her.

"No doubt the press of so much unease," he said glancing around the hushed mill of people in the hall.

Elenor leaned toward them. "It's as if they know the battle will not go well."

"I said nothing," Serena defended in hushed tones.

Elenor nodded. "I know, but we often underestimate the power of intuition in women." Elenor squeezed Serena's hand. "I think ye should take a nap, Serena."

"Like a babe?"

"Shall I carry you up to your rooms?" William said rising from the bench.

"I can make my way on my own," Serena said softly and turned from the room. She crept up the steps slowly, her mind and heart twisting and tumbling with sorrow. She was crumbling, succumbing to the despair of losing him.

Serena leaned into the roughness of the wall, letting her tears soak the granite. She hadn't replaced her gloves after eating, and she ran her hands along its hardness and strength. Serena stopped in mid sob as a spark of power surged up her fingertip as she grazed one of the chiseled mason's marks. She blinked to clear her eyes. It was the dragonfly mark.

The mark hummed with energy, and the image coalesced into that of a real dragonfly. She blinked again. Had the membranous wings really lifted from the rigid rock? Timidly she ran her palm over the space just above the image. Warmth, tingling warmth, pulled at her.

Tears dried sticky on her cheeks, and her heart pounded behind shallow breaths. Slowly she lowered her hand until it came in contact with the hot stone image. Need shot through the touch, up her arm, spreading down to her heart and up into her mind.

Need to move, to move west.

"I must go," Serena said to the stone, answering its spell. The power urged her to go, but her rational mind questioned how. The gates were lowered, only opened for needs, not desires. "Follow the marks." The words echoed in her mind as if someone had spoken them aloud.

Serena only then realized that her birthmark tingled where it lay etched in her skin. Glancing again at the rock, her eyes turned downward, down each narrow step, knowing without being shown where the next dragonfly mark was chiseled into the stone of the castle. She took several steps down, turning with the winding staircase until she found the next. Sliding her hand along its shape, she once again knew where to find the next dragonfly mark lower still. She walked on.

A mist flooded her mind, a dark warm mist like a pleasant dream. So tired. Serena's legs continued to follow mark after mark. Vaguely Serena knew that the magic must come from Drakkina, as the Wiccan priestess's mark tingled.

Maybe Drakkina could help. The woman was determined to protect her in the stone circle to the west.

Serena released her last thread of resistance to the pull. Her mind fogged over, her vision dimmed as if she truly were asleep.

Time flitted and compressed as through a dream. So it seemed only a blink before Serena opened her eyes at the bite of wind as she walked sedately through the back gardens. Her feet carried her toward the next dragonfly mark in the castle wall near a newly tilled plot for herbs.

Serena watched detached as her hand ran up the side of the twenty-foot wall until her fingertip touched the center of the last dragonfly. It was as if she watched another, not her own hand. As she depressed the small stone in the middle of the carving, a hiss of wind blew through the widening crack that meandered subtly down the wall. Serena shoved against the stone and the seemingly unmovable blocks of granite swung outward.

"Serena!" She heard her name called as if from far away. "Serena, what are ye doing?" Elenor's voice called to her as Serena slipped through the slender opening, ducking to fit under the mass of the huge wall above her.

"Stad! Stop, Serena, wait!"

She wanted to reply, turn to Elenor and assure her that she would be fine, but she couldn't turn. One foot in front of the other, Serena walked west toward a tree where a horse stood. Where had the horse come from? What was Elenor saying behind her? Another wave of need washed through Serena, dissolving the questions. Serena notched her leather slipper in the stirrup and hoisted into the seat.

Something tugged at her skirts, but she barely noticed. So tired, she would just close her eyes and rest. Serena leaned down along the strong neck of the horse. She felt the beast's strength, its blood throbbing beneath its skin. She heard her own steady breathing as darkness swirled around her. The horse's body warmed her, and she belatedly realized that she was cold without her cloak.

A frantic voice, so small, pulled at her consciousness. It was almost completely engulfed by the sound of her breathing and the heartbeat of the horse.

"Nay Serena, doona go. What is happening? How did this horse even get here? How did ye ken that crack in the wall?" It sounded like Elenor's voice. Why was Elenor here? Serena couldn't remember. The voice was insistent. "Serena, climb down."

Serena could no more climb down than she could fly. She was stuck in place, lying across her horse, waiting to go. It was time to go.

Serena felt a tug so hard that the side of the horse dipped. She clung to the mane and felt the deep whinny barreling up through the horse's neck. The rocking righted itself and another warmth fell across her back, hugging her.

Elenor's muted voice cut through the fog in Serena's ear. "If yer going somewhere, I'm going with ye, Sister."

The horse shot off into the woods behind Kylkern. Elenor's cloak surrounded Serena from behind as her friend wrapped it around both of them.

Fear soaked into Serena, Elenor's fear.

"Where are we going, Serena. Why doona ye answer me?"

Serena dragged her hand along her thigh behind to Elenor. Finding her friend's hand, she clasped it. With a gentle squeeze, Serena tried to will calm into her friend. Elenor squeezed back tightly and leaned down against Serena's back as the horse sped along through the woods.

****

Drakkina stood, arms akimbo. She watched with narrowed eyes as the horse approached through the thick forest ringing the circle. The second rider did not look like Serena's Highlander. In fact, the second rider didn't look like a man at all.

Caoch! She didn't bring the Highlander! Keenan Maclean was still somewhere out there, somewhere unsafe at a time when Drakkina felt death lurking close to them. That's why it was so imperative that they both come to the circle, where she could protect them. Instead, Serena brought a woman.

"Who are you?" Drakkina's frustration poured acid into her words. Serena and the woman sat up as if they were one, Serena blinking from the spell and the other stared with wide eyes.

"Me?" the woman asked stupidly.

Drakkina threw her hands out toward Serena. "I know who she is. Who are you, and why aren't you Keenan Maclean?"

Serena shook her head as if clearing it. "She is Keenan's sister, Elenor, and a close friend of mine, my new sister in fact."

"But where is Keenan Maclean?" Drakkina yelled, stamping her foot.

"Despite her temper, I think she means well, Elenor. Let us dismount," Serena said.

The two women slid one after another down the labored horse. Drakkina flicked her fingers at the beast, and it walked out of the circle toward a creek for water and grass. Drakkina tried to quell her anger, her fear. She lowered her voice but the terseness could not be filtered out completely. "Again, where is Keenan Maclean, Serena, your soul mate? I need to protect you both."

"Can you protect him?" Serena asked.

Elenor stayed toward the outer edge of the circle watching them.

"I can protect him in the circle, which is why I've called you here. Why didn't you bring him? He's tied to you."

"He left for Culloden before you called me."

"No! The fool!" Drakkina turned, her hands on her hips. Panic raced through as her eyes flew from stone to stone. Her blood pumped hard in her nearly solid veins. She hadn't felt so alive in centuries, nor so scared. If the Highlander died, Serena wouldn't have her soul mate. What would that do to her chances of winning in the final battle with the demons in the future? Each daughter must come to the battle with their soul mates beside them. She knew the instructions from her oracle. How could she fail with the very first one?

"Can you bring him here, Drakkina, save him?"

Serena asked softly, weakness turning her face slack as if rain had washed off the colors from her spirit. Drakkina studied her, this sadness. For several beats, Drakkina's heart clenched in pain at the despair enveloping Gilla's first born. Then Drakkina's mind took over, her determination, her resolve to save the worlds.

"Can I bring him here?" she repeated Serena's question and tapped a finger on her lips. "Well I thought I was," she said absently. "He doesn't have my mark to pull him to me like you do."

"Perhaps he willna die at Culloden," Keenan's sister spoke up from the inside edge of the circle. "He could come home."

Drakkina drilled into the woman with her fierce glare. "Death stalks all the Macleans, I feel it, I know it. Culloden will be a disaster for all of Scotland."

The woman paled and placed a hand along her throat.

Drakkina's eyes shifted back to Serena. "He loves you, why would he leave you?"

"He said he had to, had to fight with his men. Had to lead them so Lachlan wouldn't march them foolishly to their deaths."

"Culloden is certain death," Drakkina mumbled darkly, her eyes snapping back to Serena. "And you let him go!"

Tears traced down Serena's cheeks, and she crumpled to the ground. "I trusted him," she sniffed. "Trusted the plans I had for our life together. Children, vegetable gardens." She took two trembling breaths as Elenor came to crouch down, hugging her. "He left anyway."

"He will return to ye, Serena," Elenor said.

Serena shook her head. "What if he chooses to die instead, to be the sacrifice? What if he leaves me? What if our love is not enough for him?" Serena sobbed.

Drakkina rubbed deeply lined hands across her face. She had died centuries ago and yet she couldn't rest, couldn't go beyond into oblivion. The ancient Wiccan sighed deeply. No, instead she had to save this mess of a world. And even though she couldn't fully enjoy the pleasures of the earth any longer, she was still tied to it. And she wasn't willing to give up yet.

Drakkina walked past the two women toward the scrying bowl. She ran her hand across Serena's bent head. Such suffering. An ache in Drakkina's chest tightened and she rubbed at it as she continued toward the bowl. Drakkina sniffed the afternoon air. The dark calm before death stunk of anxious men and dirt and hot raging blood. The wind was full of it. "Perhaps he didn't love you as we thought," Drakkina mumbled as she dipped her finger into the glassy surface.

Serena stood slowly, straightening to her full height. "He loves me as I love him. I feel it in him still as he struggles," she said, closing her eyes and turning east toward Culloden.

Drakkina's finger froze, and she turned sharp eyes to Serena. "You can read him now?" How could it be that Serena could read Keenan Maclean? He was meant to be her soul mate. Her powers shouldn't work on her soul mate.

Serena shook her head. "No, not read really." The tears had stopped, replaced by a stronger look, determination perhaps. "But I feel his emotions. We have formed some sort of connection between us."

"He feels your emotions too?" Drakkina slid away from the table and walked closer. Serena nodded.

"What do you feel now?"

Serena closed her eyes. She took some deep breaths. Tears began to leak out from under her dark lashes. "He feels irritated, angry over foolishness perhaps. Resentment." She opened her watery eyes. "Determination."

Drakkina's mind whirled. "And you say he can feel your emotions too?"

"He has before."

"Then pull him here! Think that he must come, that he must leave."

"But I told him to stay at Kylkern. He feels he must go with his men, his clan. That I am safe and he must help save those who aren't. It is what he does, what he is." Serena nodded her head as if convincing herself.

Drakkina felt it in her, resolve. Drakkina frowned at her steadfastness, but the thought echoed in her mind. Safe, the Highlander thought her safe. "What if you are unsafe?" Drakkina said.

"But I am safe." She stared at Drakkina. "I will not lie to him. He trusts me."

"Serena, you don't understand. I need you both alive, the whole bloody world needs you both alive."

Serena faced her. "You're right Drakkina, I don't understand all that. I don't understand how you know that, where you came by that information. I know that the world has a strange way of continuing on and that prophecies are unreliable. I don't really even know who you are."

Drakkina's heart pounded, at least she thought it was her heart, or where her heart should be if she still had one. She flapped her hands out around her. "There's no time for that, woman! We need to get him away from that battle."

Elenor stepped before Serena. "Try to call to him, pull him away."

Serena shook her head and pulled the dagger from its sheath in the folds of her gown. "He left me this," she said and handed it to Elenor, "and his trusted men. He knows I am not in danger."

Drakkina focused on the blade. "Peril, real life peril. He'd feel it. By the Earth Mother, let him trust it," Drakkina whispered the prayer and walked toward Elenor.

Drakkina concentrated on the bits of energy comprising her form, turning them translucent until she was nothing more than a mist. She wafted over to the Highlander's sister. With one surge, Drakkina invaded the particles that held together Elenor's body. Between the infinitesimally minute spaces Drakkina squeezed her being until she completely joined with the stunned woman. Elenor's consciousness gagged against the intrusion, but Drakkina blocked it out, focusing her energy on moving Elenor's limbs like a puppeteer.

Had Serena seen her squeeze into Elenor? Could she read her intent? Elenor still held the dagger. Drakkina raised it high.

"Forgive me," she said through Elenor's tight voice as she plunged the silver blade downward just as Serena turned toward her. The blade sliced into the flesh above Serena's right breast. Down through muscle, between bone until the hilt lay flat against her skin.

Chapter 17

Keenan watched Lachlan slump down against a boulder in the misting rain. Keenan raised his arm, a signal to his men to halt their march. They had made it to the moor, but darkness was beginning to fall, and Lachlan didn't seem like he planned to stand again soon. His brother looked up at the gray gloom around them.

"Caochan!" Lachlan cursed into the rain.

"Take yer rest men," Keenan called. "Disperse rations." The Maclean warriors pulled the supply wagon near a copse of scraggly trees. Rus unloaded wrapped cheese, cured meats, and bannocks. Keenan sat down next to his miserable brother and handed him a lump of cheese and strips of venison.

"Ye ken, Lachlan, we doona have to continue with this foolishness," Keenan said chewing hard on the tough edge of the meat.

Lachlan stared out across the vastness of Culloden Moor. Off in the distance smoke snaked up through the tree line. Those would be King George's men, under the command of the vicious Duke of Cumberland. Scouts reported nearly nine thousand English, Irish, and supportive Scots, just like Keenan had seen on King George's map.

"I doona care what Murray and the Prince think, I've met Cumberland. There's no way he's letting his troops drink themselves into oblivion in honor of his birthday; not before the start of a battle," Keenan said and swallowed down some cheese. Lord George Murray, the commander over Prince Charles Stuart's army, had convinced the

Bonnie Prince that they should cross the moor during the night and attack the drunken English troops.

The troop of two hundred Macleans had traveled for a day and a half to reach the muddy hills of peat and bog across from Cumberland's massive troops. There were Scots spread out around the perimeter of the moor, waiting for the signal from the Stuart prince and Lord Murray. They had arrived hours ago to a haphazard band of close to five thousand Scots, no provisions, no organization. Keenan chewed his bannock. At least his men had food and blankets. Most of the other troops were becoming weak from hunger, cold and exhaustion.

In Lachlan's silence, Keenan's thoughts drifted to Serena. He had promised to be with her again. What a foolish thing. No man could promise what he could not control.

Deep in his gut, Keenan felt his nerves tightening. Fear? Never before had he worried over the start of a battle, but never before had he actually cared about living through one.

"Ye love her." Bouncing sleet muffled Lachlan's voice.

Keenan threw his blanket over both of their heads so that they sat in a small cave together, upper arms touching.

"Aye, I love her."

Lachlan nodded his head knocking the covering. He turned his eyes toward Keenan. "When?"

Keenan remembered her cool fingers as they traced his scar the night they met and then the kiss on the moor. Keenan met Lachlan's eyes. "Before I knew who she was."

Lachlan peered intently at him. He turned back to the darkening moor. "If King George walked up to us right now," Lachlan said, "to strike me down." He wiped the freezing water that ran down from his eyebrows with his hand. "Would ye step before me, Keenan? Would ye defend me, Little Brother?"

"Aye, I would," Keenan answered without hesitation.

Lachlan's eyes measured his words. "Why?"

Why? It was a valid question. Why not let Lachlan die so he could become the brother who lived? He already had the witch, why not abandon Lachlan now to the prophecy as he had been abandoned by most everyone since birth.

Keenan rubbed his dirty hands along his own wet, mud smeared face. "Because ye are my brother. Even if I doona believe in yer prince, Lachlan, I do understand what loyalty is."

Lachlan stared, but slowly his face relaxed until the hint of a grin crept along his lips. He looked back out to the slowing rain. "This is miserable business."

"Aye, bloody miserable business," Keenan agreed. The rain and sleet ebbed.

Keenan threw off the blanket and stood to shake the water from his hair. He would check on the horses. Brodick and Gavin's horse had disappeared earlier that day, and they would need every beast in this brawl.

Keenan straightened out his large frame, stretching his back when suddenly white-hot pain shot through his chest. He doubled over with a huffing sound and fell against Lachlan.

Lachlan struggled under his mass.

"Keenan?"

Keenan grabbed the right side of his chest.

"We're under attack!" Lachlan yelled. Men scrambled everywhere, grabbing swords and shields as they ran toward the brothers.

Keenan held his chest, but no blood poured from him. It wasn't his own pain he felt searing through his chest. His face paled. It was Serena's.

Keenan caught his breath. "Nay, halt! There is

no attack here." The men gathered around them, torches glowing in the gloom. Keenan pulled his tunic low, showing his already scarred pec to be unmarred by any new wound.

"But ye crumpled like ye'd been hit," Lachlan insisted.

Keenan leaned forward against his own knees trying not to fall under the crush of feelings thundering through him. Shock, pain. Never before had he felt such a connection with Serena. Resentment, remorse. Each dark color of emotion bled over him, coating him in her unfiltered anguish. Sorrow and finally acceptance. It was the last emotion that gave him the strength to move.

"Na' me, Lachlan," Keenan said, breathing hard against emotions. "Serena. She's been stabbed, here," he said rubbing his still aching pectoral.

"How do ye ken this?"

"We doona ken how it works, just that we are connected somehow," Keenan shook his head, his eyes traveling to the tethered horses.

"Are ye going?" Rus called out as the large group of men watched.

Keenan barely noticed Brodick and Gavin climbing together on another horse as Ewan and Thomas took Ewan's mount. Keenan looked back at Lachlan, standing there alone, against a backdrop of Culloden Moor. What a bloody horrible choice to make, between his clan and Serena. Guilt pulled at him, at his honor before the eyes of his men. These were men he'd trained, men who depended upon him. How could he leave them to his brother's leadership?

Keenan came close to Lachlan. "I tell ye brother, this scheme is doomed. Like I said, the Stuart prince's strategy will na' work. We doona need Serena's warning to ken the outcome of this. Come away now. We will pick a different battle with the

English."

Lachlan shook his head. "I canna leave," his words were low, only for Keenan. "It is the first time I've felt their respect," he said glancing past Keenan's shoulder toward the expectant men. "I canna play the coward anymore, Keenan. It will kill me."

"But ye will die here."

Lachlan smiled grimly. "Perhaps, but it is also the first time I will truly live."

"But the men. Think of their lives."

"I will put Rus in charge of our strategy." Lachlan nodded. "Ye trust him."

"But, Serena's warnings..."

"Ye've told me them. I remember. I will tell them all and let them protect themselves as best they can from what she saw. Or they can go."

"They willna go," Keenan said shaking his head. The pain in his chest felt so fresh that he looked down to see if blood pooled between his feet. But there was only mud and trampled grass beneath him. "Lachlan, they willna go without ye."

"Perhaps," Lachlan grabbed Keenan's shoulders in his hands and shook him slightly. "But ye, Brother, ye must go. If she dies, so does the prophecy and our chance for peace. Ye must keep our witch alive."

"Lachlan...Brother..."

"Nay, Keenan." He nodded, using his father's favorite utterance. "'Tis yer duty." Lachlan's eyes warmed with a hint of a smile. "Ye are already with her, not here, not on this bloody moor. Yer heart was never for Da's cause because ye doona respect the Prince. Finally yer heart is for something. Ye love her, Keenan." Lachlan raised his voice so all could hear. "Go to her, save our witch, Keenan. Without her alive we have no chance for peace. Ye must go to save our clan. I know ye will do yer duty."

Keenan stared into his brother's eyes and then nodded. He must go. He must reach Serena, not for the prophecy, but for himself and for her.

****

Air wheezed out of Serena's stunned lips. Drakkina drew away from Elenor's body, rematerializing next to Serena.

"Quickly, bring her to the stone table," Drakkina demanded.

Elenor looked down at her shaking hands. "What have I done?"

"You've done nothing!" yelled Drakkina as she frantically tried to catch Serena's wilting body, but the woman's form fell right through her own. Serena fell onto her side crushing the wildflowers. Serena's low moan squeezed inside Drakkina's chest. "What have I done?" Drakkina breathed softly and turned her fury on Elenor.

"Move!" Drakkina ran over to Elenor waving her arms in the air before her face. "Pick her up and place her on the stone table while I call her sister here to save her."

"Her sister?" Elenor said, her eyes wild.

"Move!"

Elenor snapped into action, heaving Serena up and wrestling her as gingerly as possible onto the stone table.

"I," she said, "I must keep her on her side. The blade protrudes from her back," she said on a sob. Elenor pulled her hands away from the wound. Blood, Serena's blood flowed down her palms, staining the edges of her sleeves at the wrist. "It was her blood she saw, her own blood."

Drakkina ignored her. "Just make her as comfortable as you can." Drakkina looked around the stones. "Chiriklò come to me," she called, and the bluebird screeched loudly as it wove in and out of the stones around the circle. Drakkina knew it had been close, never far from Gilla's girl. It flew to perch on Serena, chirping and squawking.

"No time to panic. Go to him. Find Keenan Maclean and lead him here over the bridges I'm weaving." Drakkina closed her eyes and pictured the lands between them, mountains, lochs, moors until she reached Culloden in her mind. She pulled upon the magic thick within her. The power threaded out, bending the miles, folding them into short lengths.

"Go," she ordered the bird and heard its small wings stretch as it soared toward the east. "Go fast," she said as she wove a second thread around the first, pinching together the layer of time that lay across the land. Each moment in time was in itself complete, held apart from every other instance in time. But Drakkina's magic, much like the magic the demons desired, could collapse those layers, shortening time, bringing it together.

With extreme focus, Drakkina tied off the threads, keeping the bends and twists of time and land together into a bridge. It should shorten Keenan's journey from days to perhaps an hour. If he came. She turned back to Serena.

Elenor cried quietly as she dabbed at Serena's pale face. She looked up at Drakkina with hatred seeping out with her tears. "Ye've murdered her, Demon, witch, whatever monster ye are," she spat in her direction and turned back to croon over Serena.

"It will bring him here," Drakkina said defensively. An uneasy tightness formed in Drakkina's stomach as she looked at Gilla's eldest, her chest growing red with her blood.

"It will bring him to her corpse."

"Not with Merewin helping us." Drakkina turned toward the Northeast and spread her hands wide. She wove another thread with her diminishing powers, a thread back through time. She traced the thread as it moved across time and space to another dragonfly birthmark, on Gilla's second eldest daughter.

"Merewin I have need of your magic," Drakkina called into the air. "Merewin, I need you now to save your sister." The silence twisted in Drakkina. What if she couldn't call the healer? She should have called her first. "Merewin!"

"Calm yerself old crone," a sassy female voice answered. "I am here." Drakkina took in a calming breath and lowered her arms so none would see them shaking. A misty figure stood near the inside edge of the stones. She was faint, much too faint.

Drakkina closed her eyes and focused a portion of her magic on the stones, pulling on their strength from the earth beneath them. The air began to hum as the stones pulled more power up through the earth. The wildflowers wilted, adding their life force to the power. When Drakkina opened her eyes, Merewin stood solid within the circle. Mist moved outside the stones, as if the circle sat apart from the current time, but also within it.

Merewin, tall like her father, slender like her mother, had long wavy brown hair and snapping green eyes. And they narrowed as she took in the scene before her.

"What has happened?"

"She is your sister, Serena," Drakkina answered as Merewin ran across the circle.

"Crone, I ken who she is. What's happened?" Merewin shoved Elenor aside and glanced at her bloody hands.

"The woman did not harm her. She can help you where I cannot," Drakkina said, showing how her hands passed right through the stone table.

Merewin tore strips from Serena's petticoat and wadded it against the tip of blade sticking out from her back. Serena's chest rose in short shallow breaths as Merewin laid her ear against her breast.

"A lung is punctured, I hear the wheeze."

"You can heal her," Drakkina said.

"Aye, I can," Merewin said tersely, "but I'd still like to ken what happened."

"Later." Drakkina ignored the piercing eyes of Elenor and watched Merewin pull several stones from a bag tied to her waist. Some were polished, some rough. Merewin carefully rolled Serena to her back. She gave several jagged crystals to Elenor.

"Lay the clear quartz along her stomach up her sides near the wound." Merewin held up a smoky, smooth crystal. "My rutile quartz will ease her breathing and lesson her shock." She laid it against the hilt still buried in Serena's chest. Drakkina recognized jade stones that Merewin placed in each of Serena's palms, curling her fingers around them.

Merewin closed her eyes and moved her hands gracefully over the stones. Drakkina studied her, trying to see the intricate web of healing threads that Merewin wove. Fascinating. The power to heal was one Drakkina had never mastered, but this young woman, she held complete control of the power. She used the stones to help her focus the intricate energies required in healing.

Drakkina looked at the dagger hilt. "Shouldn't we remove it?"

Merewin didn't open her eyes, and a frown creased her flawless brow. "Nay, not until I'm certain."

"Certain?"

Merewin lowered her arms and touched several of the stones. She bent low to Serena's face and brushed back her hair. "Why doona ye warm from my magic, Sister?"

"What?" Drakkina squawked. She clasped her misty hands.

Merewin didn't rise, but turned her face to Drakkina. "My magic isna' working on her." She turned back and kissed Serena's forehead. "Sister, open yer eyes, see me."

Serena's eyes flickered. Merewin smiled. "There now. Ye must open to my power, else I canna help ye."

"What do you mean, you can't help her?" Drakkina demanded.

Merewin pulled back, still smiling at Serena. "I can only heal those who want to be healed."

Drakkina wafted over to Serena and looked down at her. "Serena, let your sister heal you. He's coming. I know he is. Trust him to come to you."

Serena's eyes didn't focus on anyone in particular. "If he is to die, then so will I."

"No!" Drakkina wailed as she yanked her shawl off her head and threw it on the shriveled wildflowers. "You are not to die. Even if he does, you cannot die. Stop dying this instant."

Merewin looked at Drakkina like she'd gone mad. Perhaps she had. The tightness in her chest moved behind her eyes. She wouldn't cry. It was weakness to cry, and she was the powerful Drakkina. Reigning in her control, Drakkina looked at Merewin. "Do what you can. I must work to shorten his journey here."

Merewin turned back to Elenor, and the two of them began to pack around the wounds. Merewin dabbed drops of liquid on Serena's pulse points and dropped several drops between her parted lips. "This is Apophyllite gem essence," she said to Elenor. "It fights off hopelessness."

Chapter 18

Voices wavered in and out. Serena felt the cool weight of stones along her body. A wet rag wiped at her mouth. "Serena, ye must want to live for my magic to work on ye. Do ye not want to live?"

Serena squeezed her eyes and managed to flick them open. Large lashy eyes stared into her own. Serena was mesmerized by the warm green orbs.

"I remember you." Serena coughed.

The woman ran her hand through Serena's hair, brushing it back from her face. She smiled. "I am Merewin. We've met before, though at the time I thought it a dream."

Serena watched her lovely soft lips smile. Soft golden brown hair framed a heart shaped face. She did look familiar.

"I'm yer sister. Our mother sent us away, hid us. Do ye remember?" Merewin asked. Serena caught glimpses of a girl laughing as they danced in and out of the large stones around their cottage.

"Yes," Serena breathed. "I remember."

Merewin beamed at her. "I too." Serena felt Merewin squeeze her hand, but it felt like she wore thick mittens.

"I am cold, numb," Serena said and coughed up some more blood.

Elenor came into view, her eyes red with tears. She rubbed Serena's mouth then placed her cloak over Serena below the dagger. "Serena, ye have to live. I," she hesitated. "I wasn't the one to strike ye."

"I know."

"And I didn't want to strike you, Serena,"

Drakkina's loud voice came from nowhere and everywhere at once. Serena squeezed her eyes shut.

"This is yer doing?" Merewin snapped.

Serena opened her eyes again. Drakkina's misty form hovered over her making her gasp which led to another cough. Concern, self righteous defensiveness, and panic, floated with the priestess. "Listen to me, Serena," Drakkina's voice spoke into her mind. "It was the only way to make him leave the battle. He must have felt the attack through your bond with him." The image wavered slightly. "He will be here soon. Do not die, child. It was never my intent to harm you mortally."

"Perhaps it would be easier to die," Serena murmured. Life was so hard. She'd been fighting for normalcy her entire life and she would never truly know it. Her magic would always single her out and without Keenan she'd never know love.

"Sister," Merewin snapped above her, blocking Drakkina's floating form. Merewin's eyes were as firm as her hand that squeezed her fingers. "Ye must not be my sister, born of Gilla's blood." Serena watched her storm filled face. "No daughter of Gilla would give up so easily."

"It's so hard," Serena said.

"Do ye remember her, our mother?"

"Aye, a bit. She was beautiful. She hummed all the time."

Merewin's face tightened, a sad smile sat on her lips. "I'd forgotten that, aye she hummed." She leaned closer to Serena. "Mama fought for us, to save us, leaving herself helpless to the demons."

"Demons?" Elenor asked.

"Yes demons!" Drakkina shouted. "If you only knew how important this is!"

Merewin ignored her. "She did not give up even when they killed Papa. She fought until the end. Do not make her sacrifice in vain, Serena. Mama died for us," she shook her head, soft brown curls falling over her shoulder as she looked down over Serena. "How could ye give up on yer life so easily?"

Elenor stepped beside Serena. "Yer a warrior, Serena. Keenan told me that. Ye saved William, ye saved that boy and his mother from the Campbell. Brodick said ye stood up to yer whole tribe. Ye even lied to King George to help us."

"I did," she said looking first at Elenor and then Merewin. "Mama was a warrior, wasn't she?"

Merewin nodded, tears glistening in her once again soft eyes. "She fought for us all."

"She fought for this world," Drakkina added hovering nearby.

Serena closed her eyes, releasing the burden of her indecision. She'd chosen.

"Look," Elenor's voice wavered in her muffled ears. "The stones are glowing!"

Serena felt Merewin's strong hands touch her skin. The cool fingers warmed and a heat spread out, connecting stone to stone along her numb body. Serena gasped as the heat penetrated. Flesh and muscle tugged closed across the stab wounds inside and out. Serena opened her eyes. Merewin stood, eyes closed, forehead furrowed, hands sliding along Serena's body.

"Woman," Merewin said to Elenor. "When I say, pull out the knife in the same slant that it entered."

Elenor bit her bottom lip and nodded while she wrapped her hands around the hilt.

Serena closed her eyes against the gruesome sight. Heat pooled around the blade embedded in torn flesh.

"Now!" Merewin yelled and pain ripped through Serena as the blade yanked free. She gasped, her eyes flying open. Merewin covered the hole with both of her hands and the sharp pain dulled, blending into the numbness throughout Serena's entire body.

Merewin continued to radiate magic into her body. It crept along her limbs, nudging them with power.

The numbness awoke to pain which ebbed to discomfort and dissolved to wholeness once more. Serena struggled onto her elbows.

"Serena!" Elenor yelled and helped her sit up. Stones rolled to the table and into the grass. Merewin opened her eyes and smiled at Serena.

"Ye are healed, Sister," Merewin said, fading as she gathered the rocks about her.

Serena smiled. "Thank you. Before you go…" but Merewin was already gone. "Let us meet again," Serena whispered. Her gaze moved about the circle and she slid off the stone slab.

"Elenor, where's our horse?"

"Where are you going?" Drakkina said.

Serena pivoted, piercing the witch with a harsh stare. "To help my husband."

"No!" Drakkina shouted. "Stay in the circle where it's safe."

"Safe?" Serena yelled sarcastically.

"I feel that you and your mate are in terrible danger. It is safer here than anywhere else in this world."

"You want me to hide," Serena said and shook her head. "Damn all the prophecies and warnings of this world! I am going to my Keenan's side and we will meet fate together!"

****

Keenan broke through the tree line followed by Brodick and Gavin, and Ewan and Thomas. Keenan dodged a tall monolith of stone as he tore into the clearing. His eyes fastened onto a stone table in the center. He jumped from his horse. Red blood dried upon the stone.

He turned, "Serena!"

"She's not here now," Drakkina's voice wafted to him on a breeze as she materialized.

Fury, hot blood fury whipped through his mind, into his muscles. Without breaking stride, he pulled a dirk and hurled it toward the witch. A startled look crossed the wrinkled face as the blade cut through her vapor to clang unheeded against one of the stones behind her.

"Sometimes it's good to be nothing but mist," she said, floating nearer.

"Where is she? What have ye done, old witch?"

"Hold your blade and your temper, Highlander," Drakkina admonished and pulled back the stray curls of white hair that tossed wildly about her face. Her eyes narrowed but flushed cheeks and rapid movements gave her a flustered, anxious look. "Your wife is whole and well."

"Even though ye stabbed her."

"You know?"

"Our link is strong."

"Then you know she's headed for your battle?"

"Nay!" Keenan roared.

"The battle," Ewan said. "She goes alone." His face mirrored the horror pinching at Keenan's features.

"With the other woman, your sister," Drakkina said, looking to Keenan. Keenan turned, slamming his fist down on the blood soaked granite. Drakkina continued. "I brought you here over my temporal bridges. Serena travels back over them."

"Then we return over them," Thomas said pulling his horse forward.

Keenan had already mounted his horse. He noticed the blue bird circling the stones. "He knows the way."

"Stay," Drakkina said, her voice trembling. Keenan looked at her. She seemed suddenly old, tired, as worn as an ancient hag. "Once she sees you aren't there, she'll return. She will always return to the west." The hag dripped resignation as if she already knew his answer.

"We go, old crone," Brodick said.

Thomas climbed onto his horse. "The prophecy says that she will lead us to peace. The prophecy..."

"Is no more!" Keenan's roar filled the stone circle, vibrating off the tall monoliths to tremor through the gathered men. "I ride to save Serena, not the witch." His eyes narrowed with challenge as he looked at his faithful men. "I ride because I will it. I ride because I love her." Power and strength flowed through Keenan's body as he shed off the shackles of the prophecy. Energy like he'd never felt before rushed in his blood. He breathed in, filling his lungs as if for the first time. No longer would he try to decipher the words, the plan for his life. Only he and God could control him now. "The prophecy has damned my life, damned the lives of my family," he said, and turned his horse in a tight circle. "No more," he said, his eyes moving to the blue bird. The bird chirped once and shot off into the woods. Keenan plunged after him.

****

The dawning sun sparkled over the landscape as Elenor and Serena flew along Drakkina's temporal bridges. Serena heard Elenor's soft prayers to her God and Serena added her own silent ones. *Let him live. Let me get to him in time. Let him live.*

Up ahead a patch of air quivered. "Hold on!" Serena yelled back as they plunged off the end of the bridge onto normal ground with the momentum ten times faster than natural. The horse screeched as Serena and Elenor clung around the beast's middle. They dismounted on shaky legs.

Elenor threw her arms around Serena in a hug. "Dearest Lord, I never want to get on a horse again," she said into Serena's hair. Serena nodded and hugged her back. Feelings of thanksgiving eclipsed the fear and worry that Serena felt twining around

Elenor's heart. Fear and unease, worry for the future, but also hope. The white brilliance of hope glowed softly from Elenor, hope and trust in Serena. Serena pulled back, tears at war with the smile on her face. Elenor held only trust and sisterly love for her. There was no desire to use Serena, no wish to possess her, no anxiety that Serena's touch was somehow evil.

"Yer weeping?" Elenor frowned. "Ye are ill?"

Serena shook her head and wiped her eyes. "I am good, Elenor," she said squeezing her hand. Serena glanced around.

"The horse?" Elenor said.

"She's too exhausted to go far." Serena ducked under heavy branches. She pushed one last fir branch from her face, careful not to let it hit Elenor, and walked out of the trees.

Serena stood on the edge facing a boggy moor that stretched far before them, Drumossie Moor, better known as Culloden. Elenor stepped up beside her and gasped as she squeezed the feeling out of Serena's hand.

Men in tattered plaids walked back across the moor toward them, some limping, some walking with their heads down, some crawling.

"Is it over?" Elenor asked.

Serena shook her head while her eyes searched for one tall figure that should stand out from the crowd. "No, too many of them are still alive for it to be over."

"They look like they've been to battle," Elenor said. She sucked in breath and pointed. "That's Lachlan! And John and Angus!" Elenor cupped her hands around her eyes to see against the sun that was three quarters up to its zenith. "And Hamish...Lan and Fergus." Her head turned to scan the crowd. "But where is...?

"He's not here," Serena said, her voice numb.

"He must be here. Keenan wouldn't leave his men."

Serena looked at Elenor. "He felt my wound."

Elenor's eyes turned to her and then glanced behind them toward the temporal bridge. "Ye think he…"

"Fell for the trick," Serena finished the sentence. What had Drakkina done? She had taken Keenan away when his clan, when his family needed him most. But hadn't that been what Serena had asked of him earlier? She swallowed down guilt, the bitterness invading her spirit.

"It wasn't a trick," Elenor countered. "Ye were stabbed."

"I let my weakness, my doubt in Keenan…" Serena swallowed back her tears. "I should have read Drakkina, known what she planned…"

"Serena, nay," Elenor said.

"Would the Macleans be crawling back across a moor if Keenan had been here to lead them?"

Elenor reached for Serena's hand and squeezed. She didn't say anything as the two looked back out over the moving moor. Lachlan had made it half way across the field when the Bonnie Prince rode out on a white horse, his orders carried away from the ladies on the wind. Elenor and Serena clung to one another as they watched the men turn back around and form lines.

"Holy Sweet Mary, Mother of God," Elenor prayed out loud. "Save our men."

Save our men. Serena's prayers echoed silently. When had these Macleans become her men? It didn't matter, they were. *Save our men.* Serena thought of the wives and children she'd left at Kylkern. Their hearts full of hope and fear. *Save our men.*

"Look," Serena said and pointed to the line of red coated men at the far end. They marched as a united front, perfect precision, row upon row. A flash of fear trembled down through Serena. "There are so many."

Both women jumped as the volley of British gunfire popped in the distance, slicing through the first line of men.

"Nay!" Elenor yelled as a second volley exploded. Dust and gunfire smoke billowed up into the air. The deep boom of a cannon followed. Clumps of peat and men flew into the air where the cannon hit. Their mangled mass of broken bodies twisted in the smoke and mud.

Serena scanned the field. She caught a glimpse of the cockaded bonnet of the Bonnie Prince, retreating from the slaughter. In an instant their proud leader was gone, his leadership shot out from under him like his horse. She steeled herself against the onslaught of emotion. The Scottish fought with swords and scythes and axes, which did little against the British artillery.

Serena heard stones sliding down in front of her. "Elenor!" she yelled. Elenor scrambled down the hill and onto the moor. "Elenor, come back!"

Elenor looked back for a moment at Serena her face red and washed with tears. "He's dying out there," she said and ran out onto the moor.

Lachlan stood, blood on his hands as he grabbed his thigh. He'd been shot in the leg but wasn't turning in retreat. He must have heard Elenor's cry because he turned to watch her run to him. They were too far away for Serena to hear, but she could see Elenor pull Lachlan's arm, trying to pull him from the field. The sound was deafening. Cannons boomed echoed by screams and thumps of debris and bodies. Guns popped continuously. The deep resonance of guttural war cries lay like deep water over the moor, flooding the hurt and dying, smothering, drowning.

Serena couldn't breathe. Her overlapping hands

pressed hard against her chest as she heard the calculated popping over another deadly round of gunfire. Lachlan must have heard it too because he threw Elenor to the bloody mud and covered her with his body.

"No!" Serena screamed. "Elenor! Lachlan!" Serena jumped up and down, her fingers curling and uncurling at her sides. She took a step toward the edge of the moor and looked around for something physical that she could use for a shield. There was nothing but rocks and trees. Rocks and trees...and Keenan!

Keenan burst through the tree line and pulled his horse up quick so as not to plunge down the hill. The horse reared back, its legs flailing high in front of him. He spotted Serena immediately and something tight uncoiled in his chest, something that allowed him to breathe again.

"Keenan!" she cried and he engulfed her with his arms, pulling her into his heaving chest, so close that his legs straddled around her.

His eyes lifted over her head and he stiffened. Serena pushed against his chest. "Keenan, Elenor, Lachlan..."

Serena's words seemed to garble together as his mind, so intent on saving Serena now shifted to his clan. Her words hit him like a mace. "Lachlan just threw himself on Elenor! She ran out there to pull him off the field. He's shot and..."

He must protect them. "Brodick, Gavin," Keenan said as he grabbed his shield from his horse. "Guard her until I return."

Keenan plunged down the hill, rocks and dirt scattering under his heels. He held his sword in his right hand, his shield in the other. Thomas and Ewan flanked him.

"Keenan," he heard Serena call his name. She still feared he would die. Would she have him turn his back on his family, his clan? At the bottom he turned his eyes to her. She stood proud above him, the wind catching at her tangled curls. "Keenan," she called. "Save them, save our family."

Energy and intent billowed up into him. His muscles flexed as his legs leapt across the soggy moor toward his brother's body. He and his two men crouched down under their shields as a barrage of gunfire rained down on them. Ewan grunted. Keenan looked to his left, his friend wiped a fresh swell of blood from his leg.

"Nothing," the warrior said and the three leapt forward through the smoke, dodging British and Scottish artillery. They ran low to the ground, bent over as they hurdled fallen Highlanders and pools of fetid water tinged red with blood. Men shouted, grunted, screamed. Cannons boomed and shook the warped earth beneath Keenan's boots. Smoke and the tang of blood burned inside his nose. War, full on dirty war, what he'd been trained for, what he'd practiced all his life. Keenan's voice carried above the noise, out across the moor. "Lachlan! Elenor!"

"Keenan! Help!" Elenor's frightened cry sent another surge of ruthless energy tearing through Keenan. Raw need gave him nearly inhuman strength as he lifted Lachlan as if his full grown brother weighed no more than a child. Blood seeped through Lachlan's shirt near his shoulder and dripped from the wound in his leg.

Ewan took the unconscious Lachlan while Thomas took both shields.

Keenan hoisted Elenor against him, his arm under her knees, his shield draped over his back. He ran, his legs churning as if he climbed a steep incline, dodging bodies and sword blades, leaping over moats of water and ditches of mud and death. Elenor clung to him as if she were a wee lass, his dear sweet sister who had always stood strong in support of him, who'd showed him what love was when there wasn't any to be found.

Keenan's eyes focused on the lone woman standing tall ahead on the rise. Serena's red hair tossed wildly around her shoulders with the wind, blazing like a flame in the noon sun. Her hands pressed out before her as if feeling along a wall, violet eyes closed, forehead furrowed. The guttural growls of warriors pierced by screams of agony and death beat as his back as he tore across the mottled land toward his wife, toward his love, toward life.

Half the hill came down under his heels as he stepped up the raw, cut hillside. Serena opened her eyes. "He watched you. He's coming."

His eyes washed over her, not understanding, but feeling the panic racing through her. "Who?"

"I...I threaded through them all to find their leader," Serena said breathlessly, and Keenan realized that she hadn't the full strength to stand. She leaned against Brodrick. Keenan set Elenor down as Thomas stepped up to take her weight. Keenan pulled Serena into his arms.

"The Duke of Cumberland," she said and swallowed. "He's close and he saw you run here." She looked into Keenan's eyes. "His mind...his heart is blackness." She shook her head. "All he wants is death, Keenan. He's consumed with it and he's coming this way."

"Ye read him?" Keenan asked, and felt Serena shudder with her nod.

Serena's eyes glossed over with unshed tears. "Bloody, brutal slaughter. He wants all of Scotland dead...starting with you."

Keenan wrapped her tightly against him and turned to scan out at the field. A contingent of horses moved across the moor. Their British riders sliced and chopped at the exhausted, underfed Scottish warriors. Cumberland rode in the middle of them, protected from most of the danger. Serena pulled away to check on Elenor and the barely breathing Lachlan.

"He will die," Thomas said where they knelt near Lachlan. "Just like the prophecy said."

Tears streamed down Elenor's face. "He was defending me." Elenor looked up at Keenan. "He was defending me and now he will die and ye will lead the clan, just like the prophecy said."

The anguish in his sister's words cut through Keenan. His words were firm like the rocks around them, like the mountains of their land. "The prophecy is dead. We follow no prophecy." Serena fished out something from her pocket and placed it on Lachlan's chest near the worst of his seeping wounds.

She looked up at Keenan. "Then let us really be rid of it." She placed her hands over the wound and closed her eyes. A labored breath rattled past Lachlan's bloodied lips and then he lay still.

"Nay!" Elenor screamed and fell into Thomas's arms. "Doona go, Lachlan!"

Serena continued to breath, eyes squeezed shut, lips pursed tight. "Not yet, Lachlan."

"Aye," Keenan murmured in the stillness. "Not yet, Brother."

"Keenan," Ewan said. "Cumberland."

Keenan turned back to the field. Cumberland and his men were close enough for Keenan to make out Cumberland's sneer. His beady black eyes searched him out. The man apparently blamed Keenan for his mistress's confession before King George. Keenan had heard the man's reputation had suffered from the incident.

"Surround them," Keenan said with a glance at Lachlan, Elenor, and Serena. "Let nothing reach them."

Keenan felt a hum in the ground beneath his

feet, Serena's magic was the source. Power pulled up through the ground into Lachlan. His body twitched. Let it be enough, Keenan prayed.

"Here the bastards come," Ewan said, anticipation lacing his words as he bounced on his toes and rotated his sword.

Cumberland and his men left their horses at the bottom of the steep embankment and charged up, swords flashing, curses flying. British steel struck Highland iron as Cumberland's soldiers attacked, trying to hack through the circle around Lachlan, Elenor and Serena. Keenan's blade sang as he moved, his warrior's blood ran free as the familiar dance moved his body with deadly grace. His mind focused on protecting what lay beyond him in the tight circle. His breathing followed the cadence of his heartbeat as the familiar movements clashed and defended over and over. The dance was over much too fast for Keenan's taste, the powdered red coats scattered haphazardly across the ground. Now only Cumberland and his standard bearer stood. Cumberland brandished his sword, his narrow eyes hard and venomous.

"Strike at me and ye will join yer men," Keenan said, his stance casual.

"You are a traitor, Maclean, and will die a traitor's death."

"I protect my clan, Cumberland. I stand for what is mine."

"Against King George," Cumberland said.

"I stand against no man save my enemy."

"You support the Pretender Prince Charles."

There was movement behind Keenan and Elenor gasped.

"I support Prince Charles Stuart," Lachlan said. "Na' Keenan."

Keenan didn't move his eyes from his adversary, but relief flooded him.

Lachlan's voice was weak, but he was conscious, alive. "Keenan has tried to convince me to place my loyalty elsewhere," Lachlan said. "He is na' loyal to the Prince."

"Then stand down," Cumberland spoke directly to Keenan, his eyes never wavering.

"He will strike when you..." Serena started.

"No doubt," Keenan said more to Cumberland than to Serena. "I willna stand down until I ken my family is safe."

"I know your family's prophecy, Maclean. Are you frightened then, knowing you will die defending that family? Isn't it your duty to come meet me here and die? You Highlanders are all about duty."

"No prophecy rules my actions, Cumberland," Keenan said, his voice lethal, calm. "If ye think I will die by yer blade, then come meet me." Keenan took a step toward the duke and sliced his sword through the crisp air in a fluid figure eight. The duke's eyes opened a hint larger. Keenan took another step closer to the hedging man. The standard bearer retreated several paces. "I doona fear death and I doona welcome it." Keenan arched his sword in another fluid movement, the blade literally singing as the wind whistled by it. His eyes hardened, his body on the verge of elegant violence. "Death," he said with menacing softness, "I defeat it."

Keenan stood, his sword arm ready, waiting for the duke's response. The sun caught his blade and Keenan angled it slightly so that the sun shone into the leader's eyes. The duke squinted.

"Tread carefully, Maclean," Cumberland said lowering his sword so as not to look threatening. He glanced at Lachlan somewhere behind Keenan. "And your brother is a traitor. The king will deal with him." Cumberland backed slowly from the scene, arguing with the standard barer to leave the bodies of their soldiers. Keenan lowered his sword and turned to find Lachlan hugging Elenor. He smiled and breathed deep.

"'Tis good to see ye whole, Brother," Keenan said as he knelt before Lachlan and grabbed his shoulders.

Lachlan looked between Serena and Keenan and grinned. "Aye, thanks to both of ye." Elenor threw her arms around Lachlan again. "And ye, fair sister, are never permitted in battle again," he rebuked, though he smiled through it.

Horns sounded. Runners from the Scottish commander, Lord Murray, rode through calling a retreat. The battle was over in little more than an hour.

Keenan stepped up to Serena.

"Death," she said staring up into his eyes. "You have defeated it."

Keenan touched her chin, rubbing the soft skin with his thumb. "Nay, lass. We have defeated it." He dipped his head down to her warm lips. Serena wrapped her arms around his neck and tilted her head. She was warmth and soft woman and so much more. She was life. He pulled back.

"I love ye, lass. I will always battle to come home to ye." Serena flung herself into Keenan's arms, their kiss so deep that they didn't even hear the low chuckles of the men behind them or the sweet chirping of a bluebird overhead.

Epilogue

Kylkern Castle loomed majestically ahead of them. Sheep roamed the hillside. Chiriklò twittered with two robins in budding trees that flanked the path. Serena and Keenan walked hand in hand after visiting several of the soldiers at their homes. Spring bloomed around them as the warm breeze cleansed the air and earth. It had been a fortnight since they returned and tales of the battle had followed.

Culloden had been a massacre. One thousand Highlanders had given their lives to only three hundred-sixty-four of Cumberland's men. Thanks, though, to Keenan's training and Serena's magic, all the Macleans had been saved. Cumberland's campaign to kill all Scots earned him the name The Butcher. He continued his killing rampage, murdering the injured and Scottish innocents in his way, for days after the battle. His savagery disgraced the British army and his own reputation.

"I'd have gutted the man if I'd known." Kennan had murmured upon reading the report.

Rus jogged up and fell in line with them as they walked toward Kylkern.

"He's gone."

"I know. He bade us farewell at dawn," Keenan said. A second chance at life, Lachlan had called it. Wanted to make his own adventures. No arguing would stop him. Lachlan had left with several loyal young warriors to travel south to pay their respects to the Faw Tribe. From there Lachlan hoped to journey to Ireland or the Colonies, he wasn't sure.

"Ye are the true chief, Keenan," Lachlan had

said. He'd smiled at Serena, then. "Lead yer people to peace." A letter under royal seal had arrived the night before from George himself. Apparently the standard bearer had spoken up on Keenan's behalf. Maclean lands would belong to the clan as long as Lachlan no longer led them.

Keenan laced his fingers through Serena's, remaining silent. Serena still couldn't read his thoughts but the tightness of unease filtered to her through their bond.

"Elenor is starting a tapestry to capture the battle with Lachlan at the head of the Maclean regiment," Serena stated. Rus nodded.

Serena walked half-way through the small village beside Keenan and Rus before the eerie quiet caught at her busy mind. Windows stood empty, doors closed.

"Rus," Keenan said firmly as they neared the gatehouse. "I need to talk with ye and Brodick. With Lachlan gone, we need new leadership."

Rus nodded. "Aye, we have some things we'd like to discuss with ye, too," he said, his voice stern. They strode through the deserted bailey. Only the gateman stood watch and waved. Up the steps, Rus reached the top and pushed open the arching oak doors, letting Serena and Keenan walk into the entry.

After the bright sun, the total blackness of the corridor blinded Serena. She smelled spring wildflowers, brought in by Elenor no doubt, and fresh baked bread for the afternoon meal. As the narrow corridor opened up into the great hall, Keenan stopped abruptly, halting Serena with him. She blinked twice, astonished. The entire room, from the winding tower steps to the space before the hearth, to the tops of the long tables, was filled with Clan Maclean, silently waiting. Women, children in their arms, stood next to their returned husbands.

Mothers, fathers, old and young alike.

Brodick's thick voice filled the air above the packed humanity before them. "Let it be known that on this day in the year of our Lord, seventeen hundred and forty-six, that Keenan Maclean of the Macleans of Kylkern is proclaimed The Maclean, Chief of the Macleans of Kylkern." Without words, each man in the room slid his sword free, filling the room with the slicing sound of steel. All tips pointed upward to the stone ceiling.

Thomas stepped forward next to Brodick. "And let it be known that on this same day, we welcome Serena Maclean with our gratitude and hearts to walk beside our laird."

Gavin stepped up next to Thomas. "So that they both shall lead Clan Maclean to peace."

Rus jumped up on the bench near them. "So say I," he yelled raising the tip of his sword even higher in the air.

"So say I," Robert Mackay called from the back of the room.

"So say I," yelled Ewan at the same time as two other men whom Serena had healed along the Inverness road leading from Culloden.

"So say I," Elenor called out raising her clasped hands in the air where she stood close to William.

With that the hall exploded in an uneven chorus of shouts, three simple words that rippled through Serena. "So say I!"

In the deafening thunder of acceptance, Serena let Keenan pull her to the table. He lifted her up next to Brodick and jumped up himself. Looking down at her, Keenan smiled into Serena's eyes. She nodded briefly, and he turned out to the throng of people.

The room hushed. Keenan's sword slid free, and he raised it overhead. With his other hand, he grabbed Serena's and raised up their clasped hands between them.

"So say I," Keenan's voice boomed through the room.

"So say I," Serena followed as she smiled broadly at the sea of faces.

Again the room erupted, and Serena could no longer keep back the tears of happiness. Keenan lowered his arms, sheathed his sword, and pulled Serena into his embrace. He looked deeply into her teary eyes. "Welcome home, lass." He paused and smiled. "I think if we start tomorrow, there will still be time for yer vegetable garden."

Serena laughed and leaned into him. Their kiss, full of hope, full of love, consumed them as the celebration continued.

A word about the author...

Heather McCollum is an award-winning, historical paranormal romance writer. She earned her B.A. in Biology from the University of Maine at Machias, much to her English professor's dismay. She is a member of Romance Writers of America and Heart of Carolina Romance Writers.

The ancient magic and lush beauty of Great Britain entranced Ms. McCollum's heart and imagination when she visited there years ago. The country's history and landscape have been a backdrop for her writing ever since. She currently resides with her very own Highland hero and three spirited children in the wilds of suburbia on the mid-Atlantic coast.

Thank you for purchasing
this Wild Rose Press publication.
For other wonderful stories of romance,
please visit our on-line bookstore at
www.thewildrosepress.com

For questions or more information
contact us at
info@thewildrosepress.com

The Wild Rose Press
www.TheWildRosePress.com